One
Christmas
Morning

RACHEL GREENLAW

ONE PLACE. MANY STORIES

HQ
An imprint of HarperCollins*Publishers* Ltd
1 London Bridge Street
London SE1 9GF

www.harpercollins.co.uk

HarperCollins*Publishers*
Macken House, 39/40 Mayor Street Upper,
Dublin 1, D01 C9W8, Ireland

This edition 2023

1
First published in Great Britain by
HQ, an imprint of HarperCollins*Publishers* Ltd 2023

Copyright © Rachel Greenlaw 2023

Rachel Greenlaw asserts the moral right to be
identified as the author of this work.
A catalogue record for this book is
available from the British Library.

ISBN: 978-0-00-855893-2

For Joe. My anchor, my home.
I love you.

Chapter 1

I am surrounded by cardboard boxes. There are piles of them, heaped up all around me in an arc on the newly laid, slightly dusty shop floor. And all I can do is close my eyes, lean back against them and wish I could wind time forward. A week would do. Maybe a fortnight. Then all the items in these boxes would be arranged on the shelves, scattered artfully across the middle tables and customers would be wandering in and out, arms piled high with throws and candle holders. I allow that image to sink in for a moment.

Isn't that what you're supposed to do so a dream becomes real? Visualise it?

But it's not long before the cold seeps in through my jeans and I throw myself forward with a sigh. It's five days before we open. Five days before my dream becomes a reality, and all I feel is hot, stifling panic. My phone rings and I force myself to get up, hurriedly rustling through the open boxes, turning in a circle on the heels of my perfectly white trainers. There. It's on the new counter. I lunge for it, swiping it open as I catch the name.

'James?'

'I got the Thai. They didn't have the beef massaman, so I got chicken instead. Should be another...' his tinny voice slips away and I picture him shaking back his sleeve, checking his watch, 'twenty minutes?'

'James, the thing is... I...' My words stick in my throat, excuses glued to the roof of my mouth.

There is a pause, a beat of silence. 'You forgot, didn't you?'

A wash of shame fills my chest and I close my eyes. We were meant to get a takeaway tonight. Just me and him, alone in our flat so we could catch up, refuel. Have a date night like an actual husband and wife, like we used to. But of course, I forgot. As I got the last load of scent diffusers on the shelves for the launch, another arrived, then Diana called to say there was a delay with the printed paper bags... then suddenly it was dark outside and all I could do was sit on the floor. Just sit and stare at nothing, my mind filling with a tiredness that sleep can't cure.

I clear my throat. 'I'll be back in an hour. Give me an hour and I'll get all this put away in the stockroom. I can pop back in afterwards, after we've had dinner—'

'Eva...'

'What?'

He huffs an exasperated breath. 'I can keep it warm in the oven. Don't get back too late, yeah?'

'James, I'm sor—'

But the line has already gone dead.

A laugh claws up my throat, short and bitter, as I drop my mobile phone back on the counter. Staring blearily around at the tumble of boxes, the dustpan full of dust by the door, the till still blinking angrily, not yet set up, I feel that sharp pain again. That insistent prickle in the centre of my chest.

This is all I wanted. This is what I've been building towards for the past three years, this shop with its double-fronted sage-green-framed windows, its casually rustic timber flooring. I take a deep, rattling breath and reach for the nearest shelf. I run my hand over the photo frames, the textured napkins, letting the feel of fabric and wood ground me, anchor me. It reminds me I've got this far. That I *could* be enough, if I push harder. Try harder. I nod to myself, straightening a set of four white napkins, smoothing them down until they are perfect again.

It's all worth it. He'll see.

I have to remind myself of this whenever I feel that gnaw of doubt in my stomach. All the maxed-out credit cards, the hours at trade fairs, the nights spent glued to my laptop screen.

For a moment, I allow myself to step into the haze of what only *I* can picture. What I'm creating with this brand. The charm of a well-decorated room, the scent of the ocean, afternoon light as it dances across the floorboards. This vision of peace and calm that I so desperately needed a few years ago. That other people might need too. Then I blow out a breath. If James doesn't get it, that's fine. But this is everything I have worked for, the all-consuming distraction I have needed over the last three years, and I won't stuff it up at the last minute.

I won't fail this time.

James and I will be OK. We've just got to get through this shop launch. Then we can go back to being a normal couple, the two of us making weekend plans, going for Saturday brunch, me cheering him on from the sidelines as he plays football on a muddy pitch with his team, eating Thai takeaway like a picnic on the carpet in front of our favourite TV show. Although I guess… we haven't done that for a while. When was the last time I turned up to watch him play? I try to put my finger on a date. But maybe… maybe it's been a couple of years. I use the weekends to work now.

My phone beeps again, this time with a text from Hallie. A reminder of how to get to this Christmas house party she's organised this year. It's probably the same message she's sent to her other guests, the cheery directions, the reminder to *drive safely!* But I don't need these directions. I know how to get to the manor house, Penhallow, like following the creases of my palm. It's seared into my memory, every lane, every drystone wall.

It's the holiday home I went to every year as a child, huge and lumbering, the whole place to ourselves. The place that haunts my dreams even now. I can still remember the way the lichen spread like lace over its granite walls, the crunch of the gravel in the driveway, the endless rooms that seemed to move around in the night, as if by magic.

I shake my head, desperate not to dredge up that part of my past right now. Of the bittersweet memories it recalls. Besides, I don't have time to give in to my childish imaginings. It's the day before Christmas Eve and we're opening in less than a week. Every minute counts to making this shop a success. But I promised James that I'd go, and I can't go back on my word now, especially when I need to make things up to him.

Of course, the timing couldn't be any worse, and out of all the places, why did Hallie have to choose this one? She knows my connection to Penhallow… my family's connection. But I can do this. The shop launch, the house party, the Christmas full of ghosts. I can juggle it all and stay afloat.

The door rattles and my assistant, Diana, steps in, blowing on her hands. 'Bloody freezing! Definite snow weather.'

I groan. 'Don't say that. Not the S word.'

4

'It'll be fine. They'll clear all the snow away and grit the roads if it's really bad.'

'Not in Cornwall. Those lanes are like ice rinks in the winter. No gritter can be arsed with the moorland tracks and lanes.'

Diana wrinkles her nose, shrugging out of her coat. She knows how much I hate driving in bad weather. Especially when there's snow or ice involved. 'I can drive you, then we can catch up on last-minute prep before I head back.'

'What?'

She shrugs, not quite meeting my eyes. 'I know the area pretty well. It's no bother, really.'

'On Christmas Eve? What about your plans?' But what I *really* want to say is *yes, that would be great, thank you* to her. To push aside the niggle that I'm taking advantage of her goodwill, her wish to get on my good side. I know I should tell her not to be a workaholic, to put herself first. Of course I should.

Diana crosses the shop floor, reaches for the box closest to her and neatly slices through the packing tape. 'Aha! The sea foam throws. I thought they missed these off the manifest.'

'Diana…'

'It's fine,' she says firmly, her dark hair falling back from her face as she looks up at me. 'I need to… I have an appointment in the area anyway. Something I shouldn't really miss. The house, Penhallow, isn't it? Where this house party is? It's en route, so won't be any trouble to drop you off.' I don't ask about the appointment as I glance her way, it's not my place to pry. Her eyes catch mine and I notice the smudge of shadow underneath them, which I know isn't from age. She's a green tea drinker, mindful of her body, the wrinkles that haven't yet appeared. But she's also six years younger than me. If she's tired from this shop launch, it won't permanently mark her skin. At thirty-two, no amount of antioxidants are going to turn back the years of sugar and coffee I load into my body each day, or the number of sleepless nights.

Needing to busy my hands, I reshuffle a display of cushions, the scent of vanilla wafting up from the spritzed covers. I contemplate the fallout if I don't show up to this house party on the moors. James is leaving early to beat the traffic, and we've already decided that I should travel down later. He isn't happy about it, but I have to get set up before I leave. When I get back to London, there won't be time before the grand opening. There won't be time for anything but unlocking the doors and plastering a smile on my face.

I bite my lip, fuss with the next set of cushions. James made it clear that as long as I make it down there, he could overlook the fact that we won't be travelling there together.

I rub my eyes, tired of the constant balance of it all. What I need. What James wants. What Hallie wants. This is her house party, her closest friends and family. And as James is my husband, and *her* husband, Kian, is his best friend, I'm automatically on the invite list. Not because we've been joined at the hip since our university days; living together in cramped little flats, sharing the last tin of baked beans when we were both completely skint, fighting through everything to stay afloat in our twenties. She may be my best friend, but we've barely spoken in a year. I just haven't had the time. At least, that's what I tell myself when the guilt prickles me, when I ignore a message from her: that I don't have the time. Not because she'll want to talk, and I'm not sure I can yet. But if I don't turn up at all… it's not worth facing *those* consequences.

'If you're sure,' I concede, shoving aside my guilt. Diana flashes me a grin.

'Don't worry, I grew up there, remember? I know the roads. I can drive us down, finalise anything last minute that crops up and be back here in time for Christmas. A bunch of us are meeting up to spend the day together. Then I can get things straightened out in here on Boxing Day in time for when you get back.'

An uneasy feeling grips my chest, as I picture all the ways that this could go wrong. The needling guilt grows, that I really shouldn't accept this offer on top of her already working on Boxing Day. Then I tell myself to relax. I'm overthinking it, that Diana is a grown woman who can make her own decisions.

I busy myself with the boxes nearest the door as Diana hauls a stack of blankets through to the stockroom out the back. I'm kneeling down, carefully unwrapping a set of aquamarine vases, when a breeze brushes softly against my neck. The scent of gorse flowers, coconut and summer envelopes me. Her scent. I turn, eyeing the door.

There's a face at the window.

I freeze. Between blinks it's gone, and I spring quickly to my feet, breathing heavily. Blood pounds in my ears and I step forward to pull the door open. Outside it's a dark, silent cold. The kind that creeps inside you, burying itself deep under your skin. I hug my arms around myself, looking up and down the street.

There's no one there.

'What's up?' Diana asks from the back of the shop and I turn to see the question on her face. For a moment, I almost tell her.

Not just the face at the window, but everything. What happened three years ago. How I still see her face sometimes. How there's part of me that searches for her, combing the crowds of people at Tube stops and bus shelters. And another part that shrinks away. Hoping that I will forget it all if I keep moving forward, keep focusing on building my business.

Step after step after step.

But somehow the words are sticky, clogging up my throat. I still haven't worked out how to voice them. How to break it all down into a palatable sentence or two for other people to digest. Not even for James. So I walk back inside, fix a smile on my face and close the door.

'Just getting some air. You know, all the fumes from the new fittings.'

Diana says nothing. I'm her boss, it's not her place to ask if I'm stressed out or tired. That's why I like her company. No questions, no curiosity. Just a simple transaction between two parties. We allow each other the space to carry our secrets.

I continue unstacking boxes, filling up the stockroom, trading last-minute details with Diana as we pass each other. But as the hour ticks by, my time here running out, that face at the window haunts me.

It's near midnight by the time I get home. Silence and the lingering smell of massaman curry greet me, but no reproach from James. I'm all ready with my excuses, with the sorrys balanced on my tongue, but our home holds the silence of absence. I swallow, tiptoeing into the lounge, and find him huddled under a blanket. Our takeaway is spread out on the coffee table, two clean wine glasses waiting next to it. I pick

8

one up, the guilt knotting in my stomach. I should have been back hours ago. I should have made time for this. For him.

I crouch down, my eyes level with his as he huffs a small breath, eyelids pinched even in sleep. I move his hair away, wanting to kiss him. Wanting to feel his love. At the touch of my fingers he relaxes and I almost imagine him whispering my name, balancing it on the edge of an exhaled breath. I lean towards him, tracing the shape of his face as he dreams, the pinched tightness around his eyes disappearing. He looks so young. Like the James I first met. No longer weighed down by the last few years. I imagine waking him, curving my body into his and dozing on the sofa with his arms wrapped around me into the small hours of the morning.

But my phone beeps insistently, snapping the moment, and I hurriedly move away. I don't want to wake him. Moving into the bedroom, I shut the door with a quiet click and scroll my phone before curling up in bed.

The last thing I see as I drift off is that face, the one that haunts me still. Peering in from the cold.

Chapter 2

Ghosts are everywhere at this time of year. In the sharp, frosty air, the way the light softens and slows at four o'clock. In the green of the moorland, the grey of the sky and that jagged, closed-off chamber of my heart. I hate Christmas, loathe it in fact. But this year I have a distraction.

'What time were we meant to get there?' I ask, glancing at Diana before hurriedly tapping out an email on my phone. The car jolts as we go over yet another pothole and my heart skips. If it wasn't for Diana driving, I would have abandoned the trip by now. The roads are coated with slick, deadly black ice and every few feet a pothole jars my nerves. I imagine the local council taking one look at the lanes through the moors and shaking their heads, leaving it for the wilds to reclaim them.

'Midday,' Diana snaps. 'We'll make half one, if we're lucky.'

I can't see her face, but I know she's on edge. It's Christmas Day tomorrow and instead of being with her friends sipping glasses of Prosecco, she's here with me. In the middle of nowhere, Cornwall, England. And the drive is taking longer than we expected.

'Look, Eva, I know I said I'd drive you down, but I can only stay for an hour after—'

'You said two,' I shoot back and regret it instantly. 'Sorry, sorry. I'm being awful.' I run my fingers through my hair, twisting the brown strands away from my face. My mind is a revolving to-do list, reminding me of everything that is still undone. The shipment of paper bags arrived after we left this morning and every time I think of them, my stomach twists tighter. When Diana gets back, she'll have to unstack all of them, check the stock and just hope that there are no mistakes. She arches her neck and sighs. I'm putting too much on her, I can tell. But what choice do I have?

'It's fine. Don't worry.' She bites her lip. 'Snow isn't forecast until tomorrow, I can make it back.'

'Maybe you should turn straight around when we get there, just in case—'

'Eva, stop. Chill. Remember, I've got something I need to do here, too.'

I laugh nervously. 'Urgh! You're right. We've worked so hard on this; I just want everything to go right. And the last thing we need is for me to come to this *ridiculous* house party… Who even has a party in the middle of the moors anyway?' Something presses on my chest, a pressure point. A memory, of the last time I came to Penhallow. It was many years ago now, but it could be only yesterday. How every room gleamed with candlelight and pomanders, the scent of oranges and cloves filling those perfect days. I close my eyes, facing the window so Diana doesn't see.

I keep picturing that face at the shop window last night. The melancholy eyes, the folds of greying skin. If only I had been on the other side, if only I had caught her in time.

Diana mutters something, jolting me back to the present as

she takes a sharp right. I look up and spot the sea in the distance, a filmy line of pale blue pressed between sludge-green fields and swollen storm clouds. There's a scattering of sheep and cows across the bleak wilderness, giving way to a vast moorland. We slow as the lane narrows even more, two granite posts jutting out of either side of a gate. It's open, but the cattle grate we judder over tells us we've made it. We're on Bodmin Moor, and Penhallow should be just up ahead. I bite my lip, tapping the weather app open on my phone. Snow for days. It looks like it's going to be a very white Christmas.

I pick up the invite, carelessly discarded under a pile of drive-in food wrappers on the dashboard. It's printed on thick, creamy card, the writing embossed in a stylish calligraphy font. I run my finger over the names at the top, mine and James's. It's the same font we used on our wedding invites. We spent all weekend stuffing those into envelopes, my hair up in a bun, him making endless cups of tea. Then on the Monday morning, we dropped each one into the post box at the end of the street. I remember him counting down to the last, like it was our own little ceremony. A moment to be marked. I wrapped my hands around the back of his neck, leaving tiny ink smudges on his skin, and I remember him saying it, like he still couldn't believe his luck.

I feel like I've won the lottery, getting to marry you.

I laughed breathlessly as he kissed my throat, picking me up to twirl me around on that crisp, early morning London pavement. Knowing that it wasn't James who had won the lottery. He had no idea. It was me.

I wonder if he remembers. If he still feels like the luckiest man in the world. Probably not. Not with the way things have gone between us recently. I had to call Hallie last night, explain that Diana might need a room to freshen up. There was a beat of silence before she agreed, like I'd overstepped a line I didn't realise was there. And I haven't told James yet.

'Did you manage to get that dry cleaning? No probs if there wasn't time,' I say, dropping the invite into my handbag. Maybe I'll mention it to James, how the font is the same. Maybe he'll smile and remember that moment when we posted them too. Flipping open my compact mirror, I check my lipstick for the hundredth time. Everything about this day is putting me on edge. The shop, James, the house party. I just have to relax. Have a glass of Champagne when we arrive, make some small talk – then I can escape with Diana to get the last-minute details ironed out. The socials scheduled, the hashtags aligned. The website update triple-checked so we can launch anew in a few days. Surely James will be OK with that? Just a few hours with Diana, then he has me for the whole of Christmas. It's the longest break I've taken in three years.

'Do you even need to ask about your dry cleaning?' She sniffs, then rattles off the list of garments. 'Two suit jackets, your Armani dress, two white shirts—'

'OK, OK! World's best assistant, for ever and always.' I sigh, casting her a smile. 'What would I do without you?'

A smile breaks apart her frown, her fingers clutching the steering wheel tighter. 'Probably still be drowning in online orders and wearing sweats seven days a week, eating McDonald's fries for breakfast...'

'More than likely.' I grin. It's true.

As the narrow lane leads us further away from civilisation, a thick mist envelops the car. Diana slows to a crawl, pumping her foot on the brake as a flurry of shapes pass in front of us. Their shadowy forms, fluffy in their winter coats, disappear through a gap in the Cornish drystone wall opposite, and we drive on. I glance back, watching them hop through the gap and my heart stutters.

A face is peering back at me.

'Stop!' I screech, grabbing the steering wheel.

'What the fu—' Diana squawks. She slams on the brakes and we skid to a halt.

I fling open my door, throwing off my seat belt, and bolt from the warmth of the car. I saw her. I did. Not just a face at a window this time. She was standing right there, not two feet from all those sheep as they clattered through that gap in the wall, mist swirling as a shroud around her.

'Eva!' Diana calls over. 'What is it?'

My pulse is drumming so fast, great gulps of air shuddering up and out of my lungs as I stumble to the drystone wall…

But there's nothing there. No one. Not a petite woman wearing a waxed green jacket and a headscarf. Not her etched face, blending with the wild moorland as though she is part of it. Born from it. I place my trembling hands on the granite of the wall, closing my eyes briefly. The grating cold of the uneven stones seeps into my fingers, numbing them, burning them. I open my eyes and take a long, shuddering breath. It was her.

I'm sure of it.

'Look, Eva, we should press on…' Diana says in the kind of voice people use when they're delivering bad news. The soft, irritating sort that goes perfectly with supermarket flowers and generic, pastel-coloured cards. It's exactly the sort of sharp reminder I need to reel myself back in, fix a smile on over my teeth and shut it all away.

'We should. You're absolutely right,' I say, marching back to the car. 'I thought I saw someone who needed help. Didn't get enough shut-eye last night, between the late night and that warehouse call and—' As I catch Diana's shuffling, awkward expression, I quickly stop talking. I shouldn't have to explain myself.

We set off again, Diana sitting a little straighter, the atmosphere in the car charged with tension. She probably thinks I'm overdoing it. It does feel that way; my head is a scatter of half thoughts and memories. I have one foot in the present, one in the past, just like every Christmas since. I hoped that by timing the shop launch now it might pull me fully into the present. Into the *now*. But it's just intensified it, the stress, the disconnect. If anything, I'm more aware than ever that when I see her, even a fleeting glimpse, it isn't real.

It won't ever be real again.

'Can't be much further…' Diana mutters.

I squint, as if I can somehow peel the fog away, trying to see past the murk to what lies ahead. Then a shape emerges. 'At last.'

It's exactly how I remember it. The house is tall and imposing, built from granite with three storeys and a sweep of gravel driveway in front. Dark green ivy creeps up the wall to the left of the front door, winding in a curve, reaching for the centre windows. There's a sign by the entrance, the name of the house picked out in smart white lettering on a piece of smooth cut slate.

Penhallow.

It hasn't changed in all this time. There's already a scattering of cars outside and a few lights are on at the windows. I take a steadying breath. So the rest of the guests are already here. I had hoped that I could squirrel myself away in whatever bedroom Hallie has put James and me in and gather myself together before the party begins. I need a moment to breathe.

It's just the kind of house Hallie has always wanted to live in. She'd told me as much when I had talked about Penhallow, how grand it is, how the rooms are filled with candlelight, how it's the kind of house you want to make memories in. Her name and the label of best friend twined together in my head sends a little shiver of guilt through me, snapping me up to sit a little straighter. As though I can shrug it off. But there's also a twist of bitterness worming its way through my chest. Penhallow is perfect in my memories, I don't want to find it any less than that in reality. But now Hallie has chosen it as the setting for this house party, I have no choice but to compare the place I find today with the dream I slip into when I need to escape the world. I just hope it hasn't changed too much. That those perfect memories won't be tainted.

Apart from our hurried phone call last night, I haven't spoken to her in months. In fact, I'm not sure I can call her my best friend anymore. She invited both of us to this, me and James, but I know it's for his benefit, not mine. I've morphed from the person in her life whom she texts daily and meets regularly for brunch on a Sunday morning, to her husband's best friend's wife. And every time I think of her, my stomach twists. We've moved so far from those early days, the four of us living together in a cramped little flat in Clapham. The one that had two cupboards for a kitchen and a microwave that was temperamental at best. It's been so long since we lived in each other's pockets, closer than sisters. And now, I'm not sure how we stumbled so far from that path.

But James insisted on this. Insisted I be here, on Christmas Eve, and stay put for four whole days. He's been at the office every day, his calls and messages growing steadily sparser over the past few months and now the looming silence has become too noticeable to miss. We used to have a running conversation throughout the day, tucked away in text messages with little emojis and funny memes. Even when we were just across London from each other, he at his office, me at the shop or the tiny crooked office space I rent. But now we are ships that pass in the night.

I blink, seeing his car parked up. It's nearest the house, which means he must have arrived pretty early. I didn't even notice him leave this morning. Diana picked me up at eight, we went straight to the shop and grabbed KFC on the way down. I can still smell fried chicken when I breathe through my nose. The scent of it lingers on my clothes and suddenly, I desperately crave a shower and half an hour to give in to the swirl of long-dead things. The shadows that linger, curling around the edges of the holiday season like smoke.

But I know that isn't what I'm about to get as we crunch to a halt, Diana parking at the farthest end of the driveway. A set of curtains twitches at a downstairs window, and I catch the flurry of a person moving. They know we've arrived.

'I guess I-I'll go and say hi to everyone,' I say, getting out of the car. I straighten out my crumpled clothes, feeling the ache in my lower back as I stretch out. As I look up, I feel dwarfed by the expanse of this house. Not just the people inside now, all these people I haven't been able to make time for, but the memories of visits past. Of all the times I have been here before. The present and past clatter together, layers of Christmases all shouting in my head. I pinch the bridge of my nose, needing all my thoughts, my worries, to quiet down. Needing to get through the next few days, one moment at a time.

The door opens as I approach, letting out a gust of warmth. I spy the welcoming hallway, a chequerboard floor of black-and-white tiles that I used to play hopscotch on, the gorgeous solid wood staircase in the centre with boughs of ivy and twinkly lights running up the banisters on either side. The scent of cinnamon and evergreen wraps around me, tugging me forward. It's so similar to what I have locked away in my memories. I can almost feel her warm hand in mine, the childish elation of another Christmas spent with her in this place. I gulp, pain flaring as it always does in the wake of the most vivid memories of before. In those few steps to the front door, I pull myself back and wring the pain from my heart. I take a breath, look up.

And there, standing in the doorway, is Hallie. Her features are tense, filled with hesitance, as though she is not sure how this meeting will go. I step forward, remembering all the messages I have ignored. How our conversation on the phone last night could have been between two strangers. There is so much we haven't said, so much *I* haven't said, and in a rush, all that pain floods my chest once more. I should share it with Hallie. I should let it rush up my throat and spill out at our feet, then maybe she'll understand. But this isn't the moment. This isn't the time to break apart.

Chapter 3

'Hey,' I say, moving to hug her. 'The place looks great.'

She gives me the briefest hug back, the lightest of pressure on my arms, before letting go. She's got her dyed blonde hair loose around her pale cheekbones and shoulders, berry lipstick on and a thick, blue wool jumper and jeans. I want to compliment her on her jumper and the casual way she suits this house, as if Penhallow is the kind of home built into her bones. But the words stick in my throat.

'Just like you remembered? Did you find it OK?'

'Sure,' I say, sidestepping the first question and indicating Diana, who steps up behind me. 'Di knows the area. Grew up nearby.'

'Is that so?' Hallie says, her tone an almost imperceptible degree warmer than when she greeted me. She holds out a hand to Diana. 'Nice to meet you. Welcome. You're just here for a couple of hours, right?'

Diana awkwardly holds her hand out for Hallie to shake. I try not to notice that their smiles are so much brighter for each other than they ever are for me. 'If that's OK? Sorry to barge in. But actually, I've got to get somewhere first... all right, Eva?'

19

I nod, wondering for the first time where she's going, what this appointment is. Why she can't quite meet my eyes.

Hallie waves her hand. 'It's no bother, really. Everyone's gone out for a walk.' She steps back into the dark embrace of the hallway. 'The door will be open when you get back.'

'Thanks,' Diana says before turning to me. 'Do you need any bags out of the car, or…'

I hurriedly return to the boot, pulling out my suitcase. I open my mouth to say bye to Diana, but she's already in the driver's seat, adjusting her mirrors, avoiding my gaze. I shrug it off. She's probably told me already.

I cross the gravel, dragging my suitcase behind me as Diana drives off, and step over the threshold of Penhallow. I'm suddenly aware of how vast and echoing the entrance hall is. It feels even bigger than when I was little. Aren't places supposed to seem smaller the older you get? It wouldn't be out of place on a shoot of *Downton Abbey*. It'd been a small hotel long before I came here every Christmas, but it's since become a holiday home. There are eight bedrooms from what I can remember, all set on the first floor along two corridors that peel off, left and right.

The third floor is an attic, and I wonder if it still stores all the old treasures from past lives that I used to discover. Strings of yellowing pearls, sepia-tinted photographs, forgotten teddy bears and painted porcelain dolls… I brush my hand over an arrangement of dried flowers in a vase by the door, taking a moment as those memories twist and unfurl. The soft sheath of pale creams is like running my fingers through feathers.

Suddenly, it feels like she's here. *Gran.* I remember the second time I was here, after Granddad had passed and it was just Gran and me alone. How we arranged dried flowers in vases, the stiff little limbs coating my fingers in the scent of dust and lavender. And how when I walked around the kitchen garden at dusk, Granddad joined me for a chat about the blackbird's nest I had found. How I told Gran that night as she read my favourite Shirley Hughes poems, and her secret smile as she wished me goodnight. I still wonder about that, how I must have muddled the visits up. But those blue blackbird's eggs and the sound of my Granddad's slow, kind voice are imprinted on my heart like ink.

For the first time, I wonder why Hallie chose this place. Why now, at Christmas.

'Is James around?' I ask her, peering into the rooms that lead off the entrance hall. It all rearranges itself from my childhood vision of it, taking on life and energy. Breathing. There's a dining room, dark wood furniture arranged in a neat line down the centre. A formal-looking sitting room hangs to the right, a slice of cream-coloured sofas just visible through the doorway. There's another door that is closed at the back, tucked in against the staircase. The memory of a kitchen, molten hot chocolate, my cold fingers wrapped around a mug of it. A snug lounge with squishy sofas and leather armchairs, a chessboard always out on the coffee table. Her pale mauve knitting bundled on her lap. A fireplace crackling as the wind howled down the chimney.

My parents… absent. Elsewhere. Working away and leaving me with Gran for another extended stay. As absent as they always are, even now. I push away those memories, trying to stay grounded in today. In this moment.

'Yeah, James is here. He went out with the others.' Hallie laughs. 'Probably all found the pub by now. Anyway, I'll show you which room is yours and I guess you can help yourself to food? The staff put some stuff out for lunch at midday that should still be all right. What is it now... half past one? It's all in the snug, through that door at the back. I guess you know that though! Do you, er... need anything else?'

I nod, holding up my phone. My mind is already now on the shop, that delivery of printed paper bags still sitting outside and a thousand other small details I still need to work out. 'No, that's great. Thanks.' As I move around the entrance hall, my phone still shows nothing. No signal, no Wi-Fi... zip. I frown, standing on tiptoes to hold it high above my head. Nothing. 'Do you know where I can get service here?'

'Oh, there's none. And the internet's down, something about a faulty connection at the exchange?' Hallie shrugs. 'Anyway, you can get signal at the pub, and Wi-Fi. But it's a bit of a hike across the fields. Not that we need it, right?'

I smile, laughing nervously. No Wi-Fi? Or phone signal?! This was *not* good. Not good at all. What about the socials? The scheduled posts? I pocket my phone, avoiding eye contact with Hallie. I'm on edge. Balancing on a knife blade. And the smallest breath of wind, the slightest flip in my plans unbalances me.

I need to be alone. I need to refocus. That's all.

Hallie reaches for my suitcase but I shake my head. 'Absolutely not! No need to put your back out on the first day.'

I follow after her, feeling like a lemon as we climb the red-carpeted treads to the first floor. Glancing up, I can see the staircase is less regal leading up to the second floor, but no less festooned in ivy and twinkly lights. It's all so decadent. Expectant. A house waiting for something to happen. 'How many people are here?'

'Oh, you know. You and James, obviously now Diana for a bit when she gets back… Natalie. Kian's cousin, John. I think six of us? Dad couldn't make it. But that's about it.'

'The usual crowd then,' I say, propping the door open with my foot that leads off onto another corridor. 'And you said you have staff too?'

'The woman we hired this place from sends two for the Christmas package.' Hallie smiles. 'They live local, so they can get back to their families after they've served dinner tomorrow. I'd hate to separate them from their loved ones on Christmas Day, you know?'

I try not to think about the subtext of Hallie's comment. Diana chose this, I want to say. She wants to be in my shoes, that's what she told me eighteen months ago when I gave her the job. I warned her about the late nights, the weekends, the cancellation of holiday plans. And she agreed to all of it, grateful and determined. She wants to learn the ropes so she can start her own business, or grow mine enough that she's managing it alongside me.

But Hallie has never been interested in running a business. She's a creative, a freelancer, and prefers a slower life. I just wish she would see that it's worth it, my choices. Even the ones that lead me away from her.

'This is your room,' Hallie says, stopping at the second door on the left. 'And that…' she indicates the farthest door at the end of the corridor, 'is a spare room for Diana to freshen up if she needs to. I guess it's all the same as your last visit. The owner told me she didn't change too much when she took it on, just repairs and things. Anyway… see you both downstairs in a bit? When she gets back here?'

I say my thank yous and shuffle around before Hallie disappears back to the staircase. Leaving me alone.

Pushing my overnight bag and suitcase into the room, I flop onto the bed. Staring at the ceiling, all I see is white. A buzz of nothingness just behind my eyes. I dread this day every year. It's precious and must be marked, and yet I want to run from it. Escape these twenty-four hours and somehow wake up on Christmas Day, with everything as it was before. And now I'm alone, the weight of it settles over me.

With a sniff, I force myself up, the heaviness of my heart dragging me down. I have a miniature in my bag, one of those you get in anonymous hotel minibars. I think it might be rum, or maybe whisky. It was shoved at the back of the tea and coffee cupboard in our apartment – it could have even been a leftover from our honeymoon. I freeze for a second, picturing the James and me of just a few years ago. The hot white sand, the bluest blue of the ocean. His eyes crinkling with laughter as I freaked out over seeing my first shark in the water beside us. His hand, tanned from the sun, as he passed a cocktail to me. It might be the last memento of our honeymoon, this miniature.

I rub my thumb over it, remembering the late afternoon we walked along the beach. How the sand still held the heat of the day, the water at the tideline trailing over my toes. He leaned down, brushed his fingers over the sand and stood up, holding something out to me.

For you.

I laughed as he placed it in my palm. The palest, moon-white scallop shell.

How did you know it's my favourite?

His hand found mine, just as my eyes found his. Everything I ever wanted. Everything I needed.

I know you, Eva, he said. *I just know.*

Rummaging in my suitcase, I push that memory aside, pulling out a polystyrene cup I grabbed from KFC on the way down. It still has one of those plastic filmy lids over it and I peel it back, propping myself against the foot of the bed. I pour in the miniature, the acrid scent of the alcohol hitting the back of my throat. But it hardly matters. As long as the moment is marked.

'To you, my darling,' I say softly, aware of the tone of my voice in the thick silence. The irony of being back here, marking this day as if it's a celebration with a miniature from one of the happiest times of my life. I raise the tumbler, and down it. It stings, just as I knew it would, fire and fury wiping everything clean. I cough, eyes watering from the fumes, and place the empty tumbler at my side.

I think about the last time I saw her. All broken and wrong in that hospital bed after someone skidded on the black ice and hit her. They left her on the road, alone in the snow. It still steals my breath to think of it, how she was on her way to Penhallow, to this very place. Where she spent every Christmas, even when I couldn't make it down from London anymore. And I think about her on this moorland, that headscarf tied under her chin, a wink and a crooked smile just for me as we rub tiny yellow gorse flowers between our fingertips. The scent of coconut clinging to our skin. Her scent. I try to hold on to that image of her, instead of the bad one. The wrong one, when someone took her life from her so suddenly, so violently.

When someone took my world from me.

She was the anchor in our family, the home I ran to when

mine with my parents became too edged with sharp words and long silences. Or when they were gone for so long with work, I'd practically become her own child. She was the one stood at the side of the track on sports day. The person who sat in my parent–teacher meetings, nodding along seriously as they discussed my mock exam results, how I excelled at conversational French. I still remember the hollow pit in my stomach as my parents let me down, forgetting to collect me from a swimming lesson when I was nine. And her, driving like the clappers to come and scoop me up. Fuss over me. Make me beans on toast and pretend it was all OK. I long to hold her hand in mine, hear her voice full of witty, gentle prying, old-fashioned sayings and offerings of fruit cake and warmth.

But she isn't coming back. That woman at the side of the road, the face in the shop window, was just a mirror of my own longing. My gran, my home, is three years dead.

Now she is just my ghost.

Chapter 4

A shower is exactly what I need. As the spray hits my shoulders, every muscle in my back loosens. I breathe in, out, picking up the shower gel from my travel toiletries pack and lathering up the scent of vanilla and jasmine. After standing under the jets for an extra five minutes, I reluctantly turn them off and step out into the steamed-up bathroom. It's huge and stately, filled with fluffy white towels with a separate claw-footed bath under the window and a his and hers set of basins. The floor is that same checked black-and-white tile as the entrance hall and every tap gleams gold, reflecting in the huge mirror along one wall. I wrap my hair up in a towel and pull another one around my body to pad over to it. Sweeping my hand over the glass, my face appears between streaks of condensation.

I look exhausted. There are grey grooves under my eyes, the usual blue of them dull and bloodshot. My skin has that ghostly appearance of someone who spends too long hunched over a laptop screen, and not enough time outdoors or asleep. I untwist my hair from the towel, shaking the brown cloud of it out over my shoulders. At least I've had it cut recently. And with a bit of make-up, I can cover up most of the damage my lifestyle stamps on my skin. The doughnut runs, the all-too-frequent glasses of wine. But the red-veined lines in my eyes won't disappear.

The shop launch will make my business. Right now, it's still hidden in the folds of the internet, its reach defined by social media algorithms and sponsored ad posts. It's all about traffic, target audiences, and digital footprints. But this shop is real, I can touch it. I can breathe it in and walk around it. It's my creation, something I've made that has a *pulse*. It beats with life and expectation.

It'll all be worth it, I'm sure of it. A wave of determination, blood-hot and electric, zips through me. 'This is what I want,' I mouth into the mirror. *All I want.* Maybe it wasn't always, and maybe I had to make space in my life for it. But people and relationships are transient, ebbing and flowing like the tide.

I learned that the hard way.

I pull out my suitcase in the bedroom suite, unzipping the various travel bags inside. I like to keep things orderly. First impressions, at trade fairs and in meetings, are a thirty-second game that I am determined to always win. My capsule work wardrobe folds up perfectly into the grey bags in case I need to change before heading back to London. The various casual clothes I had already pre-packed for this holiday party are stowed in the black ones. I knew I wouldn't have time this morning to pack, so I did it last weekend.

Tossing them on the bed, I check out the room. It's got a huge four-poster bed, a thick moss-green carpet and a set of sofas in front of a working fireplace. There's a big hardwood wardrobe and two sets of drawers against the far wall. But it's the view that stops me in my tracks. Facing out from the front of the house, it takes in the sweep of driveway, then the moorland beyond. The mist has receded, the sun bathing the land in the pale hues of a wintery day. It's breathtaking. A tapestry of Cornish drystone walls cut across the green of the land and, in the distance, a craggy set of hills with white already dusting the tops of them. I can see the old ruined croft a mile or so away; it's made of granite with tumbledown walls.

Gran and I used to walk to it for our first walk each year. Our little ritual. As I press my fingertips against the pearly panes of the windows, lost in the snapshot memories of those walks, I can see why Hallie chose this place. Why she fell in love with it from the stories I shared with her and decided it would be perfect for her own house party. It's a world away from the reality of Tube stops and shops and deadlines. And underneath the calm veneer is a beating heart with all those childhood memories. They're bleeding behind the walls, ensnaring me at every turn. It's like walking through a waking dream, being back here.

This was my favourite holiday place, one that hasn't blended in with the few Mum and Dad took me on abroad, when they would stick me in a kids' club while they enjoyed mojitos and grown-up lunches. I can still pick out particular years, with Gran, that shine like tiny keepsakes. The one when Gran and I had late-night feasts when I was eight, built snowmen with carrot noses and played fiercely competitive board games in front of the crackling fire. She taught me how to play chess here. And somehow, the library always knew which book I wanted. It would be waiting for me, sitting on the table as I walked in. I shake my head now, but it seemed so real then. The magic of this place, twining through the walls, casting a web around it. It was like stepping into Narnia. I still find it hard to discern what was real, and what was made up. Perhaps, though, it was all real.

My phone pings in my handbag and I freeze, then launch myself at it. Scrabbling quickly, I dig it out to find a tumble of messages and emails. But as soon as I move, the one bar of signal disappears.

'You've got to be joking…' I mutter as I tap through the various missed notifications. Three emails from the small marketing and PR firm working with me for the shop launch. One from Hallie from a couple of hours ago, checking I wasn't lost. And a message from Mum filled with her own feelings. I swallow, quickly deleting that notification. I don't need to see it. I can't handle her feelings right now, or anyone else's as well as my own. It's not as if we're in touch anymore, or if she ever asks me how I am.

Moving on to the work ones, I find that only half of them load and I practically scream in frustration as I see the words 'issue' and 'urgent', but none of the context.

Carefully, I replace the phone where it had signal, trying to coax even the briefest flicker of life from it – 'Come on, come on…' – but it stays stubbornly blank.

I hear the thump of feet outside in the corridor, and a muffled laugh. Then the door flies open.

'Oh,' James says when he sees me, crouched over my phone in just a towel. 'I thought you'd hit traffic.'

'We got here quicker than we thought.' I straighten, making sure my towel is still firmly wrapped around me.

He glances at his feet, then over my shoulder towards the window. Never quite meeting my eyes. We both talk at once.

'Sorry, I—'

'Meant to ask—'

I take a breath, waiting for him to speak. He shakes his head, smiling ruefully, and something aches, deep in my chest.

'You said… you said *we*. You didn't, did you?' he says, pushing his hands into his pockets.

'I… the thing is—'

'Diana's here, isn't she?' He lets out a huff of a laugh, staring at the carpet. 'We had a deal, Eva.'

'It's just a few hours, she had an appointment nearby so it just made sense…' I drift off, horribly aware of how still he is. 'James?'

He shakes his head again, never meeting my eyes. 'It still astounds me, the lengths you'll go to.'

'I… that's a *bit* unfair, isn't it? I'm here! I'm right here and I'm all yours. We have a few things to go over, a few niggles…'

He sighs, opening then closing his mouth. I rush on, wanting to stop this argument before it's begun, wanting to defuse it. 'This is the last little bit of work, and Di isn't staying overnight or anything. It's no big deal! Please, James… please…'

'I'll see you downstairs in a bit,' he says abruptly.

'James, wait—'

But he's already gone.

I tighten my fists in frustration. He's mad about the takeaway last night. He must be. It's not directly about Diana, he likes her. It's because I missed our date night. But if he would only let me speak, if he would just *listen*… I sigh, turning my attention back to my phone. He has to have forgotten what day it is. The anniversary. Otherwise he would have stayed with me. He wouldn't be picking a fight, or judging me for needing to work a few more hours. I'm sure of it.

When no more messages or emails come through, I dress quickly in a white button-down and jeans. The house feels warm enough, so I don't bother with a jumper. But I take a minute to fix my make-up, filling my features with much needed colour. I fix pearl studs in my ears and run my fingers through my hair. I try to breathe some life into myself. There's a knock at the door and I open it to find Diana, laptop tucked under one arm, her folder of notes under the other.

'Shall we get ahead now, or do you need more food?'

I smile, relieved that at least *she's* on board with what I'm trying to create.

We settle into a steady rhythm of quiet, occasionally interrupting each other to pass documents back and forth. It's the best we can do without Wi-Fi. She knows my business inside out, there's no one else I would trust with this. But still, I check every detail. The bounce rates on the home page of the website. The lines of product that are performing best, the planned social media roll-out, the suppliers' next deliveries. The work calms me, washes away my frustration with James. The memories bleeding from the walls. The whisky, still burning the back of my throat. And Gran's face, her voice. The ache in my chest.

Gradually, the room changes from dim, wintery light to a glowing pink and I glance up to see the winter sun is fast disappearing behind those hills in the distance. Stretching, I check my watch and find it's nearly 4 p.m.

'We should call it a day, you need to get back,' I say. Guilt niggles at me. I haven't even said hi to the other guests, most of whom I have known for years. 'Are you all right to get back on the road? Do you need something to eat first?'

'I can grab something on the way,' she says, already packing up. She stretches, smiling briefly, and crosses to the window. I'm busily closing down documents on my laptop when she thumps the window with her fist.

'It's already started. Bugger, bugger, bugger.'

I look up, a frown creasing my forehead, and move to stand next to her. The sky is darkening quickly to the colour of misery, a thick flurry blotting out the landscape. I clench my jaw, blinking down at the cars to see a layer of snow already covering them. 'But the weather app—'

'Said tomorrow morning. Yeah,' Diana groans, turning away from the window. 'I won't make it back. Not at night-time.'

I watch her as she pushes back her hair, agitation marking every movement. I don't know what to say. It's not just her Christmas that will get messed up, it's the whole launch. *Everything.* All our plans depended on her being there. Not stuck here with me.

'It might be clear enough in the morning, the gritters...' I tail off. Of course, there won't be as many out on the roads on Christmas Day. Even if she can get off the moors safely, the ice will have compacted overnight. 'Shit,' I say, rubbing my temples. Without her there in the next few days to make sure it all runs smoothly... 'I'll have to cancel. Postpone. There's nothing else for it.'

Diana says nothing.

'I'll let Hallie know that you're staying for a couple of days, if that's OK with you? She won't mind.' I force a note of calm into my voice, even though inside, I'm screaming. I should have stayed in London. I shouldn't have left everything to fate and expected it all to go right. Especially not at this time of year.

And with no signal, no Wi-Fi, I can't even contact the PR and marketing firm to pause promotions. I can't speak to the suppliers, the warehouse and tell them to hold off on deliveries. I can't even access my own sodding emails.

'I'd better go and get changed,' Diana says, making me jump. 'Can I borrow a few things from you?' I had forgotten she was there.

'Yes, yes, of course,' I say as she quickly pulls out a couple of outfits from my suitcase then leaves the room.

I begin to pace. Everything I've been working towards, the sacrifices, the debt… it's all going to fall apart. It was a distraction at first, planning the launch for just after Christmas. I had hoped to be so busy, so *consumed*, that I might even forget. Skip over these dark days completely.

But it's also just being smart. I have to cash flow all the debt payments and it's going to be tight as it is in the next month or so. Just after the holidays is when people have Christmas money to spend; everyone's ready to escape the house filled with guests and children and wander around the shops, looking at bright shiny things. Specifically, *my* shop. *My* bright shiny things.

I stop pacing, an idea forming. What if I took the risk? What if I told James I had to leave… and just went? No worrying about Diana on the roads. It would be my car, my neck that was at risk, not hers. If I just don't think about black ice, about the terror of losing control… I gulp. I could get back by the small hours, be in the shop tomorrow morning. Warming to the idea even more, I cross to the door. I'll go and tell James.

Downstairs, the entrance hall is full of the echo of laughter and soft-voiced conversations behind the doors that lead off it. I can't pick out the deep rumble of James's voice, so instead of choosing the dining room or sitting room at the front of the house, I head for the door that leads to the back. I open it to find another web of doors and a floor made of cold flagstones. This section of the house is noticeably chillier, the cold piercing the

34

thick socks I put on. I hug my arms around my chest, reading the gold name plaques on the various doors. I don't bother with Kitchens or Scullery, or even Snug. Instead, I try the Billiards Room, hearing a deep male voice behind the door.

Inside, the room is wood panelled, a single beaten-up leather chair in the corner. It's odd that it's called a billiards room, as it has a snooker table in the centre. Perhaps it's a nod to what used to be played in here, before the snooker table was moved in and the billiards one removed. Just another eccentricity of Penhallow. Low lights hang over the snooker table. I find James squinting at me, Hallie's husband, Kian, at the far end of the room. I stutter in my determination.

'Eva! You got here,' Kian says, the dimples in his brown cheeks deepening. I cross the room to give him a hug, which he returns with real warmth. 'I thought you were stuck in traffic.'

'She got here a couple of hours ago,' James says, potting a ball. Pointedly avoiding eye contact.

Kian releases me, that warm smile still fixed to his face. But now, it looks a little forced.

'How long has it been? Six months? You're looking great,' I say. And he is. Kian is a human rights barrister, and completely passionate and dedicated. I know he stays up as late as me, but it never seems to show on his face. He's been like this since our uni days, crouched over a set of scattered textbooks in the library, teasing Hallie as she made careful notes for her art history degree. She always studied with me after we met on the first day in halls, our bedrooms right next to each other. I remember the moment they first met, it was just after James and I had started going out, and Kian brought over tea for Hallie in a takeaway cup. That dimple appeared and she was lost. It was the four of us after that, every day, every evening. Until we all finally stopped renting together and bought our own places. Even now I can still picture his favourite Snoopy mug. How he would so carefully carry Hallie's cup of tea to her each morning.

'Seven. It's been seven months. We miss you,' he says, glancing up to look at James. 'You don't bring her over enough, man.'

I catch a flicker of annoyance on James's face out of the corner of my eye and turn to face him. 'Can we talk?'

'After dinner? I just want to finish up here,' he says, barely looking at me. 'Got to beat him at least once a day.'

'Is that right?' Kian laughs, stepping back to the table. 'Because I'm about to whip that bony arse of yours.'

They get back into the game and I'm left hovering on the periphery. I could force him to talk to me now, listen to why I have to leave. But as he jokes with Kian, I shrink a little. Maybe I should have dinner first with everyone. At least show my face, prove that I have made the effort. Then whatever tale James chooses to spin about what a workaholic I am might fall a little flat. I sigh as I trudge back up the stairs.

Something has shifted between James and me. This past year has been littered with cancelled dates, hurried catch-ups on the phone between work meetings. The most time I spent with him recently is on the Tube, three stops to his office. Then the last two stops I travel solo to my own little rented office space. It's a solid twenty minutes we spent together every morning, but lately, I'm in and out of London so much that even that pattern had been broken.

As I get back to our bedroom, flopping down on the bed, I try to remember the last time we shared one. When was the last time I didn't tiptoe to the spare room so as not to wake him? I can't easily recall which side of the mattress is his, and which one is mine. It's those things that make up the glue of our relationship, that have kept us together through the last fourteen years. The rituals, the shared things like the fact that my toothbrush is always purple, his is always the green one in a new pack.

The day we met is tattooed on my heart, printed inside me like a song. I was in the domed reading room in the uni library, filled with the discreet shuffle of papers and well-shod feet. It was one of my favourite places to visit. I flashed my university ID card for the second time that week, the thrill squeezing my ribs that I could just walk in. I could wander the stacks of this hushed place, run my finger down a thousand spines and read whatever book I wanted. I was only a month into my course, that first heady freshers' week a dim memory, and after many years of escaping into the pages of stories, it was my new haven in this loud, vibrant city. And I knew just which book I wanted to find next.

He was hovering nearby, arms cradling at least ten volumes, staring intently at a shelf mark. I felt sure he worked there with all those books, the mussed-up brown hair, the glasses. I walked right up to him, asking if he worked at the library. Asking where I could find the book.

'It's by Dodie Smith,' I said.

'The one about Dalmatians?' he said, his eyes crinkling.

'No,' I said. 'The one about Cassandra. *I Capture the Castle.*'

'Oh. Of course. Follow me.'

He dropped all those books on a nearby table, his hand hovering near my elbow, just shy of touching. He was so much taller than me, nodding to almost everyone as we walked until we found ourselves in a stack filled from floor to ceiling. The scent of dust and wood polish wafted around us, every sound beyond the stacks seeming so very far away. Like we were the only people that still existed. He peered at the shelves and my heart gave a funny flip, and I wondered, just briefly, what it would feel like if he concentrated on me like that. If he looked at me, this boy in the library, as though I was the only story he wanted to read.

When he handed me the book, our fingertips brushed and it was really just us. Just us in that moment, surrounded by a world of old books. He smiled, admitting he didn't really work there. He had seen me in there the week before, hoping to catch my eye. Hoping I might appear again. He just wanted an excuse to ask for my name.

So I told him.

Eva.

There was something about him. The way his head tilted slightly to hear my name, how he clearly felt at home in this hushed, hallowed place. I asked him what his favourite book was, what he would recommend, and he grinned, striding two stacks down, searching for the right one on an overstuffed shelf. When he pulled out the book all seriously, it was almost hesitant. Like he was handing me a window into his soul. I folded my hand around it, promising I would read it there and then.

It wasn't until after I left the library, when I was tucked up on my bed, leafing through the library books, that a piece of paper fell out. It drifted onto my duvet, his name, *James*, and a phone number. No expectations. No demand for a text or a call. Just his spidery scrawl in black Biro on a torn-off sheet from a notebook. My heart still thuds as wildly as then, remembering how I wrote and rewrote that first message to him, agonising over every syllable. How I waited the two minutes, which seemed to drag like two hours for him to reply. For him to say, *Yes, I like that café too. Let's meet there.*

But somehow between that day and now we have come unstuck. The glue has worn away, and all the pieces of us are coming apart. More and more, it seems that I can't be good at both work and life. I'm not sure how we got here.

Or how to fix us.

Chapter 5

'A toast to our lovely hosts, Hallie and Kian.'

We all raise our glasses, a sea of glinting Champagne flutes all bubbling and gold. I smile around the dining room at these people, my friends. The people who make up the social circles of mine and James's shared existence.

The people I have barely seen or spoken to this past year.

'And a toast to the wonderful staff,' Hallie says, warm eyes liquid in the candlelight, 'for making this the best Christmas ever.'

Everyone says, 'Cheers!', taking another sip, and I catch the two members of staff slinking out of the dining room, having just delivered the first course. Probably to scarf down their own dinner between preparing the mains.

I cut into the scallops in front of me, the three perfect pieces melting on my tongue. I'm starving. All I've eaten for a week are takeout noodles and sandwiches in plastic wraps, crouched over cardboard boxes, my desk or the tiny pull-out tray on a train. This is like the food of the gods right now. I take another gulp of Champagne, the warm fizz relaxing my mind.

It'll all be OK. I have to promise myself that as I peek over at Diana, who is steadfastly staring at her plate. If I can sneak off to get signal, then maybe Diana can leave in the morning. Maybe I could call her a taxi. I don't need to be so reactionary, do I? Maybe I don't need to disappear in the middle of the night. Perhaps James and I can avoid the brewing storm of an argument. I can be the doting wife, ignore the memories crawling from the walls of this place and be back in London with some small excuse on Boxing Day. Two days. That's all. And I can bury this Christmas, just like I've buried the others before. The Champagne fizzes in my stomach at the thought.

'So, Eva, I saw that interview you did in the *Guardian* online,' Kian's cousin, John, says across the table. He glances up, spearing a scallop and speaking around it as he places it in his mouth. 'Must be quite a thing for you, opening the shop. Big leap, big risk.'

I flush, irritated as all eyes swivel to me. I hate being caught off guard like this, especially when I haven't been paying attention. I try to remember what John does. I know it's something in logistics. One of the big headquarters, based just outside London. Perhaps one of my suppliers goes through him?

'It's a good move for the company. Expansion, dreaming big. Got to take some risk to grow,' I babble.

'Must be a *sizeable* risk with that location,' he booms, wiping his mouth with his napkin and looking around for back-up. But Hallie is staring avidly at her plate, Diana is chewing methodically, eyes fixed on the far wall, and Natalie and Kian are tied up in their own conversation further down the table.

'No shop talk, come on,' James says, putting an arm around the back of my chair. His shirtsleeve brushes the back of my neck, sending a tingle trailing down my spine. 'It's Christmas.'

I smile at him weakly. To anyone else, it looks like he's come to my defence. But I know what it really means, the way he's putting an arm around my back, how he leans forward, a flush creeping up his throat. He hates discussing my company. Loathes it. Especially the remortgaging, the refinancing. The extra loan I had to take out just last week. It wasn't always this way, I'm sure of it. When I first started out, he was my biggest supporter. But over the past year, his tolerance has worn thin. He despises my absence as I've nurtured my business, pressing all my energy and time into its unfurling.

The only times we have talked about my work over the past year it's ended in blazing arguments, usually with one of us walking out. Every one of those heated, loaded words we've both shrieked pierces me now.

I take a piece of bread from the basket in front of me, ripping it to shreds in my fingers.

'James tells me that you're planning a ski trip,' I say smoothly, recovering as I fix a polite smile on for John.

He nods, swiping a piece of bread and slathering it with butter as he talks. 'Just a quickie. The Alps for a week. You guys are coming, right?' He looks up and grins. 'Unless you've got news we don't know about...'

James splutters and I take a quick gulp of Champagne, as obviously as I can. We can't afford a ski trip. Not the kind of trip that John likes to book. But now, if we don't go... I mentally calculate which credit cards I haven't maxed out yet and trying to ignore the churn in my stomach. 'Nope! We're totally free. Let's work out the dates.'

'Awesome,' he says, nodding to James. 'Look forward to tackling some of those black runs with you again.'

I groan theatrically, earning a short laugh from James. It surprises me, how easily we can slip into character.

'I'll never hear the end of it from Eva if I break something again,' James says, winking at me. The last time we went skiing, he fractured his ankle and had to be airlifted off the slopes. I clear my throat, pushing down the feeling of panic, the flash of that sickening swirl of snow as he went down right in front of me. How it took forever (or that's how it felt) for any medical help to arrive. Before that, we had been drinking hot chocolate at a mountain-top lodge, pulling off our ski gloves to hold hands. As James moves his arm from around my back now, I wonder if he will hold my hand, even for a moment; if he will squeeze it under the table to reassure me.

He doesn't.

'No black runs,' I say in a more measured voice than I thought I could manage. 'It's my only rule.'

John rolls his eyes and turns to Diana, sat on his left. 'You ski, right? I'm sorry, we haven't been introduced…'

'This is Diana,' I cut in. 'My assistant.'

John whistles. 'Wow, this shop launch must be *pretty* serious.'

Diana blushes, but straightens her back to hold her own. 'Couldn't get back tonight with the visibility and the roads being so icy, that's all.'

I smile politely, even as I catch the pinch of Diana's mouth as she sips of her drink. I go to take another gulp of my own, but find the glass empty. I need to pace myself. We still have to go over some points after this dinner, and James and I need to talk. I need a clear head.

James turns to the person sitting on the other side of him, Hallie's younger sister, Natalie. They start talking about her year of backpacking through Australia and New Zealand, how her girlfriend is now her fiancée. I carefully pour myself some water. I feel eyes on me and look up to find John sizing me up. For a beat, we both stare at each other and it's that naked, candid kind of stare that strips everything away. It tells me he knows what a fraud I really am. That my work life has stripped my personal one down to its bare bones, wringing every minute from me. That I've chosen to live this way, and James is paying the price. Then he turns to Diana, asking her more about her education, how she came to work for me. I tune them out, tearing up another piece of bread.

It's only then that I realise I haven't eaten a single bit of it.

The mains are divine, a choice of slow roast pork or soft, tender beef Wellington. I take a little of each, as well as the glazed carrots on offer, the roast potatoes, the fragrant gravy. I don't hold back, tucking in as the table falls under a spell of silence. Everyone is enjoying the food and wine, warm in the knowledge that they don't have to lift a finger. Moments like this still feel like out-of-body experiences for me, when, at any moment, someone will snap their fingers, and none of it will exist.

My parents never took me with them to restaurants or cafés. They would park me at Gran's and forget to wave as their car pulled away. A holiday party like this was the kind of thing I read about in novels, one of the ones I forever had clutched against my chest like a shield. It was only at Gran's that I ate like a queen and we would go to the café in her tiny hometown to order Welsh rarebit and tea. Or when she would bring me here, to Penhallow, pulling me out of my own world where my parents didn't seem to want me, and into hers where everything glinted with magic.

But now, this is my life. Every cloying, charged breath of it.

A dinging sound erupts from further down the table as the mains are cleared. Everyone is leaning back, shining eyes gleaming with the promise of pudding and a slow evening of drinks and card games, maybe a few Christmas carols around the grand piano in the formal sitting room. I blink, breathing in the stuffy scent of meats and spilled wine that hangs like a cloud above the dinner table. Kian stands, still dinging his spoon against his glass.

'You know we love you all,' he begins, those dimples making everyone smile right back, 'and we're so happy you could join us for this holiday party.' He smiles down at Hallie, whose face breaks into a sunbeam of pure happiness. It claws at my chest and I reach forward, fingers wrapping around the cool stem of my wine glass. 'So there is a *little* reason we wanted you all to be here with us...'

I freeze as Kian waves over the two members of staff. They're carrying a cake, iced white, plain and round with a tiny set of sugar-paste booties in the centre. My fingers stiffen on the stem of my glass.

'We wanted you all to be here for this. Because we've been keeping a bit of a secret from you all...' Hallie says, as Kian is cutting into the cake.

Blood beats hot in my face, my eyes fixed on those sugar-paste booties...

'We're having a baby!' she trills, laughing up at Kian.

'And...' Kian says, holding up the cut slice. It's blue inside, a bright baby blue. 'It's a boy!'

45

Cries of delight reverberate up and down the table, chairs are thrust back and everyone piles over to Kian and Hallie to hug and dab at tears with their napkins.

'Well, shit.' James exhales next to me. It's barely audible, but I can hear it. I can feel the weight of it. He looks at me, moving his hand to reach for mine. But I can't bear it. I snatch my hand away, quickly topping up my wine glass to drink deeply. It burns going down, leaving an acrid trail in my throat to curl like a snake in my stomach. When I look back at him, he's already pushing his chair back, moving up the table to thump Kian on the back. To hug Hallie. He's plastered a grin on his face, laughing loudly with the little crowd of them at the far end of the dining room. Every one of them sparkling and flushed, shining with the wonder of the moment.

With shaking fingers, I pour more wine and glance up to meet Diana's eyes. She raises her eyebrows, the bottle in my hand hovering between us. Then she raises her own glass, and drinks deeply too.

I have to move. I can't sit here, fixed to this chair while James is over there, with them. My limbs twitch as I walk over and hug Hallie, pressing her against me, breathing congratulations into her ear. I feel like I'm watching myself, as though I'm somewhere overhead, hovering on the ceiling. As Kian cuts the cake, beginning to hand out slices, I deftly swipe those sugar-paste booties.

Then crumble them to dust between my fingers.

Chapter 6

There's no way I'm eating this baby-blue cake. I pick at the lump of it on the plate in front of me, regretting downing that last glass of wine. The only thing I can manage is milky decaf coffee and I slurp it down, pouring extra into one of the tiny teacups left for us by the staff. I imagine them washing up as quickly as they can, so they can bugger off home and leave us to it.

Kian is leaning over to press a protective hand on Hallie's belly at the far end of the table and they're exchanging adoring looks. I feel the iceberg that has sprung up between James and me grow, his entire body angled away from me to speak to the others further down the table. Now seems like an acceptable time to slip away. The coffee's been served, everyone will be drifting to the snug, or the billiards room, or the sitting room at the front of the house. With the work on the shop launch, I have the perfect excuse to disappear completely. I mutter an excuse that I don't intend anyone to hear and push back my chair.

I'm halfway to the staircase in the entrance hall, my face still hot from the announcement and the wine, when I hear a voice behind me.

'Won't you congratulate me properly now?'

I spin, finding Hallie in the middle of the black-and-white

tiles. She's directly under the vast chandelier above us, angelic and hopeful as her eyes turn up to mine. There's a wall between us. Weighty and thicker than a curtain.

'Of course,' I say, slipping on a smile. It's brittle, the cold seeping from me. But I have no warmth for this moment. I can't do it. 'Congratulations. Brilliant news. When are you, er…'

'April. Twenty-fourth,' she says, a hand straying to her belly. Now I know, I can see it rounding gently underneath her camel-coloured dress. All full of hope and the promise of everything to come. I swallow, taking a step up, the staircase at my back.

'That's great. Such great news for you and Kian. Really thrilled for you, Hal.'

'Are you, though?' she says, tipping her head to the side. 'Look, I haven't seen you for months. I would have told you sooner, maybe I should have warned you—'

I wave my hand, cutting her off. 'It's just been busy, that's all. You're doing your thing, I'm doing mine.'

'Sure,' she says. 'I get that. But… why aren't you happy for me?'

'I am, you know I am…'

She moves towards the staircase and I bristle. It takes every-thing within me not to retreat another few steps. All I can see is that gentle glow radiating from her, the perfect peace concealed under her skin. I swallow, wanting to scream. It's not her fault. I have to remember that. This isn't about her. But if she corners me like this, if she makes me face it…

I take a deep, steadying breath and walk back down the staircase until we're only a few feet apart. I feel like I'm floating out of my body again, that this is happening to someone else. It makes it easier to take her hands in mine, even as my stomach churns like the snowstorm outside.

48

'I'm happy for you. Really. Everything is perfect for you. Just as you always wanted.'

She opens her mouth, a crease dimpling her forehead. 'I know Christmas isn't the best time of year for you. But I–I know when you're not telling me everything, Eva. We've known each other too long to hide things. I wish it had worked out differently for you and James, no one wishes more than me that it had happened for you. But I hoped… I hoped you would celebrate mine…'

'I… Hal,' I breathe, trying to regain some composure at the mention of Christmas. 'You know it's only me, you and James that know, I–I wouldn't want anyone else—'

'I'm not going to tell anyone, Eva. About your Gran, or about, well—'

She's about to say more when the door to the dining room opens, a wash of laughter and talking gushing out like a pail of water.

'Hal, babe, everything all right?' Kian measures us with his eyes, closing the distance slowly.

But he isn't looking at her. His eyes are pinned on me.

'I'll leave you two to it,' I say in a strangled voice, dropping Hallie's hands and edging back to the staircase. 'Congrats again, super news…'

I make it all the way to the bedroom before my legs give way beneath me. Sliding down the closed door, I tip my head back against the hard, cold wood. Then I shut my eyes and push everything away. I press my fingertips into the carpet, anything to ground myself.

Then I think of absolutely nothing.

★

I'm packing my suitcase when James finds me. He stares at me for a minute, taking in the half-filled suitcase, the carefully arranged travel bags that I've placed inside it. He closes the door, letting it click softly. The sound is so incredibly jarring in the thick, oozing silence of the past hour that I fumble over a zip, snagging the corner of my thumb on its teeth.

'Are we moving rooms?' he asks, coming to stand next to me. It's not really a question. He knows we're not moving bloody rooms.

I breathe out a sigh, standing to face him. He's taller than me by about a foot. I have to shop the petite range, whereas he goes for long. It's only in heels that I can get any real vantage. But now, I'm standing in socks and it pisses me off that I have to tip my head back to look up at him.

'No, we're not moving rooms. I'm leaving.'

'But... there's a literal blizzard outside; you've got to be joking!' He rubs his hand over his face, laughing humourlessly, and goes to flop on one of the sofas. 'Jesus.'

'With Diana stuck here too there's no one in London for the shop launch. You *know* how important it is. And I can't get any signal, it's like a blackout up here! I'm stuck. I have to be there, I have to finish this. Now.' I'm flustered, the words tumbling out as I try to plaster over what I'm really thinking. How desperate I'm feeling. After seeing that blue cake, Hallie's announcement, the cloying, perfect night where every question, every comment, hammered home each of my failures...

'You are stuck. You're right about that.'

'What's that supposed to mean?'

He waves a hand around, at my suitcase, the laptop and notebooks spilling out on our bed. 'All this. You. We need to talk about this, Eva. You can't keep avoiding me. You can't bury yourself in all this and forget. It's not just Christmas anymore. It's all the time.'

Pressure, stifling and hot, drums in my chest. My pulse quickens, fingerprints leaving clammy marks on the packing cubes as I continue to stuff them into my suitcase. There's no order anymore. It's just a mess of clothes and make-up and toiletries, all jammed and mashed into each spare pocket of space. But I don't care. I can sort it out later, when I'm back in London. Or at least, when I'm away from here.

'Doesn't it bother you?' I ask.

'What?'

I look up at him, and the question mark between his eyes fades, his gaze sliding away from mine. I feel a tiny hit of victory. So it *does* bother him. Maybe this evening got to him just as much as me.

'Good to know,' I say breathlessly. 'That's just great.'

'Don't,' he says, bringing a hand up to his face. 'Why are you doing this? *Why?* Of course it bothers me. *Of course* it does. How can you question that?'

I stare at him for a long moment, the distance between us shimmering with tension. I should reach for him. I should wrap my arms around him, like I might have done before. But I just… can't. 'I'll see you in a few days. It's not that long. And anyway, I would be up here in the room most of the time whilst you're with everyone, or going off to chase down some Wi-Fi. I have to get this work done. It *has* to go well.' I finish packing, zipping my suitcase with a hint of satisfaction. At least it closes. 'Would you mind taking Diana to the station when the snow settles, use the Mastercard for the fare? I know I shouldn't leave her, but she'll get it, she'll understand…' I eye my overnight bag, then the spread of notebooks across the bed and straighten up, moving on to those.

'If you leave tonight, we're over.'

His words strike me like lightning. I whip around, choking out a laugh. 'What did you say?'

'You heard me, Eva.'

'You can't be serious.'

'I am,' he says, leaning forward. There's a vein pulsing in his left temple, his fingers holding his wedding ring, twisting it round and round on his finger. 'Very serious.'

I stare at him for a beat in shock. Then my rage catches up. 'You're telling me, that if I don't do what you tell me—'

'I never said that—'

'That if I don't stay put, like a good wife should—'

'Eva, you're twisting my—'

'Then we're *over*?' I spit. 'Just like that?! Fourteen years together… you want to throw it all away like it means *nothing*?'

We stare at each other, breathing deeply. I don't want to back down. I can't. The heat of the fight sings in my blood, fuelled by the sight of that baby-blue cake. I no longer feel nothing. Right now, I want to scream.

James deflates, sinking back down to the sofa and placing his head in his hands.

'James…' I say, the fight cooling instantly. Thawing then freezing around us.

I don't know how we got here.

'Stay,' he whispers. 'Just stay. For once. Don't always go. Don't always hide away.'

His words are like a punch in my middle, and I fold in half, sinking to the floor. I bring my knees up to my chest, staring at the moss-green carpet. I can pick out the individual fibres, the speckled strands of lighter green. It's springy, this carpet. Like it's only just been laid. There's something about new carpet, the smell and feel of it underfoot. It's addictive, like the scent of fresh snow. Or the rush of that first perfect espresso in the morning.

My thoughts are fracturing, breaking under the weight of his words, and I force myself to look up. To meet his gaze.

His hair is like mine, a rich, chestnut brown. There are a few spidery strands of silver, but they are only noticeable to me. The thing I find most arresting about him are his eyes. Green. They gleam when he's happy, bright as the leaves in spring. When he's sad, they turn hazel, reflecting the inner murky depths of his heart. My breath catches as I look at him, into the muddy depths his eyes are now. We don't look at each other anymore. Really look. We're too busy trying to avoid all the words we cannot say.

'Stay,' he says again, setting his jaw.

I hesitate, scrubbing my hands over my eyes. 'You know what you're asking of me.'

'Yes.'

'My shop launch, this day, that… that… cake.' I suck in a breath. 'And that doesn't bother you?'

He sighs, then stands. Crossing the room slowly, he comes to hunker down next to me. I lean against him, breathing in the scent of pine and woodsmoke. I feel the steady warmth of him and allow it in. I let him ground me. We both stare at the empty fireplace across the room.

'It bothers me that it bothers you. But if you don't stay now, I don't know how else we can fix this.'

I nod, a single tear shivering down my cheek. I move my hand to swipe it away quickly before it has a chance to sting but his hand is there, his fingertips gently smoothing it away. His hand rests against my cheek, and I close my eyes, leaning into it. Leaning into the comfort, into *him*. Then I sniff, pulling away.

'It's today. The day.'

'I know.'

'You give an ultimatum like that… today?'

He reaches across again, bringing his arm around my shoulders. 'I'm sorry. But I can't see any other way, Eva.'

More tears cloud my vision but I let them fall. And we sit there, staring at the empty fireplace.

We're at opposite sides of the bed, only our fingertips touching. It's the closest we've been in months. If I'm honest with myself, maybe even years. James is asleep, but I can't switch off. I can't find peace, or any way of going back.

Staring at the ceiling, I listen to the chime of an old grandfather clock in the dark. After it chimes eleven, then midnight, I curl onto my side, facing away from James, and stare blearily into the shadows. I don't know how we got here. But I can't stay.

I can't.

James sighs in his sleep next to me, shuffling around. I glance over at him. He's a whole pillow's width away, the cover dipping between us. We may as well be on opposite sides of an ocean.

Stay.

I grind my teeth, squinting up at the ceiling rose, making out the details of the plaster in the dark.

If you leave tonight, we're over.

I turn onto my side, pressing my eyelids tight shut, trying to block out the keen hurt in his words. The ultimatum he issued. But they are still there, echoing round my head. Making me flinch.

I can't see any other way, Eva.

The chimes shudder to a stop, leaving behind a pocket of ringing quiet. The air in the room is icy against my cheeks and I puff out a breath, watching it form a cloud. I frown, feeling around on the bedside table for my phone and check the screen. Still empty of signal, or notifications. But it's exactly midnight. Officially Christmas Day. I stretch, feeling parched, and slip out from under the covers. It's freezing in the room, as if a window has been thrust open, allowing the night in. But the windows are closed and fastened.

I look back at James as I sip the glass of water on my bedside table. Suddenly, I can't feel that bond that ties us together. That draws me to him, that makes us a team. Maybe it was the argument. Maybe it's all the arguments we've had over the past year, piling up until they spell out something that's so glaringly obvious, we have to accept it. I know in this moment that I can't stay here with him.

Quickly, quietly, I gather up my things. Most of them are half-thrust into the suitcase from earlier so it doesn't take long. I slip on a long coat over my pyjamas, check that I have my car keys.

Then I look back at James.

He's frowning slightly in his sleep, a furrow forming in his forehead. I want to stoop down, shake away the bad dream. I reach out with my fingertips, brushing the hair from his forehead. It used to be so comfortable, any touch between us as familiar and natural as breathing. But now, it's stilted. He mutters, stirring slightly, and I freeze. Should I wake him? If I don't say goodbye now, is that a mistake? Perhaps I shouldn't go at all. Perhaps…

But I can't face waking him. I can't face the torrent of questions, the heartbreak that would follow. My pulse sharpens, tapping insistently in my ears, reminding me why I'm leaving. Why it's best to slip away. When I've put all this behind me; those sugar-paste baby booties, the memories, his ultimatum… surely then we can have this out when we're both back in London. When I've finally launched the shop and done something right.

It takes five minutes for me to wheel my suitcase out and reach the black-and-white tiles of the entrance hall with only the small light from my phone to guide me. The front door is ajar, allowing a steady flurry of ice and snowflakes inside. Did someone pop out to check on their car after dinner? I shiver, wrap my coat tighter around my body and begin the long walk past all the gaping doorways, the silent, watchful rooms beyond.

I remember when I was younger, I was sure the rooms of Penhallow moved around in the night. How I would wake and find myself in the attic, or discover the snug was at the front of the house. Gran used to say the house just liked playing tricks. But now, as a creak sounds in one of those rooms, it's as though the house is shifting. As though the rooms have sprouted feet, swapping places behind closed doors. I curse myself, quickening my footsteps. It's so quiet tonight. Too quiet. But maybe everyone went to bed early, ready for a busy Christmas Day tomorrow. Natalie did mention something about the annual Christmas Day dip at the beach nearby. Yes, that must be it. I have to lock away all these imaginings where they belong, in the past.

I find the grandfather clock in the dark, staring at me accusingly. The hands are stuck on midnight. I tell myself it must need rewinding. That's all this is. The only ghosts at Penhallow are in my mind, my memories. I tell myself I'm imagining the press of peering eyes, the skitter of nimble feet. This house isn't watching me. But I walk a little quicker.

When I reach the car I don't bother opening the boot. The night crowds in, as though hungry for the small light from my phone as I swipe at the snow on the windscreen. I don't want to linger on the driveway. I open the door, push my suitcase onto the back seat, climb in and swiftly lock the doors again. My hands are shaking and my whole body is jumpy as I grip the steering wheel, trying to find a measure of calm. It's just night-time. It's just a quiet old house that creaks and sighs. All the other guests are asleep already. I've read too many stories. There are no ghosts here.

It takes me three attempts to start up the engine, my breath pluming in small clouds as I swear at it. When it ignites, triumph eclipses my fear for a second before I pull out, moving away from Penhallow. I want to drive faster, put as much distance between myself and that eerie entrance hall as I can. But the lanes are slippery and coiling, the dark night devouring each tight corner. I have to crawl along and it makes me want to scream. My fingers are twitching on the steering wheel, each tiny skid making me tremble. I didn't want Diana to face this drive in the lonely dark but now, it's me behind the wheel. And as a fresh flurry of snow coats the windscreen, fear thickens in my chest, making it hard to breathe.

I keep picturing his face. How it collapsed in on itself as we argued. As though he knew there was no hope, but he clung to it anyway. This is for the best, I keep telling myself. For the best.

At last I see the cattle grid ahead and I smile, allowing the tension inside me to unspool.

There's a figure on the road.

I gasp, slamming on the brake. All I see is a face, her hands, palms held up to protect herself. The car slides, screeching as it slips over the road and I push my foot harder, powerless as it keeps rolling, keeps moving—

The car finally stops, throwing me forward. My pulse crashes in my ears, thumping wildly as I stare at her over the steering wheel. Slowly, I reach for the car door, blinking at her in disbelief. She's not wearing a headscarf anymore.

The woman is old. She has white, sugar-spun hair in a messy plait, a bathrobe tied around herself. I know this woman. I know her better than anyone else. I step out of the car, my hand trembling as I reach out to her, needing her to be real, needing to feel the brush of her cotton robe. To know this isn't a ghost I've conjured from my grief. That just this once, it isn't a fleeting glimpse at a bus stop, or a face in the window. It's really her.

'Gran?'

Chapter 7

'You gave me the fright of my life!' she says, lowering her hands. 'Or should I say, my death?'

I choke, knowing I should run, bolt for the car and lock the doors, then drive as fast as I can until I hit the motorway. This can't be happening. Am I still asleep? This has to be a dream. I must have drunk more than I thought at dinner. I look at her, my heart aching unbearably. I want her to be real. I want her to be standing here, in this silent lane on the wild moorland, like we've wound back the clock to those perfect holidays I remember.

I take a breath, the pressure building in the back of my throat, my nose, and all I want to do is throw my arms around her. Is this what stress does? Am I having a breakdown? This must be it. The moment I crack.

I step back, every part of me trembling, and brace my hands against the car bonnet. The cool metal bites into my palms. It's the anchor I need. As much as I want this, desperately clinging to the idea that she is still with me, haunting me, this isn't real. Heat fills my chest, pressing against my ribs. If I let myself break now, just fall apart on this lane… what if I never get back up?

'I'm going to get back in the car now,' I tell myself slowly.

Making myself believe it. 'And when I get back to London, it will be Christmas morning and none of this will have been real.'

'Sure, dearie. If that's what you want to believe.'

I focus on Gran, the planes of her face thrown into contrast by the car headlights, squinting then widening my eyes. I can't see an aura and there are no wiggly, bright lines, so maybe this isn't a stress-induced migraine. I am prone to them. And with the time of year and the ultimatum from James, I wouldn't be surprised if I developed one.

She's smiling at me, waiting patiently with her hands clasped in front of her, snow swirling around her ankles, her slippers. Exactly how she stood every time she knew I had done something wrong. Waiting patiently for me to explain. Like the time I poured an entire box of Cheerios down the back of the sofa to make a 'waterfall sound' for my jungle game when I was five. Or when I put on her wedding dress when I was eight and paraded around her garden in my own version of a wedding, getting the immaculate ivory hem coated in mud and grass.

'Gran, how are you here?'

She frowns for a moment, as though contemplating how to answer. Then she points behind me, back to the wild moorland, the granite-walled house growing out of it. 'Do you remember when you had that chat with Granddad in the garden here?'

'Yes. Of course, it was one of his last visits—'

'He had already passed on.'

My skin prickles, the faintest pinpricks trickling down my shoulders, along the curves of my spine. 'What are you trying to say?'

'It's the house. Penhallow. Somehow, it invited me back. I've been trying to see you, follow that thread between us. But here on the moors, it's like a door has been left open and I can give it a little nudge and walk through.'

I bite my lip, balancing this against my own experiences. How the rooms seem to dance in the night, how the library knows what I want to read. And how, when I was very little, Granddad still found a way to have those last moments with me. It's impossible, and yet…

'Why… why now?'

'Aha!' she says, raising a finger. Her eyes crinkle at the corners, the papery folds wrapping around her piercing blue eyes. 'Now that's a question worth asking. Why am I here? Why now?'

I fold my arms, waiting for her to evaporate, to dissolve into the black of the night. To curl around my grief, only for a moment, before getting back in the car and driving to London. Telling myself that I'm fine. That I can get through this.

But she seems to be settling in for story time.

'First things first. Why have you stopped taking your vitamins? I *explicitly* told you that was the number one rule. That, and *at least* an hour of real daylight a day. Not that fake stuff churning out of the laptop screen you like to work on. Very bad for your eyes, dearest. You'll get crow's feet!'

I splutter, 'I… Gran—'

She holds up a finger, silencing me. 'And why are you looking so pasty? You look like you haven't slept properly in weeks. Or had a decent meal. Self-care is queen, Eva!' She tuts. 'How can you take on the world with less than eight hours' sleep and three square meals a day? Coffee is *not* a meal replacement. Even the good stuff with that hazelnut syrup you're so fond of.'

This all sounds spookily like the last few conversations we

had in the year that she died. And that was three years ago. The year before I started my business; started hitting trade fairs and markets every weekend to give me something else to focus on other than when everything was ripped from me. I blink, trying to reset my brain. This is obviously some kind of subconscious stress reaction. Yes. I'm just overworked, worried about the shop launch and my marriage and half-asleep right now. None of this is real.

However much I want it to be.

I smile kindly at her, this ghost from my own mind. How perfect she looks, whole and unbroken. Not at all the way she looked the last time I saw her. 'Gran, I love you. I... you don't know how much I've wanted this...' I grip the car bonnet harder, the cold metal searing my fingers. 'But I'm getting back into the car now. I can't... this isn't real.' I move around the car, closing my hand around the door handle.

'You can't run from it forever, Eva.'

Silence stretches, wrapping around me. The wind picks up, whistling over the fields, through the gaps in the drystone walls. I take a breath, steadying the sudden thump and rattle of my heart. 'Gran, that's honestly not what I'm—'

But when I turn to where she was standing, there's no one there.

Did I imagine it? Am I really alone? I stare out into the night, call her name softly. But just like all the other times before, she's gone.

Shakily, I open the car door and turn on the ignition. I stare at the lane outside, the flurry of snow, the velvet darkness surrounding me. I try to find a reason why I just imagined a whole conversation with her. Why now, after years of searching for her in crowds, sure I had caught a glimpse of her, reliving that moment again and again before I remember: she's dead. However much I want it, she's not coming back to fix me.

After what feels like hours of staring, turning her words over and over, I look at my phone screen and frown. It still reads '00:00'. I pick it up, swiping to the alarm app, checking the time again. But it's stubbornly stuck on midnight.

'Great, that's all I need…' I mutter. A broken phone, on top of no signal, no Wi-Fi. In a lane in the middle of nowhere, when I'm about to take the biggest step with my business. The biggest step of my *life*.

My head is thick and pounding, jagged lines crossing my vision. I can't drive tonight. I can barely see through the windscreen. It takes everything I have to push my foot against the clutch, to turn the car around and lumber back the way I came. I breathe in and out in smooth, slow motions, the migraine wrapping my head in a storm cloud.

I stumble out of the car and find my way back into the entrance hall. I can barely see as lightning cleaves my vision, as my hands reach for the solid wood of a banister, as I drag my body up the staircase. I find a room, a bed. And slide into unconsciousness.

When I wake, there's sunlight streaming in and a steady thump, like a fist, or footsteps on carpet. I stretch out, feeling a mattress, pillows. Maybe I made it to a Travelodge last night? I can't remember what happened. I left Penhallow, drove over the moors… and something happened. Did I reach a service station? I pat the sheets beneath me, feeling the soft scratch of crisp linen. The room is filled with muffled silence. I rub my eyes again, wondering if I did in fact have a migraine last night. It's all a thick blur around me, the furniture and shape of the room lying under some kind of sleepy film. I groan, reaching out blindly for my phone. But my hand finds two items on the bedside table. My phone and… a pair of glasses. I close my fingers around them, bringing them closer to my face. They are Diana's.

'What on earth…' I say, squinting at them. They are definitely hers. Black frames, slightly squared. She usually wears them instead of contacts when she's driving, or focusing on her laptop for a long stint. Did she leave them in the car yesterday by accident? Maybe I brought them into the Travelodge with me. Grabbed everything out of the car before I locked it. I can't remember. And she'll surely need them this morning. Guilt slams into me as I remember… I left her behind last night. At Penhallow. I shouldn't have just expected James to pay her train fare and send her home, I have to phone her, I have to speak to her.

I grab my phone, bringing it close to my face to swipe up. But the face recognition won't let me in. I sigh, typing in my passcode hurriedly. Once. Twice. Three times. Then I'm locked out.

In frustration, I stumble out of the bed, and walk straight into a piece of furniture.

'Shit!' I shriek, rubbing my toe, which made a horrible crunching sound. It throbs and I close my palm around it. Carefully, I move around the bed, my eyesight still not catching up with being awake. It must be a really bad one. Even though I get regular migraines, I've never gone to the doctor. Another promise I broke to Gran three years ago. I would rather just pop an aspirin and hope for the best.

When I get to the bathroom, I splash cold water on my face, then drink deeply from the tap. Raising my eyes to the mirror, I catch a swish of dark hair. A long grey T-shirt. I always sleep in a white T-shirt, one of those ones that are easy to pack. An oversized one I can curl my knees up into. I frown, peering closer. This T-shirt is the wrong colour.

With cold, sickening dread, I stumble back into the bedroom. Crawling across the bed, I reach around with searching fingertips for that pair of glasses. When I find them, and put them on… the bedroom snaps into focus.

This is not a Travelodge.

A trickle of fear runs down my spine and I move as fast as I can, back to the bathroom.

'Holy shit!' I reel back in shock from the reflection in the mirror.

This isn't real. It isn't.

Bringing my fingers up to my face, my hair, I stare back at my reflection. At the dark sweep of hair. The pointy chin. The brown eyes. The pale dewy skin I wish was mine. This face, this person is not me.

It's Diana.

Chapter 8

This is obviously all a dream. Just a stupid, stress-induced dream. And then I remember. The grandfather clock stuck on midnight. The skittering sound of unseen footsteps in the dark. Gran. I saw her. I spoke to her. It all rushes back, flooding me, knocking the air from my lungs.

Seeing her in the lane on the moors last night, *talking* to her, and now this… I laugh, high and false, and Diana's mouth laughs back at me from the mirror. I clamp my teeth together, pushing the glasses up the bridge of… Diana's nose. My nose.

'This isn't happening, you're going to wake up any minute now,' I say, watching Diana's lips twist around the words.

Each breath is coming a little too fast, a little too shallow. I can't hold them down long enough. I stagger back into the bedroom and realise it's *really* not a Travelodge. Or mine and James's room at Penhallow. It's small, and there are no sofas next to an empty fireplace, no vast expanse of moss-green carpet. This one is a deep, burgundy red and it looks kind of tired and faded. The wardrobe is the same as the one in our bedroom in the manor house, but there's only one set of drawers and the bed is smaller. There's a general air of neglect, like this is the bedroom that doesn't get used very often.

In two steps, I'm at the window, thrusting back the curtains. 'Oh shit…'

The window is at the side of the house and faces onto a sweep of moorland with the sea in the distance. I'm back at Penhallow. I really did drive back here last night. I blink rapidly, stumbling back into the bed. This has to be Diana's actual room, the spare one that Hallie gave her yesterday. The one down the hallway from my own.

Crossing to the wardrobe, I throw it open and make a strangled kind of noise, deep in my throat. Hanging inside are the clothes Diana borrowed last night. All hung up in a neat line… in her wardrobe. I turn in a circle, surveying the room. This is all a little too realistic. I haven't even *been* in Diana's room, so if I'm projecting this, if I'm asleep and dreaming all this…

'Breathe, Eva,' I whisper, pressing a hand into my chest. 'Just breathe. This isn't real. You can fix this.'

As my racing heart slowly calms, I consider what to do next. This obviously isn't happening. But I can somehow do what I want in this dream. I've read somewhere that you can't read in a dream, not actual words. They skip around and blur, your brain can't make sense of them. So maybe I should try doing that now? I reach again for Diana's phone, wondering what the passcode is. But this time, the face recognition kicks in, and her phone unlocks for me.

'What the…' There's a torrent of notifications. Emails, messages, social media alerts. And two whole bars of signal. Then suddenly, it cuts out. I nearly scream in frustration, waving it above my head. It doesn't come back. Slowly, I bring the screen down to my nose, thumbing through the various notifications. Did she know she could get signal in here? I shake my head, pushing the glasses back up. Of course not. This is a dream, a way for my brain to reassemble actual issues, actual things into a realistic order, that's all this is, just a dream…

There are messages from a group chat. I bite my lip. Should I… read them? Is that an invasion of privacy? But it is *my* dream. And I need to know if I can read. If I can disprove that particular theory. I tap to open it, and the text fills the screen.

You can't get back at all?!

Honestly, Di, your job is a nightmare!

We'll save a cracker for you xx

Hmm… I guess this is the bunch of friends she was meant to meet up with today? It looks like the stream of messages came in at midnight exactly. And it is now… 8:22 a.m.

I pick up the phone again, prop my back against the bed and scroll through the emails. All the alerts seem to have popped up recently. And as I delve into the rabbit warren of missed social media tags and emails from the PR firm we're working with, there's one that pops out. From an unsaved number, just a string of kisses. I wonder again what she had to go off and do yesterday… was she meeting someone? Someone she didn't want me to know about?

I flick back to the messages between her and her group chat. They were all sent late last night when she must have got a flash of signal. Her admitting where she was, that she had driven me down to Cornwall. Telling everyone that she was stuck in the snowstorm, that she wouldn't make it back for Christmas.

I can't read anymore. I chuck the phone on the floor next to me, massaging my temples. I need air. I need… I need to get out of this.

I dress quickly, pulling out a raspberry red polo neck jumper, one Diana took from my suitcase yesterday, and a pair of smart-looking high-waist jeans (also mine). My jeans are the skinny kind, and they show off her perfectly streamlined body. I turn, looking in the mirror, and observe the figure that I had in my mid-twenties reflected back. It's odd, seeing the kind of body that I thought I had said a final goodbye to. Now I barely have time to complete all my work, let alone get out for a run. Finally, I run my fingers through my hair, brush my teeth and step out into the corridor.

Straight into... myself.

'Whoa!' I say, practically falling straight into Eva.

Eva, or me, or whoever this is in this weird dream, licks her lips and steps back carefully. Her hair is up in a ponytail, her dress is the red Armani one that Diana... that *I* got dry-cleaned. I never realised how stressed I look. How there is a permanent worry line etched in the centre of my forehead. How I don't meet Diana's eyes. Is that how my face usually is? So tense, so uptight. I look like I'm about to burst and scream. But it has been a stressful few weeks. And with the sudden snow yesterday, well. I have every reason to be stressed out.

'Are you ready?' this Eva says hurriedly, checking her watch. 'It's already half past. We agreed on quarter past. Have you got your laptop? The snow hasn't eased up so you can't drive yet, but we can get on with some projections, maybe try and find that pub with Wi-Fi...'

'Er... I...' I blink, not sure what is going on. But this Eva looks really distracted, and there is a lot to do, especially with us both stuck down here. I shake my head, wringing this reality out. This isn't real. These are my own insecurities, playing out in a horribly vivid twist on a version of this day. That's all. I'm not really Diana.

'Diana? Are you OK? Brunch is at nine. We can get a head start, make the most of the time.' Eva rubs her temples before refocusing on me. 'God, I would kill for a proper coffee.'

'Same,' I find myself saying, already thinking about the alerts on Diana's phone, the emails. Pushing away that needling voice in my head, shrieking, *This is all wrong!*

'Let's get some coffee sent up, press on with plan B now we're both stuck here, yes?' she says, a smile ironing out the frown, only a few worry lines lingering.

'Agreed,' I say, nodding. 'Absolutely.'

'Thanks, Diana. I don't know what I'd do without you.' Turning, she stalks back down the corridor, banging her bedroom door shut.

For a moment, I stare down the corridor, still reeling at the shock of seeing myself, walking around as a whole separate entity. Then I snap back, giving myself a shake. I return to the bedroom, picking up the notebooks and laptop and selecting a favourite pen as if by instinct. Then I stop myself. What am I doing? Am I going along with this… whatever it is? Briefly, I close my eyes, counting to ten. More laughter and footsteps shake the corridor outside. The other guests are getting up, excited to spend Christmas Day together. To celebrate the news of the baby, to eat too much food and open beautifully wrapped, carefully chosen presents.

I shouldn't be here. In this body, this house, with these people. It's all wrong, somehow. Seeing Gran in the lane last night has unhinged me. I need to wake up. I need to get back on the road, get back to London.

I press my fingertips into the bedroom door. I feel smooth polished wood and it seems real. I lean my forehead against it, the coolness seeping into my skin. I close my eyes. And see my gran, her crooked smile. That robe wrapped around her thin frame. That hollow ache in my chest returns and I wonder if I will see her again.

If I don't play along with this dream, what will happen? Will it grow and twist, turning into a nightmare? It's a fear of mine, being trapped in sleep. Losing control, not being able to get out. And more and more, that's exactly what my life has felt like. The scales have tipped so far in one direction I have no control anymore. I'm slipping and sliding, trying to grasp onto anything I can, but the scales keep tipping. I keep failing. And now I'm trapped in a dream as someone else.

Chapter 9

'Pass the bacon, would you?' James says to me and I hand the platter over, standing slightly so he can grab it from across the dining table. 'Ta.'

I sit back down, looking at the plate of crispy bacon and French toast, my cooling cup of tea. It's just after nine in the morning and I can barely eat, my stomach churning and hollow. Every time I force a bite down, my whole body lurches. As calmly as I can, I put down my knife and fork, tucking my hands under the table. I don't want anyone to see them trembling. For a dream this is alarmingly realistic.

Eva is crunching away on her second slice of bacon, studiously ignoring everyone, with a tell-tale crease line between her eyes. This version of me has a headache, I can tell. She was rubbing her temples earlier and she hasn't touched the mug of coffee in front of her yet. Instead, she's sipping on iced water and cringing away from the bright light pouring in through the wide expanse of windows. The light has that milky, glaring hue of snow and frost, the sun reflecting off it in one huge, beaming mirror. If it was anyone else, I would peg them as hungover. But I know I didn't drink *that* much last night. Not enough to be hungover, anyway.

I still can't work out what my brain is trying to tell me. But I'm going with it, for now at least. It might be the easiest way of breaking out, by accepting it.

I peer at this version of myself, who is now eating tiny mouthfuls of a poached egg, taking ages to pile the smallest scrapings onto her fork before bringing it to her lips. It's so weird, watching myself eat. Catching James glancing over, checking up on her. I never realised he did that. He even refreshes Eva's coffee mug, stirring in the perfect amount of sugar and milk. She takes her first sip without thanking him, like she hasn't even noticed. Does he always do that? Silently watch over me? Maybe it's just this morning, after our argument last night. After what he said. What we both said. Our argument hanging over us, like a bad-tempered storm cloud.

James's eyes lift to mine and I don't break away, like I should. I hold his gaze and wonder which one of us is going to crumble first. And how it became me versus him. I hold his stare for a beat longer than Diana would, and his mouth turns down into a grimace before shuffling his gaze along to the window. His hair is still slightly mussed from sleep and I want to reach over, tangle my fingers in it. Just like I might have done before. I wonder briefly if he would ever realise it's me staring out of Diana's eyes. Even if this is all a dream, would our souls find each other? I bite my lip. Perhaps once. Perhaps once we would have found each other beyond the trappings of the everyday. But not now.

'Hey! Happy Christmas! Mind if I sit here?'

I glance up, startled by the interruption in my brooding, and find Natalie beaming down at me, her hair tied up in a bun. She has that slightly concerned look that Hallie sometimes gets when she sees someone left out. Or lost-looking. I guess they're similar in that way. 'Sure.'

She slides into the chair with a groan. 'Way too much Champagne at dinner last night.' She giggles, heaping sugar into a black coffee and taking a sip. 'Perfection. So, you're Diana, right? You work with Eva? Shit luck, getting stuck here on Christmas Day.'

'It's fine, you know, I can get some extra work done, prep for the shop—'

Her mouth twists. 'Didn't you have plans?'

I think about the messages in the group chat from Diana's friends. I wonder for the first time why she isn't seeing any of her family, why she didn't try to go and stay with them last night when she knew she couldn't get all the way back to London safely.

A sudden wrench twists my heart, pulling the breath out of me. A sliding sensation forces me to gasp and I start coughing, reaching quickly for a glass of water.

'Something go down the wrong way? Here,' Natalie says, passing me a napkin so I can cover my mouth. I shrug, making light of it but I'm left panting, gulping down breaths. What... what *was* that? I hold up my hands – Diana's hands – in front of my eyes, and they're trembling. If I didn't know any better, I would say this feels like... grief? Like someone has just died.

'Thanks. Hate it when that happens.'

'No worries. You were saying about your plans? For today?'

'Oh, yeah. I-I did. Have plans, that is. But I can get ahead on some work.' The disappointed messages in the group chat from Diana's friends burn a hole in my pocket, where I've shoved her phone. 'Make up for it when I get back.'

'Huh.' She frowns, taking a small nibble of toast. I've known Natalie since she was a tween, all gawky limbs and braces. Now she updates her TikTok and Instagram with backpacking adventures, practically sponsored by brands to climb Machu Picchu with their latest travel rucksack offering, or wander the streets of San Francisco wearing a must-have pair of boots, *durable and stylish!* 'I guess there's always New Year.'

'Right,' I say, nodding. 'Exactly.'

'You know, there's a bunch of us going to the beach for the Christmas dip if you're up for it?'

I shake my head politely. 'Thanks, but I think I'll just get some work done.'

Natalie says nothing as she crunches her way through her toast, the silence stretching out between us.

When brunch is over, I slip away before anyone can catch me. I need air and silence and a chance to work out the muddle of this day. I grab Diana's coat from her bedroom, wrapping it around myself. It's thick grey wool, perfect for the city. Hopeless for a snowy moorland. It's not even waterproof. But it's warm and cosy and as long as the snow doesn't turn wet, I should be all right.

When I step outside, the world is transformed. Thick flurries of snowflakes cascade from the sky, dousing the world in pure, brilliant white. It's enough to need sunglasses. I breathe in, the sharp chill of the air nipping at my throat, my lungs. It feels wonderful. Like the first real breath I've taken in ages.

As the snow curls around me, the flurries whipping up to dust the cars and gravel driveway like sugar, I walk around the edge of the house. These boots, Diana's boots, are black patent, low-heeled torture devices. Why does she wear these? My toes already feel squished. I crunch through the fresh snow, leaving a pattern of boot prints in my wake, leaving the gravel of the driveway to step into a formal garden. It's set out Tudor-style, with gravel walkways between gated rectangles of raised beds. They are all covered in snow and frost now, but I imagine them brimming with herbs and flowers. The old kitchen gardens. This was where I last took a turn with Granddad, head so absorbed by that bird nest and those tiny blue eggs that I never realised the significance. That it would be our last. Farther off are sloping lawns, giving way to the moorland beyond. There's another gated garden, but the twisted hedges I can see from the house are all crooked and bent, as though neglected. I don't recall it being that way. Instead, I remember the gate had a key that hung from a hook in the kitchen and Gran called it our secret garden. I remember that it seemed to be sleeping in the winter, tucked up in a blanket of snow.

I'm about to take a turn around the kitchen gardens, hoping the motion of my footfalls and the sharp air will shake a plan from me, or better yet, shake me awake, when I hear the crunch of footsteps at my back.

'Di?' a woman's voice says. I turn and find one of the staff standing on the path. 'It's you, isn't it? I almost didn't recognise you. You look so posh now.'

'Hey… yep, it's me! Er… Diana,' I stutter, an uncertain smile curving my mouth upwards.

The woman's nervousness dissolves and she laughs. She's pretty and curvy, all soft lines under a navy-blue waitress-style apron, with a frizz of red hair sticking out from under a cap. A constellation of freckles dusts her nose and cheeks, her grin crooked with a mouthful of tiny teeth. A question mark hangs between us, and it's not just my uncertainty. It's coming from her too.

'I figured you had got too good for us. For me.'

'Never,' I say and clear my throat, hoping it's what Diana would say. This is beyond awkward. I have absolutely no idea who this woman is, nor how she might be related to Diana. I know she grew up around here, so maybe it's someone from her childhood? A school friend? This woman reaches towards me suddenly, her shoes crunching on the snow.

I open my arms just in time. We hug, and a deep sense of complete ease settles over me. She smells how my old school friends smelled, the combination of soap and fabric conditioner, and a slight sour tang of milk on her breath. Like she's just eaten a bowl of cereal. I have to be merging this with my own lived experiences, my own memories wrapped in this greeting. In this woman.

We break apart and she smiles shyly, gesturing to her apron, her cap. 'Obviously, I did *super* well. Got out of night shifts, anyway. The Tesco manager was putting me on all the weekend ones. Never saw the kids. But this gig, it's much better.' She sniffs. I clock a name badge, discreetly pinned near her shoulder, and relax. At least I know her name now. Sarah.

'You've got kids?'

'Two.' She rustles through her pockets, producing a battered Polaroid. Two ginger-haired boys are sticking their tongues out at the camera, hair poking out at every angle, black-and-white-striped football kits displayed proudly on their chests. 'Harvey and Milo. Six and eight now.'

I blink in shock, quickly calculating. Diana can't be more

than late twenties. So if Sarah is the same age as her, that means she had them in her early twenties. Or late teens.

'Yeah, I had Milo when I was nineteen.' She nods. 'I expect you were at university? Travelling the world on a gap year?'

I laugh uneasily. I know what Diana was doing, but only from reading her CV. We've never *actually* discussed her life in great detail, her childhood, her family. Her hopes and dreams beyond a glittering career, independence, a purpose. How she's willing to work twice as hard, bury herself in her job to get ahead. Just like me. 'I would have just started my degree course. Business and economics in London.'

Sarah puts the photo away, scraping her shoe against the snow on the path. It grates in the snow-muffled silence and I blink down at it, watching the shoe catch at the sugar-spun flakes. 'And those people in there…' she jerks her thumb at the house, 'they're your friends?'

'Yes, I mean… no,' I say, quickly adjusting, recalculating. I don't want to seem odd, don't want to make a misstep. Even if this *is* all a dream. 'No. I have to be here, for my boss. There's this big thing happening at work… at her business and if we pull it off, it'll make my career. So I have to be here. For her. I was only meant to be driving her down, but…'

'Huh. I guess you got stuck, right?' Sarah looks at me, critical and assessing as she gestures at the swirl of winter surrounding us. Cloaking us. 'Always knew you were smart. I didn't… I guess I never expected you to come back. Not really. Is it worth it? All… this?'

'A hundred per cent.' I swallow, the words sticking in my throat. But for the first time, I wonder if Diana does think that. If it is all worth it to her. If all the hours, all the missed social things, all the striving is consuming her, or driving her. I guess I never stopped long enough to ask.

I take a deep breath, the cold air like tiny needles, prickling along my tongue. A worrying thought, barely a fragment, begins to nag at me. This is all so real. How could I make up so much about this person, Sarah? Is it possible for a human brain to assemble so many details? What if this isn't my subconscious?

What if… I'm not actually dreaming?

'Well, I better get back inside,' Sarah is saying, stamping her feet. 'But seriously, it's good to see you, Di. I— we miss you. I forgot how good you look when you wear that kind of boots.'

Then she's gone, hurrying back towards the house. My cheeks flush, as though this body, Diana's body, is processing the compliment, turning it over like a shiny penny. I shove my hands deeper into Diana's coat pockets as the snow falls thick and fast around me. Turning to trudge back inside, I begin to wonder if there is a reason I've woken up as Diana today. Seeing Gran, having that god-awful migraine and now… this. Walking through Christmas Day in some strange body-swapping alternative dimension. I mean, this is just the kind of prank Gran would pull. She loves a practical joke. I stop, suddenly making the connection. Did she… do this? I shake my head and carry on trudging through the snow. No. She would want me to fix things with James, wouldn't she? So why would she make this happen?

Unless…

Maybe, just maybe, Gran has somehow given me extra time to work. Maybe, if this is all real, she's allowing me to somehow be *Diana* for a day… so I can sneak off and leave the *other* me, the one inhabiting *that* Eva, at Penhallow with James.

I pause, looking up at the house, the myriad of dark, watchful

79

windows. And a plan unfurls. I quicken my steps, heart jumping excitedly against my ribs. This must be a gift from Gran, this day. Not just some cruel practical joke. It has to be.

I scribble a quick note for Eva – *Happy Christmas! Spend the day with James, enjoy the Christmas Day dip and leave the plans to me. I'll pop over to the pub and get on the Wi-Fi!* – and poke it under her bedroom door. Diana's work laptop, her pens and notebook are all carefully hidden in the bag under my arm and I have this gleeful, sure feeling that this is what Gran wants for me. Of course she wants me to succeed, and make sure I spend Christmas with James and Hallie. And what better way to do that than go off and find this pub?

I practically skip over the fields, the stiles caked in snow. The village is nearby, only two miles away, and with every signpost I almost squeal with happiness. Gran is a genius, sorting this out for me. It's *exactly* the sort of thing she would do, and I can just picture her nodding away as I walk. In fact, I feel a touch smug that I worked it out. As I reach the pub, with its diamond-paned windows steamed up from the merriment inside, the low chatter of voices and laughter drifting out through the old oak door, I know I've made the right choice.

I busy myself with setting up in a corner table, tucked away near the roaring fireplace. The logs crackle deliciously, popping away as a barmaid brings over a plate of turkey with all the trimmings. I thank her, grinning as I turn on Diana's laptop, her phone already buzzing with notifications. With a contented sigh, I pop a bite of roasted carrot in my mouth, pen poised over my notebook, and get to work.

★

After two hours, I stumble across it. An email file, hidden in the folds of this laptop, named with only a date. At first, I think it's just another file of emails between her and the logistics firm. But then I notice the timestamps. Her hurried, misspelled email responses, always sent over the weekend or late into the night. All from her iPhone. All promising to fix something, to complete something. All dated over the last four months. I bite my lip, clicking back to our shared Google Drive detailing the workflow of the business. And it slowly dawns on me.

She's been covering up mistakes.

Any errors she's made in the run-up to the launch, all carefully rectified outside office hours. Huge swathes of work reworked correctly… without even passing it through me. I sit back, frowning. Tapping the cool side of my wine glass with a fingernail. Why would Diana do that? If I didn't know any better… these emails look like the work of a drowning assistant. Someone barely keeping their head above water. But her work output is excellent. Unparalleled. She's efficient, cool under pressure, the glue that holds my fledgling business together. And yet…

I click on the last file in the folder and an email chain pops up. It's a rival homewares business, a Goliath to my David. And they want to set up a meeting with her to discuss an opportunity. I freeze, reading the words again, then flick up to the date stamp. Three months ago. Then a short email back from Diana a few hours later, pleasant, polite and noncommittal. I release the breath building in my lungs and continue scrolling down the file. There's another email. Oh God, it's from midnight last night. Diana, her mind changed, wanting to set up a meeting with them to discuss the opportunity.

'Excuse me, miss?' The barmaid from earlier approaches, breaking my concentration. She's holding a glass of bubbly in her hand. There's a small cluster of raspberries inside and the drink is a deep shade of berry. 'Kir Royale. From the gentleman over there.'

She points in the direction of the restaurant, through a door by the bar. I catch a flash of eyes, an uncertain smile before I quickly help the barmaid make space for the Champagne glass on the table. 'I... thank you,' I stammer, head still swimming with Diana's hidden emails. The other business trying to poach her. 'Please thank him for me.'

The barmaid beams, piling up my plate and cutlery, sweeping away the two empty glasses. 'Of course.'

I sip the drink, the tart sweetness of Champagne hitting my tongue. Looking up, I see the man staring at me. Maybe it's someone who knows Diana? He must be in his sixties, wearing a Christmas jumper with a cartoon Rudolph on the chest, stubble lining his jaw. He has a haunted look about him. Features I almost recognise, but can't quite place. I smile and nod as he raises his glass and drinks deeply, before turning back to his group. Then another message pops up on Diana's phone from the same number as those string of kisses.

I'm here when you're ready to talk. Happy Christmas

Sipping the drink, I look between the phone screen and the man sat in the restaurant. She did grow up in the area. And she was pretty vague over her reasons for driving down to Cornwall. Could that be her father? I take another sip, allowing the bubbles to frost my tongue. Then I shrug it off, figuring it's probably best not to meddle, that I should leave it to Diana to sort through. Whenever that may be.

I turn back to the email chain, Diana's words flashing across the screen again and again as I read over them. Would she leave? Has it all got that bad? Unease creeps over me, stealing away my happy work glow. I quickly pack up, pay at the bar and head back out into the snow, desperate to distance myself from that email.

Chapter 10

I barely notice the stark, wild beauty of the moorland as I walk back to Penhallow. Instead of leaving me with that fulfilled buzz I was craving, the day has left me empty. Hollow. I hope now that this is a dream. Foreboding tugs at me, nipping at my heels. Why didn't Diana say she was struggling? Why hide it? I can't escape the feeling that I've somehow taken a misstep. With her and with this day. Didn't Gran want me to get to work? I picture Eva and James somewhere within these walls, chatting together, enjoying a cosy Christmas Day. Just as I planned. Just as I'm so sure *Gran* had planned. I push Diana's dark hair back from my eyes, fingers combing through wet, clinging snowflakes.

I'm halfway up the staircase, phone grasped in my fingers, when a hand clamps down on my shoulder. I spin, quickly grabbing the banister so I don't topple down. And there, with suspicion written into every pore, is my husband. I feel a flutter of irritation that he's here, on this staircase. Without Eva. I glance over his shoulder, expecting to see her hovering behind, perhaps taking an extra few minutes with the rest of the guests? But as I scan the entrance hall, I find it empty. She's not with him.

'Is everything OK, Diana?' he asks, suspicion making way

for concern. He eyes me thoughtfully, sweeping his gaze across my features, the snow still clinging to my coat and boots, and places a hand casually on the banister. Downstairs, the door to the sitting room opens, Sarah bobbing out with a tray full of used mugs and cups. She glances up at us and hesitates, as though she is about to intervene. Then she looks away, hurrying across the entrance hall.

'Everything's fine! All fine. Just got to… you know. Um…' I realise that I can't tell him I've been at the pub. He would know I've been working, and maybe blame Eva… *me*, all the more. I picture her strained, tired eyes, the weight of everything balancing on her shoulders. The argument just last night, the heated despair clawing up my throat as I fought back. A bitter knot forms in my middle, twisting my stomach. Instead, I chirp on mindlessly. 'Freshen up, you know. For dinner. Just in case there's photos or… whatever…'

'Is she working you too hard? You didn't want to drive down here really, did you?'

I work my jaw to answer. Trying to keep control of this conversation and the mental gymnastics I'm apparently playing. If this were Diana answering, would she say yes? Would she confide in my husband? I picture that secret email file, the torrent of badly typed replies. *Am* I working her too hard?

'Look, you don't have to answer that,' he says with a shrug and a forced laugh. He's nervous. He thinks he's doing the right thing, checking in on Diana, making sure his wife isn't taking advantage of her own assistant. But now he's worried that he's stepped over a line. 'She can be pretty demanding. And I know this shop launch and the new website and all are important to both of you.'

He pauses, clearing his throat. I bite my lip, wanting to interject. But he doesn't stop, carrying on. 'You know, this is a hard time of year for her, the holidays. A really tough time. And I probably made it even harder for her, dragging her here, and therefore now, you…' again, the forced laugh. 'So, I'm sorry about that.'

I say nothing, wondering where this is going. Hating the fact he's discussing my personal life, however vaguely, with my assistant. Even in this strange day I'm stuck in, it shouldn't happen. I've always kept my personal and professional lives totally separate. That's why it's always worked, there's never any blurring. This is the first and only time my two separate lives have ever had to collide, and I'm fast regretting all of it. I should have made up some excuse to James and not travelled down here; delayed delivery from our key supplier, horrendous food poisoning, sudden, unexplainable UFO crash-landing on my head…

'I should probably…' I point up the stairs, raising my eyebrows. Hoping he gets the hint.

'Right! Of course, yes. See you down there in a bit.'

I turn to go, relieved I'm off the hook, when he clears his throat.

'Oh, and, please don't mention this little chat to my wife. She gets very defensive.'

I'm fuming. Who does he think he is, commandeering my assistant like that? And spouting all that rubbish about the time of year and how tough it is on me… I'm pacing up and down Diana's room, over and over, fidgeting with the phone in my hands. He has no right, absolutely *none* to talk about me like that. Like I'm some delicate china doll he has to handle carefully. And if he's spoken to Diana, practically a stranger, then who else? Kian? Does Kian know about my… my… I stop pacing, dread washing over me. If this isn't in my head, if I'm not about to wake up, then did James… really just do that? Hallie knows. She's known since the moments after it happened, but I begged her, pleaded with her not to tell Kian. I couldn't face such a warm, kind human knowing I was in pain and treating me any differently.

I groan, turning to collapse onto the bed. This house party just gets worse and worse. Or rather, this alternative version that's playing out right now. This alternative reality that I seem to have slipped into. Maybe I'm playing out my worst fears? This is probably all a stress reaction. James speaking to Diana about my personal life, Diana apparently working double the hours crisis-managing my business. The job offer, her hasty midnight reply. Yes. That really has to be it.

The phone vibrates again in my hand and I bring it up to my face, repositioning Diana's glasses to read the text. It's another message from that unknown number. But it's not what I expect. In fact, it's a link to a song. I mouth the words, staring at the YouTube link, my finger hovering over it, just a breath away from unleashing all the memories tied to it. I know this song. It's one of my favourites, a Coldplay one that speaks directly to my heart, that I've played over and over, curled up on the sofa, hanging off every lyric.

I sit bolt upright. This is conclusive proof that I'm in a horrible dream. My brain is reorganising my trauma, or something. I'm experiencing all this from Diana's perspective, because my mind can't deal with thinking about it from my own. I snap my fingers, glad I've finally figured out the puzzle of this weird day. But… how am I supposed to wake up? Wait it out? Try and fall asleep?

I get comfortable in the bed, press my head into the pillow and close my eyes. I can smell Diana's perfume on the linens, a floral and coconutty scent that reminds me of gorse flowers. Like the ones Gran and I would find on the moors, bringing back golden handfuls to place in a bowl. I push that memory away before it sours. This scent is just like her perfume too. Like she's spritzed it all over the pillows. Turning over, I breathe in deeply, in, out. Trying to relax. If I can get to sleep, if I can just ignore that scent I'll wake up as myself again and this will all be over.

A knock sounds at the door. I grab the other pillow, stuffing it over my ear. Then the knock comes again, thudding inside my head.

'Diana? Are you in there?' It's Eva. I should probably get up. Tell her about the secret email file. The company trying to poach Diana. Make a plan for how to fix this… But even the thought of it exhausts me. The weight of the explaining, the backtracking. And if this isn't even real… what's the point? 'Just checking you're all right? I got the note… really appreciate you working today, I know it's Christmas.' A pause. 'I should have got you a gift. That was really thoughtless of me.'

There's a pause and I wait, heart thumping in the close warmth of the bed.

'Anyway,' she says, clicking her tongue, 'would you catch me up on everything before dinner? Maybe an hour before… if that's OK?' She coughs, as though covering up her uncertainty. Trying to navigate this moment where her professional and personal life have collided so horribly. 'And we can, er, check the forecast again? See if you're happy to drive back in the morning?'

I sigh deeply. I can't completely ignore her. 'Sounds good!' I chirp, the words sticking to my throat, sounding high-pitched and hollow. 'See you in a bit.'

The silence on the other side of the door stretches for a beat and I picture her, *me*, staring up at the ceiling for a moment in that red dress. Collecting myself, drawing myself back together. 'Cool.'

There's the shuffle of footsteps as she moves away. I throw back the covers, practically suffocating in the stifling heat in this room. What is it with heating systems in old houses? Freezing cold or fit to boil a lobster. In irritation, I get up. This isn't working. If I can't get to sleep to get out of this, then what if I physically just… leave? What if I go downstairs, walk out of the door and jump-start this whole mess until I'm no longer Diana? There is something about Penhallow. How it's lured me back after all these years and Gran has appeared, more real than the ghost who has haunted me. Did it whisper in the dark to Hallie, leading her to book this place? I shiver, imagining the watchful walls leaning in, soaking in all our memories and wielding them years later.

There's a tug, deep inside me. It's instinctive and keening, a physical need to escape this house. I trust it, relaxing a little now I have a plan. Now I'm sure I should leave Penhallow.

Like a thief, I move as silently as I can down the corridor. I'm half expecting to see the Eva version of me in this dream leap out, attuned to the smallest sound Diana makes. But luckily, I get to the staircase without incident and see that the door to the sitting room is still shut. The other house guests are in there, laughing and chatting, and in that moment, I feel so removed from it all. All my friends are in that room, the people I love and care about. But Eva, this Eva is upstairs. Alone and stressed. The person on the periphery.

It never used to be this way. Three years ago, Hallie and I would have sat shoulder to shoulder, exchanging gifts, toasting, laughing and hugging with our inside jokes and snorts and shrieks. But that's another person, that Eva. The one that sits firmly on the divide of before. Whereas I'm the one sat squat in the middle of the after.

I shake it off, pull on my boots again and step out into the afternoon. It's still snowing, but not as frenzied as earlier. The lemon wedge of sun filters down through the sullen grey clouds, glancing off the smooth white of the last flurry. Now the snowflakes drift down ponderously and I reach out, capturing a tiny one in my gloved palm. Each one is unique. And this one, with its delicate pattern, its flawless symmetry, is perfect. I breathe on it, watching it melt until it dies a small death in my hand. Happy Christmas indeed. Then with a sniff, I wriggle the car keys out of my pocket and head over to the car we drove down in.

The key turns in the ignition, spluttering and spluttering and that familiar feeling of panic grips my stomach. The windscreen is iced up, but I'm hoping that the turning engine will clear it. My breath comes in clouds, steaming up the air around me as I swear at the stupid car, willing it to life. Finally, it starts up. I click my seat belt into place, check my mirrors and wait an agonising few minutes as the screen clears. Then with trembling fingers I grip the steering wheel and reverse out of the space, kicking up gravel in my wake.

Penhallow soon disappears in a swirl of snow and mist in my rear-view mirror and I settle down into the heated car seat, smug in the knowledge that I'm winning. Those ghostly memories, the rooms full of people I am so disconnected from all fall away behind me. I'm getting out of this dream, this reality, whatever this *thing* is, and as soon as I wake up, I can put the whole sorry mess behind me.

Three hours later, I'm still on the moorland.

Panic has seeped under my skin, filling my chest. Every breath I take is a laboured one, trying to fight down the terror. Night has fallen, thick and suffocating, and the snow clouds have unleashed a blizzard. There's nobody else out here. No signposts, not even any sodding sheep. I'm totally and completely alone. A sob wracks my chest and I blink away furious tears.

This cannot be happening.

It cannot.

The fuel gauge blinks, the dial shifting to empty. I should have another forty miles or so, but I can't be sure. What if I'm out here all night? The heating will cut out and I'll be left to shiver alone until daylight. Maybe I'll freeze to death. Doesn't that happen sometimes? Those tragic, awful news stories when a person isn't found until days later? I check Diana's phone again, swearing loudly when I see it *still* hasn't got any signal. I pull over, leaving the headlights on to catch the bright flurries of snow dashing down.

Then I scream.

I fill my body, beating the steering wheel until the heels of my palms ache. I release all the frustration, all the fury, all my pent-up rage. Then, when my breath is spent, I lean my forehead on the wheel, sniffing and sobbing. My shoulders shake, my entire being shuddering as sob after sob rips from my chest. This is a nightmare. This day is no dream. I should never have left Penhallow and its ghosts.

Gradually, my sobs subside. I look up, rubbing away the fatigue, the fear, and push Diana's glasses up the bridge of my nose. If this is a breakdown, my mind fracturing into a thousand sharp pieces, maybe I'm catatonic somewhere. This could all be a projection. And if it's all in my head, it isn't real. This car, the night, the suffocating snow.

It isn't real.

A snowstorm won't beat me. It won't. I force my trembling hands to grip the wheel, will my foot to press carefully against the pedal. I pull back into the lane, moving slowly forward again. Sniffing occasionally, a numbness washes over me. There's never been a situation I couldn't break out of. In that, at least, I am strong. Every time I've been stuck, at home growing up, in the torturous graduate scheme at that third-rate bank, on my gap year when my only debit card was eaten by that damn machine in Thailand… I've thought my way out of every situation. And dug up. I've hardened over the years, grown a shell of armour. I have never been beaten down entirely. This time is no exception.

The only difference is that Gran isn't with me anymore.

As I round a bend, I catch a glimpse of something. The shadowed, stark outline of a building.

'Yes!' I shout, punching the air. It's Penhallow. I've somehow circled around this whole bloody moorland in the dark and found my way back to the house. Briefly, I collapse against the steering wheel, a bubble of laughter bursting wildly from my chest. Then I sit up straight, tension flowing away. I may not have escaped, but I made it back. *I made it back.*

'Well, Eva. Glad to see you've pulled yourself together,' a voice says next to me.

Chapter 11

'Shit!' I scream, heart hammering as I scrabble for the door handle.

Gran starts laughing, grinning at me as I pinch the bridge of my nose. She was always the prankster. Forever hiding one of my granddad's slippers so he would trail forlornly (and slightly crookedly) around the house searching for it; or she'd remove the crossword puzzle page from the Saturday paper, encouraging him to phone the newsagent and report a damaged copy. She would always wink at me, stifling a laugh until the penny finally dropped. I can't imagine what she was like as a teenager. Must have driven her mum up the wall.

'I don't find any of this *remotely* amusing.'

'Of course you don't!' she gasps, dabbing at her eyes. There are tears. *Actual tears.* I slump lower in my seat, waiting for her to finish. 'Ah! Most fun I've had in ages. Your face! Priceless.'

I rub my forehead in frustration. I can't believe that this is the version I'm getting of her. Not the sweet listener who guided me through choosing the right university, or the person who baked my favourite shortbread for every visit. No. I'm getting the wicked version. The least useful one in this kind of situation. But then, any version of her is better than none.

'Whatever you've got to say, say it. I'm cold and tired and not in the mood for any of this… whatever this is.' I catch sight of myself in the wing mirror, lurching forward to check again. It's my face, not Diana's. My features, my smudged, tired eyes. I bring my fingers up to my cheekbones and relax slightly at the feel of pressure against my skin where they touch. At least this awful day is nearly over. I can wake up, fresh and new on Boxing Day. Maybe I'll even give Diana a bonus. Surely I have one credit card I haven't maxed out yet? I contemplate which balance I can jiggle around to make it happen.

Gran straightens up in her robe, smooths out her plait of white hair and fixes her eyes on me. The laughter has gone, replaced with a hint of sorrow. 'My darling girl, aren't you even a *little* bit happy to see me?'

'Of course I am,' I say quickly, unfolding my arms, all thoughts of Diana and credit cards swiftly evaporating as I reach a hand out to her. My heart thumps with guilt. After searching for her in every crowd, even after I had finally accepted her death, longing for her reassuring presence in my life, this sudden twist of fate has thrown me.

I want so much to believe this is her. I gulp, a sharp pain piercing beneath my ribs.

'Gran, you don't know how much I wanted this. Even just five more minutes.' I take a steadying breath. I can't give in to this. It's stress and tiredness and deep, drowning heartache. My mind has cracked under the pressure of it, and if I give in now… what if I never get back? 'But you're not real. This car, this bloody empty fuel gauge, none of this *exists*. It's all in my head. So, you've got to be in my head too. As much as… as much as I wish you weren't.'

My breath catches and I turn away from her. I can't keep talking. The thought of her not being real, the truly logical explanation for all this… well, I would rather the illogical reason. I would rather this was all real.

'Are you sure about that?'

I open my mouth, then close it again. Her hand is in mine now, the papery folds of her dry skin held within the solid web of my own. She's warm to the touch, but I imagine that's because I naturally run cold.

'You're wearing the same robe you wore the last time I saw you… when I visited you in the hospital, Gran,' I say gently, reasoning with myself as much as with her. Pushing away the image of that broken body, the tubes and beeping and how very *small* she looked.

'Unfortunate thing about the afterlife. No wardrobe changes for these sorts of occasions,' she says with a shrug, brushing my reasoning aside. 'We have to make do with what we died in. No theatrics. I do wish I had gone out in something a bit more flattering. Even my silk robe, you know, the turquoise one with the peacock feather pattern? That would have been better than this hospital issue tat.'

She picks at the cord of the robe, tutting at it. I'm not really sure what to say. Every plausible explanation I have settled on today has somehow deftly been swept aside.

'Now we're past the pleasantries, I had better explain a few things,' she says, removing her hand from mine. A stern expression fills her features, the laughter vanishing from the creases around her eyes. 'There are a few rules. A few things you need to know. And really, I haven't got much time. It'll soon be midnight and everything will reset. Christmas Day will begin again, and you'll wake up in the next host body. But you won't get many chances at this, you really *do* have to make each one count, Eva. There are only so many Christmases to go round, before all hope for change is gone.'

I blink, trying to absorb what she's saying.

'For once, turn that big brain off. I can see it whirling. Highly distracting, like some big fairground ride.' She leans closer, her eyes capturing mine. '*Humour me.*'

I wait for a beat, considering my options. They seem fairly slim out here, sitting in the darkened driveway in a car with my dead gran, sprightly and rather well next to me. 'OK. Let's say, *hypothetically*,' I hold up a finger, 'that this is all real. That I really just lived a whole day in my assistant's body, and that I just drove around the entire moorland and nearly froze to death on some arse end of nowhere country lane.'

'Yes.'

'And that you're real, not dead exactly, but…?'

'Think of me as a guide,' she says with a flourish.

This might have all been more believable if she was wearing the turquoise silk robe, to be honest.

'A guide. Right.' I let out a small strangled sound. 'Not a figment of my stressed-out, overworked, sleep-lacking imagination. Great.'

'Don't frown, darling, you'll look *terrible* in ten years. Maybe even five the way you're going.' She sighs. 'I am your guide. I'm here to remind you who you are. What you want.'

'I… Gran. Is this a joke?' I'm trying to stay measured. Level-headed. But this is all getting a bit much. As much as I've craved even a moment more with Gran these last three years, I never pictured it being like this.

Her smile widens. 'No joke, darling! I will turn up just before midnight. Or just after, depending on how far along you've got in the day. This day has been a bit of a washout, wouldn't you say? Hot-footing it off to the pub like that, tut-tut. So I thought I would pop in early. Give you a little pep talk. We all need those every now and then.'

She pats my arm and I try not to shudder at the fact I can feel it. I can feel the slight pressure of her fingers. It exists, that touch. It's a human connection that shouldn't be there. Perhaps this isn't a joke.

'So what happens now?' I ask, swallowing down my unease. The world is tilting and I'm trying to keep a grip on it. To make sense of this moment, this day I experienced in another woman's body. But I'm finding it increasingly hard.

'You have to trust me.'

'Trust you?'

'Trust that I'm telling you the truth. That I'm doing this for *you*, Eva. For your own good.' She sighs, looking out of the windscreen at Penhallow. 'Change doesn't come easy. And I should know, I've lived a whole lifetime and every time I've realised something, and had to put in the work, it's been like wriggling through a keyhole that keeps getting smaller and smaller. Even while I get bigger and clumsier.'

'What kind of change do you mean?'

She waves a hand vaguely at me, then the manor house. The car we're sitting in. 'Look around you. Really *look*. This is where you are, right now, on this day. At this very moment. Is this what you want? Is this where you planned on ending up?'

I do as she says and look around. Up at the dark looming shape of Penhallow, the window with mine and James's

98

bedroom behind it. The memories of those perfect childhood Christmases overlaid by the rather painful one I'm finding myself living now. I look at my dead gran, sitting next to me. At Diana's phone, useless in my lap. All the years of reaching and striving have amounted to this. Every decision I've made over the past three years, all leading to now. To the shop launch. To Hallie's house party.

To this wide, chasms-deep divide inside me.

What do I want?

'Now you're getting somewhere,' Gran says, eyes twinkling in the dark. 'Now you're using that big brain for what it's meant for. Not just spreadsheets and brand guidelines and social media conversion rates. Although all those things *are* rather fascinating. Don't look at me like that, I *do* know what the Facebook is.'

I blink, fighting down a wave of fatigue. It's like a current that is pulling me elsewhere, away from my own body. Away from this car. 'What now?' I ask, desperately trying to cling to the steering wheel. To stay awake. 'I still don't understand. I have questions. I'm not ready. I-I need you.'

Gran nods, as though this is all perfectly normal. Nothing out of the ordinary. 'You'll wake up again, Eva, on Christmas Day. But not as yourself. As someone else.'

I blink and a line of light zigzags down my vision. I try to shift it, blinking rapidly, even as Gran fades in and out.

'Tell me more. Anything!' I say desperately, reaching for her. Is this the last time I'll see her? Panic grips my chest. 'Who will it be? What do I have to do? I'll go along with it, I will! Just… tell me. And stay. Please stay. Don't leave me again! Not like this!'

But Gran just smiles sadly, fading fast into the dim world

of snow beyond the car windows. And somehow, I am fading away too. A pull at my centre is carrying me forward, just as Gran fades to nothing but a glowing silhouette.

'Don't waste it, Eva. Listen. Learn. Don't waste a single second of this chance.'

Chapter 12

I groan, fighting to get out from under the duvet. It's stifling hot, weighing down on me, and my stomach twists with nausea.

Stomach. Churning. Nausea.

I'm going to be sick.

Stumbling from the bed, I clamp my hand across my mouth and just make it into the bathroom in time. On shaking legs I creep to the basin, rinsing my mouth out and groan. Oh no. Please no. Have I somehow woken up as... Hallie?

I cast around for a mirror, the fog in my head insistent and pressing, making me want to collapse back in the bed, close my eyes and sleep. The weighty clatter of bangles on my wrist draws my eye and I find a jade bracelet, thick and veined with jet. I've never seen Hallie wear something like this before. Is it a present?

My hand strays to my stomach, finding it flat and unobtrusive. Definitely not baby shaped. I breathe out a heady sigh of relief. I'm not Hallie. I don't think I could have handled it, a day with that life uncoiling inside me. A reminder of how much of a failure I really am.

So... who am I today? Who has Gran sent me back as?

There's a wardrobe in the corner, all scuffed at the edges. I fling it open and finally find a mirror on the inside of the door.

'Well, this isn't terrible…' I mutter, a smile breaking over my… no, *Natalie's* features. I turn back and forth, taking in the pyjama shorts, the silk camisole top. The messy bun of brown hair, streaked by the sun of a hundred holidays. The tanned skin, the freckles. Natalie is even younger than Diana, she's the baby of Hallie's doting family. I pull the tie from my hair, letting it fan out around my shoulders. It's glossy and smells like shea butter and almonds. My stomach churns again and the sour taste of Champagne bubbles up over my tongue. Of course. She must have drunk a lot last night to celebrate Hallie's news.

My smile drops and I watch Natalie's face crumple in the mirror. Remembering what I learned the day before. That Diana is about to be poached by another company. How she's hiding things from me. What does Gran want me to know today? How bad can things possibly be?

I make a swift mug of weak tea with the tiny travel kettle on top of the chest of drawers and get back into the bed, pulling the covers up to my chin. Sinking into the pocket of fading warmth, I tap a finger against Natalie's phone and see the screen flash up with the date. It's Christmas Day. Again. I groan, leaning back into the pillows, and think over the sequence of events of this day. How everyone would be going down to breakfast right now while Diana meets Sarah afterwards outside the kitchen. They'll go for this sea swim and then it'll be Christmas dinner. I suppose everyone will be there, even Diana if I'm not sending her off on some great escape across the moors.

What is Gran trying to tell me?

Natalie's phone beeps in my hands and I scroll to a video

message. It's from her fiancée, Olga. She's on the other side of the world, already celebrating Christmas on the beach. I laugh as she blows theatrical kisses, then says in her slightly husky way how much she loves Natalie. How she'll love her for ever. How being apart for so long makes everything less vivid. Less beautiful.

I cradle the phone against my knees, watching the thirty-second clip again and again. Trying to put James in this video in my head. Wondering if he would blow me kisses like that if we were apart. The knot forming in my stomach tells me everything I need to know. This is how we were, years ago. How we were after our honeymoon, when we couldn't bear to say goodbye on the Tube platform each morning. How his hand would tuck the strands of my hair behind one ear as commuters brushed past us, muttering distractedly. We would cling to just a few more moments together, my fingers laced through his, murmuring about nothing, our dinner plans, what was on TV later – anything to delay and bask in that bubble before we went our separate ways. How we would text throughout the day, making plans for the weekend, plans to meet up with Hallie and Kian. How we would actually stick to them.

I drain the last of the tea, placing the mug decidedly on the bedside table. If Gran wants to torture me with this perfect relationship, so be it.

After a shower, I pull on the loosest-fitting clothes I can find in Natalie's wardrobe, a sloppy red jumper and leggings, and go out for a walk. I stuff a hat over my head and grab a croissant from the breakfast table on the way out, eating it quickly and dodging around anyone I come across. Luckily,

I manage to avoid Hallie and Kian. I'm not sure I can face their perfect happiness too right now.

I need to be alone.

The moorland is the dull white of old porcelain, the kind stuffed in charity shops, clattering together on brimming shelves. I don't stop to catch snowflakes in my hand, marvelling at their symmetry. I've already grown tired of this rabbit warren of more questions than answers. I want to get to the part where I know what I'm supposed to learn and find a way out. All I seem to be seeing are my failings. How I work too much. How Diana is overworked and I missed it. And now, clearly, how I neglect my marriage.

Instead of heading to the gardens at the back of the kitchen, I stride out into the fields. This bleak day doesn't feel like Christmas. There are no cosy vibes, no soft morning light as snow glitters frostily against the blades of grass. There is only snow and mud-churned fields, narrow lanes slick with treacherous black ice and the building frustration inside me. I drop over the stile, kicking up a patch of ice and mud to coat Natalie's shiny green Hunter wellies. There's something satisfying about trudging across this field, the trail of my boots dimpling the snow. My breath forms clouds around my face, these muscles protesting gently as this body works all the Champagne out. If I walk a little faster, push a little harder, maybe the tension will drain away. Maybe I'll find some peace.

But I know, deep in the four chambers of my heart, that peace only comes if you earn it.

So instead, I give in to it. All the rage, all the bitterness simmering just under the surface, always. Forming snowballs in my gloved hands, I chuck them steadily, one after another, watching them explode against an old drystone wall.

'*That's* for giving me an ultimatum.'

THUMP

'And *that's* for making me eat that bloody cake.'

THUMP

'And *that's* for stranding me in a sodding blizzard.'

THUMP

'And that's for making me face this… alone.'

THUD

I screw up all my anger, all my sadness and hurl it as hard as I can against that wall. Over and over, until I'm panting and aching. I've scooped up all the snow from around the wellies, exposing an ugly smear of scrub grass and mud beneath. With a sniff, I look back at Penhallow, shoving my hands into my coat pockets. There's no anger left now. Only cold emptiness, seeping into my bones. I would rather the anger. I would rather feel something, anything, than this yawn of wide nothing that I keep returning to.

I walk back to the house, savouring every crunching boot print. It's like cracking the top of a crème brûlée, and I take my time, zigzagging across the field until there's no smooth nothingness left. My boots have left an impermanent tattoo, tracing the path of my thoughts until the next snowfall conceals them. Until it all melts away.

John is in the entrance hall and I spot Hallie, sporting her best hostess smile. Then an arm circles her waist, Kian's smile dimpling his brown cheeks as he angles his body towards hers. Loving her. Protecting her. They share a secret look and carry on chatting to John. And Kian's arm stays around her. It hits me in the chest, seeing that. That simple act. I can't remember the last time James did that, just flung an arm around my shoulders as if to shout to the world, she is mine.

No, that's wrong. I can remember. It was when… I gulp. When I had that same sickening glow Hallie has now. It was three years ago, and we were in the corner shop at the end of our street, searching through the fogged-up glass windows of the freezers for our favourite ice cream. I love the Ben and Jerry's cookie dough, he prefers raspberry ripple. It was December, the days slipping away until Christmas and festive songs were blasting out of unseen speakers. I found his favourite flavour first, gripping the door handle in triumph to open it, and, as I stood back up, wiggling the carton in my hand, he snaked his arm around my waist. And I thought yes, this is our next step. This is the path we've chosen. We're doing it.

But now, however many cartons of ice cream I cram into our freezer, it feels like we've strayed from that path.

As I hover on the periphery, shrugging out of the coat and wellies, from the corner of my eye I catch James walking down the stairs. He's troubled, his shoulders hunched and hands shoved deep in his pockets. He's wearing my favourite of his shirts, it's pale blue with tiny white buttons. But today it's untucked and so rumpled I know it hasn't seen an iron.

My heart lurches and before I know what I'm doing, I reach out to him. As my hand lands on his forearm, surprise lights up his features, the dark murk of his eyes. So brown today. A deep, brooding hazel. There's barely a drop of green in them. I bite my lip, unsure of what to say. How to act around this man I feel is slipping further away.

'Um… happy Christmas?' I manage, glad at least that the

small group gathered in the entrance hall is around Hallie and not me. Kian nods at us, then follows Hallie into the lounge where Sarah is serving coffee and tea, a tray of tiny spice biscuits by the door.

'Happy Christmas, Nat,' he replies, smiling down at me. 'Do you by any chance, er… know where Eva went? She didn't come for the dip at the beach.'

'Sorry, no. I went for a walk…' I drift off as his brow furrows and my heart sinks a little. It's happened again on this version of Christmas Day. I've fled, probably sequestered myself somewhere with my laptop, anything to steal just a few minutes for myself. He looks so lost, so out of place in the midst of Penhallow that I want to put my arms around him. Drink in his scent and tell him it's all going to be all right. 'Do you want to… play a game? Snooker?'

'Sure.' He shrugs, as if resigned to a Christmas Day alone. Without his wife. 'Didn't know you could play.'

I can't. Which is painfully obvious two minutes into the game. We close the door on the billiards room, instantly killing the hum of voices from outside. This room is all wood, leather and low lights, the table itself in the centre. It feels like a confessional, or a secret. Somewhere to unburden my soul as I play. But as I'm gearing up to talk to him, ask him how things are going, he drops his head into his hands.

'James?'

'I know, I know,' he says, his voice muffled and distant. 'I shouldn't talk to you about this stuff. But I guess, you're removed from the situation, right? You're not Kian. Or Hallie. I know I shouldn't be dragging her little sister into my mess too… Man, it feels like only yesterday when you used to stay with the four of us in the flat at the weekends. Time flies, I guess? And now you're all grown up and about to get married.'

The image of Nat as a gawky, Bambi-limbed tween surfaces. James and Kian would spend hours teaching her to play chess, taking her to the skate park, and Hallie and I would spend money we didn't have buying her glitter hairspray and magazines.

'Is everything OK, James?' I find myself saying, gently prising out his thoughts, his words.

He is quiet for a moment, a frown line deepening between his eyes. 'The thing is, I can't keep doing this, Nat.'

I blink, pushing back the memories of our early twenties and reach for the cue, testing its balance and weight in my hands. I keep a measured expression, trying not to allow the panic to wash over Natalie's features. As though my whole being hasn't filled with a sudden flood of foreboding. 'What… what do you mean?'

He straightens, looking me dead in the eye. The low lights pick out the brown sheen of his hair, the shadows that crease his features. My breath hitches as he forms the words I dread to hear.

'I–I've done something terrible. Unforgiveable. And I think I have to leave her.'

Chapter 13

'Wh-what?' I stutter, the life draining from me.

James sighs, covering his face with his hands. 'I kissed some-one – well, someone tried to kiss me. This woman at work. And the thing is... I *wanted* it. I wanted her to kiss me.'

I stare at him and the world slows around me. I'm aware of everything. Every tiny little detail. The breath as it warms my lips. The staccato tremble of my heart. The scraping of Natalie's jade bracelets against my wrist. His hands lower from his face, slowly. Too slowly. He looks at me and the guilt has wrung him dry. Drained the colour from him, the life and warmth I love so much.

'But... you... you stopped it?' I manage to say, my voice sounding unnatural. High and false. 'The kiss?'

'Of course. Of course I did,' he says, placing his hands on the back of his head. It's what he does when he's anxious about something. Like when we went to Venice for my birthday and a pickpocket stole my purse, along with our hotel room key, my credit card, everything. I can still feel the warmth in his chest as I hugged him, waiting for his arms to drop around my waist. Like they always did. Like they never seem to anymore. 'But it's the thought, isn't it? I wanted to. That's the line – and

I crossed it. I couldn't ever imagine, even for a *second* wanting to. I mean, it's us, isn't it? This is me and Eva we're talking about. She's my constant. I'm not making excuses, you have to believe that, Nat. But you've seen how it is, right?' He breaks off bitterly, leaning across the snooker table to ricochet another ball off the white, the tiny crack as they collide echoing harshly around the room. 'She barely acknowledges my existence now. I could be a coat rack and she would pay more attention.'

I open and close my mouth. I don't know what to say. The floor tilts sickeningly and I stumble to a leather armchair, pressed into the corner of the room.

I need air.

I know I got in the car to leave, to drive to London and face the consequences later. I was desperate. I never truly believed. But this, this is different.

'If I didn't go home for a week, I'm not sure it would bother her. Or if she'd even notice.' He shakes his head and sighs. 'Even this house party is all about the business, whether she can be back in time for the shop launch. I'm proud of her, but... I just... I'm not sure I fit into the picture anymore. This was the one bit of her time that I wanted, you know? Just a few days. That was all.'

'You want her to... notice you?' I say, finding my tongue. Not only is my assistant considering leaving, my relationship, my marriage is foundering. It has to be Lauren from marketing. I've seen her eyeing him up, waiting until I'm chatting with someone else at one of his work dos. Bloody Lauren and her perfect horsey grin, those rows of white teeth.

He gave me that ultimatum on Christmas Eve, yes. But a part of me didn't believe he would ever go through with it. That he really wanted it. I thought he was just being reactionary, that it was only a step up from our regular arguments. That it might have been due to the time of year, that maybe he felt the same pressing grief I did. I believed that even getting in that car and driving away wouldn't end us. In fact, I never thought beyond reaching London.

How wrong I was.

'Not so much notice me... I need her to participate. I need her to look up from her laptop and ask me how my day was. Talk to me, tell me what's going on in her head. Open a door and let me bloody walk *through it*.' He pockets another ball and rubs his hand over his face.

As he stands staring at the table for a beat, the shadows gather around him like a cloak. Half of me wants to reach for him, smother him in all the love I can offer right now. But the other half is louder. More insistent. That half is telling me to give up. Because what's the point in fighting for something that's already failed? How much can one person divide themselves up, give all of themselves at work and at home? But I'm afraid. So afraid. I don't want this to be the end of us.

He sighs, straightening up. 'Is it so much to ask?'

'No,' I say immediately, the word hollow and too loud in my head. I feel like I'm playing a part, that this is all a scripted piece. 'I suppose it's not too much to ask.'

'You're away a lot from your girlfriend, right? Where's Olga now, off on a beach somewhere, isn't she? Surely that takes its toll, being apart so much.'

I think back to that video message from this morning. Olga's husky voice. The sureness in the way she said *I love you*. Their time apart didn't seem to cast them adrift. Like their foundations were solid granite, and in contrast, ours had been plunged into loose sand.

'What would you do?'

I look up at him and blink. 'What?'

'If you were me, if this was your marriage. Would you end it? If it were you and Olga?'

I bite my lip, tearing my gaze away from his. My fingers are tied in a knot in my lap, a dull ache radiating under my ribs. What would I do, if it were the other way around? We've had our problems, James and I. But we're built on something solid, something lasting. Not just sand, I'm sure of it. We've been a team for over a decade, fighting for the same things. Fighting together.

I felt our foundations locking into place the day that it rained and rained in our first year of university in London. It was the middle of winter, water streaming down the windows as though the clouds had crowded directly over the launderette. My hair was a damp muddle of waves that I had hastily twisted in my fingers, wringing as much of it out as I could from the dash through the streets to get there, all whilst grinning at him. This boy I had met only three months before. His hair was just as damp, with fog steaming up his glasses. He never wears them now, instead he chooses contacts. But I remember him in those glasses, how he would take them off to rub the lenses with the corner of his T-shirt. How it would lift up slightly, revealing the taut skin beneath.

He was handing me piles of those T-shirts he liked to wear, band ones that you buy at gigs with big capital letters sprayed across them. I was chatting about nothing, maybe the rain, as I folded and he said the words so quietly, like a sigh, like he'd been holding them in forever.

I love you.

My breath hitched, heart thumping loudly, so loudly I was sure he could hear it. And I carried on folding, as though my whole world hadn't just ended. And this new, perfect one had begun in its place.

Later, when we lay with the sheets all tangled around us, my fairy lights glittering in a web overhead, I waited until he closed his eyes. Until he frowned in that funny way, his eyelids crinkling for a moment. I waited until I was sure he was sleeping, and I whispered back.

I love you too.

And his lips twitched, like he'd been waiting a lifetime to hear it.

But that was back then when we were like giants, when we thought anything was possible. When the world hadn't buried us in all the things that could go wrong. In the last three years... I shift uncomfortably. He's right. I have shut him out. After Gran died and my heart was ripped apart, I scraped together whatever was left just so I could carry on. I wasn't ready to open my heart to him. I couldn't talk to him about any of it. I turned inward. All I could do was build something new, nurture a project that might actually breathe and grow and live. So I started my business, painstakingly building it brick by brick. It's the anchor I've clung to throughout the storm. The only worthwhile thing I've produced in the years since she died.

But I never let him know that.

I never whisper my secret thoughts to him in the dark anymore. We have stopped making those everyday plans, stopped existing beyond our own work ambitions. I swallow, separating my fingers to hold them against the cool leather of the armrests.

'Maybe she just needs more time,' I blurt.

His eyes shine in the low lights as he smiles grimly. 'She knows what she wants, Nat. She makes time for the business, the shop… I wish she could save some of that time for us. For… for me.'

'Then tell her that.'

'What?'

'Tell her you need that from her.' I sit forward, bracing my elbows on my thighs. If James wants an honest conversation, I can do that. I think. If I want us to work, I have to. 'Make her let you in. Get her to open that door so you can start to talk again. Like you used to.'

'She's still raw though, you know? If I make her actually talk, will she even be able to say it?'

'About her gran?'

'About everything. About that whole Christmas and what it did to us. Not just her gran, but… everything. The avalanche of it.'

I reel back, the words cutting like a knife. James ambles around the table, pots another ball then leans against the cue, eyeing the table. 'It was all too much.'

I shake my head. I don't know how he can talk about that Christmas so calmly. Like it's an everyday thing that happened to us, like getting caught in the rain on the way to work. Or losing the house keys. Everything halted that day after we drove back from the hospital. After I held Gran's hand until her body gave up. Just picturing her, and what happened in our flat afterwards… I shudder, leaning back once more into the armchair. 'She lost everything, all at once. You have to see that. Her family, her past, her hope…'

'But she doesn't want—'

'She *does* want you,' I breathe. I frown, trying to straighten out my muddled thoughts. Because I do want James, don't I? I do. 'She does. She wants the you from before that Christmas, when there was still hope. But she's afraid of failing again. There's no safety net this time…' I swallow. 'Gran's not… she's not coming back.'

My throat thickens and I turn in the chair, hiding my face with my hair. The tears are so close to slipping free, they're pulsing. A gentle, cool hand pushes back my hair and James kneels in front of me. 'Hey…' he says, reaching for my hand. 'What's up, Nat? Do you want me to get Hallie?'

'No,' I sniff, trying to gather myself. 'No, I'm fine.'

I don't need Hallie. I need James. I need his concern, his cooling touch. I need him to hold me and stop the world from spinning away. 'I'm just hungover, that's all,' I say, attempting a weak smile.

James stares at me, confusion pooling in the corners of his eyes. 'For a minute, I swear you sounded just like Eva. You know it's funny, she used to talk about this house and the strange, unusual things that would happen. I didn't really believe it but then I swear I woke up this morning and her gran was in the kitchen, humming this song she used to sing. She called it the pancake song.' He laughs quietly and my blood freezes. I haven't heard that song since the last time we stayed with Gran. Four months before she died. 'Maybe this house does play tricks.'

I stare back at him. What if I just… told him? If he remembers the things I told him about Penhallow, maybe it'll make sense to him… maybe this is how we find our way back.

'James... actually, there's something you need to know,' I say. 'Don't freak out.'

'What do you mean?'

'What if I told you that... that Eva is stuck in this loop. That she saw her gran and then she woke up as Diana and now somehow she's... well I'm... *me*.'

James blinks once, twice. Then stands abruptly, taking a step back. A grin splits his face and he points at me. 'Nice one, Nat. You nearly got me there. Did Kian put you up to this? Where is he? He's hiding here somewhere, isn't he? Kian! Yeah, you can come out now!'

'No, James, really—'

'Nearly had me fooled,' James says, shaking his head and laughing. 'Good one.'

As he goes back to the snooker table, talking about the time Hallie and Kian tricked him into thinking it was his final exam day at university, when really it was still a week away, I collapse back into the armchair. For a single, charged moment I felt sure I could reach through all this and grip his hand. That I could tell him the truth, unburden myself and he would be there, ready to understand. I was ready.

But as he reminisces about uni days, clearing the table of all the balls, I know I am completely alone in this. I have to figure it out by myself. And maybe James will be there at the end of it all. But perhaps, after hearing him out, after listening to how he's just as alone as I am... that maybe he won't be. Maybe he's ready to move on with someone like Lauren from marketing.

And maybe that is what Gran needs me to know.

Chapter 14

I sit through Christmas dinner in a vacuum. I eat, I chat, I even crack a few jokes. But the food is ash in my mouth. All I keep thinking about is the ultimatum and how James might have meant it. That if I had truly left last night and driven back to London as I planned, it might have been the end of us. Does he not want me to succeed? Does he really need my time so badly that he's already looking elsewhere?

I shudder, covering it up with another sip of wine, and steal a glance at him. He's talking to Kian, nodding as Kian discusses something at work. James asks the occasional question, letting him speak, and I'm struck by how thoughtful he is. How he'll give his time and attention so freely, so willingly.

In contrast, the Eva sat at this table is pushing turkey around on her plate. I guess this Eva must have found somewhere to hide away with her laptop for a few hours, then rejoined everyone for this meal. She's barely touched her food, and the green paper Christmas hat perched on her head looks garish in contrast to the pallor of her skin. John is talking on the other side of her, discussing the merits of different ski resorts for their upcoming trip. I slump back in my chair, watching them both. So separate. So far removed from each other.

I never considered that he wouldn't be there after this shop launch. I thought he understood the time I had to pour into it.

'Missing Olga, Nat?' Hallie asks softly, slipping her hand into mine on the table. She squeezes my fingers and I turn to her, her warmth and the familiar scent of her perfume. All amber and vanilla and smoke. But instead of relaxing me like her presence usually does, it prickles. I remove my fingers from hers and swallow down the wash of bile on my tongue.

'Miss Olga? Yes, yes of course.' I cough and quickly take another sip of wine. 'But she's having a great time, you know? Two people can be apart for a while without it being a big thing.'

Hallie nods, a slight crease appearing in her forehead. 'You're allowed to miss her, darling. Even if you are happy for her.'

'Yes, I mean…' I blink, thinking of what Natalie would say. 'She sent me a video message. She's having a blast and when I see her in a few weeks, it'll be like no time has passed, right?'

Hallie nods encouragingly. 'That's a good way of looking at it.'

I toy with the stem of my wine glass, focusing on the slip of golden liquid inside. 'Hal, what would you do if you found out that Kian wanted to kiss someone else?'

'That's an interesting question. Why are you asking me that?'

'No reason!' I chuckle and pat her hand. 'Just hypothetically.'

'Well… I suppose at first I would be upset,' she says, tilting her head to one side. 'Then I guess I would wonder how we got there. If he had changed, if *we* had changed… I don't know. It's not really Kian, is it? He's not like that.'

'True.'

'Olga hasn't…?'

'No! God, no. Nothing like that.'

'All right.' Hallie smiles, clearing away her frown lines. But it still lingers in her eyes as she watches me. Watches Natalie.

My left temple twists, beginning to throb with the beginnings of a headache. I put my cutlery carefully together and down the last of my wine. 'Just going to nip to the room for something… be back in a bit.'

I don't wait for Hallie to respond. As I walk through the quiet manor house, everyone tucked downstairs in the dining room, I think about James. He confided in Natalie because she's so far removed. He probably won't see her again for six months so she's a safe place to tuck a secret into. I reach the top of the staircase, turning right towards Natalie's room. The light flickers overhead, bathing the landing in broken darkness. I hear someone humming and realise it's coming from behind the door at the top of the staircase. 'Library' gleams discreetly on a brass plaque, the room beckoning like a crooked finger. I grip the handle and turn it, pushing the door inwards.

Inside, the scent of old books and wood polish plumes across the threshold. I breathe in deeply, smiling at this treasure I have found. The room that holds some of my most rose-tinted memories, reading in a nest of blankets on the rug, finding books that lit my soul on fire. I close the door behind me and the room seems to ruffle, as though sensing a disturbance. The leather chairs and side tables look untouched, as though no one else has explored this room either. The windows are dark, red velvet curtains drawn part way across them, and the shelves of books stretch from floor to ceiling along every other wall. I run my hand over the nearest one, the volumes on land management, poetry, Dickens. Then my hand lands on a book I haven't read in some time. *I Capture the Castle.* My heart stutters as I pull it from the shelf, tracing the shape of the lettering on the front cover, lost in the moment when James handed this book to me in our university library. When I knew meeting him would change our lives forever. I place it back where I found it, running a finger along its spine with a smile.

And slowly, another memory unfolds. Of when I hid in here the first time I stayed with Gran. How I found a book of fairy tales and read it while Gran made dinner in the kitchen downstairs. The illustrations seemed so real, and I desperately wanted to believe. To believe that fairies were real, that this was my house, my collection of books. That Gran and I never had to leave.

'You loved this room,' a voice says, and I know it's her. She's next to one of the windows, hand on the curtain, staring out. 'I tried to find that fairy book you loved so much. Couldn't find another copy, not even in Waterstones! Ah, it was the first time you had really sat down and read a whole book. Every page.'

I sink onto one of the chairs. 'I remember. I ran down to where you were making a chicken pie in the kitchen. I startled you and you dropped the wooden spoon on the floor.'

Gran chuckles, turning towards me. 'I was so proud of you. Still am.'

I sigh and look down, finding the jade bracelets gone. 'I'm not Natalie anymore?'

'You're yourself again. Can't you tell?'

She's right, I can. The way my heart beats is different to Natalie's. Slower, more ponderous. Gran comes to sit on the armchair opposite me, eyeing me carefully. Waiting for me to talk first.

'So… James.'

'James.'

'You always liked him.'

'He's good for you. Straight-talking, no nonsense. Good heart. Solid.'

'That sounds like you're describing him for a job interview.'

'How would *you* describe him?'

'Funny? Easy-going?' I bite my lip, peering into the events of the day. How he was in the billiards room. His confession. 'Although not so much lately. I suppose we're arguing a lot. Little, niggly ones mostly. He's quieter. And… I don't know. We're distant.'

Gran says nothing.

'I… I didn't realise he actually meant it. That if I left he might actually—'

'Divorce you?'

I reel back, that word hitting me in the chest. 'Don't say that. Never say that.'

Gran sighs. 'Nope. You're still in denial.' She gets up, shuffling over to a bookcase. 'I wonder if that fairy book is here… now why didn't I think of looking sooner?'

'Wait, what do you mean, "in denial"?'

'If only I could remember the author's name… Baker, was it? Maybe Barker…'

'Gran!'

She eyes me thoughtfully. 'You think you can still snap your fingers and he'll come running, don't you? That this is all a blip. That you can put your energy into your marriage at any point and recharge it like a battery. Well, it doesn't work like that.'

I stand as well, crossing to the window. The dark outside is impenetrable. Deep and flinty, unyielding tonight. 'We've just had a few rows, and people stray all the time, and he didn't actually *kiss* anyone. I–I can't hold that against him.'

'Can't you see it's cutting him to bits?'

'Gran, I really don't think it's that serious—'

I turn to look for her, but she's gone.

In a fit of frustration, I march towards the library door, determined to find her. To wring some truth out of all this and stop playing this game. 'Gran! Come on, this isn't helping. Just let me go back, let me launch my shop, sort this mess out with Diana.' I pull open the door, cross to the top of the staircase. 'James and I are fine. Truly. I–I have to believe that. We're going to be OK.'

I hit the stairs, walking down them two at a time. But after five steps, my limbs stop working. However much I try, I can't move any further. A cloud, a mist forms around me, pluming like smoke until it covers everything.

'Gran—' I cough.

Then there is nothing.

Chapter 15

My fingers are tangled in bedsheets. I roll them around my fists, the heavy cotton twisting, cutting off the circulation in my wrists. I wake slowly, the world around me filling with soft, white light. Turning to the side, I check I'm alone and release a sigh of relief. I am. Gradually I ease my legs out from under the covers, shifting my body to place my bare feet on the floor. A thick carpet, moss green like the one in my own bedroom, greets me.

I blink and look up, staring around. This room is bigger than mine, and through an open door I can see a separate sitting room with period furniture and huge paintings in heavy gilt frames. Dust motes trail in a slice of dim light that cuts across the room from the half-open curtains. It's morning, and it must be Christmas Day again.

I gulp, feeling the dry scratchiness in my throat and bring a hand up to rub it. My stomach twists and I groan. Have I eaten something bad? This is like motion sickness. Worse than in Natalie's body, far worse. This sudden lurch, the tumble and queasiness, as if I am moving too fast. I crash onto the floor as bile rises up my throat. I need a bathroom. I need a toilet. *Fast.* Dashing across the room, I wrench open the door I *hope* is the bathroom—

And see Kian completely naked in the shower.

I only just manage to reach the toilet before I'm sick. Gripping the seat, my whole being writhes like a wave, over and over, emptying even the stomach acid from me. A warm, damp hand lands on my shoulder, rubbing it gently. I recoil, smashing my head against the toilet seat.

'Shit!'

Kian laughs, helping me to my feet. I can't look at him. *Ohmygod*. I just saw my best friend's husband *in the shower*. Naked. It's basically tattooed behind my eyelids. I keep my eyes on my feet, mumbling about needing my bathrobe as he thrusts a glass of water into my hands. I'm shaking. My mouth and throat are on fire from the stomach acid and all I want to do is crawl back into bed.

'I'm fine, just give me… a sec…' I manage, wrenching myself away to stumble back into the bedroom.

I take small sips of the water, panting and trembling. There's snot dripping from my nose, my eyes are watering and I'm sweating. Actually sweating. My stomach is still rolling queasily, making me wonder if I need to dash back into the bathroom. Taking small, pathetically slow steps across the bedroom, back bent like an old woman, I pull on a bathrobe and find a tissue to blow my nose.

I know who this is. This body I'm in. But as I turn to the mirror, seeing Hallie's face staring back at me is still a shock. I take a deep, shuddering breath, trying to calm my leaping heart. It can't be good for a pregnant woman, can it? Raised blood pressure and all that. A wave of bitterness engulfs me, nothing to do with the morning sickness. All I can do is stare.

Hallie's belly is rounded, hips curved and full. And the bra she's wearing is basically strapping her in, but I can feel the weight. My chest aches with it. I rub my hands over my eyes, Hallie's eyes, turning away. I can't bear to look. Hallie must be what, just over twenty weeks? Over halfway. You usually find out at the twenty weeks scan if it's a boy or a girl, and she knows she's having a boy.

That is, if you make it that far.

I'm not sure I can do this. Of all the bodies to wake up in, of all the people to pretend to be for the day... a pregnant woman. It's torture, the swell of this belly, the nausea stirring once more at the back of my throat. I can't do this, I can't handle this, I have to get out—

'You OK, babe?' Kian says, walking out of the bathroom in a shirt and jeans. He's doing up the buttons, eyeing me with concern. I swallow, looking away. James hasn't looked at me like that in years. I've forgotten what it feels like to be looked at like that. That raw, unguarded love. The kind that never shies away, or flinches. It's just as painful as being in this body. An unborn child pressing against these bones.

'Fine. Just, you know,' I say, smiling for his benefit. I try to keep the hitch from my voice. I don't want him to worry. Even as my stomach churns sickeningly, my mouth still full of bile.

He nods, understanding. 'Shame you've had this all the way through. Let's get you some toast, yeah? Should help. Do you want me to ask one of the staff to bring it up?'

'That's really sweet...' I say, then stop. I square my shoulders. The way Hallie would. 'But all our guests will be up. I'm all right. Honestly.'

He bites his lip and I watch the war play out behind his eyes.

He doesn't want to put his foot down, but he's worried. But why? Isn't morning sickness pretty normal? It can happen the whole way through. It's unlucky, but there's no harm for the baby. As far as I know.

'All right. But if you get tired, even for a minute...'

'I'll be straight back up here, tucked up in bed with a book and a plate of toast.'

'You've got it.'

I cross to the bathroom, needing to use the basin, and shut the door firmly behind me. Does Hallie feel like this every day? She gave no indication. She always seems so happy and serene, the image of calm contentment. Is it all a mask? Or is she... I swallow. Is that what someone looks like when they've got everything they ever wanted?

When I've made myself slightly more presentable, showered and clean, the sick and sweat scrubbed away from my body, I amble over to the dresser in the bedroom. Racking my brain for the memory of what Hallie was wearing when I last saw her. When I was Natalie. A dress, perhaps? But then, does it really matter? Surely I can wear whatever I want. Whatever feels comfortable. Gran said I shouldn't waste a moment of this chance. She never said anything about what I should or shouldn't wear doing it.

'Babe?'

'Yeah?' I say, whipping around so fast, the room lurches, taking a moment to catch up.

'Happy Christmas.'

I smile, practising my very best impression of Hallie-esque serenity. Even as inside, I want to leap out from this skin. 'Happy Christmas.'

I can only manage plain toast and a watery smile at breakfast. My stomach is still churning, but you couldn't tell from my face. I barely had to apply any make-up, Hallie's skin is glowing. Just like all those wholesome, sugar-sweet adverts tell us it will. Must be all the hormones. Or she truly has got it all.

'Try some of this,' Kian says, putting a spoonful of scrambled egg on my plate. 'You usually wolf it down.'

I can barely breathe, I'm trying not to smell them. Everything is so much stronger, the breakfast foods, Natalie's cloying perfume, the scent of wood polish. I could inhale that artificial scent for ever, and I didn't want to stop brushing my teeth earlier. The taste of toothpaste, the feel of the brush on my gums… I could go upstairs and brush them again right now. Dutifully, I take a bite of scrambled egg. Pregnancy is very weird.

I catch glimpses of myself, Eva, here on Christmas morning, sitting further down the table as people lean forward then back again, chatting and pouring coffee, helping themselves to more pieces of bacon. Another slice of French toast. The same hollow expression haunts her face as it did the day before yesterday. Or rather, today, but when I was Diana. James's holds the same sort of ghosts, tension lacing his features in place.

I eat some more scrambled egg, watching him as he chews and makes small talk. I hadn't noticed that he's lost weight. Maybe not around the chest or middle, but definitely in his face. He looks gaunt, scarecrow-like, his chin pointed and high over his shirt collar. I want to get up and pour him a glass of orange juice, give him a bowl of granola and raspberries. Tell him he works too hard, that he needs to take care of himself. That it's Christmas Day. That I still love him. It's still there.

That I haven't given up.

I snap out of it, staring down at my empty plate. I've just eaten half a plate of food, lost in thought about my husband. Blinking rapidly, I hope no one noticed that I was staring. What would Kian make of it? Trembling, I pick up my teacup, taking a sip of the herbal tea in there. It's lukewarm and tastes like pond water. I grimace, setting it quickly back down.

Was there something Gran didn't tell me? Is there some consequence to all this that I haven't quite grasped yet? Maybe I have to stay in character. Be Hallie for the day, observe myself through her eyes. Yes. That would make sense. But there's no action to that, no way of changing the course of the day. No way of enacting this big change that Gran seems to think I need.

I reach for another teapot, hoping it's different to the tea I was drinking. I pour it into a clean teacup, the steam swirling towards my face. Taking another sip, my whole body relaxes with the soothing taste of peppermint. Perhaps I am an observer today. The press of another body inside me, taunting me with what might have been. Just watching my life crumble away across a pile of breakfast foods, powerless to stop it. Maybe I'm meant to face it. A tremor runs through my fingers, the teacup rattling against the saucer.

'How about you and me go for a walk before we head to the beach then unwrap presents? Just the two of us,' Kian asks, leaning over to whisper in my ear. I smile and cringe away. It tickles and feels far too intimate. Not even James whispers to me like that.

'Sure,' I say, hoping I sound suitably Hallie-ish. Compliant, easy-going. Happily pregnant. Fulfilled.

'We could check out the wilderness down by the lawns? Let the others go to the beach and meet them later?'

I know where he means. The walled garden that didn't used to be so wild. Not in my memories of my last visit, anyway. It was a beautiful place and I pretended it was the secret garden, that magic was spun through its roots and shoots. That all we needed, Gran and I, was to turn the key in the lock and enter.

'Are you going to bring your guidebook with you?' I crinkle my nose so he knows I'm teasing. One thing I do know about Kian is how into botany he is. A neglected gated garden will be like catnip to him. He spends almost every weekend exploring different neglected parts of the countryside, talking animatedly to James about some species of foxglove, some uncommon strain found in Surrey. That sort of thing. He's told me before that it's because he didn't have a garden growing up. He's a London boy, through and through, and the most they had was a balcony to catch the thin slices of sunlight throughout the summer. The herbs his mum grew in little pots.

'You got me.' He laughs, leaning back to rest his hands on the back of his head. Smiling adoringly at me. His wife. Love of his life. Mother of his unborn baby. This is so weird. 'I'll grab it from our room and meet you downstairs?'

I nod, taking my last sip of tea. I'm still not sure why I'm supposed to be Hallie today, why I have to suffer through a day in this body. But Gran told me not to waste a second. And if I'm honest with myself, I haven't done so well this far, have I? In Diana's shoes I rushed off to get work done, forgetting that maybe this was a chance to observe James and me. I caught snippets of us at mealtimes, the way this Eva is so drained and withdrawn. How James still pours her coffee, discreetly checking she's eaten enough. As Natalie I learned that we're nothing like her and Olga, we've lost that honeymoon phase magic. James wanted to kiss someone else. Just the thought of it leaves me breathless. Now I realise how very precious he is. He is one of the pillars that holds me up, and yet I'm so close to losing him. Even if I am an observer and shouldn't meddle, I can listen. I can learn. So I intend to find out.

Then I can get back to myself.

Chapter 16

We set off across the lawns, Hallie's wellies hugging my feet. They are so much more comfortable than Diana's boots. I feel like I should gift her some next Christmas, maybe fur-lined ones, or fleece… the thought pulls me up short. Those secret emails, the strain she must be under. I need to speak to her. To understand what's really going on.

I pinch my lips together as a frosty breeze cuts across my cheeks. Everything to do with Diana I file away for later. There are still more questions than answers. And I have to focus on the now, this body, this walk with Kian.

'Great to see James and Eva here, isn't it?' I say as Kian opens the rusted gate for me. It's slightly ajar, the keyhole rusted over from neglect. I enter a labyrinth of overgrown walkways, dead branches clawing their way across the paths. Their spindle limbs crunch underfoot, splintering as we walk. It doesn't look how it did in my rose-tinted memories. This garden is tangled, forgotten. Kian looks around adoringly, as though this isn't a thicket of brambles and death, but a garden with a beating heart. A place long abandoned which whispers with promise, with plants hidden like secrets in the beds.

'Well, it's great to see James.' He laughs, closing the gate behind us. It screeches on its hinges and I wince.

'Not Eva?' I prod.

'You know how I feel about that,' he says quietly, taking my hand in his. But I don't know. Maybe Hallie does, but I don't. And maybe this is why I'm Hallie today. This is what I'm meant to find out.

'Shall we try clockwise?' he asks, stepping to the left.

'No,' I say, stubbornness kicking in. 'Let's try the other path.'

He shrugs, ever the agreeable Kian, and follows after me as I trudge along the gravel walkway. It's not neat and orderly anymore, the gravel is half scattered in the beds, revealing layers of mud beneath. In places it looks like someone has tried to rake it over, even put down some new stones. But mostly, it feels like it's slumbering. Like it's waiting for a gardener with as much passion and care as Kian to come and wake it up.

'It must have been a winter garden. Perhaps for the mistress of the house to enjoy?' he says, consulting his guidebook. He's peering at a holly bush, the berries a slash of red against the grey of the wall they are planted against. 'So much potential. You can see all the plants, still tangled underneath all this weed. It's choking them.'

'Maybe the owner will fix it all.'

'Maybe,' he says, smiling up at me. He straightens, snapping his guidebook shut and offering me his hand again. 'How do you feel about seeing Eva? I know you were split on whether to invite her.'

'Can't invite James without his wife, I suppose?' I try, seeing if I can get a reaction. I hope that isn't how Hallie really feels, that we haven't reached that step.

'Oh, Hal,' Kian says, squeezing my arm. 'Don't be bitter about it. It is what it is. She's preoccupied, that's all. And yeah, you know we can't invite James and not her. Even if it isn't the same as it used to be. However much... however much we want it to be.'

I frown, taking my hand from Kian's to stuff them both into my pockets. I hate that I have become an addition to them. A titled add-on, a person invited out of politeness. A bitter lump forms in my throat and I regret pressing for this. I don't know if I want to hear anymore.

'You know it's not all Eva,' I say. 'James kissed someone else – someone from work. At least, he wanted to. Which is just as bad.'

'What?'

'He didn't tell you?' I bite my lip, looking up at him. Kian's eyes are clouded, troubled.

'No. He did not,' he says quietly. 'He told you?'

'Yes, er, yesterday.' Realisation hits me: I'm Hallie. I'm still Hallie and Kian's staring at me, underlining my misstep. 'After... after dinner. Eva doesn't know.'

Kian swears under his breath, shoving his hands in his pockets. He stares silently at the ground, as though assembling his thoughts. Reworking this new information into the image he holds of us, of the James and Eva he knows. 'She... she's been pushing him away, working all the time, it was a moment of weakness, he doesn't want that...' He swears again, turning away from me.

I sigh, placing a hand on his shoulder. Kian sounds just as shocked as I feel. It's almost a betrayal, of us, of the four of us. The way we were before.

133

'Hal, she's pushing everyone away,' he says quietly. 'How would we get her back?'

I move my hand from his shoulder as he turns back towards me. Takes my hand in his. His troubled eyes have given way to sorrow, and I wonder just how much he and Hallie have spoken about me. What Hallie is really thinking.

'I need to speak to her,' I say softly to myself. Meaning Hallie. 'I need to understand.'

'What is there to understand?' he says, dropping my hand to carry on walking. 'The woman puts work before everything. I mean, Christ! She made her assistant drive down here. That girl – what's her name again? Debbie? Dana? – is like a wet weekend. I would be too if I had to spend Christmas with my boss. I mean, I'm not excusing what James has done, you know that…'

'Maybe she had her reasons. This shop launch sounds pretty import—'

'Ah, come on, babe!' He nudges my shoulder. 'We've been over and over this. She's expanded that business of hers so fast, it's like she wants to hole herself up away from the world. She's *created* the work. She's built a wall of work to surround herself with. Drown herself in. I love Eva, she's one of us. She's part of our pack, you know? But I don't like how miserable James is. Or seeing you cry every time she blows you off.'

I stop, my heart lurching in my chest. He thinks James is… miserable? And his confession to Natalie, that's definitely something we need to deal with. But maybe I thought it wasn't so obvious. That maybe we could move past this without anyone suspecting how close we were to crumbling. And Hallie… my stomach fills with knots. I can't believe I've made her cry.

'James isn't miserable… he can't be.'

He realises I've stopped and gives me a strange look. 'You saw him last weekend. Poor guy hardly said a word. Just sat there at the pub quiz, staring into his pint. That's not the James I know.' He looks away, staring wistfully through a gap in the wall, as though he's watching something else, a scene from our past. 'That's not my friend.'

I gulp, breathing through my nose. Trying to separate my thoughts from this conversation. Stay rational, be the observer, stay as Hallie-like as I can. I need to understand. These two people, Hallie and Kian, are part of our team. More than that, they're our family. They've held up the corners of us since our university days. We shared a tiny flat in our third year, and crammed into our first house-share as our careers began to grow. Hallie was the person who persuaded me to move from the grad scheme bank into the industry I'm in now. It's what gave me the spark of the idea to start my own business, to branch out from the corporate world three years ago and build a brand in homewares that played to the social media age. To create something meaningful, then expand until I could open my own shop. Until I could hold something up and say, There, *look*, I can create something. I am not barren in every way.

We've been inseparable ever since we found each other, the four of us. Unbreakable.

Or so I thought.

I'm beginning to wonder... is this all down to me? Have I pushed so hard against every wall in my life that now the ceiling, the roof, *everything* is caving in? Is this why Gran is here? To show me that my life is like this garden, that I'm the weed choking our friendship?

'I mean, just look at her assistant.' Kian is tutting, still staring through the gap in the wall. I rise up on tiptoes and spy Diana speaking to Sarah just outside the house. A jolt runs through me. I know what they're saying. I had that conversation, just two days ago. Or today, rather. Diana is shuffling awkwardly, taking the tiny Polaroid from Sarah to stare at it, before handing it back. I can see the puff of pride on Sarah's face, even from this distance.

But there's a raw sadness in Diana's. A yearning, a haunting. She's staring at Sarah with something more than nostalgia. Like she's lost something that she knows she'll never get back. I drop down from tiptoes, biting my lip. Is that why I was Diana? What *is* Gran trying to tell me?

A flurry like little nudges drums in my middle and I gasp. Pressing a hand just below my stomach, I nudge back. Was that… the baby? A rush of adrenalin and wonder floods my veins. Is this how it feels? All the morning sickness, the aching back, the throat slick with bile… this is what it all builds to?

Of course it is. This is the beginnings of a new life, the breathings of hope, nestled inside this body. I wrap my arms around this belly, the gentle pattering of tiny feet. The adrenalin, the rush sours inside me, leaving a trail of nausea. Surely Gran didn't intend for me to feel this. It's a taunt, a whisper telling me what could have been. If only I had been enough.

All I can see are my own failings. Suddenly, I need to get out. I need to crawl out of this flesh prison that I'm trapped in. I need to leave this day and this perfect, wholesome family, still blooming and shiny and new. I need to crawl back into my own skin, down several vodkas and sleep for ever.

'…so uncomfortable, you know? Like I should say something. Have it out with her.'

'What?' I wasn't listening to Kian. So wrapped up in my own shock, my own discomfort. My need to be anywhere but here, facing the mirror held up before me.

'Diana. The assistant. I feel like we've enabled Eva's behaviour, you know? Indulged her.' Kian crouches low, reaching for a tiny seedling, brushing a brown leaf away carefully. It's so tiny and perfect, like the green of James's eyes.

I swallow, pushing James to the back of my mind. 'You think... we're indulging Eva? By letting Diana stay here?'

'Yeah.' Kian smiles back at me sadly. 'If we all collectively put our foot down, lay it all out, maybe we'll get her back. Maybe she'll stop vanishing and actually be present for once. We could all get her back. Then, you know, James might be better.'

'Or scare her off for good.'

Kian sighs and straightens, brushing his hands off on his trouser legs. 'I don't like it. I don't like any of this. What happened to us? The four of us. I know it isn't about me, I'm being selfish. But she was my friend too. And now I have, maybe, one awkward chat with her every six months at best? It's not enough.'

I open my mouth to say something. I wait for the words to pour out, for the dam to burst and a river to engulf us. But I'm already drowning in it, all those words I cannot say. They're fighting over each other, too tangled up and worn out for me to make any sense of. I wouldn't even know how to string it all together. To explain the past three years, and all the years before those. To lay them out like a wall, build them brick by brick into something concrete we can all stare at and examine.

I realise that's been the problem all along. With Kian and Hallie, even with James, I don't know which words to use so

137

that they can understand. It's easier to push them all away. And maybe that's it – I don't need to find the right words as Hallie today. All I need to do is give us a chance to mend. To see if the four of us can be as strong as we once were. If there's enough still there for us to salvage.

Chapter 17

I make sure that Eva and James are sitting next to us. Kian's frowning, obviously troubled, but he goes along with it anyway, shuffling around name cards and placing Eva's beside my own. The dark has drawn a curtain around Penhallow, the light waning to nothing but absence after six o'clock. I need us all to be together for Christmas dinner. All four of us, like we used to be. It's the only way I can start working back to that. Finding my way, reaching a hand out into the dark and hoping I grasp Hallie's fingers in return.

I'm feverish with it, this need to reunite us. To stick a plaster over the sorry mess of our relationships, get us back on track. How hard can it be? And once I've done this, surely I can go back to myself and end this whole thing? Gran will see that I can have a lovely Christmas with them all. That I *am* listening. I am learning.

The staff have excelled. Turkey, a great joint of roast beef and a honey-glazed ham sit in platters down the centre, slices freshly cut for us to serve ourselves. The heaps of parsnips, carrots and even Brussels sprouts are so divinely tempting. I love Christmas dinner, always have done. The crackers with the paper Christmas hats, even the terrible jokes rolled up on little bits of paper. I have already perched a green paper crown with pride on top of Hallie's head and note that I'm wearing one too, the Eva that's the real me, sat at my side. Her cheeks are tinged a rosy pink and there is laughter on her lips. As I reach for my glass, my fingertips tingle with it, this need for it all to go well. Without a hitch or a hiccup. I wonder if she's worrying about the shop launch? If she's only trying because of the ultimatum from James? I hope she's not.

I hope *I'm* not.

'Remember that Christmas on Old Cherry Lane? The one when James got all the timings wrong?' I say, leaning over.

Her face lights up and I hold my breath, crossing my fingers under the table. 'When we ate turkey at midnight in our pyjamas?' She laughs and takes a sip of wine. 'How could I forget?'

'We all toasted at midnight with those gross white enamel mugs. And that bubbly!' I shudder. 'James is *never* allowed to pick, ever again.'

'Agreed,' Eva says. 'Total piss water. He must have got it out of some bargain bucket. Spent the rest on scratch cards.'

'Such a gambler.'

I grin and she grins back and I wonder if maybe, just maybe, I'm right and this dinner will fix us. And we can all go back to normal. I mean, she's happy here, isn't she? This Eva. She's talking to Hallie. I'm making her smile. How hard can this be?

Kian loads up my plate, checking, *sotto voce*, if there's anything that I can't manage. Anything that turns my stomach just to look at, or smell. But this is Christmas and I'm going to push through the nausea, even if Hallie would be side-eyeing the rich food, the dark brown gravy drenching the crisp roast potatoes. Isn't a hearty meal a good idea for a pregnant woman? All those calories and protein. As long as I can keep it down.

'Eva, what happened to your assistant?' Kian asks, glancing along the table. 'She's not upstairs scribbling away, I hope?'

There's a strain to his joke that I don't like, an undertone. Her fingers pause, mid-cut, as she's loading up a forkful of turkey. I know just what I'll be thinking. Pure irritation, laced with a hint of a question.

'No idea. She took off for the afternoon. It might be safe to drive back later, or tomorrow, and I figured she needed to get out for a walk.'

I smile and nod, totally satisfied with what this Eva is saying. It sounds perfectly reasonable. I'm sure Kian will see that and drop it.

'Are you saving a plateful for her? Seems kind of sad that she's missing out.'

I shoot a glance at him, subtly shaking my head. But he doesn't notice, too focused on Eva and mashing gravy into his potatoes. Kian is *really* digging and I want him to stop. Eva's face is already shutting down, the shadows forming at the corners. This was our chance, this meal, and I'm losing her. I'm losing this opportunity for us all to make up. Why can't they all see that it's Kian that's doing this, not Eva? She hasn't done anything wrong. I bite my lip, wondering how I can reel us back. Side track Kian so he drops this and moves on. Come on, Eva, I think desperately. Shrug it off. Make a joke out of it.

I take a sip of iced water, my chest tightening. Diana could be anywhere. It's not like we keep tabs on each other. She may well be asleep upstairs, glad of a break from a house full of strangers. Well, as long as she isn't setting up an interview with that company… I shift in my chair uncomfortably. Come to think of it, she could be doing that. I glance at Eva, the worry lines, the frown, and my heart goes out to her. She doesn't deserve any of this. She doesn't have a clue about those secret emails, or some woman trying to snog James. And now Kian is laying into her. I huff out a breath, determined to get this back on track.

'She's probably just relaxing. Taking a break,' I say to Kian, keeping my voice as level as possible as I place a hand on his arm. Hoping he'll take the hint. 'Anyway, not everyone celebrates, right?'

'It just seems a shame,' Kian says pointedly to Eva, completely ignoring me as if I hadn't spoken. I remove my hand from his arm as my stomach turns, like a wave washing to the shore. I sip some more water. Breathe in and out, as slow as I can manage. Kian and Eva carry on trading spiked sentences and I sit back, my clothes clinging to my stomach. They feel too tight, the room too airless. The fizz and hope of a swift reconciliation, of us all falling into our usual patterns and banter disintegrates before my eyes. I'm not hungry anymore. And with the nausea building, I can't concentrate on the conversation. In fact, I need to find a bathroom.

I stand shakily, breaking up the conversation around me. 'Sorry. Keep eating, honestly. I'll be back in a sec.'

'You OK, babe?'

I smile as convincingly as I can at Kian. 'Just, you know. One of the joys of drinking more than a glass of water in an hour!'

James and Kian laugh politely and I wobble towards the door.

'Hal, do you need me to hold back your hair?' Natalie asks, catching up with me by the door. I glance at her earnest face, the deep concern. Why couldn't Eva leap up and offer that? She's still eating her food as if nothing is amiss.

'I'm good, thanks,' I say, smiling as warmly as I can. She nods, patting my arm, and closes the door behind me, sealing the noise and the scent of food in there.

I'm through the bedroom door when I clamp my hand over my mouth, vomit clawing up my throat. I make it just in time, slamming the bathroom door open and throwing up in the bathtub. It's just like before, my stomach emptying everything I've eaten until there's nothing there to retch up.

I sink down, resting my back against the bathtub and close my eyes. My whole body is shivering, tremors prickling along my ribs. This is miserable. If Hallie's had this the whole way through... she's a saint. An actual saint. One day of this torture and I'm ready to admit defeat, to climb into bed with a can of Coke and a bag of ready salted crisps and wait out the rest of this misery in peace.

After I've cleaned up, I contemplate going back downstairs. But I'm afraid that the smell of food, the closeness of all those bodies will trigger it again. So I peel off the fancy Christmas dress I'm wearing, shrug into an oversized T-shirt and leggings and pad through to the sitting room. There's a TV on the wall and a mini fridge with small cans of Diet Coke. I crack one open gratefully, the fizz and the taste calming my stomach.

Curling up on the sofa opposite the TV, I feel something dig into my back. Reaching down, I pull out a notebook. It's plain with a pale pink cover and I settle back, flipping the TV on with the remote. As I flick through the channels, finally settling on some home design programme with a couple sporting pristine white teeth, I open the notebook. When I glance down, I see what it is.

143

It's Hallie's journal.

Pages and pages of carefully detailed notes, interspersed with dates. It looks like she started it a year ago, tracking the amount of water she was drinking, the supplements she took, the exercise she did... but also her thoughts. Everyday things: appointments, lunch dates, films and books she loved. It's a window into her world, a time when I haven't been around that much. A glimpse into the inner workings of her day-to-day. But as I find my name on one of the pages, my heart stops.

It's a careful, detailed account of the last time we met up. It was a brunch date, at this little café in Clapham. I wondered then why she chose it, the street spilling over with designer buggies and baby clothing shops. It set my teeth on edge just being there, surrounded by all that pink and blue happiness. I eye the date. It was six months ago, a sticky June day made for lidos and ice cream. Not the city with its greasy tarmac roads and shouty adverts everywhere. I stretch uneasily, smoothing down the pages. I'm trespassing. These are Hallie's private thoughts and I should not read this.

I set it to one side, get comfortable and switch to a new programme, bored instantly of the brimming enthusiasm of the home design show. I settle on the Christmas edition of some familiar sitcom with canned laughter, engaging and mindless all at once. The pages of Hallie's journal are calling to me. Would it be so bad if I glanced over them? It is about me, after all. And maybe this is why I'm in Hallie's body, experiencing all this? This might be exactly what I'm supposed to read. The key to everything.

Yanking the journal back with my fingertips, I bring it up onto my lap and read the first line.

I can't tell her.

I blink and frown, placing my fingertip on the words. Can't tell me what, Hallie? As I carry on reading this account of the last time I saw her, it all becomes horribly clear why. The last time we met, the guilt was eating her alive that they were trying. And she didn't want to tell me. Of course, she knew what happened three years ago. She was part of my inner circle, one of the two people I told. I picture that baby-blue cake and my stomach twists, my hand straying to my baby bump. No, not mine. *Hallie's* baby bump.

Jealousy, sickly and green, flares inside me and I struggle to swallow it down. I'm glad she didn't tell me. Just the thought of it… I blink, picturing that day in Clapham. Surrounded by all the baby boutiques and buggies. That smug froth of happiness and hope. The little nudging sensation starts up again, pattering and bubbling. She never told me she was trying for a baby. That she even *wanted* to have kids. We never talked about it. But I wanted them. And she knew that.

And now this journal is all that connects me to her. It's a message from the past, stretching across these last few months, written in a way that makes me feel like I don't know her. And that maybe, I don't know myself either.

What do you want?

Gran's words echo in my mind, circling over and over. I flip the journal closed, staring at the TV screen without really watching.

What do I want?

Suddenly, I'm angry. Not at her so much, more with myself. Hallie is my best friend, and I've pulled away from her. But she's pulled away too. She didn't try to reconnect with me, this is the first time she's tried, at this house party full of other people, other lives. This house party is an olive branch flung at my feet, tossed down with a half-hearted shrug. A last-ditch effort to prove she did try but it was me that was difficult. Me that never showed up, or left early, or never put in the time. And perhaps I didn't. This journal proves it, that the last time we met was six whole months ago. And I was more consumed with the past than the present and what Hallie needed to say.

I wouldn't have cared that they were trying for a baby. In fact, I *would* have cared. But not in the way she thinks. I stand up, needing to shake off this needling heat building under my skin. I'm so frustrated with myself, with the way I have allowed her to slip from my life, that I want to jump out of it. I want to escape all this, escape Penhallow and fix things with her. This woman I practically grew up with, navigating adulthood hand in hand.

I cross to the window. Flinging it open, I gulp down the late afternoon air, wind whispering around my throat. It's crisp and freezing, the taste of snow lingering at the edges, dousing the fire in my heart, my blood. Already, the flurries are thickening, the moorland blotted out like a blank piece of paper.

I dig my fingernails into the wooden window frames, the white paint softening under my nails. So many questions. So many more than this day started with. And if I'm not careful, they will consume everything within me. They will burn and burn until I am nothing but paper and smoke, leaving behind only my charred regret.

Chapter 18

'You missed one hell of a feast, babe,' Kian says sleepily, leaning his head against the back cushions of the sofa next to me. It's half past seven, he must have wolfed it all down to get back to me. To Hallie. 'Next year, you'll be able to eat everything. It won't be so tough. No nausea, no bump.'

'Just a tiny human clinging to these boobs.' I laugh. It's been a little under an hour and I'm grateful that Kian left me alone with my thoughts. Left me alone to rage and burn, to run a finger over the lines of Hallie's carefully joined up words. To try to make sense of how we got here, to this day. To remember why I need her, how I always needed her in my life. To see past my bitter disappointment that she's given up on me. That maybe I gave up on her first.

They've obviously got it down, Hallie and Kian. Giving each other space when they can sense the other person needs it. But still being there, within reach. Just in case. I know how rare a quality that is. How, without it, those bricks that built the foundation of a relationship can crumble away to nothing but dust all too quickly. I don't want to think of how James and I compare. Especially the strained relationship we have now.

I ready myself for the next round of questions. Of searching for answers. The day is waning, and I need to squeeze more time from it. 'Did Eva behave herself?'

'She actually took off soon after you,' Kian says, turning to look at me. 'I kind of wondered if she came up here to speak to you.'

'No, she didn't.' I purse my lips. I don't know why, but it bothers me that she (that I) didn't. It was obvious when I rushed off that I needed some space. But we were best friends. Maybe the gulf between us has grown too big. Am I so disconnected, so focused on building my business that I'm missing all the details that exist outside of it? The thought makes me uncomfortable.

'You got your journal out?' he asks, holding it up. 'Thinking about the IVF again?'

I blink, a questioning look forming on my face.

'I know, I know. You didn't want to talk about it all again during the pregnancy.'

I feel like a bomb has gone off. A whooshing sound rushes through my ears, heat creeping up my neck. I take the journal back from him, flipping to a random page earlier in the year.

Injections.

Of course. The little tick mark against each day is her recording the fact that she injected herself. I bite my lip, face growing hot. I had no idea. Absolutely none. Did she try to tell me that day in Clapham? Did she choose that brunch spot to surround herself with the hope, with all that cloying baby-ness, that one day it would be her walking down the pavement with a designer buggy? Her navigating the narrow doorways, picking up dinky knitted mouse-shaped teddies with fairy wings for twenty pounds a pop?

'It's OK. We can talk about it,' I find myself saying. It's an invitation. An open door for Kian to walk through. I want to know more. I need to know more about this woman who used to be so close to me. About how she got here, to this place with the tick boxes and the injections and the baby growing in her belly. Because I don't know her, this Hallie. The biggest shock is not the IVF. It's reaching for this person, searching through the mist of the last three years and finding she's different. It's not just me that's changed.

Maybe it's all of us.

'I'm glad we're past that, I've got to tell you,' Kian says, eyeing me. 'I don't regret it. You know that, babe. But I didn't like you turning into a human pincushion.'

My mouth goes dry. I hate needles. Whenever I have to have a blood test, I look away, focus on a patch of the nondescript GP surgery wall and pretend I am far, far away. But Hallie had this every day. She didn't rely on someone else to do it, she injected herself, over and over. There's a certain kind of courage and belief that comes with that. And I had no idea.

'But we got our baby boy,' I say, mouth forming the words I know Hallie would say. Leading Kian to keep talking, to step through that open door and show me exactly who Hallie is now. The person I guess I'm missing out on. Maybe this is what Gran wanted me to find out.

I tap my finger on the journal, the page resting open on Christmas Eve. The big announcement, the baby-blue sponge inside that iced white cake. This wasn't just a few casual months of dreaming. This was the end of a long, harrowing journey for them. This house party, this gathering of friends and family – it was to draw us all together around their miracle. The one they fought for, bled for. My eyes smart and I sniff. A hot, bitter taste fills my mouth and the tears spill over, tracking down my cheeks.

I couldn't breathe, staring down at that slice of cake. Everything rushed back and it was all so unbearable. But for Hallie, it was everything. Her world, served up on a plate to share with us all. My jealousy, so immediate, such a sickly shade of green seems so shameful now.

'Hal…' Kian says, passing me a box of tissues. 'Those damn hormones.'

'I know,' I squeak, then laugh. He laughs as well and places his hand on my stomach. The baby moves, leaning towards the warmth of Kian's touch. I still can't get used to it. I cover my eyes with the tissue, wiping away the tears, and sniff again.

'We worked so hard for this,' he says. 'It's OK to cry.'

Kian goes off in search of a supper plate for me, promising that he will be back. Making me promise him that we don't have to watch a chick flick. I laugh, chucking a cushion at him as he dances out of the room. There's so much of Hallie in this room now. I relive the moment she announced last night. The hit of pure pride she must have felt as the white cake with the sugar-paste booties was carried in.

The night rewrites itself from my perspective to hers. She had wanted this, needed this for so long. There are moments in this journal, moments she's never shared with me. Hallie crying on the bathroom floor at their flat in London, tears peppering the page like rain as she writes about her deep, aching need. Hallie gazing longingly at babies in the park, her takeaway coffee growing cold in her hand as she stares, frozen. Unable to tear herself away. Then I find a torn-out article from a magazine about a woman's experience of IVF. The page it's tucked into is one of the first in this journal. About how she showed it to Kian. Asking him if he was all in. The utter elation when he said yes.

Guilt needles me as I remember my reaction to the cake. How Hallie followed me out into the entrance hall, so desperate to share the joy with me. How I couldn't stand it. I cringe, wishing I could take that back. Pull her into my arms and hug her properly, tell her I'm proud of her. Tell her I'm sorry.

When Kian returns, we watch an action film, something mediocre that we can still talk through and not lose track of the plot. I eat crackers and apple slices, sat on the floor with my legs straight out in front of me, the sofa at my back. It's the first time I've laughed in ages, listening to Kian talk about the time he went out with James. How they dared each other to sneak a glass out of every bar they went in and ended up with a cupboard full to surprise Hallie and me with the next morning. How Hallie insisted we take every single one back, and I stood there, lips twitching, trying not to laugh.

There was one stolen glass James has never returned. It still sits in our kitchen cupboard, shoved at the very back, spiders casting their webs over it. It's from the first pub we went to together, the first time we shared a drink, and later when he walked me home, James surprised me by revealing the hidden glass I'd drunk from in his coat pocket. He'd kept it as a memento, joked that he couldn't believe he was jealous of a glass that had better moves than him. I couldn't resist his corny lines and under the amber glow of a street light we shared our first kiss. I had forgotten about that. The tiptoe of sparks that tingled over my lips, how he dipped his head to mine. How his forehead rested for the space of a heartbeat against my own.

And how the next day, I felt sure I had dreamed it. That this boy, this tall chestnut-haired boy was mine.

We couldn't have been more than twenty-two or so the night they stole those glasses. Fresh graduates, in those schemes with the glossy marketing and shit pay, trying to figure out who we were. Pretending we had it all, that we did know how to do the whole grown-up thing.

Trying to figure out who we would become.

I flip through the journal as we carry on watching, skimming the entries over the last six months. There's one entry from a couple of weeks ago that stings like a needle. Hallie had messaged, wanting to meet, wanting a catch-up. She even offered to come to the shop and help me do some last-minute decorating. I was frantically trying to fix some of the paintwork, dabbing it and hoping it wouldn't look uneven under the new wicker shade lighting. And I ignored her. I pretended late that night that I hadn't seen the message. And running my finger over her words now, that needle stings like it's slipped between my ribs.

She wanted to tell me about the baby. To warn me before the big announcement. To give me time to process so the pain would dull before we were all together here. She wanted to tell me that she chose Penhallow because of me. Because of every memory I shared with her, and how she hoped it would knit us back together.

How she hoped it would knit *me* back together.

I stifle another wave of tears, guilt-ridden and bitter, then close the journal, cradling it in my lap. By the end of the film, my legs are going to sleep and Kian's eyes are dipping. I wait until his breath evens out and I know he's snoozing. Straightening out, I know what I've got to do. Who I have to go and see. I need to see what Hallie sees when I look at her, when we talk to each other. If I have any hope of saving this, us, then I have to go and see for myself. The Eva of today, the me that's still stuck.

I leave as quietly as I can, throwing on a jumper before I leave the room. There are people downstairs, carols being sung around the piano. It's a little after nine and dinner will have drawn to a close, everyone stuffed and sleepy from the feast we devoured.

Eva and James's room is in the east wing corridor, whereas Hallie and Kian's is in the west wing. I cross the top of the staircase, picking out James's voice in the mêlée downstairs. I waver, listening to his words, the rumble and patter of them. With all that's still between us, I want to go to him and smooth us out. Hold his hand in mine and savour every last drop of his attention, his love. But in the end, I turn away. I'm still in Hallie's skin, still breathing her air. And hopefully, if I can mend this, I'll have our whole future ahead to feel warm and safe again, wrapped in his arms.

I knock on my bedroom door, bracing myself.

And when Eva comes to the door, I barely recognise her as me. It's as though another person has taken on my legs, my arms and eyes, is moving through my life as a replica of me. There's a fog to my face, as though I was so deep in the layers of business plans and spreadsheets that I'm still down there, buried. My grasp of the real world loose and fleeting. She freezes, betraying no emotion. Just stands there, staring at me. Her pen is twisted in her hair, it's what I do when I'm thinking. Twist it up, around and around until I'm left with an ungodly tangle.

'Hello, Eva,' I say softly. 'Mind if I come in?'

Chapter 19

For a beat, she hovers. There's a brief second when I think that this version of myself, this Eva standing on the other side of the threshold, might shut the door in my face. But then she retreats from the door to let me in. I hover by the sofa, waiting for her to offer me a seat. She doesn't. All she offers is pinched lips, frost and the atmosphere of a morgue. I wonder when I got so cold, so distant. I'm so removed from my own self already after a day walking in Diana's uncomfortable boots and another living in Natalie's head, not to mention carrying another life through Hallie's, that I can't make myself out. This Eva is an enigma.

Paper and folders smother the bed and coffee table. A notebook, pens and several used coffee mugs are strewn around the space, lending the room an air of student-like neglect. The air smells of burnt coffee grounds and stale sleep. It looks like this Eva has been working for most of the day, not even bothering to let the world in through the window. The curtains are drawn tight, she's created a fortress made of spreadsheets and projections and caffeine. There's something so sad about that. That I could be at this beautiful manor house, in the rugged heart of the moors of Cornwall surrounded by friends, and yet bury myself in work.

'Looks like quite a party,' I joke, trying to trick a grin out of her.

She sighs, clearing a space on one of the sofas to sit down. I take my cue, doing the same opposite her. Her eyes keep straying to her laptop, no doubt another note she's made, a tiny hiccup in how she's planning the next few weeks to roll out. Anxiety plumes from her in a cloud, the toxic tendrils reaching across the space between us.

To her, I'm sure it's huge, this glaring error that must be rectified. Maybe one of the new staff members she hasn't rotaed on in the shop? A defunct hashtag she needs to remove from the brand guidelines? I can imagine myself, already playing out the scenarios of what could go wrong if I don't change that tiny detail. What might play out in the shop launch and website refresh, what my business could stand to lose if I don't get this exactly right.

I can feel her straining towards it, this tiny detail, wanting me to leave. Am I always like this? This woman is pale and tired, dark circles feathering out under her eyes. She won't look at me, not directly. And I'm supposed to be her best friend. Hallie is my best friend, and I'm letting this chance to reconnect slip through my careless fingers. She's lost her way, this version of me.

I've lost my way.

'How did we get here?' I blurt out without thinking. Like it's a conversation we've already started, one we've been silently passing back and forth between us for the last seven months. Maybe even the last three years.

She drops her face to her hands, rubbing her eyes. This Eva is crumpled, worn thin by too many late nights, too many early mornings. Barked email commands, hastily tapped out notes, striving, always striving, bitterness at the thought of failing uncoiling like a snake inside her.

I want my business to flourish. I deserve it. I've worked myself into the ground to reach the next level, jumping through so many hoops I've lost count. I've had to sacrifice a lot to make it work. I can picture myself, signing the lease on the next shop and the next, hiring more staff, turning a tidy profit, forging a new direction. Paying off that extra mortgage, celebrating with Champagne. This is my chance to banish those lingering ghosts. I don't want to fail at this too.

But is this the price I have to pay for it?

'I don't know,' this Eva says quietly after an unnerving stretch of silence. 'I don't know how we got here, Hal.'

'Can I make a suggestion?' I say, leaning forward to brace my elbows on my knees. 'Close your laptop and maybe just... listen to me. Can you do that?'

She flinches, but leans over, snapping her laptop lid shut. 'Of course.'

'OK.' I draw in a breath, choosing my words carefully. One clumsy sentence, one hastily spouted phrase and I could destroy this moment. And I need this as much as Hallie does.

Maybe this is what Gran wanted me to do.

'I think you need to go downstairs for a bit. Chat with everyone, make the most of being here. *Then* get back to all this. It'll still be here. Remember that first Christmas we had, just the four of us? We went to the pub on the end of the road, drinking eggnog from those tiny glasses...'

Eva smiles, the smallest quirk of her lips. 'I think I still have the photos somewhere.'

'And you could go down there now, we could recreate that,

you know? Imagine that, just half an hour, just to get some new memories—'

'Hallie, I—'

'Go on,' I say quickly, cutting this Eva off before she has the chance to say no. I need to hear this. Hallie would say the same, I'm sure of it. Even though she hates conflict. She would walk into it for me. Maybe only once, but she would. I need to believe that. I need to engage. To listen. Not just for the sake of our relationship, but for myself, too. 'Take a break. When was the last time you and James just hung out?'

'Doesn't this count?' Eva says, irritation flickering around her eyes, her lips. 'I'm here, aren't I? I-I was there at breakfast. And at dinner. I've done exactly as you all wanted. I put *my* life on hold to celebrate yours. So, if that's all I really have to—'

'I had IVF.'

This Eva reels back as though a fist has found her chest. Any colour in her strained features drains instantly.

That's it. That got through to her. To me. This is what we need to talk about. We need to say the raw things, the uncomfortable things. Or we'll never find our way back to each other. I'll never find my way back to myself.

'I had IVF, and I've wanted this for a long time. This holiday party, this baby, all of you being here… it means a lot to me. *You* mean a lot to me.' I lean back, bracing myself. The words I'm saying, I know Hallie will be thinking. I know that's why she wants us all here. And somehow, this gets to me, cutting deep into my heart, that this is what she wants. What she's desperate for. 'And you can't even celebrate for one day.'

'I didn't know you had IVF.'

'Well, obviously, I didn't tell you.'

157

'But why not, Hal?' Eva says, flinging up her hands. 'You brought out that cake, that baby-blue cake and served a slice of it up for me. Put it right under my nose and expected me to *eat it*.'

I recoil from the flint in her voice. The hurt. This version of me, of Eva, spits out those last two words like poison. And it's true. That's exactly how I felt being served up that cake. Like it was being rubbed in my face. On an anniversary I would give anything to skip. But now I've walked a day in Hallie's shoes, I can see her side.

'You couldn't be happy for Hal— for me?' I find myself saying. I run my fingertips over the sofa, the material pulling against them. Grounding me. After reading Hallie's journal, experiencing a day as her, I want to stand up for her. 'You know I tried to meet up a few weeks ago, but you were always too busy. I wanted to tell you – to prepare you. But you're never available.'

'You couldn't have pulled me aside? Maybe whispered it quietly beforehand? Given me a little bit of…' She looks away, blinking rapidly, and I imagine her throat closing up. I can feel the knives, twisting a little deeper, reliving that moment. But this Eva has to see past that. She has to see a bit of Hallie's side, too.

'Eva… this Christmas isn't about you. It's a celebration. I wanted you to be here, I wanted you to remember your gran the way you've told me she was at Penhallow when you were little. I wanted… I wanted you back.' The last words scrape up from somewhere buried inside me. As though they came from Hallie too, as though her soul, her kind, beautiful soul is nestled in this body. And the moment I say it, I see how

Hallie was trying to bring me back. It was just a misstep with the cake. All an honest mistake.

'I-I can't do this,' Eva grates out. She stands abruptly, her face shutting down. 'It's haunting being here, Hallie. She's everywhere. It's too much, it's overwhelming. And I-I've got a lot still to do, and *somehow*, I have to find Wi-Fi tomorrow to get these amendments back to the PR and marketing firm. Yes. *That's* what I have to focus on. And somehow, Diana or I need to get back to London and launch the shop, and you don't understand I'm *trying* to hold it all in, hold it all back—' She chokes on the last word, her hand flying to her mouth. And my heart, my ruined, hopeless heart shatters.

'Eva...' I try to reach for her, try to hold her hand in mine. This grief is never-ending. It's an endless snowstorm I can never leave.

'It's probably time you leave. Wouldn't want to tire yourself out... it's for the best...'

I stand reluctantly, stomach churning. It has nothing to do with the baby and everything to do with this. This destructive mess our relationship has become. Her words ring in my ears, turning me hot then cold, the hurt in them. The drowning mess I have become.

'We're in tatters, you know that, right? This is our last chance,' I say, imploring her. And I'm not sure if I mean me and Hallie, or just me. Me, and this version of me. The one who has lived inside this storm for so long.

'Then you should have thought about that!' Eva snaps suddenly. 'You and James and everyone else have expected me to drop everything and be here, at Penhallow, in this house of all places, for you to announce in the *cruellest* possible way that you've done what I could never do.' The last words choke off into silence. She releases a small sob, pressing her fingertips to her lips. As though trying to push all her pain back inside.

'We can get back from this, we can—'

'No we can't… I–I need time. I need to get away from here,' Eva says, crossing the room to open the door.

She won't even look at me. I stand too quickly, black spots dusting my vision like stars as my heart lurches in my chest. This isn't how it was meant to go. Hallie and I can't end like this. We love each other.

'I'm happy you're pregnant. I'm happy for you that your life is on track, and that you've got everything you've ever wanted. Now please… please just leave me alone.'

I can't believe I'm speaking to Hallie like this. That it's me in there. That I've lost all sense of what really matters. Of all perspective. That my failures have shaped me into this person.

'I'm not going to stop trying,' I say as tears well in my eyes. Dammit, Hallie's body cries easily. 'And I'm here. We can get through this. We *have* to.' I walk across the room on trembling legs, until I'm back in the doorway. A threshold, a roaring chasm dividing us. But this isn't about just Hallie and me. This is about this version of me, this Eva and my true self. I can see how far I've veered off from who I am, *what* I am. How haunted I've become.

And that scares me more than anything.

Eva hesitates, like she's about to say more. As though maybe a part of her regrets what she said. What she's doing. I hold my breath, hoping there's something left inside her. That we can get back from this, that we can find a way.

But like a light blinking out, all the hope fades to nothing.

'I'll leave tomorrow so this isn't awkward for you. Even if there is a bloody blizzard. So you can have your happy celebration without me ruining your party.'

'Eva, you're not—'

But she's already closed the door, very firmly, in my face.

Chapter 20

The lock clicks. Heat floods my face and I stumble back along the corridor, eyes stuck to the floor. That went so much worse than I expected. Seeing myself sitting there, crumbling to dust, refusing to allow my best friend in as I watched helplessly through Hallie's eyes has left me stunned.

When did I become that person?

I'm still carrying too much around in my heart. I have to change. My business is important to me, and I'm driven. There's no shame in that. I was desperate to create something, to bring something to the world. But in the process of reaching, clutching each opportunity with the tips of my fingers, I have lost all perspective. I have tried to bury that Christmas three years ago, but somehow, it's creeping back in. Warping my life in unexpected ways.

The cake was a mistake.

And if I get another chance, if somehow this day becomes my own, I will tell Hallie that. But I will also hold her, love her. Tell her how perfect and giving she is, how much I miss her. How full of sorrow and rage I still am, even now, three years later. How that has driven me, stalked my every waking moment as a curse. A haunting.

But as I place my hands on the worn wooden door that separates the corridor from the top of the staircase, I realise it isn't about the cake. It isn't about the colour of it, or Hallie and Kian's excited announcement. It isn't even about her pregnancy, or the IVF, or the not knowing.

It's about everything I've lost. Gran. My anchor, my world. Gone.

I'm still adrift.

I pass a hand over my face, trying to remove the exhaustion. The tangle of complicated, thorny thoughts in my head. If I don't learn to strip it all back, clear everything away until I am just left with the truth, just the single beating heart of all this, then I have no hope of changing anything. I will be forever haunted, seeing Gran at crowded Tube stations, turning down invitations to Hallie and Kian's because I can't stand the comparison of what our lives have amounted to. I have to shake this off. I have to face it.

Everyone moves to the snug after ten and I go to join them. Diana stays in her room, and I leave her to the quiet. Even though it's late, nudging closer to midnight, finally I can sit comfortably in this body, cosy on an oversized leather couch, and reflect on the day and what I want. There's a fire popping and crackling in the hearth, Natalie's handing out glasses of fizz as a nightcap and Kian is shuffling through the channels to find a film for us all to watch.

'*Casablanca*?' he asks, eyeing everyone for approval.

James chucks a cushion at him, laughing. 'God, no. Nothing black and white. Or anything I have to concentrate on. *Elf*!'

My breath catches as I steal a glance at him. He's in one of the armchairs on the other side of me, grinning at Kian as he chucks the cushion back at him. And laughing. James is actually *laughing*. It's so rare, it sends a flutter along my ribcage. I want to press my mouth against his and feel that bubble of laughter trailing along my own lips. Kiss like we used to, when nothing else in the world existed but us. I miss that.

'Earth to Hal!' Kian is saying and I whip around.

'*Elf* is good!' I say, sticking one thumb up like a loser. Natalie grins and everyone else shouts Kian down. He rolls his eyes and we all settle down, even though it's late, even though we're not students anymore, to watch *Elf*. It's just as silly as I remember. But somehow, the storyline hits me differently tonight. How Buddy wants his dad, his real dad, so desperately. How he finds a fractured family and draws them all together. I want that too. I want that do-over, that perfect family that I didn't get when I was young. That James and I were going to create together. We were going to form our own, give our children that perfect childhood that I was always so desperate for. Actually give them our time, be there for them. Not like mine, with all the good memories contained solely in my time with Gran, at this manor house each Christmas, or eating shortbread at her kitchen table.

Why can't I have that? Why did it have to happen?

A sob rattles my chest and I dab at my eyes, pointing at the film and shrugging when Natalie raises her eyebrows. She laughs, passing me tissues. Kian calls me soft. James has drifted off and is snoring away, head bent against the back of the armchair, mouth slightly agape. His hair is mussed, the strain of the daytime dropping away. He looks so young. Like he did when we first met, when I whispered, *I love you too* under the simmering glow of the fairy lights.

Gran used to sleep like that too. After every meal, she would fall asleep on the sofa afterwards, hot cup of tea turning tepid in front of her. I used to balance objects on her, see how many I could pile up. My record was twenty-three. I snort, a wave of giddiness overtaking my sobs. Grief is funny like that. Sneaks up on you like a thief, stealing the breath from your throat. I look back at the film, watching the colours bloom in reds and greens. But I'm no longer really watching. All I can feel is the pattering kicks against my ribs of Hallie's baby. And I desperately want this feeling to be real. For it to be mine.

I never got to hold my baby.

Never got to see them grow. Find out what colour their eyes would be, if he or she would have hair like mine, or James's. We nearly announced on Christmas Eve three years ago, just like Hallie. But in the end, our Christmas was hollow. Full of strained silence. James never blamed me, but he didn't need to. I always blamed myself. I wanted that perfect family *so much*, to pour all my love into that one tiny being. For James and me to be a forever team, perfectly whole.

I wasn't showing yet. But we'd had the twelve-week scan. We'd watched the flutter of a heart. Listened to its staccato beat. I had the scan picture, all ready to show Gran. She was the first person I wanted to tell and I was waiting – I insisted on that before we announced. But then, she died before I could share it with her. I'm still so bitter. How that was taken from us too. And the next day, the day after I said goodbye, I had to say goodbye again. The heartbeat stopped.

Why couldn't I have that happily ever after? The business is my creation. Something I breathed life into. But it isn't the same.

It will never be enough.

The tears grow hot and thick, blurring my vision of the TV, and I wipe at them furiously. The film finishes, credits rolling down the screen, and Kian scoots over to me with a fresh batch of tissues in his hand. Natalie frowns at me, mouthing, 'Are you OK?'

'Why are you still crying? It was a happy ending. It's all good, Hal.'

I blink, not realising I still was. I point to them all, vaguely indicating Hallie's bump, James slowly waking up. The happy family around me. 'Because this is everything I've ever wanted.' The words drip like tears from that hollow place in my heart. That place I've tried to close off, to shut down and ignore. I hadn't realised just what a sorrowful, dark place it had become. Full of thorns and bitter, half-formed yearning. So many tears, they could drown the world. 'This. Being all together. Being a family.'

I should have this. I still want this. Despite everything, the miscarriage, Gran's sudden death, the rift between James and me, my heart yearns for the grip of my own child's hand in mine.

My tears are jagged streaks on my face as the room reassembles itself. I gasp, rubbing furiously at my swollen eyes, my nose. I stand up, peering around into the gloom. It's cold, with no warmth from the fire casting a heated glow over the snug. Kian, James, even Hallie are all gone. I'm back in my own body, my own salt-clad tears creating lanes and tracks down my face. I turn slowly, this new reality falling into place. I'm still in the same room, the snug at Penhallow.

But Gran is sat watching me.

I walk over to her, sinking into the armchair beside her. My breath stutters in my chest, making me hiccup. She's holding her knitting, mauve wool and two clacking needles, which she places in her lap, reaching over to grip my hand. Her skin is warm and soft, and it makes me cry even harder. I can hardly bear it.

'You're early.'

Chapter 21

'Better than being late, I suppose.'

'Is it?' Gran says, releasing my hand and straightening out a bit. She pulls the cord on a table lamp at her side, flooding her features with soft light. 'Only if you're truly ready. Only if it's not at the expense of your happiness.'

I chuckle softly, the tears sticking in my throat as they wash away. The warmth of watching the film with everyone still lingers in my heart, but now fingers of frost creep into it. Reminding me of my own life, my current path. How far it is from the happy family I wanted so desperately to create.

'Perhaps I shouldn't have pushed you into this. Maybe you weren't ready. Maybe—'

'Gran.'

'All right,' she says, sighing. 'All right.'

I clasp my hands in front of me, the tears still fresh and raw on my cheeks. I'm back in my own body now, my own skin and hair and clipped tones. It's like coming back to an old friend, the feel of the air in my own lungs as it rushes down my throat, the click of my hips as I cross my legs. How different these perspectives are, the way a body moves and feels. The muscle memory, the thoughts hidden, as though locked away in a chest. Scraping at the back of my mind. I am oddly calm, settled and ready. Now I have admitted what I want, that deep, aching need for a family of my own, it is as though a poison has been swept from me. I have recognised that within myself, and *why* I want that. That my fear of failure has held me back from trying again.

Will it be enough?

'I admitted something. To myself.'

'And what's that, dear one?' she asks gently.

'I do want a baby. I don't want to lose James or Hallie. I don't want to lose any of them at the expense of my business.'

'Yes. Go on.'

'But being Hallie, seeing the way she was, the way others spoke to her, so thoughtfully, so respectfully… and James, how sad he is, how desperately unhappy… and seeing how happy Natalie is, which when you compare it to our marriage, well…' I take a breath. 'It's not going well, is it? This obsession with work. I've convinced myself it's enough, that I don't need anything else. Or anyone. But the truth is, the truth… I still want the same things. With James. A family of our own.'

Gran nods. 'Well done.'

'And now someone else has tried to kiss him and he might leave and I've driven him to that.'

'Let's put that to one side for the moment. You can't control his choices. Only your own.'

I nod, trying to do what Gran says. Trying to shift that terrible moment from my mind in the billiards room. Knowing he might not be there after this Christmas. That I can't ignore how unhappy he is and I might not be able to repair everything.

'Let's talk about your work. Yes. Do you think you'll look

back on this Christmas in twenty years and feel happy with how you spent it?'

'You mean, working up in the bedroom?'

'Precisely.'

'Probably not.'

'And why is that?'

I cross then recross my legs. Trying to get comfortable. Only, it's not about this armchair. It's being comfortable with the choices I'm making every day.

'It's become toxic. My relationship with my business. It's not fulfilling me how I wanted it to. How I need it to. It's draining all the colour from my life. It made me feel human again, but now… I just feel anxious. I guess… I guess I've used it as a kind of shield to hide behind. But I've hidden from everything, the good stuff and the bad stuff. And that's the problem.'

'Yes.'

'But how do I change that? How do I find balance?'

Gran shrugs. 'That's down to you, isn't it? Growing a business out of nothing is a huge achievement. *Huge*, my dearest. And you're right, it was your lifeline. But it needn't be your *only* lifeline.'

'It's the only thing I've got right,' I say, breathing the words out, letting them expel from my lungs in a rush. 'The only thing I can truly control. And I do love it. I really do.'

Three years ago, I curled my fists around the seedling of a business, gripped it tightly and refused to let go. It was three days after Gran died. Two days after the bleeding started and we knew there was no longer a heartbeat. We had been trying for over a year, each month growing hopeful, but not discussing it. Never discussing it. As if we might scare it away, this possible baby. And then, miraculously, a positive pregnancy test.

We began to talk again, James and I. About the future, about a nursery, maybe even a little house and a garden? Selling up, moving to the commuter belt. Did we like Market Harborough, with the new fast train link? Or maybe south, maybe Kent, all that salty sea air and freedom…

Then blood. And cramps and all my hopes, every dream I had allowed to slip into my heart, spilling over in those giddy whispered conversations with James in those few precious weeks, all shattered overnight.

So, I closed the door on it all and threw myself into this idea. It was welcome, the distraction. The daily triumphs as I created mood boards, talked to suppliers, formed a business idea. The spreadsheets and train journeys, the air-conditioned buildings full of stalls and wares, the first zip of energy when I watched my website go live. Nudging that heartache aside. The loneliness, always lingering at the corners, pushed back by the light of my laptop screen. If I just found that perfect supplier, took this perfect flat-lay for Instagram, then the next, then the next… I never had to stop. It was intoxicating. I could keep moving forward, propelling myself further into the after. And maybe those shadows and failures would no longer linger. I didn't have to always fail.

I would begin to forget.

'You tried and it didn't work out,' Gran says, gentler still. 'It's not a failure, dearest.'

'It's what I'm designed for,' I say fiercely, wiping away another swelling tear. 'To have babies. To make a family. If I can't do that, what's the point of me?'

'Many things!' Gran says, leaning forward. 'You are capable of many things in this life. Just because you are a woman, it doesn't follow that you *must* procreate. Creating – yes. Things of value, relationships, art, matters of business...' She sits back. Fusses with her knitting. A pause. 'But to assume your only value is to bring a new life to this world undermines everything you are. Do you want a child because it hasn't happened so far?'

'No,' I say quickly. 'No. It's not that.'

For a moment, I'm back there, just after we returned from the hospital. When the heartbeat was gone and my own stuttered to numbness in my chest.

'I want it,' I breathe. 'To hold my baby in my arms and watch them become themselves. To know your, your death...' I swallow, my words tumbling into the silence. 'That it wasn't the end of the family I love.'

They are the truest thing I've said in years. At last, I've spoken them aloud. Thought them through, as a whole complete sentence. Not just a fragment to shy away from. In case it might be true.

'But you must find balance, dearest. Between your wonderful work, James and all these other people in your life. You must realise that they are family too? Family isn't defined by blood alone. I'm not saying it'll be easy, finding this balance in your life. Nothing worth fighting for ever is.'

I nod rapidly, still reeling from what I've admitted to myself.

'Will this all stop now?' I sniff. 'Haven't I done enough? Diana, Natalie, Hallie...'

'Not quite,' she says, rising from the armchair. 'There's still the small matter of the last three years. It's one thing admitting what you want, quite another working out how to fix things. Tricky game, this, isn't it? Seems as though we know less and less what we *truly* want as time goes on. It becomes lost to us. We lose our balance.'

Balance. I don't even know what that means anymore. The scales tipped, and I kept leaning on them. Piling things on, more and more, until they creaked and broke, stuck in this position. On the middle of a moorland, in the darkest depths of Cornwall. In a manor house, surrounded by ghosts.

'I'm sending you back because you're not done yet,' she says, turning so her back is to the fire. She clutches the dressing gown tight to herself, her eyes crinkling at the corners in the way I know so well.

Can I have both? A family *and* a business that I don't pour my entire soul into until it becomes a weight, rather than a release? I picture the kind of buzzing life where I'm fulfilled from my business and juggling the family stuff with James at home. How we could be happy if only we find that elusive balance. But I don't know how to even begin finding that.

'You'll find the next perspective interesting, Eva. A little shift, a little outside view. I think it's time.'

'How will I know when I am done?' I ask urgently, noting the edges of her fading. The smouldering coals in the fireplace flare quickly, as though an open door has allowed a draught to sneak in.

I'm losing her. I'm always losing her. No matter how many bodies I wake up in… she's never going to be there when all this is over.

I move to stand, but my edges are fading too. My clothes, my limbs are falling away. I'm falling into the next body, the day resetting itself. I reach for her, my fingertips fading into nothing. As I disappear, I hear the thread of her voice in the enveloping mist.

'When you're ready to fix it. All of it.'

Chapter 22

An alarm jolts me awake. I fumble for it, trailing my hand over a duvet cover, then a bedside table cluttered with a lamp, books and a box of tissues. I find the phone and jab at it. Silence yawns blissfully and I close my eyes again, leaning back into the over-stuffed pillow. Just five more minutes. Long enough to slip inside a dream, carried away on a wave of—

'Mummy, you're taking up too much space!' a little voice says. The cover is yanked away, leaving me to groan and roll over, finding a patch of warmth. I huddle up, sharp fingers of cold air tiptoeing across my skin. The dream, the distant warmth of sleep seem so far away. Slowly, I open my eyes. And staring back at me is a small, freckly, very ginger imp. 'Mummy, how long have dinosaurs been dead for?'

I blink, reaching again for the phone. There's a picture on the lock screen of two boys in matching football strips. Squinting, a memory surfaces slowly. I've seen this image before, but not on a phone screen, on a Polaroid—

'MUM'S AWAKE!'

I clap my hands over my ears, falling off the bed with a thump. Two faces appear above me, giggling behind their hands. 'Not funny...' I say groggily, picking myself up off the carpet. In

174

fact, not just a carpet. Practically a floordrobe. I have landed on a pile of jumpers, jeans and long-sleeved shirts. Whoever I am today, I'm pretty messy. But then again, with two small children… maybe just too busy?

'Can we go and see if Santa's been?' the oldest child says. 'Please, please, pleeeeeease!'

'Um… yes?' I say, wondering what the time is. I find the discarded phone halfway down the back of the bed and grasp it, just as the two boys career out of the bedroom, thumping quickly down a set of stairs. I tap the phone screen, lighting it up. It's six in the morning.

My fingers fly instinctively over the lock screen, typing in the passcode. I'm getting used to the fact that some things in these bodies are muscle memory. That in some instances, their actions are bleeding through into my own experience of living their life for the day. I do wish that I had their thoughts though. Their memories. But perhaps that is part of it, this grasping for the truth, this unwinding of the hours to find my own place within them. And where I must fight my way back to, when all this is done.

There are a few text messages on this woman's phone, a few Facebook alerts, and the only emails are in full, shouty capitals reminding me to *SHOP, SHOP, SHOP WITH 50% OFF* and *ENJOY A MERRY CHRISTMAS!* I shudder away, closing that app down immediately. But when I tap on the Facebook app, I find the name of the owner of this phone. I scrutinise the profile, scrolling down to click on pictures, funny quotes and events this person is interested in. I know this person. Not super well, not like Hallie and Diana, or even Natalie. But I have met them. Today, I'm the staff member working at Penhallow Diana knows.

175

Sarah.

I sit back down on the bed with a whoosh. Why her? What can she show me that I don't already know? I don't know her. She is not a part of my life, save these few days I am spending at Penhallow. I gaze around in a fugue of dazed tiredness. Sarah did not get a lot of sleep last night. I wonder if it was something to do with those two boys. Or if she had to stay up later than planned at Penhallow, catering to all us guests.

I take in my surroundings. There is a cheap pine wardrobe which is listing to one side with clothes spilling out of it. One window sits next to it, the curtains half drawn with a row of terraced houses facing me. The sky is a swirl of night and stars, it's not even dawn yet. But the chimney in the house opposite is already piping wood smoke, ashy-grey plumes of it curling like fingers. Opposite the wardrobe there is a chest of drawers with a collection of silver jewellery, make-up and perfume bottles all muddled up together.

There's also a notebook and I grab for it greedily, searching for any clue as to who this woman is under the uniform. It's full of research. Holiday cottages, hashtags, marketing angles… there's carefully documented notes from classes she must be taking. It's all digital marketing, growth models, target audiences. I raise my eyebrows. It's impressive, Sarah's obviously working hard on this. Perhaps a distance learning course?

I eye the jewellery again, wondering if I should choose something to put on. Instinctively, my fingers raise to touch the chain fastened around my throat. It's thin and delicate, with a heart pendant resting in the centre. I can feel that there is a catch, a raised notch of metal. It must be one of those ones that holds tiny photos inside. Probably of her children.

I reach over, pulling a beige cotton dressing gown off the hook on the back of the door, and shrug it on. It smells faintly of her, Sarah; a berry-scented perfume, maybe some fruity body lotion. My hands are dry and callused, these are workers' hands. I'm not used to it, not with the hand creams I buy. I bite my lip, shoving these hands deep into the robe pockets. Perhaps I do have a lot to learn in this body. What was Gran saying in the snug? She was reminding me to find balance.

'Mum! When's breakfast? We're starving!' a voice hollers up the stairs.

It jars me into action. 'Coming!' I yell back, dashing out of the bedroom and immediately tripping on a small mound of Lego on the landing.

Downstairs looks like the inside of the Christmas aisle in a supermarket. Shiny foil tinsel winds along the edge of the ceiling, around the banister and in criss-crosses over the lopsided Christmas tree. Fairy lights wink around the window and the tree in a spectacular array of garish colours. And at the heart of it all are Sarah's children, tearing into brightly wrapped parcels.

'Hang on!' I say, rushing over. 'Are you supposed to open all those straight away?'

The oldest one eyes me strangely. 'It is Christmas.'

'When else do we open them?' the youngest one says, fingers ripping into a well-wrapped box.

'Have some breakfast first? Spread them out a little!' I realise I sound like my own mum and cringe. 'Oh, just go ahead. Go wild.'

They both grin and I roll my eyes, deciding to leave them to it to go off in search of a kettle, and coffee. The kitchen I find is a cupboard. Barely enough room to swing a cat, I can stretch my arms wide and almost touch either wall. But the front of the fridge is filled with so much love. School certificates, photos, fridge magnets spelling out things like, 'BuM' and 'Luv U mUM'. I crease up when I spot a painting, buried underneath a load of neon fridge magnets. It's meant to be a picture of Sarah holding a mop, but it looks more like... a pole dancer. She's stuck a note underneath it, 'Harv's artistic impression of my day job. Age 6.' I chuckle again, opening the fridge to search for the milk.

Sarah's phone vibrates in the pocket of my robe, and I pull it out to find a message from 'Nan'.

Be there in 15.

The phone vibrates again, and this time it comes up with 'Naomi'.

Bring jam with you, never mind if it's not posh. we've run out and the bloody shop is shut! I'll come and get you at half 7. Merry Christmas!!!

I figure this must be the other member of staff.

The text message brings me up sharply, like a rap over the knuckles. It's muscle memory, an automatic reaction, this tension tightening across my shoulders. All firm and no nonsense. Is she her colleague, or her boss at Penhallow? I make a quick cup of instant coffee, carry bowls of Cheerios through to the lounge for the boys and whizz back to cram a slice of toast into my mouth. The doorbell rings and I figure it's Nan, so I disappear up the stairs to get ready.

★

178

The next hour races from under my feet with crackers at break-fast, quick hugs with the two boys and the woman, Sarah's nan, reminding me at the last second to take the spare pot of jam from the cupboard. She blows me a kiss on the way out and I feel a tug. It wraps around my heart, anchoring me to the carpet. Sarah doesn't want to leave.

I don't want to leave.

This explosion of tinsel and wrapping paper, of red and green and twinkly fairy lights, is the most homely home I've been in all year. Maybe even since I was little, staying at Gran's house. I hover, just for a moment, in the doorway. Taking it all in. It's small, this house, and noisy with the TV blaring out a Christmas film, the boys with new electronic toys that have far too many buttons and batteries, and Nan sitting on the sofa, laughing and pointing at them with a mug of stewed tea in one hand. Nothing matches. Not the sofas, the wall colour, or the collection of dolphin ornaments on the mantel above the wood burner. But it works. Nothing is out of place.

I breathe it in, the smell of soggy cereal, of unwashed children and instant coffee. Sarah's made an attempt at introducing something nicer with a plug-in air freshener, and I can just taste the tang of the artificial scent as I inhale. I want to linger here. I want to open presents, eat pigs in blankets and watch old Disney films with this family.

But then Naomi pulls up outside, honking the horn on her car. I steel myself for the day, jar of jam wrapped firmly in my fist, and dash outside. Back to Penhallow and the me locked inside it. If Gran's sent me back as Sarah, this has to mean something. Nerves patter in my stomach, hastening my steps, and for the first time, I'm glad of this chance. Because if I'm Sarah then I'm slightly removed, able to observe more, understand more. And maybe it will give me the chances I didn't have as Hallie or Natalie or even Diana to find the people I love and shake out a way of fixing everything.

Chapter 23

'Only got strawberry,' I say, shaking the pot of jam as I get into the car.

'Seeds?'

'Seedless.'

The woman, Naomi, grimaces and quickly shifts gears to rev up a steeper section of the lane. I'm thrown backwards in the passenger seat of the old, beaten-up Range Rover. 'Probably not posh enough, but if we serve it in one of those little dishes they might not notice.'

Naomi is older, late forties, with streaky bottle-blonde highlights that have gone a touch brassy and dry. She's wearing brown-framed glasses and a pout as she focuses, navigating the old country lanes to reach the manor house. Her white button-down shirt and black skirt, the uniform we both wear, is carefully smoothed and prim under a waxed jacket that reeks of Labradors and cigarettes. She's a study in contradictions.

'Are you with your family later?' I ask, trying to work out what Gran wants me to get out of this day as Naomi crunches through another gear change, swearing in a puff of cold breath. She's got her window wide open, blasting in icy air. I'm glad of it; I still get car sick and the smell of cigarettes sours my stomach.

'Only Lindy,' she says. 'And that's a Skype date. As if that counts, right?' She rolls her eyes at me, seeking agreement. I nod with a serious frown and she seems satisfied. Even though I have no idea who Lindy is. 'Felix couldn't make it down to Cornwall. Gone off on some ski trip with his mates, so it would have just been me and a TV dinner. And obviously since the new girl called in sick...' She shrugs, raising her eyebrows. 'You're stuck with me for this whole shindig, and only me.'

'Oh,' I say. Clearing my throat, I lean forward to catch a glimpse of Penhallow. We're nearly there. The sun is just coming up, painting the sky in pale pastels and stark whites. I reach down into the footwell for my bag, and spy a small, white business card. Nudging it with the toe of my shoe, I see Naomi's name on it. And, underneath, the name of the company Hallie rented this house from. Of course. She's the owner. That's why she's so pissed off about working over the holidays.

'I guess I'm on pot-wash duty again?' I chance, glancing at her slyly.

She winks at me. 'Bingo. I'll cook, you serve and clean up.'

My red raw hands tingle at the thought of it.

Over the course of breakfast prep, I listen to a fast stream of monologue from Naomi. Complaints about her two adult children, Lindy and Felix, who never visit, the properties her husband and she acquired and renovated in their twenties and thirties, before he divorced her a year ago. Leaving her with a ton of debt and the two properties in the portfolio that were the hardest to run: this one, and another on the Cornwall–Devon border. She complains about the price of heating them, the constant shit she gets from the guests ('I ask you, who wants a phone call at two a.m. to say the hairdryer in their room has blown a fuse? Sit by the fire or go and borrow one from another room!'), and the fact she has to drop everything, like *now*, because the Gen Z kids she hires have no work ethic.

I nod along, keeping my head down, and think about Sarah's life. Those two boys at home, waiting for her to finish her shift. The bank alert I got earlier on her phone, saying she had overdrawn. Again. And this boss who clearly thinks of her team in terms of their work output only. Not as individuals, not as Sarah, the person.

As I serve breakfast to the guests, spying myself, this version of Eva and Hallie and Diana, all carefully avoiding eye contact with each other, I wonder who got it right. Did I? I'm planning on working Christmas Day, just like Sarah. But I don't have that cosy family to go home to afterwards. Just a cold bed, a bitter taste on my tongue and a joyless marriage, where we've swept all the words we cannot say firmly under the rug. At least Sarah has her family. Those Christmas hats, the foil decorations, the home strewn with scrunched-up wrapping paper and two boys fit to burst with wonder. Amidst all that chaos, has she somehow found balance?

'Did you take out the bacon? It'll go cold,' Naomi is saying as she dusts the French toast with cinnamon sugar. 'And that coffee pot wasn't hot enough. It has to be *piping*. Remember, if they rebook next year, you'll get that bonus!'

I say nothing, dashing back and forth from kitchen to dining room, my head a whirl of the guests' requests and Naomi's barked commands. It doesn't take long for me to make mistakes and I curse myself. Sarah clearly needs this job, and a bonus would certainly help her out. If she's a single mother, which I'm fairly sure by now that she is, then she doesn't have a second income stream to rely on. Just herself, a mug of strong coffee and the drive to drag her tired bones through another shift. Another day.

By nine thirty, they're all eating and I take ten minutes to sit in the kitchen before going back in to clear away. Naomi is standing by the back door, dragging on a cigarette. The smoke plumes from her lips as she eyes the garden critically. 'That gardener hasn't been here for a month. I can tell, just look at these weeds!' She tuts, tapping the ash from the end of her cigarette on the ground. 'Can't get the bloody staff.'

I think about what Kian said when he went on the walk with me as Hallie. The wilderness garden, brimming with potential. It had always seemed so magical when I was younger, enchantment dancing just beyond my fingertips. 'Have you thought about the walled garden? You could prune that back, revive it. It would be a great feature. All those interesting plant specimens and maybe you could renew a meadow to rewild the grounds. Especially if you put in a hot tub as well on the terrace, somewhere to watch the shooting stars on clear nights.'

Naomi cuts me a look and drops her cigarette on the ground, grinding it to dust under the toe of her shoe. 'Not a bad idea, Sarah. Not bad at all.'

I shrug, warming to the theme. 'If you need to earn more from this place, it would only take a small tweak here and there. Get some PR interest, a few socials and you'd have a place like Soho Farmhouse. Everyone would want to come here to get away. Take selfies on the lawns, bang on about "hashtag explore more" and "darling weekend" to their followers.'

She laughs drily, pointing a finger at me. 'How do you know about socials?'

The notebook in Sarah's bedroom, the carefully documented pages and pages of relevant hashtags and research flood my vision. Sarah really has done her homework, and I understand why, now. It's for this very conversation with Naomi that I've somehow stumbled into. She's googled similar properties, similar companies. She's even thought of an account name, put together a set of campaign ideas and thought about the target market, from what I read this morning. I feel that familiar fire simmering in my chest. The one I've been chasing in my own business, craving a hit of the passion I first found when I started it. Perhaps Sarah and I are not so different.

'It's that open university course, isn't it? That one you mentioned a while back...'

I smile and nod. 'That's right. It's er... digital marketing, I've been researching. Thinking about the business model.' This all comes so easily to me. So naturally. And I'm reminded, this is what I'm good at. This is why I have loved building my business. These are the kinds of conversations I crave. The positive ones, the ones building plans.

'You completed the degree last month, I remember you talking about it now!' Naomi snaps her fingers and looks at me. As if she's seeing me for the first time. As if Sarah isn't an interchangeable staff member. I hope I never make Diana feel this small. This needy for a single ounce of praise. 'Took you six years, that's right, isn't it? All by Skype and online research while you looked after those boys.'

I'm staggered. Sarah's completed a digital marketing degree... at home? I know what it is to study around a full-time job. It's how I got my Masters in Business and Economics. But I didn't have two young children at home, needing me. She must have done it while she breastfed, or prepared dinner, or ironed endless piles of laundry in that tiny front room. How has Naomi not seen it in her? Her drive, her ambition? Her steel.

Everything suddenly makes total sense. Sarah's shyness as she spoke to Diana. Her tiredness, the bone-deep kind born of years of lack of sleep. Not just a single night. Her willingness to do just about any job to get by, even as she burned the candle at both ends at home. It was eating her up, this desire for more. To push past what life had dealt her, but not just for her boys.

For herself.

I allow myself a moment of brief victory before hauling my tired self up to go and clear away the breakfast things. Maybe this is why I was meant to be Sarah today. To gain a bit of perspective on what it means to get ahead, with a family at home. How she balances it all. How maybe I could do it too, without pushing Hallie away. And without losing James for good.

Chapter 24

Diana is right on time. She's edging towards the kitchen gardens, her shoulders hugging her ears. The stress is palpable, it radiates from her. I quickly drop the dirty dishes in my hands, leaving the dishwasher gaping open. Checking Naomi is still consumed by the phone call she's on, I slip out through the back door.

'Di?' I say. She turns, her eyes narrowing as I stand in the middle of the path, wiping my hands down the sides of my skirt. For a moment, I see her flicker of uncertainty; she doesn't know who I am. Who Sarah is, beneath this polyester uniform and the blobs of food dotting my hem. Is it me in there, too? Are we just playing out this loop, or is it truly Diana? I don't dare find out, in case it breaks everything. 'It's you, isn't it? I almost didn't recognise you. You look so posh now.'

Her eyes light up and she steps forward. Maybe it isn't me. Maybe this *is* truly Diana.

'Hey, Sarah,' she says, a smile curving her mouth upwards.

My uncertainty breaks away and I laugh. 'I figured you had got too good for us.'

'Never,' she says.

We hug, and a deep sense of complete ease settles over me. She still smells like Diana. The combination of that floral scent, and the nip of her favourite mint toothpaste. I have travelled in enough cars with her, huddled next to her at our tiny, shoved-together desks, to know her scent well.

We break apart and I smile shyly, gesturing to my skirt, the cap Naomi insists I wear. 'Obviously, I did super well,' I babble, focused on being Sarah, not myself. Trying to keep this natural. 'Got out of night shifts, anyway. The Tesco manager was putting me on all the weekend ones. Never saw the kids. But this gig, it's much better.' I sniff. I think I do a fairly good impression. I hope so, anyway. I'm fairly sure this is how the conversation went the first time when I was in Diana's shoes, staring back at Sarah.

'You've got kids now?'

'Two.' I rustle through my pockets, producing the battered Polaroid I know will be in there. Sarah's two ginger-haired boys are sticking their tongues out at the camera, hair poking out at every angle, black-and-white-striped football kits displayed proudly on their chests. It's the same image that is the screen-saver on Sarah's phone. 'Harvey and Milo. Six and eight now.'

Diana blinks in shock. Pain flashes across her face, so fleeting I might not have caught it. But it was there, that flinch, around the eyes, the tensing of her mouth. I wonder what it means.

'Yeah, I had Milo when I was nineteen.' I nod. 'I expect you were out at fancy dinner parties? Travelling the world?'

Diana laughs uneasily. 'I would have just started my degree. Business and economics in London. Lots of dreary Tube journeys and not knowing if I could make up the rent.'

I put the photo away, scraping my shoe awkwardly against the snow on the path. It's falling faster now, clumps forming around us. I ran out here in just this uniform, and I realise I'm freezing. 'And those people in there.' I jerk my thumb at the house. I need to know what she thinks of them. What she thinks of… me. 'They're your friends?'

'No!' Diana shudders. 'No. I have to be here, for my boss. There's this big thing happening at work and if we pull it off, it'll make my career. So I have to be here. For her.'

'Huh.' I look at her, critical and assessing. 'Always knew you were smart. Is it worth it? All… this?'

Is it everything you ever wanted, Diana?

'A hundred per cent.' She swallows, visibly reeling herself back in. 'Just got to keep going at this point, right? Nothing's ever easy.'

I nod in sympathy, even as my insides turn to ice. I hate the tiredness creeping over every syllable. Is she thinking about those buried work emails?

'And your boss, is she… OK to work with?' I blurt out, needing to know. Trying to gauge what she's thinking.

Diana makes a face and shrugs. 'She's anxious at the moment. Stressed out. We get on well usually, but…'

'But?'

'You know how it is with bosses.' She laughs uncomfortably. 'She's a little unreachable. I find it hard to get through to her. And lately… I don't know. I'm a cog, you know? I feel like I just serve a purpose. Plug a gap.'

I nod, absorbing everything she's saying. Am I really that distant? I don't want Diana to feel like she's a cog. Or that I don't care. Because I do! She flicks back her hair, drumming her boots against the snow. 'Well, I guess I'd better go and get ready. The others are going to this swim in the sea thing, and I kind of want to, but…'

'Work?'

She grins. 'Exactly.'

'I better get back inside, stop holding you up,' I say, stamping my feet as well. Trying to process everything she's said. 'But seriously, it's good to see you, Di. We miss you.'

As Diana shuffles away, my body, Sarah's body, twitches, turning to glance back over a shoulder. There is a thread running between them, deep but whisper thin. As though it has been stretched out and frayed over time. But it's still there, creating an ache in my chest. Sarah doesn't want to walk away. She wants to linger in this snow-drenched garden, chatting with Diana. And perhaps I feel this connection, this thread, because it's how I feel too. I don't want to lose Diana. I need her to know how very special she is.

I spend the rest of the day turning over what Diana has said. How she sees me, what she really thinks. Anxious. Stressed out. Unreachable. All the qualities I like least in a work colleague. And now... she's right, isn't she? That's me. That's the me I've allowed myself to become.

I try not to dwell on it. I try to shake it off, be the work colleague I know I can be. Those words simmer at the back of my mind, so I force myself to be the opposite of them. Because if Sarah can do it, it's possible. I have to try. My mood is infectious apparently, and by 5 p.m. when we're getting Christmas dinner on the table, Naomi is singing carols in the kitchen next to me. I know this isn't all me, this is Sarah. Her day, her family permeating my mood, reminding me to stop and relish the moments strung in between the big events of life. I imagine her here now in my stead, her laughter, probably a quick sense of humour, an ability to turn a dull day of work into a short shift glittering with banter. I forgot that side of myself from before three years ago and I love to see Naomi now as I spin out a carol, dancing around the kitchen with platters balanced in my hands. She's drinking in the atmosphere like the finest Champagne. In our own way, we're creating an unforgettable Christmas.

When we've finished serving and clearing, I nip to the main rooms; the snug, the billiards room, the library, anywhere that might need a little freshening up. I'm in the library, collecting a couple of empty tumblers, smoothing out the sofa cushions and allowing my gaze to wander over the titles on the nearest shelf when the door opens abruptly. I jump, twisting quickly to find James framed in the doorway.

'Sorry, have you seen my wife? Er, Eva? She's sort of short, brown hair, wearing a red dress...'

'I haven't,' I say, drinking him in. He looks so wan, so ready to fold in on himself. It takes everything within me to not cross the space that divides us and wrap my arms around his waist. Lean my head against his chest and listen for the sure, steady rhythm of his heartbeat. 'I can... would you like me to look for her?'

He deflates further, scrubbing a hand across his chin. 'It's all right. Thanks... Sarah, isn't it?' His smile looks a little forced, the polite kind we use for near strangers. 'How's Christmas going for you?'

'All right,' I say, smiling tentatively back. 'Well, quite good now, actually. It wasn't at first, but I feel like it's improving? I...' I swallow, remembering who I am, who James is to Sarah. Nothing, really. And perhaps... perhaps this is an opportunity.

I fidget in my pocket, pulling out the photo of Sarah's two boys. 'Left these rascals at home with Nan. It's tough, you know? I have to work, and I do love working. It gives me purpose. But they're what I love, who I do it all for.'

'Your people,' he says, glancing at the photo. He sighs, sinking into an armchair. 'What's it like, having children? I know that's a big question…'

I laugh, leaning against a bookshelf. 'Um, well, I suppose… chaotic? Hard? Amazing?'

'Everything all at once?'

'Yes, I guess so,' I say, my smile widening to a grin, picturing Sarah's boys this morning. How much I didn't want to leave the cosy nook of a home she's created. 'But so worth it.'

'I-I suppose I'd quite like children. But Eva—' He bites his lip, cutting himself off. 'It hasn't happened how we hoped, let's put it that way.'

For a beat there's silence and I feel the very air waiting. As if we are standing on a precipice, gazing over a vast abyss. Just James and me, and our world of feelings.

'You could still… try. Or you could, I don't know…' I edge towards him, my heart tugging me across the room. 'Remember how much you've already built together?' Then I remember who I am and quickly add, 'Sorry, it's not my place to say, so forgive me if I'm stepping out of line…'

'Yes,' he says, nodding. 'Yes. I mean, I was hoping I would see more of her today, spend some time together, maybe go for a walk or something, just the two of us? And try to get back what we had before. I wanted the day to be perfect, for her to just forget about work for once. I wanted… I *want* to see her less stressed, more engaged… I want her to remember how much she loves me. At least, I hope she still does. Because… because I still love her. As much as I always have.' He gives an awkward laugh, blinking quickly, as though clearing a mist from his mind. 'I'm sorry, I'm keeping you. Sure you want to finish up, get home to those boys…'

'It's all right,' I say, moving back to give him space. Remembering who he sees me as. 'She loves you. You should know that.'

He gives me an odd look. 'You know, Eva talks about this library like it's something from a fairy tale. I don't know, meeting you here, seeing that photo…' He shakes his head. 'Thank you. I mean it. And I hope you're right.'

My heart is two sizes bigger by the time Naomi and I pile into her Range Rover as night crowds over the fields of bog and gorse. The lanes are thick with snow, like icing. It muffles everything, drawing around us like a blanket, and I hope Naomi is savvy enough to navigate her way off the moors. Unlike me, that night as Diana.

'I'll transfer your bonus in the morning,' Naomi says, steering carefully away from the gravel driveway of Penhallow. The house is lit up behind us, the guests laughing and chatting in the snug at the back. Everything as it should be.

I blink in surprise, swivelling towards her. 'But we don't know if they want to book again next year yet.'

'Doesn't matter.' Naomi winks at me, the creases forming at the corners of her eyes. 'You made this day bearable for me. I laughed, the guests are happy and you took my mind off everything. Off Lindy and Felix and the bloody heating bills! Thank you.'

I sit there, slightly choked up, thinking about the overdrawn alert from Sarah's bank this morning. How by tomorrow morning she'll be back in the black, and able to enjoy the last few days of the year with a sense of security. What a burden that will take off her shoulders.

'Thank you.'

Naomi frowns at the lane. 'I *want* to. It'll give this old Scrooge a bit of joy. You've earned it. And I saw you lining up those shots on your phone of the Christmas spread. Very nice. That degree is clearly handy.'

I grin, dipping my forehead as heat flares across my cheeks. This is what it feels like, to feel proud about your work. To be fulfilled by it. Not consumed.

'Now you go home to that precious family of yours and you cuddle them and love them and not think for even a moment about work. Trust me. I wish I could have that time back. I wish I could turn back the clock and have even a *moment* of what you have. It's everything.'

Tears prickle behind my eyes and I sniff. I glance at Naomi out of the corner of my eye. She's probably going home to a cold house, huge and beautiful and very lonely. There might be a few gifts for her. Perhaps even that promised Skype call with one of her grown-up children as she heats up leftovers and pours a glass of wine. But it won't warm her heart. It'll leave her hollow. She'll toast another Christmas, frittered away, and maybe she'll grow a fraction more bitter.

Is this what I'm meant to see? The contrast between Sarah and Naomi, and what will happen if I keep pushing everyone away? I settle back into the car seat, frowning at the expanse of white, white snow. And I know with absolutely certainty. After speaking to James in the library, after hearing him so tentatively admit he loves me, I don't want a divorce. I will fight and fight to get some balance in my life. To find my way back to James and work on creating the family we've both always wanted.

Because I can see now, it's possible. Sarah makes it possible every day. Maybe not perfect, and maybe some days are a struggle. But she balances her work, her dreams and her family and keeps fighting. Keeps forging her own path. I release a sigh, an overwhelming sense of relief overtaking me. I can do this.

Chapter 25

I blink and I'm no longer in Naomi's Range Rover. Gasping, my hands land heavily on the edge of a basin, cold porcelain jarring my bones. It takes me a moment to adjust, feel my bare feet on cold tile, the scent of soap and steam lingering in the room. I stare at my reflection in the bathroom mirror, a pair of glasses firmly pushed up my nose.

I have gone backwards. I'm a different person, another face staring back at me that isn't mine. There's no Gran sat fussing with her knitting. No cosy midnight chat. Why has this loop shifted so suddenly? Why is she not here?

And why am I Diana again?

I shake my head, staring down into the basin, Diana's black hair falling in a waterfall around my eyes. I've admitted what I want more than anything. It was painful, but I did it. The experience of being Hallie, the close-knit love she has every day with Kian finally got through to me. And James's confession, that he was thinking of leaving… it shook me to my core. I can see now. From spending time as Sarah, how she juggles her family and work and dreams. How it isn't something to be afraid of. That I am capable, that I can push for it. I can find balance between all those things. Maybe not every day, but on the whole, I can do it. I am more than the sum of my fears.

But Gran said I will go back when I'm ready to fix all of it. And I'm not quite sure I know what she means. So I am in Diana's body, yet again. Diana's breath warming my lips, her chest rising and falling, the restless limbo of her limbs not quite connecting with my own mind as they should. How long will this go on for?

How long will I be stuck in this cycle?

I reach for Diana's phone, frowning at the torrent of emails and alerts. There's a bar of signal but as I move the phone, it disappears completely. I scan through the work ones, swiping away as I realise I've read them all before. In fact, I've actioned every point in them, sitting in that pub on the last Christmas Day I was in Diana's uncomfortable boots. And that didn't change anything, or make anything better. So what does this mean?

Exasperated, I flick through to the messages, hesitating for a beat before pulling open the messages from the unsaved number. It's the link to the Coldplay song that niggles at me, the same one James sent me that Christmas Day three years ago. It's so much more than a song to me now. Just as a scent evokes whole people, whole pasts, this song folds me under a memory. An afternoon, a moment. A polished coffin being carefully lowered under frost. I sit back, clicking on the link and close my eyes. And as the track begins, I'm there. Under the watery winter sun, James holding my hand in his firm grasp, mine clinging on to his. My breath pluming in steady clouds as we listen to this track at her graveside. Fulfilling her final wish, to be buried at the church near Penhallow. The place we were happiest. I tremble now as I did back then, three years ago.

The day we buried one of the loves of my life.

I haven't been able to listen to it since. But now, I listen to the whole track, every lyric, every soft space between breaths. It reaches through the phone, pulling me back to that day as I trace each syllable, each haunting note. It's about all the things they tell us when we lose someone. Someone precious and irreplaceable. That we still hold them in the hollow of our hearts. That we will love them until the end of our days. The ache floods my chest, threatening to overwhelm me as it has done so many times before. But this time, I relax into it. I allow my mind, my chest to be flooded with pain. I remember her, the alive, beautiful her, and I embrace it. The song draws to an end and I lock the phone, twin tears tracking down my cheeks. I close my eyes and huff out a breath, allowing a small piece of her to slip away.

Then I open my eyes and remember where I am. Who I am. And how if I want to get back, I can't stay here, tethered to the past.

With a jolt, I realise something. Leaning forward, I scroll back through the messages, every word, every syllable holding new meaning. I scroll back and back, sending a silent sorry to Diana. This isn't the way I wanted her to share this with me. But I can imagine her peering at the messages too, willing me to carry on. Staring blankly as they move up the screen. I know this feeling. I know it too well.

Then I find it. The message that explains it all. The personal days Diana took a couple of months ago were not because she had the flu. She was reliving, revisiting some of the worst days of her life. A sob catches in my throat, but I'm not sure if it's mine. It's Diana, rising up from the depths of this body, clawing at me, her grief pushing up like a wave.

I take a deep breath, pressing a hand into my chest, heart wild and relentless beneath my fingers. This body knows the bone-deep sense of loss, of longing for someone who is no longer there. What I can't figure out is who. Who has Diana lost? Suddenly the walls are too close, the room too hot and stuffy. I need to get out.

I dress quickly, pocket the phone and stride down the corridor. No one stirs, no one whispers from behind the closed doors and I cross the entrance hall quickly, throwing open the front door for a gulp of frost-laden air. It cools me, quenching the heat under my skin. I walk out, not bothering with a coat, turning my face up to the sky. I close my eyes. The first flurry of snowflakes kiss my mouth, my eyelids and I breathe deeply, in, out. The song slips away, no longer gripped like a fist inside me, tangled with my own memories, my own wanting.

This is a new day. A new chance in this body to understand, and to put things right. I replay the events of today from every perspective. I walk through Diana's day in my mind as I crunch slowly through the snow, taking a turn around the walls of Penhallow.

She was desperate to leave yesterday, as much as I was. Together we pushed against the boundaries of this... whatever *this* is, and slipped into the dark of night. But it didn't work. I ended up back here, in Natalie's body, then Hallie's, then Sarah's. My stomach twists involuntarily, remembering the nausea of Hallie's body. The heightened sense of smell, the tiredness dragging down every fibre of my being. The will and the courage to keep going, to bring everyone together. Seeing myself through Hallie's eyes was the most devastating of all.

I shake myself, laughing softly as I reach the kitchen door. Sarah's already inside, I can see her through the back window. She's with the other member of staff, arranging breakfast foods on platters, stirring a huge pot of porridge on the stove, and there are neat rows of bellinis, all ready for a Christmas Day toast. Why am I here? Why am I Diana again today? It can't just be to listen to that Coldplay song. To relive the bone-deep cold of those moments by Gran's graveside, feeling how wrong it was, how I would never be ready to say goodbye. I have to work it out. Even if that means disrupting the order of things. Of what happened last time I walked through this day as Diana. I draw a breath and grip the door handle before stepping inside.

'Need a hand carrying all this through?' I ask as Sarah turns. Her face lights up when she sees me, recognition igniting her features. As her old friend, Diana. She raises her eyebrows and shrugs as Naomi eyes me thoughtfully.

'Naomi?' Sarah says. A question flitting between them. She shrugs and turns back to the range cooker, stirring the pot, adding some cream. Then Sarah picks up two platters and points with her chin to a third. I guess I am helping.

'We're serving early this morning,' she says, backing up to the swing door to push through into the corridor beyond. 'So you can all get out for a walk, maybe even go down for the annual dip if that's your thing.'

'The sea swim?' I ask, placing the platter I'm carrying on a sideboard. It's crammed with breakfast rolls brimming with egg and avocado. My stomach rumbles as I look up at Sarah. I remember when Gran took me, so many years ago. When we kicked off our wellies and danced in the shallows while everyone ran into the water. I couldn't stop laughing that morning. Every breath was snatched away in pure happiness. 'Someone mentioned it at dinner last night. That's what the plan is?'

Sarah eyes me thoughtfully, her face softening. 'That's right. Your dad still goes. Even after... well. She did love the sea, didn't she?' She hesitates, and I wonder who this 'she' is. I wonder, for the first time, if it's Diana's mother. Then Sarah seems to make a decision and carries on. 'He talks about you whenever I see him. Boasts like mad, and it always sounds like you're someone else. That you aren't the same girl I swapped notes with in chemistry class. Or smuggled a bottle of Martini into Jess's sleepover in a sleeping bag. I-I don't know. I nearly didn't recognise you. You're so... different. Polished. And... well.'

I stumble over a reply, rehashing a bit of the conversation I know they've had before outside, the last time I was Diana. But all I can think about is this puzzle of why I'm here. And who the *she* is who loved the sea.

Past tense.

Diana hasn't seen her father in a year. Other than a strained meeting, in her own words. She told me on the way here and I forgot until just now, it was so swiftly said, quickly glossed over. I *let* her gloss over it. In a way, I knew. I did this to her. Weekend work, bringing her along to trade fairs, expecting her to drop dinner plans and order takeout so we could go over a set of figures, social media stats, just one more time.

I pushed her into this, this half-life that she's grown to hate. I used to be her role model, the person she looked to, whom she would dress like, act like.

But now, I can see that there was growing resentment. If

I examine my memories in a different light. That maybe her work had twisted her into someone else. Quiet at first, a stewing mass of short, tight words and thoughts. Then it grew bigger. Until the personal days, when I demanded she give me a reason why she wasn't coming in to work, yet again.

'I guess I am someone else,' I say with a sad smile. I have turned Diana into me. She is a reflection of the work me; the persistent, bossy, over-caffeinated, overstretched me. The one that can't blot away the bloodshot eyes from lack of sleep, or in a few years will not be able to trick her skin into being anything but dull and grey. I want to grip Sarah's arms, shake her and promise her that this isn't the whole of me. This isn't the sum of all my parts. That ambition does not equal burnout. It doesn't have to.

'There's still a little Diana in there though, right?' Sarah says, breaking through. She's tilting her head to one side, assessing me. 'You know, it's not my place to say. And you're welcome to pretend I never mentioned it, but you could visit him. Just drop by. I know it's been a while, but he won't care.'

I find myself nodding. If this is all actually happening, then maybe this is what I'm supposed to do today. I think of the last time I was Diana. How I left for the pub and spent the whole day working. Then I think of Sarah's balancing act, how she made time for both work and her family. And really, I should always have known what choices to make on this day.

'Will he be there, do you think?'

'At the dip? Yeah. I expect so.' Sarah straightens, reaching for the door. She casts a sad smile my way and sighs. 'Just like he always is.'

Chapter 26

'It's not a *real* skinny-dip, is it?' Hallie asks, forehead wrinkling as she stares out at the frothing waves. 'I mean… it's freezing. Must be below zero.'

'Nonsense,' Naomi says brightly as she hops out of the front seat of her Range Rover. 'Water's lovely! Like going to a spa. And it *is* tradition.'

She slams the door closed, leaving us in ringing silence. The local beach is a short drive over the moors, the cliffs parting to reveal the secret pebbled cove. Only locals really go there now, Naomi informs us. The tourist centre hasn't really caught on, or featured it on their Instagram posts. It's closely guarded, this beach. There's no bumper-to-bumper line of cars, perfuming the air with fumes and irritation. Apparently, pebbles aren't quite as sexy as sand in the summer sun.

The grey wall of sky meets the even greyer tide, spray dashing over the pebbles to froth in gleaming rivers. There is already a crowd on the beach. Lots of cherry-red Santa hats topped with white pom-poms, blanket-wrapped bodies and steaming enamelled tin mugs of mulled wine. I gulp, crossing my fingers that I might be able to get out of this. But as John and Natalie pile out of the other taxi that followed after us, laughing and slinging on Santa hats, I realise the best option might be to slug down a mug of mulled wine and just get on with it.

Heat catches in my throat as Kian wrenches open the door, revealing James hovering directly behind him. I hesitate, eyeing his troubled frown. I, that is, Eva, did not come along for the dip. James has got his mobile in his hands, jabbing away with quick fingers, biting his lip.

There are lines around his eyes and a permanent crease in the centre of his forehead. Were they always there? Or have they crept in, insidious, over the last three years, deepening as the gulf between us grew? I want to reach out to him, tell him I didn't mean it. Take his hand and pull him into the sea, Santa hats askew on our heads as we brace ourselves for the sharp, sudden cold. I nearly do reach out. My booted foot hits the grass and mud underfoot before I stop myself.

I'm not in my own body.

I am still Diana, lurking like a tumour in hers, staring out of her eyes. And all I can do is watch as he thrusts his phone into his pocket and turns away. It's the most painful thing, doing nothing.

'Coming in, Diana?' Kian asks, nudging me and grinning. Does this man ever stop being positive and lovely? We could be in a volcano, lava drenching the landscape and boiling everyone to a crisp, and I'm sure he would shrug and say, *At least we got to see an active volcano!*

Hallie is already pulling on a wetsuit, leaning against the Range Rover and laughing as Natalie tugs it up her legs. Her bump protrudes and she rubs a hand over it, telling her sister it's bump's first taste of the sea. I smile at Kian, remembering why I'm here. To see if I can find Diana's life in the midst of this cold, December day. And in the process, find mine.

I hope I am back in my own body soon though, as my feet strain to walk over to my husband. To speak to James and try and work out how to fix things. How to draw him back into the relationship that's falling apart.

'Try and stop me,' I say to Kian, blinking away my muddied thoughts and shove the Santa hat on my head. The white pom-pom bobble at the top flops into my eyes as Kian pushes the car door closed.

'That's the spirit!' he says. 'Good thing you didn't disappear straight back to London. You would have missed out.'

I smile, taking this reason as my motive for sticking around. Maybe it isn't what Diana would really do, but it's clear I can't fix everything if I leave this place.

Luckily, I had the foresight to wear a swimming costume underneath the high-waist jeans and shirt that I lent Diana a couple of days ago. I don't know why she packed a swimming suit, but thank God she did. Today could have got *really* awkward.

'Last one to the sea has to strip!' Kian hollers and we all scream, dashing over the pebbles.

A laugh bubbles up over my lips, curses fresh on my tongue as the cold, rough pebbles bite into the soft underside of my feet. I spread my arms out, trotting from one spot to the next in a bid to not be last. The waves wash in, gasps and shouts ringing out as each of us hits the water. I squeal like a child as the water rushes over my toes, reaching up with frosty fingers to wrap around my calves, then my thighs. When the water reaches my waist, I take the plunge.

It's so cold, it burns. I gasp, launching myself forward as a handful of other people flail on either side of me, all of us choking on the shock of the cold. I start swimming, a swift doggy paddle, keeping my head above water as I sip the air in short bursts, unable to gulp it down. It's so cold, I can barely feel my feet, the fizz and rush of the tide slipping over me…

But then I find my rhythm.

And the last three years fall away.

The shouts and calls around me fade into the background and it's just me and the sea. I start a steady breaststroke, making my way in an arc with the others, all of us circling the safe confines of the beach. For the first time in years, I'm free. Truly, exhilaratingly free. Not just my limbs and blood and bones, but my mind. All that exists is the tug of the waves, the salt in the water, buoying me along, and the gentle whoosh of my breath. In, out. In, out. I'm flying.

My body adjusts, the shock of the cold receding until I'm almost warm. The air around my cheeks and ears is colder as I cut along the edge of the beach. Why don't I do this every day? Why can I not feel this pure, meditative detachment in my own life? My toes snag on a pebble and I glance up to find I'm nearing land. With a wrench, I find my footing and lift myself up, out of the water. The cold nips at my skin, tiny needles a sharp contrast to the fire in my blood. I hop out, laughing and breathing fast as I make my way back to Naomi, a stack of blankets at her side.

'That was amazing!' I say, grabbing one to wrap it around myself. I can't stop grinning. My elation knows no bounds. 'What have I been doing with my life?'

Naomi laughs and hands me a mug of mulled wine. 'Beats spreadsheets and social media, right?' she says with a wink. 'Happy Christmas, girl. Chin-chin.'

I sip on the mulled wine, the heat and spices warming my chest. Turning around to face the sea, the pebbled beach is awash with flailing limbs and shining eyes. I want to do this every year. This should be a tradition, me and James, bowling down to Cornwall to sprint into the freezing tide—

I pull myself up short. But what if... what if it's too late? What if we are past the point of making traditions, and plans and the thousand small ways our lives have meshed into one over the years? I take another drink of the mulled wine, the cold suddenly seeping deep into my bones. What if this day is our final chance?

I'm shaking. The cold of the sea and the winter have permeated every part of me, curving around the marrow of my bones to make my teeth chatter and clack. I finish the last dregs of the mulled wine, thank Naomi and start to walk back to the Range Rover, and my pile of dry clothes. I'm picturing roaring fires, hot chocolate and thick wool socks when a voice cuts through my daydream.

'Diana?'

I blink, noticing a man standing a few feet away, wrapped in his own tartan blanket, Santa hat plonked on his head. He's guarded, face shadowed and uncertain, with grey hair and stubble lining his jaw. And I remember. He was in the pub, the first time I was Diana for the day. He brought me – *her* – that drink, raised his own glass across the bar in a toast. 'You never did like the Christmas Day dip, love. Didn't think I'd see you here again.'

I guess who this is immediately. Why he bought me a drink in the pub. It's the way his gaze is sharp as a razor, the tilt of his nose, the shape of his eyes. 'Dad,' I breathe, the sound scraping up like a sigh from somewhere deep within this body. From the same place that wanted so desperately to leave, then the snap of loss, like a shattered bone when I read back through those messages on Diana's phone. Of course, they were from him.

He scratches his chin, pointing at a group on the other side of the beach. 'It's good to see you, Di. Been a fair while, never expected...' He stops, shaking his head. Then his gaze drifts away as he points to his friends some distance away, as though needing to focus on something else. Anything but this moment with his daughter. 'We all made a pact, me and the boys, after... well, you know. Twice a week, meet for a swim in the sea, no matter the weather. Even if we only go in up to our knees. Get in there, swear our heads off and hop down to the pub after for a swift one.'

I nod and smile at his group of friends, who are eyeing us carefully. As if I am some mare that might bolt. I don't know how to *be* around Diana's dad. It's clear they don't see each other much, or really speak. What happened that drove them apart? I hope it wasn't all me and my relentless need to work, dragging Diana along with me. That song. The sense of loss needles me. I need to know if it has anything to do with this. Because Diana's life choices are beginning to look just like my own.

'Listen, we're heading down the King's Arms in a bit. Maybe you can persuade your friends to go too? We can talk.'

'I'd like that,' I say without thinking, the piercing sadness of this reunion catching in my chest. I really don't think they know each other anymore at all. If this is what it looks like when Diana is turning into me, then I don't much like it. Or myself right now. There really isn't any balance. It's all so toxic.

'Great. See you in a bit, love,' he says, taking a few steps away.

He hesitates, working words around in his mouth, chewing on them to spit them out. But I see him swallow them back down. 'You look good, Di. The sea suits you. Just like, well. Just like her.'

I watch him trudge across the grey pebble beach to his own group, all old men who clap each other on the back, passing a hip flask around to warm them. They trail in a line off the beach and Diana's dad looks back at me. He doesn't smile, doesn't blink. Almost as if I am someone else entirely.

'Hey!' Kian taps my arm and I spin to find everyone getting changed under blankets, shuffling around to pull on jumpers and jeans. 'We're having a quick game of rounders to warm up. A few of the locals are organising it. You in?'

I check around, searching for James, and spot him tugging on a sock, hopping on one leg, and grin. 'Sure.'

'Great! That makes… yeah, just enough for two teams. Field or bat?'

'Oh, bat,' I say, sizing up the rest of the group. My competition. 'Definitely bat.'

I quickly change, taking my place behind the first batter. My heart stutters when I see it's James, roped in by Kian. The fielders have fanned out around the four posts, ready to catch the ball and reach the post before the batter. I hop up and down, joining in as everyone shouts, 'Come on! Give it some welly!'

Hallie holds the ball, sizing him up, and throws it underarm. It flashes, falling towards James as he swings back the bat—

'Hit!' I yell as he stands there, watching it. 'Drop the bat! Drop the bat!'

He chucks me the bat with a whoop, launching himself towards the first post, his competitive streak roaring to life.

I hop up and down, cheering him on as he hits first, then second, the fielders finally plucking the ball out of a gungy patch of seaweed…

'Stop!' I shout, waving my arms. 'Stop on third!'

He does a theatrical feet-first slide across the pebbles, crashing into the blanket we're using as third post, seconds before the fielder reaches it with the ball. It's Kian, and he's laughing, clapping James on the back as he hops to his feet. I get in position, the spark of competition flaring inside me. I love games like this. I love the anticipation, the adrenalin, the split seconds of luck as you swing back the bat…

It cracks, the sound echoing across the beach, the bat connecting perfectly. I whoop, rushing for first post, then second, flying as fast as I can over the pebbles. I see a fielder, Natalie, streaking for third post and I run past her, charging for fourth.

'Home run! Home run!' James yells, clapping at fourth. I pick up my pace, laughing, and hurtle into him, gripping his arms to steady myself.

'I did it!' I breathe, as my lungs catch fire, struggling to gulp down enough air. James is laughing too, still holding my arm and as I look up at him, grinning, his face suddenly tightens.

'Eva?'

I freeze. The beach, the rounders game, everything falls away. And it's just me and him in this moment. 'James,' I say, looking up at him, wanting, *needing* him to realise. That it's me, that it's the me of before. That we can get back to us, that this proves it. He stumbles, our gazes locking and my heart picks up a faster beat, warming me against the winter chill. I reach out, my fingertips grazing his.

'Eva…' he says again, softly, tentatively. And I realise it's no longer a question. My breath flutters in my throat as he leans forward. His mouth merely inches from mine. So close I could close the space between us and kiss him, ever so lightly. For a weighted heartbeat, I nearly do it. I nearly press myself into him, allowing his warmth, his touch to ignite this moment. To burn everything away and for it to just be us.

Then he shakes his head, as if clearing water. He blinks, stepping back, a flush creeping up his neck. And I see him reel himself back in as the sound of the beach and the game around us steadily rises like a tidal wave. Sweeping our moment away.

He claps me on the back, not quite meeting my eyes. 'I swear you looked just like her, Diana. We used to play this on the green at uni and for a moment… for a moment you sounded just like her too. So strange. Sorry, I didn't mean—'

'It's all right,' I say, catching my breath. Concealing my disappointment that we didn't really share this. That it wasn't the real me playing this game with him, sharing our victory on this grey pebbled beach. But this is what we're missing. Moments like this, moments that take us back to times we weren't so weighed down and caught up in other things. 'It's really all right.'

Chapter 27

As we drive to the pub I can't shake the almost-moment with James. I wonder if I would have broken this cycle, like a spell, if I had only reached out, finding his mouth with my own. I brush my fingers across my lips, imagining the kiss that could have been as I stare out the window. Trying to turn my thoughts elsewhere, away from that moment we nearly shared.

The image of Diana's dad filters in, how there's something there between Diana and him that I'm missing. Perhaps I should speak with him again so that I can connect the dots. Naomi doesn't take much persuading to stop off at the King's Head en route. The others pile out to join me; Hallie and Kian, Natalie and John. James stays by the car, forcing a smile as he tells everyone to carry on without him. That he's going back to try and get Eva out to join us. I bite my lip, wondering if I should persuade him to stay, to have some fun. That knowing how I was before all this, it's unlikely I'll leave the room. But I'm swept into the pub with everyone else and he gets back into the car with Naomi. Back to Penhallow, back to me.

A blast of heat greets our little group, instantly relaxing me. I step forward into the hubbub of chatter and activity, narrowly avoiding a waitress holding two brimming bowls of fragrant beef stew and soda bread.

'So sorry!' I say, holding out a hand to steady her. But she's already swerved, ducking under a wooden lintel and walked into a dining room. There's a bar in front of me, a roaring log fire to the left and dark wood tables and chairs scattered in clumps across the flagstone floor. A couple of dogs are sprawled in front of the fire, their tails lazily thumping the floor. They look like retrievers, maybe lab crosses with their sandy fur and dopey, content faces. I cross the floor, reaching down to run my hand over their heads and I am rewarded with an extra tail thump or two.

'Diana, what will it be?' Hallie calls over, smiling. I glance up, noting the slight flush to her cheeks, the way she clutches her bump. My heart lurches and I stand, making my way back to the bar. I wonder if she's feeling nauseous after that car ride. She doesn't show it.

'I'll take a half of the local ale, whatever it is,' I say, joining her to peer at the taps. The brass is gleaming, the bar smooth and polished with beer mats dotted along to soak up the spills. They advertise a local cider press, with a lime-green snake peering up from a red background.

'Don't touch that one, whatever you do.' Hallie laughs, poking her finger at the beer mat in front of her. 'Lost a whole night a couple of years ago to the stuff! Lethal.'

I laugh back, linking my arm through hers without thinking. The press of her arm against mine sends my heart lurching again and I scramble for something to say. To fill the sudden, Hallie-shaped void inside me that I wish was still alive and well with everything that makes us a pair.

'Did Eva not want to join everyone today?' I ask lightly, avoiding eye contact. I sound like I'm snooping.

Hallie hesitates, clearing her throat and frowning slightly. I loosen my arm from hers and look at her, searching her features for even a glimpse of care or affection. 'I think she wanted to press on for a bit this morning. Said to James she would join us later. Anyway...' She shrugs, the quick smile she points at me doing nothing to warm her tense eyes. 'We'll see whether she actually does or not. I suppose you know more than me how well her shop launch is going.'

'Didn't you two... used to be close?' I ask, picking up my freshly poured drink to sip. It's rich and full, with a hint of bitterness. Just what I wished for after the freezing sea water.

'We used to be like sisters,' Hallie says quietly, the words rushed out in a huff of breath. 'I'm not so sure anymore.'

I take another sip of my drink, the words thudding in my chest. *Used to be.* Not anymore, not in Hallie's eyes. How have I left us to drift so far apart? 'You could find your way back. She's swamped, you know. She just needs to be reminded—'

'Look,' Hallie says, fixing her best hostess smile on over her teeth. 'You're a sweet person, I can see that. You're considerate. But Eva... she's driven. Beyond driven, she's fixated on this goal she's chasing, and she's shoved all of us aside to reach it. Even her husband. It's not just about what happened... it's a pattern. She can't seem to break out of it.' Hallie presses the back of her hand to her forehead, smile faltering. 'I'm speaking out of turn. You're the last person I should...'

'It's fine,' I manage to choke out. My throat is closing, tears threatening to rise up, to spill down my heated cheeks... I take a breath, focusing on a point on the other side of the pub.

Trying to detach myself from all this. 'There's no one closer to her than me right now.'

Hallie laughs abruptly. 'Yes. Don't we all know it.' She raises her drink to me, braces my arm with her hand then turns away. I watch as she weaves through the throng, Kian's face lighting up as she reaches him.

That would have been my place, over there with them both. But instead, I'm stuck in Diana's body and powerless to paper over the cracks in my life as they grow ever wider. Gripping my glass tightly, I breathe deeply, the ache of loneliness filling my chest. I can't move forward, but neither can I go back. I'm stuck. James was right. I'm stuck in this loop, spiralling further and further away from my life, and I have no way of getting free.

I finish my drink standing at the bar, alone. Trying not to glance over at Hallie and Kian with everyone else. Or at the group of friends across from me, huddled around a table next to the fire, white and grey hair gleaming over their creases and wrinkles and smiles. Laughing as though this is the first day of their lives, and they have an endless abundance of days ahead of them. A lump sticks in my throat and I shudder, the cold of the sea still sloshing around my chest. It's time to go. There's nothing more I can do or learn here, I'm only torturing myself with the things I cannot mend. I hoped to find Diana's dad here, but he's not with this group of men sat across from me, or anywhere else I can see in the pub. I decide to try and call a taxi outside, get back to Diana's lonely room at Penhallow and curl up with the curtains drawn.

But then I catch sight of him. Diana's dad. He's in the dining room section where the waitress walked through to earlier. He's with the same group as on the beach, all of them holding pints and chatting, nursing full bellies of stew and soda bread. The empty bowls and plates are being cleared away, a small team of waiters and waitresses gliding back and forth. He's watching me. Or rather, he's watching Diana, his daughter. I smile and raise my hand, and he raises his back. Would Diana want this? For me to go over there and talk to him? Maybe they fell out. Or maybe he was a crappy dad and she hot-footed it out of this county the first second she could.

But somehow, I doubt it. I can feel the weight of unsaid words stirring under Diana's skin and without thinking, I propel myself forward, crossing the bar to his table.

'Mind if I sit?' I ask, indicating a dark wooden chair next to him.

He sits bolt upright, a sudden spark dancing behind his eyes. 'Be my guest.'

I get myself settled, smiling around at the group as Diana's dad introduces me. I note the guarded looks, the careful shuffle as they give us some space. Diana's dad has talked about the relationship he had with his daughter with these people – or lack thereof. I'm sure of it.

'So what's new, buttercup?' he says, keeping his tone light. But there's an edge of steel and brittle nerves underneath, which I pick up on immediately. I've learned how to read people since walking the floors of trade fairs, feeling out suppliers to see what they are prepared to part with. The small tells that seal a deal, the imperceptible shifts in body language and voice. But apparently, I'm tone deaf to the needs and wants of the people in my inner circle. Including Diana.

'Not much…' I say, tucking a strand of hair behind my ear.

'Just here with my boss, working on a big project. I got stuck… the snow.'

'Well, here's to you!' he says, taking a gulp of ale and wiping his mouth. 'Will you introduce your boss to your old man?'

I smile despite myself, his accent is so thick, I only just follow the words. 'Maybe. If there's time before we head back. We don't… we're not close work colleagues. She decided to stay behind today, catch up on some stuff.'

'Well, don't go getting any ideas from that one! Christmas is important, Di. It's a time for people we love. Not work. Leave the other fifty-one weeks of the year for that!'

'Yes,' I say, blinking. I can't quite meet his gaze. It needles me, as if he's speaking directly to me, somehow.

I draw in a breath, wondering if I should take the leap, reveal something real. Not about Diana, but about myself. Because maybe I should hear what he has to say. There's a hesitance, my heart thumps quickly, but I take the plunge anyway. 'Actually, er… Dad, I've sort of buried myself in work lately. I can't seem to quite… I don't know.'

His face instantly falls, his hand reaching out to grasp mine. His palm is warm and comforting, the touch sends a jolt through my skin, right to the bitter centre of my heart. It's not something I'm familiar with, having a dad that cares like this. It was always Gran who took that role. Forever Gran who stepped in, catching my hand to fold me into her warmth. 'Oh, sweetheart.'

'It's OK.' I sniff, because that's what we're meant to say. It's OK. It's all right. It is what it is. But my own heartache; Gran dying so suddenly, the miscarriage, the weight of it that I've been balancing on my shoulders for so long presses down. Tears smart in my eyes, blurring the happy scene of the pub around me. I blink furiously, shaking my head. Diana's dad's hand tightens around my own. He doesn't want this for his daughter. That's all. This isn't about me. Or Gran. Or my own anxiety.

'Let it out,' he says softly. 'Sometimes it's the easiest way. Burying yourself in work isn't the answer, is it? When your mum—' He frowns suddenly, a shadow forming then dissipating like mist. 'When your mum got sick, I bottled it up. Does no good, does it? You know that. Can't run for ever from our own skin. And now she's not here… well. I can't tell you how much you looked like her on that beach today. It was like looking back twenty years. And Di… I know it hit you hard. Don't… don't try to deal with it alone.'

I blink, the last puzzle piece of Diana falling into place, forming a picture I can look at. It *was* Diana's mother Sarah was talking about earlier. The same grief as when I listened to the Coldplay song twists in my chest. It was her mum who died. Her mum was ill and now she's drowning herself in work to escape it. To try to move past it. She's distanced herself, throwing up granite walls around her heart.

Just like me.

Chapter 28

It all makes sense now. Diana's estrangement from her dad, her reluctance to return to Cornwall for the holidays. The way Sarah is so guarded and unsure around her. The reason for Diana wanting to drive me down here must have been to visit her mum's grave. To say Happy Christmas to her. And maybe even take that step and close the distance between her and her dad. A bitter knot forms at the back of my throat as I realise how much I've overlooked. Or how much I've chosen not to notice.

There was a catalyst, an event so huge and life-altering that she swerved left instead of right and now she works for me. She's fighting tooth and claw to get ahead, always striving, always yearning. Because someone, one of the pillars in her life, is no longer there to hold her up. I know what that is.

I *know* what that is.

I take a deep, shuddering breath and nod. 'You're right. It's no good at all to bottle it all up. It's horrible and sad and it's made me angry every damn day since.'

'Those feelings will eat away at you, Di,' he says, releasing my hand from his to pick up his pint. The absence of it leaves me cold and I want to grasp it again. To feel the warmth and love from a parent that desperately cares. I only ever had that from Gran. And it's gone for ever now.

'How did you cope with… with everything?'

'Well as you know, I didn't at first.' He smiles sadly. 'I didn't at all. All those years, the chemo, the surgery… I wanted it all to get better. I didn't check on you, I was so focused on her and only her. I'm still mad at myself for not seeing what *you* needed. It's the biggest regret of my life.'

'It's OK.'

He laughs. 'There you are, you said it again. And it means it's really not OK, doesn't it?' He takes a gulp of his drink and sets it back on the table. 'But anyway, for what it's worth, here's my top tip, sweetheart. Something I've learned from my own mistakes. Talk about it. Pick up the phone and talk. Doesn't have to be about the why or the what of it, you can even chat about the rain. But talk. And slowly, it'll start to make sense to you.'

'You're very wise,' I say, smiling up at him. I tuck his words away for later. Knowing I might need them in the days and weeks to come. Knowing I could have done with them three years ago. 'She meant so much,' I say, picturing Gran. 'She was my everything. I didn't realise how much I needed her until… she wasn't there anymore.'

Diana's dad nods, allowing me the space to voice some of my muddled thoughts. The ones I haven't known how to voice with Hallie or James. He sits and he listens, patiently, calmly. And eventually, I talk myself into silence and look at him. There are ghosts in his eyes. He's haunted still. Just like me, just like Diana. It catches in my throat, making my chest ache. Does this grief ever stop burning? Does it ever go away?

It's painful, seeing this person who clearly loves Diana so much give all his energy to her – to *me* – without a thought of taking a single thing back for himself. If she's built a wall between them, he knows this could be the last conversation they have in years. I can see it, that twisted agony shifting out of sight behind his eyes. This could be the last time, and he is patiently telling her how to rebuild herself. Without asking to see her, hear from her or making it about him. My heart grows so big, expanding inside my ribs to the point I can't breathe. How can she turn away from this? All this unconditional, selfless love? It's what I lost when Gran died. But she still has it, right here.

'You better get back to your boss,' he says, fixing a smile over his teeth. 'Sounds like a big deal, this work project. I'm so proud of you. Your mum would be too.'

I can't speak. He's letting Diana go, just like that, without a thought for himself or his own needs. I nod and scrape my chair back.

I want to say more, to spill all the things rumbling inside me, to watch them tumble from my mouth and feel that release and calm I'm desperate for. But that's up to Diana. Not me. This is her life, not mine. But now I know, I can change things for her. I can make sure she doesn't become like me. And I can take this advice and change myself.

Naomi picks us up an hour later, all of us piling into her Range Rover. This day has gone so differently to the last time I was Diana. And I'm glad of it. Glad I took a chance and stepped away from my laptop. Because it will still be there tomorrow, and the next day. But I'm not sure if these people will be.

'Oh no…' Hallie says as we pull into the driveway of Penhallow. I look up and my insides turn cold. There, standing on the driveway, is… me. And James. Our faces twisted in an argument.

I reach for the door handle as Naomi pulls to a stop, swinging my legs to step out.

'I wouldn't get involved,' Kian says, shuffling out of the other door. Hallie, Natalie and John quickly move past them into the house but Kian stops, crossing his arms and shaking his head as he stares at them. At James and Eva arguing just a few feet away. Kian's right, I shouldn't get involved. I'm not meant to.

I move around the car to stand next to him, watching in horror as we have the biggest fight of our marriage. We have always avoided public displays, believing them distasteful and attention-seeking. But apparently that has gone out the window today. This is bigger than decorum, or embarrassment. This is the fight that could end it all.

But I'm trapped, not in the fight, not in the weight of words I cannot take back. I'm trapped on the outside, looking in. And there's nothing I can do to reverse it all.

'I asked you for two days, three, tops!' James shouts, holding out a hand for emphasis. 'How is that so hard for you?'

'You're being completely unreasonable—'

'I'm being unreasonable?'

'You don't support me, you're always judging me—'

'I just want *you*, Eva!' James sighs in frustration, stepping in circles as Eva folds her arms and scowls up at him. She opens her mouth to keep going, her words twisting her expression. I look between them, back and forth, the pain radiating from them. After the rounders game on the beach only hours ago, there's now such a sharp contrast in James.

I rub my hands up and down my arms, chest seizing up. I can't believe what we have become. Suddenly, there isn't enough breath in my body. My heart, my lungs, my very bones are aching and I have to get out of this day, Diana's body. I can't breathe.

'Whoa there… easy,' Kian says, catching me under my elbow. He peers at my face, his own features drawing into a frown. 'We better get you inside.'

He steers me towards the heavy oak front door, away from the heated words this Eva will never be able to take back. My fingertips are tingling, sparks dancing at the corners of my eyes and I wonder if I'm having another panic attack. Last time, James held me on the bathroom floor until I could make sense of the world again. Until the cold tile, the steady whoosh of the shower and the gathering steam sharpened around me. Until I could feel his arms, anchoring me. Until I could hear the words he whispered, how he loved me, how I was safe. Always safe. That was just after the bleeding. Just after Gran died.

But this time I'm untethered. Weightless.

Eva is next to the car, the door open at her side, but James is blocking the view of her face. He has his back to me and Kian, his whole frame huge and tense under a thick brown jacket. I want to reach for him, spin him around and tell him I don't mean the things I'm saying. This Eva has taken the wrong turn and forgotten what she cares about. I want to tell him that she isn't the real me anymore. That I remember the why of us, how we are meant to be together. How we are twined together, him and me, that we are always meant to be. That I love him with my whole being.

But I'm stuck, staring at my marriage falling apart in the cage of Diana's body. And if my assistant intervenes, I know it'll drive an even bigger wedge between us.

I'm powerless.

Kian exhales a breath at my side, hesitating before taking me inside the entrance hall. I glance up at his storm-clouded eyes, the tight tick in his jaw. He hates this. I remember when Kian and I used to joke about how Hallie and James were better matched, and that he and I were so similar. We would be the ones to circle a party, chat to everyone, get a hit off the energy and atmosphere. Hallie and James would tuck themselves into a corner, sip quietly on their drinks and exchange a few pleasant words. Comfortable in silence, able to recharge in the quiet. How have I turned myself into everything I'm not?

James and I have always been the opposite ends of a magnet, forever attracted, forever gravitating towards each other. But now we're repelling. Gravel crunches beneath Kian's feet and he releases my elbow to take a hesitant step forward.

'Don't,' I say quietly. 'This is up to them.'

'But they're breaking up,' Kian says, the war evident on his face. Ever the placater, he wants to step in, to defuse the bombshell of our marriage. To place a steadying hand on each of our shoulders and ask us to talk this out.

And he's right. James is issuing a stream of wild ultimatums, Eva's pale face crumbling in hurt as she sweeps her body into the front seat of the car. James's hand moves to the car door, talking quieter now, gesturing with his free hand. But then the engine fires up and I'm already moving before I think it through. Before I remember that I'm here to notice, to learn. Not to interfere.

I close the distance between me and them, placing a hand on the car bumper. 'You can't go!' I say desperately and Eva's face snaps up in the car. It's so strange, seeing myself through Diana's eyes. The pinched mouth, the black smudged mascara. My hair a cloud around my cheeks. I've been crying. I'm a mess.

'Diana…' Eva sighs. 'I'll send a taxi for you. We can launch the shop together. Deal with it all together back in… back in London.'

No request, no apology. No acknowledgement that I've messed up my assistant's Christmas. Just a simple, razor-sharp focus on the business. On what I can control. Even when everything else is in flames around us, burning brilliantly. She's not even going to fight.

But I can fight.

'Stay. We can do it here. I–I can pack. We can go back inside and—'

'No!' Eva shoves her hair behind her ears, lip trembling. She glances at James, then down at the dashboard. 'It's time for me to go. This is all pointless. Like I said, I'll send a taxi.'

I look at James, the hurt, the destruction playing out in shockwaves over his features, the realisation dawning that his ultimatums are no use. That this time is the final time. And he has to follow through. 'It's over, Eva,' he says, clipped tones slicing like a knife. 'This is it. We're done. If you leave now…'

I stagger back, the snow and cold blurring at the corners, filling my vision in a steady, endless swirl. My fingertips are tingling again, my head light as cloud, as though I'm finally turning to dust.

'I'll be gone before you get back to London. I'll pack my stuff up and move out,' Eva says to James.

'One more day, Eva! Just one more—'

But the engine starts up, tyres crunch over gravel and the tenuous tether to this body snaps. The ground, the sky, this body I'm in all fall away.

Chapter 29

'It's the end, isn't it?' I manage between wracking, ceaseless sobs.

Gran's papery hand brushes my hair back from my face. It's sticking to my cheeks in salty, tear-filled clumps as I hug my knees tightly to my chest. We're back on the staircase, the bone-deep chill of the hall sinking into me. But I can't move. I'm frozen to this spot, this in-between space where it's always midnight and never the next day. I might be able to see how much Diana needs to rebuild her relationships. How Sarah has shown me it is possible to find balance. What it is to love and want with your whole heart, unguardedly like Hallie. And how Natalie loves fiercely, beautifully. I can see all this, but I'm still losing James. It's still the end of us.

'It nearly is, yes,' Gran says quietly, smoothing her hand down my arm. 'You've reached a point you can't return from this week. It's pivotal, this moment.'

I sniff, turning to look at her. 'I can't see how any of this ends well. Not the shop launch with Diana and me both still in Cornwall, or my... my marriage...' I shudder, the involuntary spasm running up my spine in a wave. 'Or me and Hallie. I haven't been paying attention, have I? Even Diana has had enough.' I deflate, leaning my forehead against my knees, picturing the secret file of emails, the way she must have been struggling silently for months. 'I don't blame her one bit.'

Gran sighs as well. 'It is a pickle, I'll give you that. Now can you see why I intervened? You're not the same woman I left on this earth three years ago. You've lost your way. You've fallen into these destructive patterns that you keep repeating, again and again. It's been hard to watch, I can tell you.'

I wipe my eyes with the corner of my sleeve, the itchy rawness of the delicate skin around them scraping against the material. On any normal day, I would already be trying to shut this down. To splash my face with cold water, towel-dry away the evidence of my tears and stare at my own dead eyes in the mirror, willing my brain to snap back in line. To focus on whatever work goal I'm chasing. Not to dwell on the past, or what I can't hope to control. To keep a lid on it. Shut it all away.

Only, I *can* control this. And I can't keep a lid on it all anymore. The last few days have shown me that. In fact, I've actively played a role in my own destruction, ignoring what was most important. And failing to nurture what would help me succeed. I want to have it all. The work life, the marriage, the small, love-filled family album, complete with snaps of weekend wanders and sunny beach holidays, ice cream dribbles down a toddler's chin. I want it so much, that family photo album, full of perfection, that my chest aches. And try as I might, burying myself in my business and endless takeaway cartons in my too-small, packed-in office, that dull thud of longing will never go away.

'What do I do now? What happens next?'

Gran bites her lip. 'You have to see everything I'm afraid, my darling.'

Instead of inspiring hope, her words fall like a curse. 'There's more?'

She nods slowly.

Then something occurs to me. 'Is this a cycle? Will I ever get out?' Panic suffuses my voice, clawing up my throat. 'Have I trapped myself here?' I picture an endless loop of days and perspectives. Not one Christmas morning, but many. Hundreds. My heart shattering over and over as I realise what it is I have created. A monster. And that monster, that person so far removed from who they once were… is me.

'There is a way out, even if you wake up tomorrow and this is finished with… know that you can still make a difference,' Gran says, gripping my arm with sudden intensity. 'But you have to listen carefully now. You know you need to change. You can see the effect you are having on the people you love most. How you push them away. But you still don't know what your next steps are. You can't see a clear path out of this maze you've created for yourself. You aren't ready to accept the things you cannot change. To move past them.'

Like the miscarriage. That's set in stone, etched on my soul in a way that will never be removed. On James's too. But I never appreciated that. Never thought about how it had affected *him*, how he might have felt as keenly as I did, when our sugar-spun dreams collapsed into ash and dust. I have to accept that I can't change what happened. It'll always be a part of us, woven through our shared past, binding us in a way we never wanted to be bound.

'If I leave here though,' I say quietly, turning to her, 'I'll never see you again.'

Her smile crinkles her eyes and she pats my hand. 'Another thing you will need to learn to let go of is me.'

A lump forms in my throat, sticky as honey. I struggle to swallow it down.

'All got a bit much, didn't it? That Christmas,' she says, shaking her head. 'My father would have called it a "testing time". Told me to have a stiff upper lip, dry my eyes and just get on with it.'

'But I did that. All of that.'

'Yes. And that's the *problem*.' Gran pats down her dressing gown pockets and fishes out two toffees, offering one to me. I accept it gratefully. We sit in silence as we open the packets, the gentle rustle of toffee wrappers calming my frantic thoughts.

'I should have talked to James more, shouldn't I? And Hallie. Even Kian.' I twist a lock of my hair around and around, winding it until it sits neatly against the side of my face. Then I smooth a few strands back from my temples, clearing my head of the stuffiness of my tears. 'I should have been more considerate to Diana. Shown her it is possible to get where I am without cutting people out of my life.'

'Not only that, you need to *celebrate* more. You are forever looking to the next thing and the next. Never turning back and stopping, seeing what you have created,' Gran says. 'Look at how far you've come! I could never have hoped to do the kind of work you do. To stretch my brain in such a satisfying way. To be the boss! But you can. You do, every day. I don't regret a lot in my life, love. But I do wish I could have had even a *fraction* of the exciting career you have. It just wasn't done when I was your age. You should talk about the miscarriage, yes. But there's so much more besides to talk about.'

'You wanted a business like mine, Gran? You never told me.'

'I was actually a secretary at an ad firm, before I had your mum,' Gran says with a twinkle. 'Most exciting place to work in London! There was a bunch of us, clacking away on typewriters, pushing our way into meetings to get our ideas on the table. There was potential, possibilities. And your granddad was so proud of me.'

I picture a different Gran to the one sitting next to me. Younger, with her famous auburn hair twisted into a chignon on the back of her head, wool jumper and plain skirt carefully pressed and fresh. Expectant, beady eyes hiding a myriad of quick little remarks and comments. If only the world had been different back then. She would have ruled it all. 'What changed?'

'I had your mum, and it was already uncommon that I hadn't left the office when I got married. It wasn't the done thing, you see.' She tuts. 'All these men and their ideas on what we are, how we should act. What we should value. It hasn't changed enough, in my opinion. There's still a lot of work to be done.' She winks at me. 'By bright sparks like you, Eva. Just takes a bit of teamwork.'

'But James and I aren't a team anymore. We're a train wreck. We can't spend one Christmas together without falling apart.'

'Then go back to before. What did you used to like doing together? Why *him*? Weren't you a good team before?'

I think back to the me and James of our late twenties. The cream cheese bagels and coffee in little artisan cafés on a Sunday morning. The Saturday paper, how I wanted the business section, and he went for travel. How I would talk about starting my own business, breaking away from my job, as I read through those articles, and he would always encourage, always listen, buying us another round of coffees so I could talk it out with him.

Then I think back to our early twenties. How we would surprise each other with spontaneous trips, weekends away at B&Bs by the seaside. How I booked train tickets to Edinburgh once and we just hopped on after work, finding a place to stay when we got there, a hotel at the edge of town that played holiday music all year round. How it rained and rained and we bought those clear plastic macs the tourists wear, posing for photos with dissolving ice cream cones and soaking clothes. How happy we were to have adventures.

We were happy at every stage, wearing our relationship in like a pair of slippers. Talking about the future, making memories we wanted to keep. So contentedly happy.

'I expect you're feeling a bit hopeless,' Gran says, straightening slightly. 'Oooh, this staircase really isn't good for my poor bum. Needs a bit of soft carpet.'

I straighten too, fresh determination filling me. I can't let what I saw today really happen. Seeing it all end with James and me on the driveway of Penhallow is the breath-stealing wake-up scream I needed.

'Am I going back to fix things this time? Really change things?'

'Not exactly... going back,' says Gran, eyeing me with something close to regret. 'Buckle up. The next bit will be the hardest.'

Chapter 30

I wake with a bitter taste at the back of my throat. Stretching, I blink and the velvet darkness wraps around me. It's before dawn, or maybe still night. A body shifts next to me and I freeze, turning my head to see the faint outline of a back and a thicket of hair. I clear my throat, reaching with my foot to find the edge of the bed, then the floor. This body feels… familiar. As I shuffle out from under the covers, I knock into the lamp on the bedside table, only just catching it before it falls. My heart swoops as I place the lamp back in its place, my fingertips brushing a phone left on the bedside table next to it. When I jab a finger at it, the screen lights up to reveal a couple with toothy grins wearing ski masks and jackets. It's a picture from four years ago.

Of me and James.

I grab the phone, dimly registering the two bars of signal. The irony of there being signal now, when it's all too late. And the date. I gasp, registering the tiny date, highlighted on the calendar app.

It's Boxing Day.

Using the light from the screen to navigate around the edge of the bed and into the bathroom, I shut the door quickly, switch on the light and stare at myself in the mirror.

'At last,' I breathe. I'm myself again. The face staring back at me in the mirror is exhausted, hair sticking out at all angles, eyes a bloodshot hue. It's odd being back, using my hands to turn on the tap, to splash water over my skin. But it's comforting. There's a lacy, delicate cobweb in the top right-hand corner of the mirror that must have formed since Christmas Eve. A spider, spindle-legged and dark, rushes under a corner, as though expecting to be flushed from its web. This tiny detail seems insignificant, but it marks the passage of time. That time has moved on from that loop of Christmases I was stuck in. I splash my skin again with the cooling water, the shock of it sharp on my face. Blinking, it wakes me up enough to feel a surge of trepidation. After the fight I witnessed between us, why am I still here? How did I end up back at Penhallow? I must have decided to stay after all. Maybe the fight I watched only yesterday eventually fizzled out; maybe that Eva chose to walk back inside with James to try to talk it out. To find a way through.

I keep going through this cycle, waking up in other bodies, but I'm not prepared to be back in my own skin. I'm facing each new day, sure that I know what I want now… but with each fresh perspective, I don't know how to get there. To change the course of the day so it falls in line with what I need and what I'm seeking. And now I'm myself again… what if I've already messed it up? A finger of cold runs down my spine. What if this is all real now?

I take a quick shower then grab a towel to wrap around myself. A door bangs outside the bathroom as I'm about to walk back into the bedroom, then through the thin walls I hear someone coming very quickly down the corridor. Dragging what sounds like a wheeled suitcase. I bolt from the bathroom, jamming my elbow painfully against the edge of the door. James isn't in the bed. By the time I reach the corridor, he's gone. Muttering, I wander back into the room, sleep still thick and cloying, clouding my head. Rubbing my elbow, I move around the room to find my side of the bed.

There's a note crumpled on the pillow.

With a jolt, I realise it's my own hastily scrawled words, my penmanship bleeding across the page. Ending everything. I scramble for the bedside lamp, switching it on to flood the room with soft light. Then I sink down on the carpet and read. It's only two paragraphs, barely enough words to end over a decade of our relationship. I accuse him of not supporting me, of having a total lack of regard for my well-being. Of not being there for me when I needed him. Of not caring enough to give me the space I deserved. He must have read it while I was in the shower and left.

I've severed us, broken us on a flimsy piece of A4 white paper with a blue Biro. I must have written it yesterday, before the fight in the driveway, and left it for James to find. So now, he must have read it. One final, horrible goodbye. Was last night the ultimate end of us?

'No, no, no…' I sigh, crumpling the page and dropping my forehead into my hands. How can I end things like this? While I've been hopping from one body to another, the real me, the Eva that's locked inside my own body, has stayed static. Buried in work. Drowning in the lies she's telling herself, never growing, never holding up a mirror and really *seeing* herself, confronting all the pain and moving past it… and this is the result. A failed marriage. A friendship cracked apart. The pieces of my life lying in jagged ruins at my feet.

It's all my fault.

In a rush, I dress, dragging my hair into a hasty bun, throw a sweater over my head and fly out of the door, softly calling his name. But I don't know where he's gone. I flutter at the staircase, deciding to check the driveway. When I step outside, the crisp air reaches under my clothes, dragging nails of frost along my skin. I shiver, wrapping my arms around myself and stare at his car. It's still here. He hasn't left Penhallow yet. I release the breath I was holding, my shoulders sagging. There's still a chance. I'll compose myself, smooth out my hair, my clothes and find him at breakfast. Yes. There has to be a way to mend this.

When I head downstairs for breakfast after making myself more presentable, everyone is packed up to leave. The breakfast table is almost silent, everyone hastily chewing on toast and taking brief bites at conversations. I sink into a chair across from Natalie as she finishes up a bowl of granola. James is the only one notably absent.

'You look like shit,' Natalie says, raising an eyebrow.

'Can we switch lives for a few weeks?' I chuckle drily, pouring myself a much needed coffee. I add a spoonful of sugar, stir and then gulp it down. 'Where are you off to next?'

'Nowhere too glamorous. Just Dad's.' She smiles sheepishly. 'Given Hallie wanted me here for Christmas, I felt like I should head over for New Year because he couldn't make it.'

'But it's in the middle of the Cotswolds. No all-night parties…'

She laughs. 'Gotta give the old man some time before I meet up with Olga in Norway. Haven't seen him in a couple of months. You know what we're like...' She shrugs. 'Thick as thieves. Family is everything.'

I pause whilst I'm buttering a slice of toast, take another sip of my coffee and glance up the table. There's Hallie, daintily nibbling on a croissant, listening avidly to Kian as he talks quietly about something I can't hear. I wonder if she's already been sick this morning. 'You are pretty close-knit, I'll give you that.'

'She's wanted a baby for so long,' Natalie says quietly, staring at her too. 'But she still sees the value in everything I do. She checks in every few days, wherever I am. Like a third parent. She doesn't have to, and she never talks about herself. Just wants to hear about where I am, what the food is like. If I've managed to get Wi-Fi long enough to post a block of Insta stories to get paid. She... she binds us together, you know?'

'She's special.'

Natalie turns to look at me. 'She *is* special. Don't you agree?'

I blink at Natalie, this boho version of Hallie with plaits and a jade bracelet. I remember what it was like to be her, even if just for a handful of hours. All that love in her heart. 'I see it. I just... I got lost. I forgot.'

Natalie sighs and nods. 'That's evident. But Hallie will always be there, you know? She's that type. It's all about family. The blood one, and the found one. She's a one and done girl. She chose you, and she's never going to move on. Even before she left for uni, I never saw her really get close to anyone. Sure, she had friends, but no one she was overly bothered about. Then as soon as she met you, click! That was it. This whole side of her emerged that we never saw before; the fun side, the chatty side. You were the catalyst for drawing her out. She would come home in the holidays full of stories of you and James and Kian. She's the same with a pair of boots, her husband, her family…'

I bite my lip, guilt prickling my chest. Hallie really is a one and done girl. And out of all the people on this planet, the many best friend candidates she could have picked at uni, she chose *me*. The girl who flitted around London, window shopping my way through life as fast as I possibly could, the polar opposite to Hallie and her quiet, contained ways. The girl who never realised what a jewel Hallie is. What I'm so close to losing. Natalie thinks I drew Hallie's true self out. But the truth is, it was the other way around. She gave me calm, she took my hand and told me I didn't need to go to every party, every event, every occasion. I could just… be. And now this whole situation, the way I've detached myself from everyone, including her, is most likely completely devastating. This isn't just about me.

'I need to repair us. I know that.'

Natalie clicks her tongue, pushing her chair back to stand up. She eyes me for a beat, rubbing her lips together, then shrugs. 'Good luck, Eva. I truly hope you find your way back to her.'

I eat my toast in silence, occasionally glancing down the table at Hallie. Even if I manage to repair things with James and get our marriage back on track, there's still my best friend. I would like to think it's not too late, that we have the kind of relationship that I can pick back up. That Natalie is right and I can somehow mend it and bind us back together in a way that is more permanent than ever. But it's clear that Hallie is almost at the point of moving on. That through my silence, my wall-building, I've hurt her very deeply. She's already grieving the loss of me and her.

With a sigh, I scrape back my chair. Now I'm back in my own

body, it's so full of pent-up, tortured energy I can hardly bear it. I feel like a Champagne bottle, one twist and I'll fizz over. Checking my phone screen, I see it's already nine o'clock. An hour until checkout. James hasn't shown for breakfast, but he has to be here somewhere. I have to find him. Because if I wake up tomorrow in my own mind and body, it'll be too late. Even now I'm not sure if I'll have another chance this Christmas, if the damage I've done is irreparable. Gran wasn't clear. So does that mean that the last loop stuck? That everyone else went for a Christmas Day dip, then came back to witness that hideous argument between James and me on the driveway? I shudder.

Summoning all my courage, I walk to the other end of the table, to where Kian and Hallie are sat. Kian looks up in surprise, his eyes instantly becoming guarded. Is it just my imagination, or does he angle his body towards Hallie?

'Kian, is James still here? I thought he would be here for breakfast. I heard him leaving the room this morning, but his car is still here and—'

'He's in our room,' Kian breaks in. He goes to say more and stops himself. 'We're planning a quick run before we all head off, I'm meeting him outside in a few minutes. You haven't got long if you need to... you know...'

I smile, covering the hurt behind my eyes. Kian is treating me like a stranger. Like his best friend's ex. Polite, distant and dismissible. My hands shake as I step back, keeping that smile on my face to paper over the cracks. 'Thanks. I only need him for a minute.'

Kian just nods. Hallie won't even look up, busying herself with her full cup of peppermint tea. Her fingers hold a slight tremor as they clutch the porcelain and it tugs at my chest.

'Hallie, can we talk when we get back to London? Meet up?'

Hallie glances up at me, then swiftly drops her gaze, staring at the teacup. 'If that's what you want.'

'It is, really, Hal…'

She sighs, looking back up to fix me with a frank stare. It's so unlike Hallie, I step back in shock. 'You'd best go and find James right now though. After yesterday.'

'Right, yes,' I stammer, taking another step back. 'Of course.' I turn to go, heat flushing my face.

Chapter 31

I don't want to have this confrontation. I want it all to be fixed and for us to be OK. I want to take a breath of frosted air, place my thoughts in order and unwind everything that's happened at Penhallow.

But I must speak to James; I don't have the luxury of time. I've ruined this Christmas for him and I cringe as I think of how we spoke to each other yesterday. We never treat each other this way. It's just not us.

I wait for him outside, the chill settling along my skin as the sun pushes through the grey and white clouds. Diana's finishing packing upstairs, waiting to drive us back. The snow has settled, the flurries less insistent. Everyone else must be getting ready to do the same after a quick breakfast to beat the traffic. I picture my own journey back to London, how I will probably pull over in some service station, hanging on to the thinnest threads of Starbucks Wi-Fi and tap restlessly on my laptop. Maybe eat a soggy breakfast roll, maybe just drink coffee. It's so miserable, it's jarring as I stand under this pleasant bowl of sky.

I shake my head. It's not the life I want, this endless chase after perfection in my work. I want to get ahead, to extend my business and reach my potential, but I don't want it to consume my every thought. Or be at the expense of everything else. I don't want it to be my only creation. It's a balance, I can see that now. One that's been tipping too far one way for far too long.

And I hope I've seen that before it's too late.

James appears, wearing a pristine white hoodie and grey joggers. 'We're not in the gym anymore.' I laugh, trying to make a joke. James toes the gravel on the driveway with his trainer, my attempt at lightening the mood falling hopelessly flat.

'It's the only thing I packed.' He shrugs, stretching one arm over his ear, focusing on the far horizon. 'Kian's meeting me in a sec. Is this going to take long? I'm pretty sure you said everything you needed to say.'

'No. Not long at all,' I say, wincing at his tone. Gathering my thoughts. I bunch my hands into fists, watching him look anywhere but at me. Like I'm no longer *his* person. The one he chose, above all others.

'What happened yesterday—'

'You mean when you screamed at me in the middle of the driveway?'

So that *is* the loop that stuck. Despite everything I learned, everything I did, that's still the outcome of us. I swallow as a flash of anger glints in the muddy depths of his eyes. His jaw, his whole being, is tense and edgy. I reach out, brush a hand against his arm and he recoils. It sends a jolt thundering through my chest, leaving a jagged hole in its wake. Is this really going to be the end of us?

'I was wrong. I'm… I'm sorry. Please, don't be like this.'

'Be like what?' he says, shaking his head. 'What did you

expect? We barely see each other for weeks, and then the only thing, the *one thing* I ask of you is to be here. For us. For our friends. And you behave like *that*?'

'Please, James… I didn't leave yesterday, did I? I know we argued. I know I've been too focused on work, on the shop—'

'I don't give a shit about the bloody shop!'

I gasp, stepping back. 'What?'

'It's all you ever talk about, and that's only when you actually bother to come home. I swear if you could, you would have set up a bed in that office of yours. You only come home to sleep and shower.'

'That's not true.'

'Isn't it?' James is almost shouting now. Bracing his hands on the back of his head, his eyes snap to mine and suddenly his whole focus, all his rage, is on me. And I can hardly breathe.

'We can get through this,' I say, voice shaking. 'We can, we can mend…'

'Or we can just admit defeat,' he says quietly, closing his eyes. 'I can't keep fighting for you. I don't even know what I'm fighting *against* anymore.'

I open my mouth, but no words fall out. My whole being is twisted up into poisoned knots, choking every thought, every word. This… this is too much. Not this. I can't lose him too. I can't have failed at this, after everything else.

'I love you, James. I really do. I've been so wrong, I can see that now. That note means nothing. I'll burn it. Tear it up.' I grab for his hand. 'We can rebuild. We can get past this.'

Footsteps sound on the gravel behind us, pausing a few feet away. I turn my head, hiding the tears, the pain tearing my world to ribbons.

Kian clears his throat awkwardly. 'You ready, James? If you guys... need a minute...'

I look at James, my hand hovering over my mouth, trying to hold myself in. Trying to keep myself breathing. But his face is flint. There's nothing there of the person I love. It's like a light that has burned so bright for so long has finally gone out.

He barks a short laugh, staring at the sky. 'No. No, we're done here. It's too late.'

I can't move, can't think as I watch them both start their run. As he disappears over a stile, jogging up the field opposite the driveway, I gasp. Drawing in a deep, painful breath that burns in my chest. Here, at Penhallow, full of ghosts and haunting memories, this is where my marriage breaks apart.

This is the end.

I don't know how I get back upstairs. The world has tilted sideways and as my shaking fingers grasp a hairbrush, a jumper, a notebook, it's all I can do to pile them up in the suitcase. All I ever seem capable of is failure. With a clutch of maxed out credit cards in my purse and a wage bill to pay in a few days, I need cash flow. I need to launch my shop and get some customers through the door. They'll say I was headstrong, over-confident. That I rushed and didn't keep an eye on the details if I can't keep up with all the bills. If I burn out. I poured so much of myself into it, and it was never enough. And now Gran has left me with all this... like the aftermath of an explosion.

I sniff, more tears burning a path down my cheeks. There are far too many details that I should have been paying more attention to. Namely my marriage. James. I gasp, a wave of pain clawing up my ribs, and it's all I can do to kneel on the floor and breathe. I gulp down air in panicked sips, pushing a hand against my chest.

Some part of me knows what this is. What is coming. Like a part of my mind is locked away from the rest of me, watching at a distance as I crash. Dark specks appear at the corners, crowding like bees around me. I try to do what I'm meant to do, I push my fingers into the carpet. I feel the wiry strands, scratching gently against my fingertips. I smell the scent of James's aftershave, still clinging to the room. I focus on my breathing. I focus on what I can control.

Gradually, I anchor myself.

My hands are tingling as I finish packing and I can't bear to look in the mirror when I splash water on my face. I'm detached from this sequence of events. All I can think about is moving from one thing to the next, controlling each one of my movements as I zip my suitcase up and turn to face the bedroom door. I take a deep, shaky breath, locking my spine as straight as I can. I will walk out of here. I will leave Penhallow and this holiday season and I will not fall apart until I'm home. Back in London. But I have to make it back there. I have to.

I open the door and walk straight into Hallie.

'Whoa,' I say, staggering back and bump painfully into my suitcase. Hallie blinks at me, registering the suitcase, then my face. It's still puffy, my eyes bloodshot. There's nothing I can do to hide that.

'We need to talk.'

I've wanted this. Dreaded it, but tried to make it happen whilst I was in her body, controlling her movements through her day. But now…

'Hal, I-I can't. I want to, you have to believe me, but can we do this when we get back to—'

'You've broken up, haven't you?' Her whole face tenses, eyes widening. 'Is this it?'

I know what she means. She isn't asking about me and James. She's asking about *us*. Me and Hal. I take a deep breath, manoeuvring around her into the corridor. The door bangs closed, cutting me off from the moment just before, the moment my heart shattered. When the panic swallowed me whole. I bite my lip, trying to rally my scattered thoughts.

'No. It's not. It's absolutely not the end. I'll call you. I'll… I'll message. Set up a date. But… I have to go. I can't stay here…'

I don't tell her it's strangling me, the failures, the past. How the only way I can carry on treading water is to bury myself in my work. To surround myself with spreadsheets and conversion rates, brand guidelines and shop shelves. To disappear in the rumble of consumerism. To hope it heals that part of myself that's lost. That I know I should have held on to James and her.

That I know it's too late.

'You're running away,' she says, the words twisting in her mouth. 'After everything… I hoped.' She swallows, blinking back tears. 'I hoped we could get back to each other. You won't call. You always say that, but you never do.'

I stare at her in despair, a sound like the wind whistling in my ears.

I can't bear the weight of another heartbreak as it cracks my chest open. I nod, fresh tears obscuring my vision, filling my senses like poison. I can't speak. I have to get out. In a rush, I extend the handle on the suitcase, running down the corridor.

'I'm sorry,' I gasp. 'I will call. I promise. I just can't do this here. Not now. It's too much.' I can barely see, the tears are coming again, the panic flooding my lungs, clawing at me—

'Wait! Eva, wait!'

As I trip down the stairs, one, two at a time, the suitcase running away from me as I hit the last tread, I'm dimly aware of movement, of Hallie rushing behind me. But I can't stop. I can't fall apart here, in the middle of Penhallow. I'm not sure I'll ever be able to pick myself back up again. I reach for the front door handle, readying myself for the welcome cool of the moors—

A thump sounds at my back. I freeze, turning around to find the unthinkable. Hallie, tumbling down the stairs. It happens in slow motion, the sound of each tread she hits ricocheting around the entrance hall.

I am powerless.

When she stops at the bottom, everything goes very, very still. Then the world speeds up.

I run to her. I think I call her name. I'm down on my knees, brushing back her hair, my trembling fingers finding the pulse at her throat.

Still breathing.

I can barely speak, barely form words as Natalie lands on her knees beside me.

'Don't… don't move her!' I choke out. 'It could be her spine.'

Natalie sobs, saying her name over and over.

Hallie garbles something, a whisper on the edge of her breath, and Natalie arcs her body over her, as if she can protect her. As though she can shield her from this.

I rush to the kitchen, grabbing the corded phone attached to the wall. It's only meant to be used in an emergency, and this is it. I can't rely on my patchy mobile network for such an important task. My fingers punch the numbers and I wait for him to pick up. The one person who needs to be here. Who has to fix this. It's a lifetime before he answers, the minutes stretching to hours, days in my mind. Then his cool tone, his heavy breathing from their run. Somehow, my voice comes out steady.

'Kian? Can you hear me? It's… it's about Hallie. Don't freak out… but she's had an accident.'

Chapter 32

'You need to get back here.'

Kian inhales a sharp breath, the sound crackling down the phone line. 'What kind of accident?'

He listens as I stutter out how she fell down the stairs. I repeat that she's breathing, that we are making sure she doesn't move. Then he abruptly cuts in, telling me to call an ambulance, before hanging up.

I dial 999 and the person on the other end starts reeling off instructions. I don't know how I get through that call, and when I return to the entrance hall, I keep one hand stroking Hallie's hair. But I need to know she still exists. That her heart still beats.

It doesn't take long for them to reach us. Natalie throws the door open, hovering on the driveway, pacing back and forth between us, then the gravel. I can't move away from Hallie. I bend down next to her, murmuring that she'll be fine. That the ambulance is nearly here. To hold on.

'Kian and James are back!' Natalie calls from the driveway. 'And… yep! The ambulance!'

I release a breath. The ambulance must have been nearby, on some shout. We're lucky. The nearest ambulance could have been miles away, it's a vast moorland. I should know after that night driving around in Diana's body, fighting back panic and despair.

'Eva rang 999,' Natalie says, voice high-pitched and scared.

Kian circles her, heading straight for Hallie, and I step back, giving them space. He cradles his body around hers, careful not to move her neck or spine. We've all heard the horror stories. She turns her face to his as James gets through the front door. He stutters to a halt, eyes widening. I catch John backing away from Hallie too. He's got his hands over his face, eyeing her like he's scared. I blink. Why are they all so unnerved? If she can move her head, surely she hasn't broken anything vital? Then I get a good look at Hallie. The dark arc around her. It must have spread whilst I focused on her breathing, her face. My heart falters, sparks forming before my eyes.

The blood.

I take another step back, not wanting to get too close to them. I don't know what to do, where to stand. All I know is that Hallie is hardly moving, pale and clammy. And her voice is a thin, barely there reed. Like she's already floating far away. James is a few feet to the side, shoulders hunched, arms crossed. I suddenly realise how cold this entrance hall is, so cold that I'm shaking. Should I get towels? A blanket for her? I don't know what to do.

The ambulance draws up in a spray of gravel and urgency and I stagger towards it, watching as two paramedics step out. A man and a woman, she looks young and fresh-faced, a wash of blonde hair tied back across her shoulder. But he's older, greying at the temples and he's already sweeping the scene, assessing.

As soon as he sees Hallie on the floor, he reels off a string of commands. 'Danni, get the stretcher ready, get the bag, scoop and the neck brace.'

Danni turns around, moving with certainty to the back of the ambulance. The male paramedic steps straight to Hallie and kneels beside her. 'Hello, I'm Mike. Looks like you've taken a tumble, yeah? Can you talk to me a bit? Tell me your name?'

Kian drops back onto his heels, watching Mike's eyes as they dart over Hallie, as though there's some checklist he's working through. Hallie stutters through her name and what happened, all the while getting paler. Weaker. The young female paramedic, Danni, gently asks us all to move back as she sets up on the other side of Mike. I step back with John and Natalie, hovering in the doorway to the lounge. I can't take my eyes off her. All the blood.

'I'm going to check your blood pressure, OK, Hallie?' Mike says, picking up her wrist, attaching and inflating a cuff of some kind on her bicep, keeping his eye on a dial as it whirls. I hold my breath. A chill creeps across my skin and I shiver, wrapping my arms around myself. This isn't happening. It can't be. We were just here, all of us, and Hallie was fine. What if I hadn't been rushing? If only she hadn't followed, if only we hadn't…

I gulp down a breath, pulling my arms around myself. None of this can be real. It's a nightmare.

Mike loops a stethoscope around his neck, plugging it into his ears and holding it against her chest. He frowns, focusing on the beat of Hallie's heart. I wonder if it's faint. If he strains to hear it, or if it's fast, too fast, galloping off a cliff. I can't watch. But at the same time, I can't look away.

'Blood pressure eighty over forty,' Mike mutters to the young woman, Danni, tapping the dial that's clipped to the cuff on her bicep. She pinches her lips together, noting it down quickly on a chart. I can't take my eyes off the pencil, the rapid scratching as he says some other numbers. Her heart rate is 120. It seems fast. I can't remember, did I learn that at school? Or on *Grey's Anatomy*? I want to turn to James, hold his hand in mine, feel a slip of the familiar in this world that no longer makes sense. But with a jolt I remember we aren't together anymore. There's no longer an *us* to draw comfort from.

Danni lowers her pencil. It's blue. One of those stubby, standard issue ones that's getting soft and rounded at the end. All I can see is a loose thread on the arm of her uniform, which is forest green and a bit bulky – I wonder if she has to wash it herself. If this is all just a standard day for her. If she sees arcs of blood like this all the time. Why am I thinking about that now? Mike unhooks the stethoscope from his ears, placing it neatly back in the bag. Every movement is practised, precise. I can't stand it.

Then they are moving Hallie onto a stretcher, using the scoop which they slide under her in two halves, clipping it together before gently moving her. She whimpers and I flinch, clenching the teeth in my jaw until they ache. Kian stands, placing his hands on the back of his head, moving slowly from foot to foot. Then they're putting Hallie's head in a neck brace, silent tears tracking down the sides of her face. We all know what this means. What this could mean. I turn away, not wanting to see the place she fell. Not wanting to see the blood and despair tattooed on the black-and-white tiled floor.

Time speeds up, the paramedics wheeling Hallie out, loading her into the ambulance. Kian's hopping in, turning back to us, telling us to follow. John's already running for his car, Natalie and James with him. I turn in a circle, not knowing what to do. If this is really happening, I have to be there. I can't leave her.

'Do you want me to take you in your car? Hey, Eva…' I'm suddenly aware of a hand on my arm, shaking me. I glance over and find Diana there. I start, an apology tumbling from my tongue. I forgot she was even here. 'I can drive you to the hospital, if you know… you're not up to it.'

I nod, clearing my throat. Wishing it would stop my head from spinning. 'She… Derriford. They're taking her to Derriford hospital.'

Diana raises her eyebrows. 'Could be major trauma then. Shit.'

We hurry to the car and it's not until we are blasting along the winding lanes that I remember my suitcase. It's still in the entrance hall, abandoned by the front door. Should I tell someone? Will they be checking us out? I feel like I should tell someone. But when I reach for the phone in my pocket, I remember I left it in my jacket, which is also discarded in the entrance hall.

'I left… I left my phone back there.'

Diana nods and bites her lip, giving me the most cursory of quick glances. 'It's OK, I've got mine.'

We are quiet on the drive. We get off the moors, closing the distance between us and the ambulance, then it stretches out as we hit the main road. It's not a motorway, just a single lane, and everyone in Cornwall seems to be leaving. But it is just after the holidays, when work and real life picks up its steady, relentless beat. We were so lucky an ambulance got to us quickly. To Hallie.

I'm restless, drumming my fingers on the door handle, needing my phone. Needing a screen to fall into, that world of lies to occupy my mind. Diana switches on the radio, some power ballad from the eighties filling the car. I tune out. Stare at nothing. Count silver cars, read registration plates over and over, the letters and numbers losing all meaning. Wonder if everything is my fault. If I could have stopped all of this from happening. If this is what Gran is trying to show me, how my world will fall apart.

We get to the hospital just as the ambulance is unloading and Diana slows, circling around to the car park. I crane my neck, seeing Kian hop out after the stretcher, a group of doctors and nurses ready at the hospital entrance to take her straight in. My breath catches, a sickening realisation dawning. They actually think their lives are in danger. But not just the baby she's carrying. They are concerned about Hallie, too. What if she… what if…

The car park is crammed with cars, other people circling like us, hoping for a space to open up. It's an agonising ten minutes before we find one, tucked as far from the entrance as we can get. I won't know which ward she's been taken to, I won't know where James is…

'That one!' I shout, already unbuckling my seat belt.

Diana pulls into the space and I throw open the door, already running.

Chapter 33

'Hi, how can I help you?' the receptionist, a woman in her mid-fifties asks. She has the steely look of a veteran and as I lean on the counter, I force myself to stay calm. To focus.

'I… my friend just got brought in. She's pregnant, she fell—'

'Name, dear?'

'Me? Eva Glass.'

'The patient, dear.'

'Oh… Hallie. Hallie Sharp.'

The receptionist pinches her lips together, dropping her gaze to the screen in front of her. There's a thrum to this place, a pulse. It's electricity and heart monitors and the ever-present threat of death, hunkering down in the corners. I swallow, already tasting the bleach. The artificial aroma, like forced sunshine.

I've never liked hospitals. Nor does Hallie. I bet she wanted a home birth, with one of those blow-up water birth baths and an earth mother doula reminding her to breathe… I realise with a shock that I never asked her. We didn't get a chance to talk about her plans, her hopes for the birth. I never gave her the space to. I never asked her if she's already buying baby clothes, if she's chosen a buggy. And now it's all crashing down around us. So fragile. So impermanent. So familiar.

I force myself to focus as a lump wells in my throat. I can't cry. Not now. Not when there are strangers passing back and forth and Diana coming over to lean against the counter beside me. Not when I need to keep my eyes from blurring, my chest from caving in so I can follow the obscure signs and directions that will lead me to Hallie's side.

'She's already been admitted,' the receptionist says, looking up to meet my eyes. She blinks once, a strand of grey hair coming loose from her bun. 'Resus, in the emergency department. Follow the green line.'

I thank her, noting the slight wince as she smiles. A coil of heavy heat writhes in my stomach, forcing its way up. I think I'm going to be sick. Quickly, I turn away, drawing in a deep, shaky breath. Sparks dance at the edges of my vision and I close my eyes, chin dipping down.

'It's OK,' Diana says and I feel her hand on my back. 'Just breathe. Breathe.'

I take a minute, my entire body shuddering.

I find a scrap of steel deep inside myself and straighten. We're not there yet. We're not. There's still time, we got here fast. *She* got here fast.

'I'm good,' I say and Diana offers up an unconvincing smile.

'You look like shit.'

I laugh, the sound ringing hollow and untrue. That's not the first time I've been told that today. 'Hospitals. Never been a fan.'

'Yeah,' she says, scrunching up her nose. 'You and me both. Spent far too much time here when Mum was… anyway.'

I flick my gaze to Diana, putting my hand briefly on her shoulder. Her smile doesn't quite reach her eyes as she looks back at me, but her eyes say it all. There are too many ghosts in this place. My heart twists, aching for both our losses.

We start walking, following the green line on the floor, past a clutch of gift shops selling merchandise covered in roses and cartoon teddy bears. We pass a coffee stop and start the long hike down multiple squeaky-floored corridors, gradually losing the press of the crowd. The only people we come across are in scrubs, or visitors shuffling around wearing oversized coats and sorrow. We are getting closer.

'Ah.' I exhale as we reach a door with a keypad entry. In the thin strip of glass set into the standard hospital-issue door, I can see a nurse station, curtained partitions and doors leading off to side rooms. I press the buzzer and an artificially loud voice asks us a few questions before buzzing us in.

A nurse greets us, ushering us towards one of the side rooms. I barely have time to thank her before the door clicks and Kian leaps up from a chair, only to deflate when he sees it's just us. No doctor bearing updates, or hope. James is standing by the window, hands clasped at the small of his back, staring out at the huddle of trees, the cars parked in neat rows. I want to go to him. But I can't. I look at Kian, who nods at me. It's the tiny sign I needed to know that I am welcome here, despite everything.

'Kian,' I breathe, sliding into a chair one over from him. The room is sparse, like a teachers' lounge with veneer wood chairs and squidgy seats upholstered in scratchy blue fabric. There are posters dotted around the walls, stuck up with Blu-tack and curling at the sides reminding us to *Wash your hands!* and asking if we *Need to talk?* There's a small table in the corner with a stack of polystyrene cups, sugar packets and coffee and tea sachets and one of those push-down dispensers labelled 'hot water'. I hope it's been topped up recently, I could use a tea.

Kian looks up at the ceiling, then flashes me a quick smile. 'Nearly threw up in that ambulance.'

'I forgot what a wimp you are,' I tease in an attempt to draw him away from his panic. Kian is the worst passenger. Always has motion sickness, he turns green on a train if he is facing backwards. 'Was she OK... on the way?' I don't want to ask. I can't form the words, the ones I really want to say.

Is my best friend still alive? Is her baby? Did the bleeding stop?

'No news yet. They left us in here and said they'd come and update us.' He brushes a hand down his face. 'They're prepping her for surgery. Natalie and John have gone to get a few things for her, in case... in case she needs them.'

I nod, turning my face away so Kian doesn't see the unease growing there. I can't hide a single thought, they always flash up like a beacon. I stand abruptly and move to the hot drinks table and Diana jumps in the chair opposite. I guess we're all on edge. 'Tea? Coffee?'

'Whisky on the rocks,' Kian says, laughing hollowly.

I shrug. 'Fresh out. Priorities, eh?'

He smiles back but it doesn't reach his eyes. I make a round of tea, handing one to Diana and Kian, then pressing one into James's hands before sitting back down to sip mine. James barely registers it, still staring out of that window. There's a white plastic wall clock by the door, ticking the seconds away, and in this charged silence it's louder than a bell. I'm tempted to yank it off and pull the batteries out of the back. Draining my tea, the dregs of it awash with flakes of tea leaves and milk, I glance over at Diana, who is restlessly tapping her leg. She shouldn't be here, to witness this. She doesn't need to be here anymore.

'Diana, if you want to shoot…' I say gently.

She clears her throat and nods, trying to hide her relief. 'I've got your car though. And all our stuff is back at the house still.'

I take a quick look at Kian. He's zoned out, staring at the wall, his tea grown cold in his hands. I can't leave him. 'Will you pick all our stuff up? Bring it back here? Only if it's not any trouble.'

'What about your car?'

'Keep it.'

'No. You'll need to get home… after this.' She stands, shaking her hair back from her face. 'Maybe drop me to the train station when I get back? I can look up the timetable on the way, grab a ticket online. It's only a few hours from Plymouth.'

I smile gratefully and open my mouth to thank her, but she cuts me off. 'Don't. It's the least I can do.'

There are no updates. Occasionally a nurse pops her head in, asking us if we need anything. If we're comfortable. What are you supposed to say to that? I'm losing my mind, show me to the nearest pub? I'll never be comfortable again. Tell me what's happening, I can take it. Whatever it is, I can handle it. It's the not knowing, the minutes and seconds ticking by that's breaking me. Give me all the science, all the medical terms, every Latin name under the sun.

Just give me *something*.

Kian pours two more hot drinks, stirring them restlessly and pacing. Always pacing. He starts reasoning it out, googling for answers. I'm tempted to take his phone away – Dr Google always delivers the worst-case scenarios. But if it's how he can cope, then I have to leave him to it. So I just nod, listen and pitch in occasionally. James turns and does the same. Kian has to analyse everything, every word, every angle. It's part of what makes him a great barrister, this endless thirst for knowledge and reason. His passion for people.

At some point Natalie and John get back, laden with clothes and toothbrushes and snacks. Natalie instantly begins to worry that she's forgotten something, and heads out to the shops by reception.

When Diana slips back into the room, I brace my hand on Kian's shoulder, just for a moment. 'Phone me if there's anything. When she's…'

'Of course.'

'You'll be OK?' I eye James and John, their faces buried deep in thought. It's enough of a support system for the next half an hour for Kian. But as James's gaze meets mine, I find only pain. We've been here before, James and I. In this very moment, waiting to know if our baby's heart was still beating. If there were any complications, if there was anything wrong with me. I want to go to him, curl inside his arms and tell him that he has me, that I love him and we can get through this. Tell him those haunted days will fade. Or maybe, just say nothing. Just stand with his arms wrapped around me, sharing his agony.

Kian sighs, snapping me back to the present. 'Sure.'

I hate leaving him there. To stew in the *what ifs*, the *if only I had done this…* we torture ourselves constantly with what we cannot change. No more so than in hospital waiting rooms, the scent of cleaning products and instant coffee permeating the stuffy, tense air. I wrench my eyes away from James, forcing myself to leave the room even though everything within me is screaming to go to him. To comfort him and smooth his frown away. But I can't. We're no longer us.

'Did you manage to get a ticket?' I ask Diana, trying to keep my voice level, to remain measured and controlled as we walk through the automatic doors at the front of the hospital, a gust of frosty air hitting my face. I drink it in, the car fumes, the coolness.

'I did. It's an open one, so I can hop on any train. I left your stuff in the car boot.'

'Thanks.'

'No problem.'

I get in the driver's side this time, pushing back the seat, adjusting the mirrors. Diana's taller than me, she needs more legroom, different angles. I already feel like I've been away from Kian and James for too long, leaving them both alone with that ceaseless ticking wall clock. And the compact casing of this car is not helping.

'How far is it?'

'Only ten minutes away,' Diana says, rubbing her hands together. 'I can direct you.'

We barely talk on the way there, just her injection of directions. It's not until I pull into a parking space and unbuckle my seat belt that she begins abruptly, 'Eva… we need to talk.'

'Yeah?'

'I can't think of a worse time to do this, but I don't think I can say everything I want to over text with you. It's better if it comes from me in person… I just don't think it can wait much longer. I know this is unprofessional, but…' She takes a deep breath. 'I have to quit. I can't do this anymore. The launch, the hours, the weekends… it's not what I want. What I need right now.'

I gulp, dread filling my veins like ink, and steal a glance at her. Diana has become one of my people. I don't want her to go, I don't want to lose her. I think, given time, I could even say she's a friend. An ache floods my chest as I realise I never took the time to show her she means more to me than an employee.

'I appreciate all you've done, what you're going through right now, I truly do…'

'It's OK,' I say, turning to her. The emails in that secret folder shuffle before my eyes. Everything she's been trying to hold together. To keep it all going, like a frantic swan paddling faster and faster. All I could see was her gliding along. In a way, I chose not to see how much she was struggling. Dread pools in my stomach, but I don't allow it to taint this conversation. I have to do something right today. 'I appreciate your honesty.'

'You don't need to be so—'

'No, really…'

'I'm sorry,' she says, regret filling her face. And guilt. She slides my mobile out of her pocket, the one I left at Penhallow, then her work one and places them both in the glove compartment. I stare at it as the catch clicks. The finality of it. 'The truth is, I've been offered another position. I'll clear out my desk before you're back, I'll leave all my notes. I-I have to do this… it's better this way.' She opens her car door, swinging out into the car park, and I do the same.

I can't leave it like this. What if this is my chance to turn the tide? 'This hasn't been a great year, I know. But… think it through first. Take some time at least…'

Any hint of warmth or regret stutters out in her features. 'I've made my decision. Goodbye, Eva.'

I watch her as she hurries towards the entrance to the train station, another integral piece of my life slipping away. But in a way, I admire her. Even envy her. She's made a decision to move on, to place the past firmly in the past and start afresh. I've failed her. I can see that now. And in doing so, I have failed myself.

Chapter 34

My mobile phone starts ringing in the glove compartment on the way back to the hospital. I scramble for it, one hand on the steering wheel, and swipe at it quickly to see who is phoning. A missed call from James. My heart thuds in my ears, drumming wildly as I speed up, desperate to get there. I kill the what-ifs circling endlessly and focus on the next steps, getting back into the hospital car park, finding a space, running for the door.

'Breathe, Eva,' I whisper into the quiet of the car. 'One moment, then the next. Just breathe.'

There are empty food packets and disposable hot drink cups strewn everywhere in this car, but it's not something I really care about right now. When I glance in my mirrors, I see Diana's work laptop and her own folders of paperwork for my business on the back seat in a discarded heap. Diana must have shoved them all there – I didn't notice when I dropped her off. This detritus speaks volumes about my life right now.

I can't shake the memory of this morning from my head, I keep replaying it. That blood and the sickening thud as her body hit the entrance hall floor. I grip the wheel tighter as I spot the turn-in sign for Derriford hospital and quickly switch lanes, the gentle whoosh of the car's movement sounding like static in my ears.

I reach the car park, circling like a vulture and spot a space to wriggle into. The parking meter churns out a ticket and I drop a handful of change in my haste to open my purse, cursing the world and the brightness of the day. It's a low winter sun that digs into the back of my eyes and I feel a headache forming at my temples. With shaking fingers, I plaster the ticket to the dashboard and race for the hospital entrance.

I'm directed to a different place in mere moments, a ward away from the emergency department. I'm out of breath and babbling until a kind nurse with a dark fringe and a blue uniform guides me to another side room. Through the slim glass panel, I can see Kian inside, holding Hallie's hand and leaning over her body. I can't breathe.

'She's alive. It's OK,' the nurse says and a sob rattles my chest, drawing up my throat and spilling over. I clamp my hands over my mouth and lean against the wall, closing my eyes. She's alive. Not dead. Still here, breathing the same air as me. It's not over yet.

'I-I don't want to interrupt,' I manage and the nurse nods, understanding. She leads me back to the waiting room, pours me a sugar-filled tea and leaves me with the ringing, awful quiet of my own thoughts.

A few minutes later I spy James in the corridor, speaking to Kian, and know that I should get up. I should. I should go to them and be one of the four, but I'm rooted to this chair. Untangling what has happened, what has been said over the last few days. And in the harsh light of this day, I cringe away. Gran hasn't reappeared and she never said I was still in the loops, the endless cycle of different bodies. And it's Boxing Day. Which means that this is all real. It has to be. And I'm afraid to face it all. I'm too afraid to try and fix everything and end up doing it wrong again.

My phone is stacking up with notifications and missed calls, from the PR and marketing firm and the suppliers who are seeing how the shop prep is going, but I don't care. It's as if I exist in a vacuum, and everything else is very far away.

'Hey,' Kian says as he pokes his head around the door half an hour later. His eyes are guarded and shadowed, because of me or from the horror of what has just happened to Hallie, I'm not sure. 'She's tired from the surgery, and kind of out of it. Natalie and John have seen her, and gone to get some lunch… but she wants to see you. She's been asking for you.'

I leap up, upsetting the drained polystyrene cup and hastily grab it, stuffing it in the bin by the tea and coffee table. Kian smiles, not quite meeting my eyes. I spot James behind him, hands in his pockets, studying the corridor floor. He can't even look at me. I tuck my hair behind an ear and focus on Kian. One thing at a time. 'You OK?'

'Yeah,' he says, nodding as if he's trying to convince himself he is. 'Mostly.'

My heart rattles painfully against my ribs when I enter the room. Hallie is too pale, lying against the hospital pillows. There's a tube attached to the back of her hand with tape, blood and bruises already forming around it, and a probe clipped to her finger which connects to a monitor, bleeping endlessly next to her. I stare at the green line, the numbers which mean nothing to me all blurring into one, and take a seat at her side.

That synthetic smell of heartache and bleach stings my nose, but I push it aside. Everything I am, all that I have, is focused on Hallie.

'How are you doing?' I ask, moving my hand towards hers. She smiles at me and my chest cracks open. It's all I can do not to weep, seeing her pale, exhausted face.

'I'm OK,' she says in a reedy voice, trying a smile. It stretches too thin and I wince. 'A bit out of it still. I can't feel anything past my hips, so that's something, I guess.'

'I should have stopped to talk to you, I shouldn't have—'

'Shush,' she says. 'It was an accident. Could have happened anywhere. Could have happened on the stairs up to the flat at home. I was rushing. And you stayed… for me. That's what… that's what matters.'

I pull her fingers into mine, curling them inside my cold fist. We have been drifting for months, moving further and further away from each other, to a point which I didn't know how to get back from. It was me. All me. But right now, none of that matters. I just need to know she's all right.

'The baby?'

She closes her eyes and my heart finally breaks. She shakes her head.

'Hal…'

Her face caves in, tears tracking down her temples. 'I don't even know what to do, what to think…'

'Oh God,' I say, using my sleeve to wipe away my own tears. 'Hallie, I'm so sorry.'

'We wanted it for so long, I can't…'

She sniffs and whimpers, more tears tracing down her skin. There's an ache, bone deep in my centre, sharpening to the point that I can't breathe. This is wrong. This is all so wrong. How could I let this happen? How can this be our future?

We sit in the quiet with our tears and I try to make sense of this. I don't know how to make this better. How to bridge the ravine that has gaped open between us, yawning and tearing until we are too far apart. How do we come back from this?

I stand abruptly, gulping down air. 'I have to fix this. Hallie, I'm going to fix us.'

She smiles at me pityingly. 'Eva, it's OK. You can't fix this… us…' Hallie sighs. 'Maybe it's better this way. Maybe we've just run our course. Not everyone stays friends for ever, do they? They… they drift. And we were drifting, weren't we? It's what you seemed to want.'

'No, no it isn't.'

'It's OK,' Hallie says, reaching for my hand one final time. Then letting go. 'It's OK.'

I love Hallie. I love her far more than I love myself or what I want. And this human, this person whom I have laughed with, shared secrets with, cried with over the past fourteen years, is slipping away. And I've let her. I've let her slip beyond my reach… and now there's no way back. I should have swallowed down my panic at Penhallow. I never should have rushed off. I should have waited for her on the landing.

'Hallie, you have to know that I love you. We all do. And you can get past this, you can.'

She turns her head away with a hush of a sigh. 'I don't think so. Not this time.'

I start crying again, a fresh wave of pain hitting me, breaking me. 'Hal, if we don't… I need you to know that I love you. That Kian loves you. That… that you don't have to be like me. To do what I have done. You don't have to go through this alone.'

Cold permeates the room, as though it isn't just the baby that's died today. It's our friendship. The bond that I've pulled at and tested beyond its limits has finally snapped. She withdraws from me like a bloom seeking sunlight elsewhere and I know I have lost her.

Stumbling, I get up and walk from that room, moving past Kian, James, the nurse, everything. I hear James calling for me, shouting my name, but I don't stop. I can't.

I leave the ward and start running, pummelling the empty, strip-lit corridors, and I don't stop until I get outside. I get in the car, scrubbing my hands down my face and lock the door.

'Gran? Are you there? You have to change this. This can't happen. I can't let… let…' Hallie's pale, smudged face swims before me. 'It's all my fault.'

I turn the ignition, reverse and pull out of the car park, driving as far and as fast as I can to put some distance between me and the train wreck of my life. Not Hallie's baby. Not this. Of all the things that I've fucked up, this can't be something that happens because of my choices, my actions. All because I wouldn't stop and just listen. For *once*.

I keep driving until I hit the moors, light fading fast from the world. It starts snowing again, flakes flooding the windscreen, and I switch on the full beam of the headlights. I can't stop. I have to get out of this day and fix this. I need to go back.

'Don't let this be it! I'll do better. Give me a second chance, I'll go through it all again, as many times as it takes, I'll stay here for ever, please…'

The drystone walls loom on either side of the road, narrowing it until it's just a muddy, stone-filled track. I keep going, blinking as the petrol dial falls. I'll run this car until it's empty. Anything to get to midnight, and reset this day.

'I'll go through the loop again,' I repeat, louder and firmer. 'I'll be kinder, I'll be better. I'll do anything. Anything. Just not this. *Not this*. Shatter *my* life. Take it all, take James away, take the shop, my business, my future… but not… not Hallie's.'

There's no moon, no stars, just the window of snow and track in front of me. The ceaseless drumming in my ears, the curses rattling my breath.

'I get it now. It's not about me. It's about everyone around me. I should have listened, I should have been there. I've spiralled, I can see that. I keep repeating the same pattern, over and over. I've buried myself too deep.'

I know what it is to lose the life inside you. For the dreams, so close to being tangible, touchable, to collapse into so much ash and dust. I wipe my eyes, swerving to avoid a pothole as the fuel gauge blinks to empty. For a second I take my eyes from the snow-spun track and when I look up, there's a figure standing there.

A woman.

'Shit!' I scream, slamming on the brakes. I spin the wheel, snow and track swirling and circling—

Chapter 35

The air bag explodes in my face, punching into my chest. I gasp, coughing as I shove it back down. It takes me a panicked moment to remember where I am in the pitch darkness. And what made me swerve and crash. I feel for the door handle and push it open, staggering out onto the rough track. The cold is like a knife, searching through my clothes to rob me of any warmth. Shivering, I spin in a circle, searching for the woman.

'Well, that was a bit daft,' a soft voice sighs. I blink, finding Gran peering at the front bumper. At the mangled mess of scattered glass and scrunched metal. 'No tow truck is going to come out in this. Guess we'd better start walking.'

I lunge for her, grasp her shoulders and peer into her eyes. 'Gran! I could have hit you! Are you all right?'

Gran shrugs me off, fixing me with a no-nonsense look. She doesn't seem hurt, in fact, she seems amused by my crash. And a little judgemental. 'Calm down. I'm clearly *completely* fine. Can't say the same for your car though. Honestly, Eva, you are *extremely* jumpy.'

'You were standing in the middle of the road!'

'How else was I meant to get your attention? Hmm?' She tuts, walking around the car to plant her feet in the middle of the track. She's wearing the same dressing gown, but now she has a pair of wellies on her feet. The same pair she would wear each year without fail, a sturdy old green pair of Hunters. 'Best get going, Eva. Haven't got all night.'

Fumbling for my phone to turn on the torch on it, I note the time. Frozen at midnight. I glance back at Gran, who is now hopping between snow flurries, making her way into the dark abyss of the moors.

'It's midnight,' I say, holding the phone up to throw sharp light along the potholes, the patches of ice, the jagged rocks. 'It was only six o'clock, if that, I'm sure of it.'

'I love midnight. My favourite time of the day,' Gran says with a wistful sigh as we start walking. 'Anything can happen. Or nothing. Or everything. Who knows? We used to have midnight feasts when you were little. Do you remember? White bread rolls and tuna, cherry biscuits and cups of silver tea…'

A burst of surprised laughter springs from my lips. I'm still shaken, my nerves jagged and raw. But I do remember. In fact, Gran made us a feast at the kitchen at Penhallow every Christmas. We sat there in front of the range, toasting bits of bread and slathering on butter. I was so tired, everything felt rose-tinted and fuzzy. As if coated in magic. Our midnight feasts were the best.

'You made all my favourite memories.'

She smiles back at me, a little sadly. 'I know, dearest one. I know.'

I blow out a breath, watching the steam curl away into the night. The only sound in this snow-muffled world is the crunch of our boots. As though we are the only people that exist in the whole world. I wonder if Hallie is asleep now. If Diana made it home. If James is still nearby, or already back in London. I hug my arms around myself, sniffing the sharp air. I'm not sure where to go from here with anything. If Gran's here, does it mean it isn't over? That it will all reset again? I allow the hope to slip in, that maybe the miscarriage hasn't happened. That maybe it's all been erased. But the hope doesn't last, because if she's here, this could be it. I might not see her again. This could be the last time her breath plumes from her mouth, the memories thick between us.

I swallow the lump in my throat, trying to stay in this moment with her. To stop my mind from racing over every detail of the day I've just lived through. 'Where are we going?'

'To the nearest village,' Gran says. 'It's not far, promise. You won't freeze if that's what you're worried about.'

'But what about Hallie? And Kian? I need to get back to them, make sure they've got everything they need... and James—'

She waves her hand impatiently, cutting me off. 'They'll keep. They are in the same loop as you, and if you want any of this to work out you need to just walk with me for a bit.'

I pinch my lips tightly, unease creeping all over me now, sliding over my skin. I thrust one hand deep inside my sleeve, the prickle of cold already feeling too much like heat. The false, treacherous kind. My toes have gone numb inside my inappropriate suede Chelsea boots, the snow soaking into them. I should have stopped to grab something warmer from the stashed clothes in the car boot. But I'm not thinking clearly. I have completely derailed.

The village is a clutch of houses with dark windows. A lonely street light stands sentry, casting a splash of light over the single road winding through it, bathing the snow in a false amber glow. I can't tell if it's a nice village, or a down-on-its-luck one. I can barely see two feet in front of me, even with the phone torch lighting our path.

'Any of this look familiar?' Gran asks, tipping her face up, beady eyes meeting mine. 'You've been here before.'

I look around, peering at the houses, the snow-crusted cars. There's nothing that stands out. Only slumbering lives, deep in the thick of mid-winter. Probably enjoying the last night of sleep after a Christmas holiday, ready for work and early starts once time resets.

Then I spot a house. It's an end of terrace, two up, two down, with a fence circling the front garden of grass and weed. There's no car parked on the short driveway next to it and the windows are dark, curtains drawn against the night. I know instantly, it's Sarah's house.

'This was your favourite perspective,' Gran says. 'The one that made you feel most complete, even more so than in your own skin. Why do you think that is?'

I shuffle from foot to foot, the numb feeling in my toes blooming into sharp, insistent pain. I need to warm my feet soon. 'Her family life, I guess. And the fact she's found balance. She hasn't shoved anything out of her life. She's somehow… made room for it all.' I rub my face with one hand, massaging blood flow back into it. 'Look, aren't you getting cold? We should probably find somewhere to shelter.'

'In a minute. Tell me about what a house like this might mean to you. A family life. Balance.'

I sigh and shoot her a hard look, thinking through what it might be about Sarah's life. She isn't well off, that's plain. The house is small and cramped, the tinfoil decorations I can see through a slender gap in the curtains are the kind you find in a budget supermarket. But deep in my bones, I know it doesn't matter.

All that she has, her boys, her cosy family, her dreams and goals, all made her day such a joy to live in. She was content, it was clear from the way her boys treated her, the way her home was set up. I press a hand against my chest, the place that's hollow and cold. I envied her. I wanted that cosy domesticity. The humdrum of the ordinary. To stop having to *fight* all the time, stop having to push past my failures. Mostly, I wanted my own family, someone to care for and love and feel the weight of in my arms. My breath catches, the image of Hallie's broken body on the entrance hall floor of Penhallow playing out in my mind. How can I fix this for myself if she's lost everything? Have I left it too late for her?

'She… she's happy. With her family, with the ordinary. With a life where she strives for better, but not at the expense of what's right under her nose. I-I want that. That balance she's found. That contentment. It was bittersweet, living a day in her shoes… but it was a good day, as Sarah. She… she embraced her failures. In fact, she didn't view them as failures at all. She… she wasn't afraid of them. She drew the people she cares about closer. Rather than pushing them away.'

Gran nods, satisfied. 'At last.'

'But I've realised too late, haven't I? And it's not just me that's lost everything; the shop launch, my best friend, my marriage…' I swallow back the lump threatening to rise up my throat. 'James lost everything too. And Hallie and Kian. Even Diana.' I draw in a sharp breath. 'How could I lose sight of the everyday? I've been racing and racing to get away from my life, put as much distance as possible between me and the miscarriage and you dying… that I lost track. I somehow thought that if I cut every tie, I could start afresh. And it's all gone so wrong.'

'There, there, darling,' Gran says, patting my arm as I sob into my hands.

My phone is a harsh edge against my cheek as I clutch it in my hand. My whole body convulses in a gasp. 'I've lost everything.'

She lets me cry it out, leading me away from Sarah's house, back towards the dark, unforgiving moorland. When I stop crying, I shiver, my chest aching from the tremors as the cold seeps into the very marrow of my bones. We walk and walk, a steady trudge through the ice and snow, and I lose all sense of time or place. My mind is a blank sheet, the memories and regret washed away. All I know is the steady rhythm of our walk, my breath, the tremors that wrack my aching limbs.

'Are you ready for what comes next?' Gran asks, pulling me to a halt. 'Are you *truly* ready?'

'I… did yesterday happen, Gran?'

She watches me, saying nothing.

I nod, sniffing. 'I see.' Time to face the reality I've created. In whatever shape it takes. To wake tomorrow in my own body, my own life, and try to rebuild from the rubble. 'I think I'm ready.'

'I think you are too. But you're holding onto a sadness that only time will heal. Fix things, yes. But also break the cycle you keep repeating, year on year. You have to acknowledge your grief, stop calling it a failure. Learn to let go.'

I nod again, staring at the ground. I know what she's talking about. But I've held my grief trapped in the chambers of my heart for so long, I can't imagine setting it free. I can't imagine a life where I don't carry around that needling sadness, one where I'm not constantly trying to bury it. Flooding my days with distractions so I don't have to deal with it, with the constant ghosts. If I let go of that grief, I'm scared that I'll lose the woman before me. My heart splinters as I reach for her hands, the papery folds of them, the memories they hold. Can I really let her go?

'Best of luck,' Gran says, breaking into my thoughts. She's fading fast, mingling with the snow and the vast night around us. So fast I can't hold onto her, I can't keep her here with me. Her hands fade to nothing within mine, leaving only cold emptiness.

'Gran, is this it?' I croak, looking up into the steady blue of her eyes. 'Am I going back for good this time?' They crinkle at the corners, the only colour in this deathly night. She steps away, and all I see is white. I gasp, reaching out to where she stood as her voice, the last words I might ever hear from her lips, wraps around me.

'Perhaps. If you're ready to let go.'

Chapter 36

I awake as though drowning, a gasp on my tongue. Clawing at the covers, I blink and splutter, sitting up to free myself of their stifling embrace. A thin grey light filters into the room, the curtains half drawn against the frosted windows. I reach greedily for my phone, hoping with every fibre of my being that I am in my own body. That the loop of perspectives and days is over, and I can finally begin to fix my life.

The phone screen is my own, an image of James and me lighting up the space around me. I release the breath I was holding and slump back against the pillows. A body moves next to me and I freeze. Would James have driven back to London with me? Are we somehow… OK? Are we at home together, after Hallie's accident? I swipe open my phone screen, catching the date on the calendar app. And I choke. A sob tears from my throat and I can't stop wheezing. Leaning forward, I drop my phone on the bed, forehead crashing into my palms. I heave and heave, weeping into my hands. I can't believe it. It can't be possible.

It's Christmas Day again.

'Oh my God, Eva? Eva! Are you OK?' James says, voice still thick with sleep and confusion as he bolts upright, his arm circling around my shoulders. 'What's happened? Are you hurt?'

I know what he's thinking. That Christmas, three years ago. How I couldn't stop crying. I can't let him think it's happening again, I can't.

'I'm OK, I'm OK,' I gasp, sniffing and wiping at my face. 'More than OK… I—'

'Eva, what's going on? Is it a bad dream? Should I get some—'

'James, really,' I say, fumbling for the bedside table, flicking the switch on the lamp. I turn back to him, grinning through my tears. His tense face relaxes and he pulls me into a hug.

'Jesus, you scared the shit out of me…'

I laugh, then gulp as my body shudders. I can't believe it's Christmas Day. Does this mean… do I get a do-over? Do I get to make this right?

'James, is Hallie in the hospital? This is important…' I struggle away from him, needing to see his eyes. To read him. 'Is she OK? The baby?'

'She's fine, as far as I know,' James says, a crease appearing on his forehead. 'Maybe you're overworked, that bloody shop launch… should I get you a tea? Or… or a glass of water?'

'Stop fretting!' I say, laughing and batting him away. His face breaks into a smile and my heart swoops, rattling in my chest. I'm with James, it's Christmas Day and Hallie is OK. I have to screw my eyes tight to stop myself from crying again, sniffing and laughing. The relief is so strong, such a shock of white-hot heat, that my mind isn't catching up. I scramble for my phone again, checking the time. It's 8 a.m.

'Look, we need to talk,' I say, cupping my hands on either side of his face. He stares back at me, bewildered, still too close to the heady haze of sleep. 'But first, there's a few things I have to do.'

He groans. 'At eight in the morning? Surely you don't need to work today of all days.'

'No, no. It's not that at all,' I say, shaking my head firmly. 'Just… trust me.'

He nods as I release his face. 'Of course.'

'In fact… would you keep the morning free? Instead of going down for breakfast with the others, come and meet me?'

'Where?'

I rack my brain for the perfect breakfast spot. Somewhere in Penhallow we can begin the rest of our lives together, just me and James. A place we can start as I mean for us to go on. 'The library. Meet me there in an hour?'

He nods, capturing my mouth for a kiss. 'What I said, last night—'

'Was exactly what I needed to hear,' I say softly, running my fingers along his jawline. My fingertips snag on his stubble, and it reminds me of all the other times. Every day I have kissed him good morning, accepted a cup of tea and run my fingers along his skin. How could I have nearly lost this?

Shimmying out of the bed, I take a deep breath. James falls back onto the pillows, a faint smile on his face as I brush back my hair, grab a dressing gown and some thick socks to shove on. I pause at the door, turning back to him. His cheek has a crease mark from the pillow, hair mussed from sleep. His eyes are heavy-lidded, I can't quite see the shade of them. But I imagine them green today. My favourite colour. 'James?'

'Yeah?'

'I love you. More than you know. Happy Christmas.'

★

Diana is still asleep. I knock at the door for a second time, glancing along the silent, dark corridor. Restlessly, I shuffle from foot to foot, until the door opens abruptly. Diana's features instantly slide into a frown when she sees it's me. I plaster on a smile. Does she really think I'm going to get her up to work at eight on Christmas morning? Actually, that's probably exactly what she's thinking.

'Happy Christmas,' I say, steeling myself. 'Can I come in for a minute?'

Diana looks like she's about to slam the door in my face and tell me to come back later. I wouldn't blame her. Getting stuck here, even if she did offer to drive me down, must be so grating. But despite that, her professionalism wins out and she steps back to let me in. 'Sure.'

I follow her into the small bedroom, letting the door click shut in my wake. We're both wearing dressing gowns, messy hair still straggly from sleep. Her bed is unmade, she must have staggered out of it to answer my knock. I perch on the end of it, feeling uneasy. But I need to have this conversation with her. And it needs to happen now.

'Look, I know this isn't where you want to be,' I begin, taking a breath. She raises her eyebrows, shifting a pillow aside to sit on the opposite end of the bed. 'And I don't blame you. Not one bit. In fact, I don't think you should be here either.'

Her eyes snap wide open. 'Are you sacking me? Look, Eva, this isn't a good time, it'll look terrible—'

'No, no!' I say firmly, waving a hand. 'Don't be daft. You're the best assistant I could ever want. My first member of staff, the backbone of my business, really. I owe you so much, Di.' I clear my throat, refocusing on her. 'In fact, I haven't given you enough credit. I should have given you more support, and well, listened. I'm sorry. I've been a control freak and I haven't been available enough. That was wrong of me.'

Her face settles back into shuttered-off confusion.

'You've been trying to do the work of two people, haven't you? Trying to cover up any mistakes, make them right before I even notice.'

Diana flushes and I'm hit with a dose of pity. This isn't her.

'All this to say…' I sigh. 'I'm sorry.'

'What?'

'I have done you a great disservice. I've been selfish and demanding and exactly the opposite of what a good boss should be. I haven't encouraged you, or allowed you to flourish on your own. I haven't enabled you. And now we're having this chat on Christmas Day, in our dressing gowns, in a manor house in the middle of nowhere!' I laugh, the humour of it escaping me in a small hysterical burst. 'Really, how have you not shoved a hairy spider under my pillow yet?'

Diana cracks a small smile. 'It's tempting.'

'One of the big ones that lurk under the bathroom sink.'

'Maybe even two…'

We grin at each other, slightly nervously. This is all new, untested ground for both of us.

'What I really came here to say is… I think you need to take some time off.' Her eyebrows shoot up again. I hold up my hands, speaking quickly. 'Not because I'm forcing you out of the business or feel you aren't good enough, but it's Christmas! And you had plans, didn't you? With your friends? And those personal days you took, Di. They were for a reason, weren't they?'

'I-I… they were,' she says haltingly. 'My mum. I didn't know how to… that is, I only drove down to visit the grave. To put down her favourite flowers. I didn't want her to think I don't care.'

'You don't need to tell me, it's OK,' I say softly. 'That's your personal business. We can talk when you're ready, if you, you know, ever want to. About your mum. Or anything. But for now… just take some time? Decide if you want to work for my business and what you want your role to look like. If maybe we need to hire some more support? Or if you want to jump ship. And think over what's happened. Process it. Trust me…' I sigh. 'Everything works out better if you take time to process and find some balance.'

Diana nods, running a hand through her hair. Her eyes stray to her phone, still on her bedside table. 'Thank you, truly. I hope it's that easy but… I don't know if it's as simple as that.'

The song lyrics, about hope and new beginnings in that message. I want to hug her, tell her it's OK to cry. Tell her it's OK to delete that message, and rage at me for being such a nightmare boss. For not understanding that she was in pain. And still is.

I settle on, 'It never is simple, but I can make the work side of things easier. I'll take on some of your workload so you don't have a mountain to return to. And we can look at hiring an intern, or another assistant. At least in that, I can set things right.'

'But I won't be your only assistant anymore…'

'And that's OK. We can discuss your role and what's reasonable. What's practical. *If* that's what you want.'

She blows out a breath, not meeting my eyes. There is a bone-weary tiredness about her that she hides so carefully.

But now, in this room, I can see it clearly. How did I miss it before? 'You know, this year has been really shit.'

I smile, looking away. 'Then it's about time we turn that around, don't you think? Take my car when the snow has cleared enough, get back to London and take a few weeks. I'll deal with the shop launch, and brief you on your return. If you... if you return.' I hesitate, but plough on. 'Reach out to your family and friends, Diana. The ones you left behind when you moved on.'

She bites her lip, not meeting my eyes. 'Sarah, who was working here last night? She's an old friend. I haven't spoken to her yet, but it's so weird, I got this rush of... of memories and things I used to think about, and want...' She shrugs. 'I never wanted to move backwards. Only forwards. And then when Mum died...'

I nod, not wanting to interfere any further. This is her life, her choices. I can influence her work life, but the rest is up to her. 'In the nicest possible way, I expect you gone as soon as the snow thaws enough. After you've had a chance to catch up with Sarah, of course.' I don't mention her Dad and the sea swim. I'll leave that up to her. I stand up, the joints in my knees creaking in a way they never did in my twenties. Reminding me I need to do yoga or something. Eat spinach and avocado. Whatever it is millennials are supposed to do in their thirties.

'Eva?'

'Yes?'

'Thank you,' Diana says, cool gaze meeting mine. Already pulling herself together, taking the next mental steps. I admire that about her, that resilience. 'I'm glad we can begin again. I'll see you soon.'

Chapter 37

After I leave the keys for my car with Diana, I shower and dress as quickly as possible. If I hurry, I can catch them before they go down to breakfast and the day's events unfold. Christmas Day wasn't the day when Hallie fell and lost the baby, at least in the loop I was stuck in. But it did happen when I pushed Hallie away, fortifying the wall I had built between us.

It's time to break that wall down.

I leave James still showering, calling through the door to meet me in the library, and with a steely breath I march over to the west wing.

Hallie opens the door with a pale, reluctant face. I dart a look at her middle, the swell of her pregnant belly still there. Still alive and well and growing. It takes me a second to adjust to that, I have to place my hand on the door frame, feel the slick surface of the cream-painted wood. This is real. She hasn't lost the baby.

I reach back in my mind to what happened on Christmas Eve between us. To what was really said. Pleasantries. Just pleasant, surface-level congratulations that I offered her on Christmas Eve, even when she wanted me to genuinely express an emotion. To break through the barrier between us because she knew every word I said was false. I hold that in my mind now, her hopeful face with the halo of light from the chandelier above her, and I cringe. I have to be honest. Even if it means we are no longer the *us* of before because of it. I owe her that much at least.

'Can we... talk?' I ask hopefully, Kian singing behind her as he rambles through to the bathroom.

Hallie nods, like she's been expecting this. A strange muddle of dread and relief mingles on her features and it's awful to know that I am the cause of that. 'We've got a separate lounge, I won't inflict Kian's high notes on you.'

I chuckle nervously and follow her. I don't know where to put my hands, clasping them in front of me, then folding my arms before finally releasing them to my sides to bunch into fists. Out of all the conversations I need to have, all the first steps I need to take over the coming days, this one is the hardest. Our friendship is like porcelain right now, delicate and brittle, easily broken for ever. I need to handle it with care. I don't want it to shatter.

Hallie sinks into the sofa, closing her eyes briefly. I wonder if she's already thrown up this morning, if her stomach is still churning with that unwelcome nausea. I can feel the ghost of it, the memory of it washing through my own body at the thought. I shuffle uncomfortably, wishing I could take that away from her.

'How are you finding it?' I ask, sitting on the other end of the sofa. A whole person's width between us.

'Honestly?'

'Honestly.'

She deflates a little, fussing with the sleeve of her jumper.

A shadow passes over her features, then a tightening, as if she has made a decision before she answers. 'I'm tired and anxious every day. And when I smell something even remotely bad, or taste something I don't like… I usually end up running for the bathroom. Sometimes it happens even without that, my body just revolting against being pregnant of its own accord.' She scrunches up her nose. 'I can't even drink tea or coffee. Or eat chocolate, it just makes my stomach churn. That's actually the worst part.'

'No visits to your favourite café on the corner then?'

'No flat whites, even decaf,' Hallie says, summoning a smile. 'It's the first thing I'll ask for when this little one is out. Takeaway coffee and a chocolate croissant.'

She grins and I grin back. 'Well, you still look gorgeous. Must be that inner glow.'

Hallie shrugs, then her eyes widen. 'Oh! Baby's waking up.' She lays a hand on her belly and I hold my breath, a tug, like a tether around my heart pulling me closer. 'Still can't get used to it. How it feels.'

'You know… I need to talk to you about…' I close my eyes. I'm not sure how to form the words, even though they should be easy by now. But somehow, they never get any easier to say. When I open my eyes, Hallie is waiting patiently. Just as she always is, for all of us. Especially for me. I've never been so grateful for that as now. 'You know I had a miscarriage. Three years ago. And James and I… we haven't been able to get pregnant again since, despite trying.'

Hallie swallows. 'I remember. And seeing me like this—'

'It makes me so *incredibly* happy,' I say quickly and firmly, grabbing her hands. 'You have no idea. Seeing you like this,

287

with Kian… everything is as it should be. Except the caffeine aversion, obviously.'

She draws in a breath, glances at the door to the bedroom. 'We never talked about it, did we? Not properly, and maybe I should have thought more, maybe I should have tried more.'

'I know. It's OK.'

'But we couldn't *talk* to each other, there was this barrier, a wall between us…' She blinks. 'I should have though. I should have tried. If I had only fought harder, *made* you talk to me. Even when you were being impossible. But you were always so busy with the business, always working late, never at home… or just straight up blowing me off.'

I nod, biting my lip. 'I'm sorry. So sorry for pulling away, for not being there when you needed me. And for not… not talking to you.' This is harder than I thought. It's opening up that part of myself that I've kept locked and hidden, releasing it into the harsh, bright light for us to examine. But this has to be done. 'I can't fix the last three years, but I can fix this, this Christmas. I can be better now. I can let you in and talk to you. We can try to get back to us. I-I really closed myself off after the miscarriage… and Gran's death… I was afraid. I needed to be in control of my life. But I took it too far.'

Hallie squeezes my hand, a real smile breaking over her face. The kind that makes her eyes darken, her skin pearly and flushed all at once. She's always had a glow about her, this happy warmth that spins out in wide circles, surrounding the people she loves most. The ones she invites in, like Kian and James and me. It's like a secret club, Hallie's love, but this past year particularly, I've shied away from her. From her warmth and her love, from everything that connects us and makes us... *us*. How could I ever take that rare love for granted?

'You're here now. That's what matters. Even if it's a tough time of year, you're still here for me. And I'm here, you know. To talk or listen or just go for a walk... maybe more of a waddle.'

I laugh, wiping away a startled tear. 'There's always herbal tea. Have you tried peppermint?'

'Are you making a date with me?'

'Maybe. Tea and a waddle next weekend, at Richmond along the riverbank.'

'Yes,' she says quickly, grinning. 'Yes please.'

'That cake though...' I blink, looking away, the moment still painfully fresh in my mind despite it feeling like a lifetime ago now.

'I'm sorry,' she says, taking my hand. 'I can see now how thoughtless that was. I wanted it to be here at Penhallow because it's a special place for you, and I wanted to find somewhere Kian and I could build memories. I kept seeing the house everywhere, advertised online, in magazines... it was like it was beckoning me. And you used to say it was magical, and I wondered if... if some of that magic would rub off on us, you know? I figured we could all have a good Christmas here together. But it was all too personal, wasn't it? Too wrapped up in memories of your gran and the baby... I've messed up.' She shakes her head. 'You know I love you. So, so much. I can't bear not feeling close to you anymore. Can we just... start Christmas over? Start again?'

'I would love that, Hal,' I say, putting my arms around her. I feel her relax against me, like she's releasing a three-year-long sigh. 'More than anything.'

We talk about the true things. The things we've carried with us. My gran and how I miss her every day. The way I've buried myself in work, like sinking sand. How Hallie's journal, that tracking of careful tick marks, was the only thing that kept her going this past year. How she has gone to message me a thousand times, then remembers that I'm not really there anymore. That it's been a jagged heartbreak, losing me. Losing the person she turned to, even before Kian sometimes. How this road has been a lonely one. And all she wanted was this time, these precious few days for us all to be here, together. That maybe it would turn the tide, and bring us back. I had no idea she felt like this.

'I'm hoping the snow clears enough that Diana can get back home,' I say, then put my face in my hands as I groan. 'What was I thinking? I should never have agreed to her driving me down. She would never have got stuck here. I'm amazed she didn't stab me with a cake fork, it's completely messed up her Christmas.'

'You *might* have deserved it.' Hallie laughs. 'Poor girl was sour as a grape about being stuck here.'

I laugh. 'Pretty much.'

'But what about the shop launch?' She clicks her fingers, brow furrowed. 'And all the… what's the word you used for it…'

'The promo work? The socials?'

'That's it.'

I shrug, as if that will shift the workload off my shoulders, as if I couldn't care less. I do still care. I care about the river of debt that could well flood my life, about the reputation I've built. About the shop, half unpacked, totally abandoned just before the launch. I shrug all of those things off, I know I can deal with it all when I get back. That this Christmas is important to Hal, so it has to matter. It has to be important for me, too.

This is about balance, and priorities. And right now, my priority is Hallie and James and Kian. This Christmas and this life we need to rebuild. 'It'll get done. I might need to push the launch back a week, but it'll be OK.'

'But you'll lose money, right? You won't get those early January sales shoppers?'

'No. Probably not.' Hallie looks thoughtful and I shake my head. 'No, you're not allowed to worry about that! My problems are *not* your problems. Remember? I am choosing to be here. I choose *you*, Hal. You.'

She smiles, eyes sliding to the coffee table. They have a shine to them, which she tries to blink away. Her voice is thick when she replies. 'Good point.'

My phone buzzes in my pocket, startling me. I pluck it out, frowning at the sudden bars of signal, the torrent of emails, the notifications…

Then I see an email that turns me cold. The subject line is all caps, from our main supplier.

URGENT CALL ME

I stare at it, swiping to the date, the timestamp. They only sent it half an hour ago. It must be a serious issue if they've sent an email on Christmas Day.

'Everything OK?' Hallie asks.

'Yeah, I mean, I think so… apparently we have Wi-Fi again.'

'Maybe the owner got it working?'

'Right. Yeah,' I say. I bite my lip, reading over the email. How the supplier has delays with ten lines of product, then asking how we want to proceed. I calculate, realising the products I already have in the shop are the bulk of the available stock in that case. That once we're sold out, I'll have empty shelves.

I wrench my gaze away to look at Hallie. Then again at my phone screen. There are more notifications pouring in now from Instagram and Facebook, a huge number of comments, questions, everything that I usually painstakingly go through and answer, one at a time. In fact, it's all the same notifications and emails I read when I was Diana. When I disappeared for the day to prioritise all this. It felt so pressing, so important to respond immediately. But I know now, it can all wait.

That time is not now.

With a deep breath, I tap out an out-of-office response, flag the two emails that I need to address when I have five minutes to myself, and turn my phone to silent mode. Then I flip the screen over, burying it under a cushion. I smile up at Hallie. 'Hazard of running a business that's just about to expand.'

Hallie grins, shifting around so she can stand up. 'As long as you're sure…'

'Positive,' I say, standing next to her. I pick up my phone without looking at it, popping it in my back pocket. They can all manage for one day. The world will carry on turning. But if I bury myself in work right now, my own world might not. 'Let's get you down to breakfast. I'll join you in a bit. I've got a date I can't miss.'

Chapter 38

Sarah helps me carry a tray of breakfast things to the library. Two plates, two cups and a candle from my shop's winter collection. I always carry product spares in the boot, samples to show people. And it's perfect for this morning. I set it all up in the hushed space and light the candle. In moments the candle gently scents the room with fir trees and cinnamon, creating the perfect setting for James and me to begin some new Christmas memories.

He taps on the door and walks in. He's hesitant, guarded, his eyes seeking mine. Then he sniffs, his gaze travelling to the breakfast tray, the candle flickering in a slight draught.

'What's all this?' he asks, still on the threshold.

I swallow, stepping forward, hoping he'll meet me halfway. Hoping this will be enough to open the door between us. 'I thought… well, this library is special to me, and I wanted to share it with you, take a moment just for us.' I point at the breakfast things, biting my lip. 'Tea? Or I can ask Sarah if she doesn't mind bringing up coffee?'

'This is nice,' he says, shuffling just past the doorway. 'Tea sounds good.'

I pour us both a cup, adding in milk and one sugar. Just how he likes it.

'It's like the day we met,' he says, closing the distance between us. I look up, taking in his wary smile, the crinkling at the corners of his eyes. And my heart unspools. He's wearing his favourite shirt, untucked and slightly dishevelled, the pale stripes creased on the background of white. It is like being back in the library all over again, my whole being filled with butterflies.

'Minus your Clark Kent glasses,' I say, laughing.

'Should I get another pair? I reckon I could rock that look again…'

I reach forward, taking his hand in mine. 'You're perfect just as you are.'

We sit down in the armchairs, leaning forward to pour tea and eat pieces of hot toast smothered in butter and blackberry jam. James gets a bit on his cheek and I lean over with a napkin, dabbing at it with a corner. He catches my hand, kissing my wrist. And I press the moment into my mind, like a wildflower between the pages of a book. Grateful to have some of the old James back, the old version of us, which I didn't realise how much I'd missed until it was nearly too late. And, I hope this moment, of us together, will be just as beautiful each and every year. That gradually we will collect more moments like this. More memories of Christmases well spent to spin us into the future.

'I really thought you would leave last night,' he says quietly, his gaze holding mine. 'We don't have to talk about it now, but I want you to know how glad I am that you didn't.'

'Me too.'

He sits back, watching me. 'There's something I have to tell you. Something which happened and I feel you should know about.'

I brace myself, fairly sure what this is. 'If it makes you feel better, tell me. You know you can always be honest with me.'

He clears his throat. 'I… well, you know Lauren? At work? Well, she tried to kiss me. I nearly didn't push her away. I–I'm so sorry, truly—'

'James,' I say, cutting him off quietly. 'It's OK. It's really OK. I trust you. I love you.' I draw in a quick breath, wanting him to know that this is a new beginning. That we can move past the last three years. 'In fact, I have a present for you…'

I reach beneath the table, pulling out the present wrapped in brown paper and tied with a green bow. I found it in the bookshop around the corner from us recently, then hastily packed it into the suitcase before I left home, forgetting about it until this morning, when I had to dash around trying to find wrapping paper. 'I was going to give this to you later, but I want you to open it now. I think it'll mean more.'

He smiles uncertainly, accepting the present. As he carefully unwraps the paper, the title of a book emerges. 'It's… It's the book I recommended that day in the library… you… you borrowed it…'

'It is,' I say. 'The exact same edition.'

He laughs, finding the slip of paper inside. 'You kept it.'

'I did. How could I not?' I say as he spreads out the creased corners. It's the note he left for me, just his name and phone number, pressed between the leaves of *I Capture the Castle* that day. The same one I've carried with me in my purse since the moment I found it. I slipped it inside the book this morning as a way of showing James I'm all in, that I'm fighting for our marriage. Our love.

He raises his head, finding my eyes on him. And my breath

hitches. His are soft and shining, more green than I've seen them in a long time. 'You remembered.' My heart thuds, a dull ache radiating from my chest. But not the broken kind. The mending kind. 'I'll do better, I promise,' I choke out, tears suddenly thickening in my throat. 'I promise.'

'I know.'

He gets up, coming to kneel at my side, and I press my forehead against his. We stay like that for a moment, and I make the promise over and over in my head.

'Shall we go and join the others?' he asks gently, moving away slightly so our gazes are level.

'Yes, I'd like that,' I say, kissing his mouth softly, the taste of blackberries fresh on our lips.

James goes to tidy up after our breakfast date when I stop him. 'I'll clear this up later. I want this to be the perfect Christmas – and we've got a dip in the sea to do together.'

'Only if I can dunk you.' He grins, pulling me out of my chair. 'But first… you know what I love most about this room?'

'Oh, what's that?'

'There's a lock on the door.' He leans down, his mouth brushing mine, and murmurs, 'I don't think they'll miss us if we're a little bit late…'

I make this day the perfect Christmas, taking all the best bits from the loops. I go for a freezing cold Christmas Day dip with James and we swear our heads off, laughing as his Santa hat gets carried away by a wave. We play rounders on the beach, stopping off at the pub afterwards for a swift drink, my fingers laced through his. I hold Hallie's hand as she presses it against her bump, her eyebrows raised with hope that I'll feel it. The wonder she feels. We exchange gifts, tearing off wrapping paper under the Christmas tree, each ornament reflecting back our smiles, over and over. I take a moment to breathe in the evergreen scent, to admire the decorations weaving through the whole of Penhallow. I feel an echo of the magic from years ago.

I sit close to James, Hallie and Kian at dinner, soaking up every memory made with them. It's almost like it used to be. We pull crackers, pop on our paper crowns and delve into roast meats, crispy roast potatoes, veggies smothered in butter, and the warmth of it all thrills me.

Natalie FaceTimes Olga and we all close in, yelling Christmas wishes as she giggles and blows kisses under an Aussie sun. James kisses me, his hands circling the small of my back as his mouth finds mine, sending trails of heat across my skin.

I sing carols with everyone around the piano, John playing a tune and leading with his deep baritone. I help Sarah clear the table so she can get home early to her children. I catch her secret smile as she checks her bank balance on the app on her phone. And at the end of the day, as the clock chimes midnight, I sit in the cosy snug with James, his arm around my waist, my head resting in the nook between his arm and his chest. I don't worry about the business for an entire day. I start as I mean to go on.

The next morning at breakfast, I'm giggling with James, firming up our plans for our ski trip. I feel unbeatable. Invincible. With a renewed energy inside me, I'm so ready to launch the shop when I get back.

'Kian…' Hallie says suddenly, her eyes widening. I catch the look they share, her cheeks draining to the colour of spilled milk. 'Something's… something's wrong.'

'What do you mean?'

'I don't… I just…' She looks down at her lap and gasps. Her head shoots back up, cracks appearing in her eyes. 'I'm bleeding.'

My heart stops. The fork in my fingers clatters onto the plate in front of me as a whooshing sound fills my ears. The world slows to drip like syrup as Kian reaches for Hallie, as James shifts back to give them space. Hallie's breathing turns sharp and short as she stares down at her lap, then up at Kian in horror.

'I-I… I need to get up.'

All at once, the world speeds up around us to a more normal pace and I blink, readjusting, gathering myself. I slide over into Kian's chair as he stands, pain blooming in my chest as I catch sight of the dark spill of blood in Hallie's lap. Just like the last Boxing Day. I swallow, moving my hand to grasp Hallie's. Her fingers are limp and cold in mine.

'What do you need?' I say quietly. Natalie comes to kneel on Hallie's other side, rubbing her arm in slow circles. The fear on her face is like a mirror of my own. This can't be real.

'I need… I need to… to get to a bathroom,' Hallie says calmly, only a slight tremor on her lips. 'And then I want to go to the hospital.'

I nod, trying to keep the shaking from my hand as I hold hers. But I don't trust my voice not to reveal it. I swallow again, glancing away as my stomach twists sickeningly. All I can see is that arc of blood on the black–and–white entrance hall floor, Hallie lying there, so still. I take a breath then nod at Natalie and we both help Hallie to stand.

I can't look at the blood. I can't believe it's anything but a small complication. Something that can be fixed, and mended. This probably happens sometimes, this sort of thing. I'm sure

I've heard of women having unexplainable bleeding, about doctors reassuring them. And then it's all fine, and the baby is fine. I try to convince myself of this as we get Hallie through the entrance hall, into the bathroom near the snug.

She locks herself in and we hear her small sobs through the door. I can't bear this. I can't bear that it's happening again, that despite everything… it happens anyway. That there are some things I can't fix. Natalie and I hover by the basins, not looking at each other.

'Is Kian ready?' Hallie asks in a small voice.

'I'll check, Hal, OK? Natalie's right here,' I say back, placing my hand on the door. It has that same, cream-painted slick feeling as the doorframe to her bedroom. The cool touch grounds me momentarily and I move quickly to the main bathroom door. Kian is standing outside, hands in his pockets, a frown line digging deep between his eyes. James turns as I walk over, my shoes unbearably loud in the silence.

'How is she doing? Has it stopped?' Kian asks hopefully, taking his hands from his pockets, looking over my shoulder, as if she might be there behind me. As if this might all be nothing.

'She's…' I begin, my tongue tying in knots. 'She's ready to go to the hospital. Should I maybe get her a robe, or something? Clean clothes? Some towels?'

Kian nods, passing a hand over his face. 'Yes. Yes, good idea. I'll get the car started, scrape off the snow. James… shit. Will you…'

'I'm on it,' James says, already striding for the kitchen. Most likely to ask the staff for a scraper, some warm water. Anything to get the car ready for the drive across the moors.

I hover for a moment as Kian staggers towards the front door.

He turns for a second, as if he's forgotten something. Then he shakes his head and carries on walking, straight into the cold of the day.

We don't all pile into Kian and Hallie's car. James and I drive in his, Natalie in the back. We are all silent, as though a spell has been cast over us, one where we're all in our own heads for the whole drive. James is slow, muttering darkly as we skid a little on black ice patches and I cling to the door handle until my fingers turn stiff and bone white. I don't realise until halfway there that I've been clenching my jaw and I pull in a breath, trying to redirect my fear. Clinging to the belief that everything will be all right.

'We have to hope, right?' James says, eyes fixed on the windscreen. On the expanse of white and winter, so bleak it feels unending. 'It can't be uncommon. Maybe this happens a lot.'

'Maybe,' I say back. I can't bring myself to say any more than that. To lose that same slice of hope he nurtures. But somewhere deep inside me the intuitive chill has set in, the knowing that this will not end well.

We pull into the car park and as I fish out change for the parking meter, I again drop my purse. I bite my lip, scooping up the rattle of coins, thrusting them into the tiny slot. I don't want this to be a sign. We are directed by a receptionist to an antenatal ward, a different small waiting room. It's not the same one as the last time I was here but there is still a sadness that lingers. The corridors are too sterile, too brightly lit. The strip lights make everyone seem tired, that same washed-out hue I saw in Kian's face last time. I didn't want to ever be back here again.

I drink the tea in the Styrofoam cup, the same metallic taste coating my tongue. I watch James as he stands by the window, clasping his hands behind him. Natalie is pacing, texting their dad and swearing softly as the messages roll in. It's so similar to last time, I have to lean over my knees until the sparks stop dancing at the corners, narrowing my vision. I have to breathe through the needling pain, pressing on my ribs. We are all stuck here, trapped. Waiting for a miracle.

The door opens and I leap up, the tiny dribble of tea left in the Styrofoam cup spilling over my red dress. I brush it away as Kian closes the door behind him, leaning against it. He's aged ten years in the last hour. I tense as he focuses on us.

'She… she's delivering him.'

'What do you mean? He's going to survive?' Natalie asks quickly, sinking into a chair.

Kian shakes his head, staring down at his shoes. 'No. It's… too early on. He can't survive.'

I gulp, a rush of heat filling my stomach as it twists. I'm vaguely aware of James crossing the room to Kian, of him dropping his head into his hands. The whooshing begins in my ears again and I get that same odd sensation that I'm floating away from my body. That I'm detached from this situation, like it's a film I'm watching. That it can't possibly be real.

This isn't right.

Chapter 39

'Miscarriages aren't common at this stage,' the doctor says, addressing us like a class of students. He has spiked hair, a face so young and new that I keep wondering how old he is. If he's just finished medical school, if this is his first job.

'So why... why did it happen?' I manage to get out, my voice ringing untrue in my ears, as though it isn't really mine. I grip the sides of the blue padded seat, as if it will stop me from floating away.

The doctor clears his throat, bouncing on the balls of his trainers. 'We imagine that Hallie experienced something called cervical incompetence. It's when the cervix can't cope with the pressure of the growing, er, foetus and it opens up, breaks membranes and will result in an unviable... foetus.' He looks around at all of us, blinking slowly. 'Sadly, there's nothing anybody could have done.'

Those last few words echo round and round, taunting me. Nothing anybody could have done.

Nothing anybody could have done.

As the doctor excuses himself awkwardly, leaving us alone once more in the waiting room, I slouch down into my chair. So it has happened. Again. A tingling begins along my arms, unfurling down to my fingertips. As Natalie leaves the room to go and see Hallie, I sit here, staring at a poster on the opposite wall. All the words and pictures blur together, the slightly curling lower right corner transfixing me. I want to go and smooth it out, make it perfect again. Fix it. I blow out a breath, shaking my hair back from my face. But I can't fix this, can I? This is something that was always going to happen. However much *I* change, however much I try… there is always going to be something I can't fix.

I couldn't stop Gran dying. I couldn't stop my miscarriage. And now I can't save Hallie's baby.

I stand up, crossing the room again to pour a cup of coffee. I load it with sugar, stirring and stirring it, the wooden stick scraping against the inside of the cup. Finally I blink, toss the stirrer in the small bin under the table and pick up the cup to carry it over to the window. I'm so aware of every one of my precise, clipped movements as the room around me dulls and dims. I sip it, staring out of the window at the snow and the cars. I don't know how long I stand there for, just staring.

I start when someone touches my arm. It's Kian, an odd detachment carved into his features. 'She wants to see you.'

'Of… of course,' I say, my voice emerging as a croak and I sniff, smoothing back my hair and dress before following him out into the corridor. Over to the room where Hallie is recovering.

She's facing away from the door, her head so small and delicate as it rests against the piled-up pillows. I swallow, the ache in my chest telling me to run. That I can't face this. That I'm not good enough to handle this moment. But I take a sip of air and push that ache away. This isn't about me. This is about Hallie. It no longer matters whether or not I can handle it. I just have to.

'Hey…' I say, rounding the bed to take a seat beside her. Kian closes the door, pointing to the corridor to indicate that he will be right outside, and we are left alone. Her face is so drawn and pale, her eyes glassy and dull. But she still summons up a small smile, closing her fingers around mine. There's a cannula in the back of her hand, a tube wound up and around to attach to a bag next to the monitors. I blink at it, reading, yet not reading the label. Some kind of saline drip. 'Do you need a drink? I can get you some water, or…'

'No. I'm OK,' she says, her voice a thin whisper. 'I just want to lie here.'

I hunker down next to her, resting my elbow on the pillow, so we're as close as sisters. She closes her eyes, the papery skin of her eyelids creasing, and a single tear tracks down her face. It's the most heartbreaking thing I've ever seen, this quiet sorrow. 'I can't even hold him. It's not… it's not possible. He's not a baby yet.'

I sigh, wanting to jump in and smother those feelings, to somehow cast a spell and give Hallie her fight back. But that isn't how this works. We can accept help and support from those we love, but ultimately, we have to want to fight for ourselves. So I wait patiently as she struggles through her thoughts. I have to give her this space to process. 'It's one thing, wanting it, and fighting for it. But we got there, didn't we? I–I don't know if I can fight anymore.'

I squeeze her fingers as she seems to sink even further into the pillows. This day has been so devastating. Everything they've worked towards, longed for… taken away with a finger snap.

'You don't have to fight today, Hal. You just have to be. You just have to keep going, until tomorrow. Then the next day. Then the next. Until one day, you're ready to fight for it again. Until you're ready to hope.'

I say all this, and it opens up that hollow place in my heart. My breath catches as I realise what I'm doing. Hallie is almost a mirror, and I need these words as much as she does. We're there, together. Except I never started fighting again. I closed myself off and began a pattern of self-sabotage that nearly ended everything.

'This moment is the very worst moment,' I say quietly, smoothing her hair away from her face. 'And once it's passed, that's it. It's over. And you can grieve and heal and find a way to keep being Hallie.' I smile at her. 'You're stronger than you think.'

'I feel right now like… like I'm letting a piece of myself die as well. Like some part of me died today, too,' Hallie says, dipping her chin. 'I can fight and be strong, but I'll have to give something up to do that. And I'm tired of giving up pieces of myself.'

I nod, the excruciating pain and honesty of her words reverberating through me. She's so right. But this moment, the darkest one, is the one Hallie has to go through, and not keep looping back to. She has to reach for that light. 'Mark this day, Hal,' I say. 'It's a piece of you. And Kian. I know it's something you never wanted to mark…' I draw in a breath, picturing myself, back in that shower again, water cascading down my back, dripping from my forehead. 'And this isn't going to be easy. Or straightforward.'

She looks up at me, her eyes still holding that dull sheen.

But there's something at the corners now, the pain and grief seeping in. She's *feeling* something. She's letting herself feel it. 'I need you to promise me something, something I have no right to ask of you. But I need you, and I'm going to make you promise anyway.'

'Anything,' I say.

'Don't leave me again. Just don't. Don't shut yourself away. I couldn't bear losing you as well.'

The desperation in her voice breaks me. I nod, even as tears slip down my face. I drop my forehead to hers, letting all of her sorrow, all her pain wash into me. And I say, meaning it more than I've ever meant anything else, 'I promise. I will never leave you.'

Chapter 40

James is waiting for me.

After we check that Kian has everything he needs, that Natalie and John have got it covered, we walk the long corridors back into the bright December day. I cringe away from the starkness, the contrast of that lemon wedge of sun and the landscape of white. It's slowed now, the snow, it's more of a trickle, and the cars have churned it into a murk-coated mess. But there are patches of it even here, surrounded by the city. And all I want to do is fill my lungs with clean newness. With the moorland and the silence of deep, slumbering things.

'Do you want to maybe… take a walk somewhere?' I say, turning to James. It feels like we're still new ourselves, like this is the first walk we're taking. The first time we're holding hands all over again.

'Sure,' he says, staring down at me. 'I know this is a rough day, and if you're not up to it, just say. But,' he glances away, 'your gran's grave isn't too far from here.'

I bite my lip, processing this.

'We could pick up some flowers. Stop in the village car park and walk over the fields to the graveyard – but don't worry if you're not—'

'No. I mean… yes. Yes.' I take a breath, reminding myself to accept it. That it's time to move forward. I flash James a quick smile. 'It's a good idea.'

We pick up the only flowers we can find at a service station. Carnations, with a plastic wrapper and a reduced sticker covering the label. I crinkle my nose at how forlorn they look, but Gran doesn't need my flowers. She needs my presence.

We drive in near silence, punctuated by the sat nav instructions and the odd comment on mundane, everyday things. I have turned off the notifications on my phone, leaving it on ring only for Kian to contact us. This visit is too sacred for technology.

James takes my arm as I step out of the car and, across the fields, I can see it. The day is bright and peaceful around the little church, the snowflakes settling in layers on the ground. The air is scented with green and moss and new beginnings. It's sharp and cold, burning my nose, my throat. But I gulp it down, letting the weight of the past few days slip from my shoulders as we walk. This, James and me and this December day, is more important. Far more precious and fragile. Something to nurture and protect.

We reach the graveyard, the iron gate swinging open that divides us from the dead. There are old gravestones, some so bleached and worn by time and rain that I can't make out the names. Only a scattering of letters, blending with the landscape, the ghosts merging with the world around them. I know where her gravestone is. I walked this path three years ago, despair numbing me to the point where I could only stare. Stare at the grave as the crowd of us stood in a semicircle. But now, now I embrace my grief. I accept it. I let it rattle against my ribs, filling my heart to near bursting. And I take a slow, releasing breath.

James hands me the flowers, dividing the bunch into two sets. I look at him enquiringly.

'One for your gran and one for… for…'

Of course. One for the baby we never had.

We lay the flowers before Gran's grave and step back. James seeks out my hand and in this cold, lifeless place, I accept it. It warms my chilled fingers and I lean into him.

I let him in.

'I haven't been entirely honest with you,' I begin as we make our way back to the car.

'We haven't been entirely honest with each other.'

'That's true.'

We take a few steps in silence, the crunch of frost underfoot breaking up the pattern of our breaths.

'You know, I've never heard you talk about it. Not with me, not with anyone. And I wish…' James sighs. 'Even if it isn't with me… I wish you would.'

'Kayleigh,' I say quietly.

'Kayleigh?'

'That's what I would have called her if she had been a girl. It's Gran's middle name. Hadn't settled on a boy's name.'

James sniffs and I don't dare look to see if he's crying. I can't bear it.

'I need to talk about what happened. You're right. And about what it is I want. For… for us. For me and you and the future.'

He's silent, bowing his head to allow me the space to speak. To let me form the words twisting in my heart, that big world inside me, the blizzard I have been hopelessly lost in for too long.

'I do want a family with you. I do. Ever since we met, I knew we were moving to that point. When we bought our flat, and we measured the hallway, and it wasn't just to check how much shoe storage there was. How your cheeks were all flushed and we looked at each other, can you remember? I thought, there it is! Like this current connected us. Like we were thinking the exact same thought. We were both picturing a buggy there, weren't we?'

He bites his lip, pain flitting across his features.

'So when we decided to try, we thought it would be easy. At least, I did. Everything else had been easy. Well, not easy *exactly*, but I had always known that if I worked hard enough, if I followed the steps, then I would get there. I took the vitamins, didn't drink, and nor did you. We went out on those runs around the park every weekend, remember? Park run. With all those other couples, like we all had that same purpose. That same finish line.' I laugh quietly. 'And you gave me your gloves when my fingers got cold. And then we got a smoothie afterwards at that little café by the park.'

'I remember,' he says quietly. 'You always had blueberry, kale and banana.'

'And you had peanut butter and almond milk.' I pause for a moment, gathering my thoughts. 'But then it all went wrong. I was so happy. You have to know that. I was so *unbearably* happy. I think that's what it was, no one is allowed to be that happy. It can't last. It's like a balloon, it swells and swells, and then… it has to pop.' I wipe away a tear as it traces down my cheek. 'That was me and you. We were too happy. We had everything, and no one can be that lucky. And one day… it all went pop. And… and I failed.'

His arm, still wrapped in mine, stiffens. 'I'll never forget that phone call,' he says softly. 'You've never cried like that before. Or even since. Like your whole being was cracking apart.'

'It was. It did.' I sniff. 'And I didn't heal properly. I've left it as this gaping wound, as if it could mend itself. Just closed the door on it, so I don't have to see it. But it's still there. It doesn't work like that. I don't know if I'm making any sense…'

We reach the car and he turns to me. He turns his whole body towards me and holds my face in his hands. His eyes are that thrilling green of spring, of new life. My breath hitches.

'You never failed. Please don't think that.'

A tear tracks down my skin, running between his fingers. And I know. I know in that moment, we are built to last. *We* are family. Me and James. Us. We did that. We created that. He gently wipes my tears away, running his thumb across my cold skin. Leaving a trail of warmth, taking the sadness away.

'I nearly destroyed it. Us,' I breathe. 'Because I couldn't bear the thought of—'

'I'm still here. I'm right here, Eva. I'm not going anywhere.'

I close my eyes as tears wash down my cheeks, as his lips search for mine and we kiss. His arms circle around me, pulling me in to his warmth and his steady, beating heart and I let go of all of it. All the fear, all the pain. James is my family, the one I wanted all along. And we did create it, we built it. As I let go of all these years of lonely walls and sorrow, I give myself to him. Every broken piece of myself.

When we step apart, I feel like we've crossed the divide I created. The past three years melt away and I see him. Really see him. 'I love you,' I breathe, leaning my forehead against his chest. 'I can't believe I nearly, that we nearly…'

'Hey, it's OK. We're OK,' he says, brushing my hair with his fingers. 'It's not the end.'

'No, no it's not,' I say. I step back, taking his hands in mine. His eyes are now a deep, serious green. The rare kind, jewel-like and wondrous. Burning with the love that still makes my breath catch, even all these years later. 'Things need to be different. I need to put you first more. Not work every evening, every weekend. Stop chasing my work dreams like they are the only ones that matter. I do want the business to flourish, desperately. But it's a hollow thing without you there with me. It's meaningless.'

'Are you saying we might…'

'We should try for a baby. Again,' I say, swallowing down my fear. Refusing to give in to it. 'Even if it's hard. Even if it's not in the shape we always imagined. We have to *try*.'

James blows out a breath, a smile lifting his whole face. 'That's all I want. To try. And if it happens again… if it gets too much…'

'One step at a time, right?' I say, smiling back sadly. 'But I have to tell you, if it does work out? I want to carry on building my business. I don't want to lose that part of myself. We need—'

'Balance.'

'Yes.' I grin. 'Actual work–life balance.' His laugh booms in the echoing emptiness of moorland surrounding us, echoing across the snow and frost. I cringe. 'I sound like I've swallowed a self-help book.'

'No, I get it. Work–life balance. We should frame that, point at it when we lose track. It should go on the fridge.'

'Which will obviously happen, it can't always be perfect, we'll get it wrong at some point.'

'We'll slip up.'

'Work too late.'

'Maybe it'll happen again.'

We smile slowly at each other. I'm floating, ten times lighter than I was even minutes ago. I forgot how much I love this human. How intertwined we are, how I could have lost that. The family we created. 'The important thing to remember is that I'm always right.'

'Ohh, *really…*'

I shriek as his hands find my sides, my neck, the places where I'm most ticklish. As I gasp for air between giggles, batting him off, I know that we are not quite there yet. There's more work to do on us, on our lives. On the day-to-day way we walk through them. But there is no one else I would rather be working it all out with. Every day, the two of us.

Together.

Chapter 41

It's close to midnight and even my bones are weary. We have one final night at Penhallow, one final night to say our goodbyes to this place. After what happened, I couldn't face the drive and Naomi offered Penhallow to us, telling us to take our time.

I thought I had made my peace with everyone, and everything. Ready to move forward when we get back to London. But now, hours later, my circling thoughts about Hallie and everything else that happened are weighing on me like granite. James has nodded off next to me, his kisses still fresh on my swollen mouth. That we can fight to stay together, that he can call us a family all our own has filled me with a deep sense of calm. Of purpose.

And as I lie here, watching the shadows play across the ceiling as snow-laden clouds move over the moon outside, I know what I want to do next. How I want the next week, the next month, the whole year to unfold. And that deadweight of failure that is constantly dragging me back down is no longer tethered to my back. Even if I fail, at being a businesswoman, a wife, a best friend, I can get back up. I can keep going.

A chime rings out, sounding muffled and far away, and

I wonder. I wonder if I will get my second chance at that too. If I can finally have my goodbye.

I shimmy out from the bed, the cold creeping with snatching fingers along my ribs. Shivering, I shrug into a dressing gown and make my way out of the bedroom as quietly as I can. She's not in the entrance hall, or the snug with its grate filled with rosy glowing coals. I find her in the kitchen, sitting at the big farmhouse table. Polishing off a thick slab of Christmas cake.

'That girl, Naomi, makes it just right.' She sighs with contentment. 'Lots of brandy fed into this one. Make sure you get the recipe, love. Worth its weight in gold, a good Christmas cake recipe.'

I slide into a chair next to her and take her hand in mine. I cradle it, this hand. It's helped me through so many times, picked me up when I skinned my knees when I was small. Helped me move into halls at university. Picked the phone up and listened as I griped and moaned about inconsequential things in my twenties. My dependable, always there rock. My family. The woman I aspire to be like, more than anyone else in the world. My gran.

'I didn't think I would see you again,' I say, voice already thickening with tears. 'Did I fix things? Did I do it right?'

'You did,' she says with a wink. 'Don't worry, no more body-swapping. No more loops of Christmas Day after Christmas Day. You look more yourself already. Did you speak to James?'

'I talked to him about… about…'

'You can say the name. It's OK to name them.'

'Kayleigh.' I smile, the name a tight pinch in my chest. I wonder if I will always feel that. 'Maybe wouldn't have worked if she had been a boy though…'

Gran laughs, sliding the last slip of marzipan and white icing onto her fork. 'Well done. I'm so proud of you.'

'You came back at just the right moment,' I marvel. 'How do you always know?'

She shrugs, dropping the cake fork on the plate, letting it clatter and settle. 'When it comes to you, I think we have a tie. Some kind of tether that I just can't shake loose. Not that I'd want to, it's nice checking in from time to time. Although now I'd like to see you live a bit more. Get that spark back you always had. That certainty.'

'I think I'll be a weepy mess for a bit longer. But I'll try, Gran. I really will. No more being so scared of getting it wrong. No more shutting myself away. Probably not *exactly* what you had in mind, all the blubbering.'

'You know what goes well with tears? Tea. And long walks with a friend. Someone like that nice girl Hallie. Nothing like it.'

'But Hallie… she… the baby…'

Gran finds my eyes with her own, making sure I really listen. 'Some things you cannot change. Some things are going to go horribly wrong and there isn't anything you can do about it. All you can do is work through it, day after day afterwards. She'll need you, you know. She isn't you, so she won't react the same way. Grief is funny like that. No two people tread the same path through it. But we *all* go through it.'

I swallow, nodding to show I understand. That there are some things outside my control. And it's not my failure if they fall apart.

'I couldn't have done it without you,' I say, even as my throat closes up again. 'And now you're going to leave again and I can't—'

'Yes, you can,' she says firmly. 'Because now you know, I'm always here. And not to spoil the surprise, but you're going to have a beautiful life, Eva. It's going to be very, very wonderful.'

My nose twitches, the tears starting. I don't want to let her go. How can I, when I know this is the last time I'll see her? The last time I'll hold her hand in mine, the last time we will sit together, talking as though nothing exists beyond this. This moment that feels like I've stolen it. Cheated somehow to get her back for this final, magical midnight.

'Now enough of that sniffing, dry your eyes. Go on, that's it.' She hands me a handkerchief, embroidered with her initials in the corner. 'You'll get those awful frown lines. Self care, Eva—'

'Is queen,' I finish with a small smile. She grins back and squeezes my hand.

'Let me tell you a story, dearest one.'

And I sit there, the warmth of her voice washing over me. Holding Gran's hand, I listen to the soft patter of her voice. One final time. And then, when she fades away, when her edges are a blur, her hand a ghostly shape in my own, I whisper into the night, 'Goodbye, Gran. I love you.'

And when I stand up, I finally feel some peace. After three years of searching for her in every crowd, at every Tube stop, sure that if I look hard enough she will somehow still be alive…

I let her go.

Chapter 42

Twelve Months Later...

The evening is scented with snow. As the last customers leave the shop and I close the door in their wake, turning the sign to 'Closed', I face this place I have created. Every neat line of candle holders, the plump bundles of cushions. I step forward, running my hand over the blankets piled neatly on the centre table. The pale blues and sea-foam greens, the patterns I chose and had manufactured.

Every item in this shop holds a memory. A history of where it began as an idea, a sketch, a wish. Every single thing here has been carefully curated by me to create a space that reflects everything I am. Everything I have fought for. And all the ghosts of ideas that died before they were made. I can see them too, what might have been, what could have been. They are layered behind and all around me.

It's nearly the one-year anniversary of my shop launch. The physical place that I piled all my hope and dreams into, and far too much of my life. It's taken many months, setbacks and striving to get that balance right. To get back on track and move forward, after last Christmas at Penhallow.

I walk behind the counter, going through the cashing-up

process for the day. Then I look again at my laptop, the email from the manufacturers containing the final illustrations and dimensions for a new product range launching in the spring. It's a range of candles, scented like the wild places our hearts always return to. The wild gorse flowers of the moors. The sharp scented air of the ocean. The loamy darkness of a forest. I breathe in deeply, my chest swelling with all the pride I can hardly contain. I have created this. Me. And in a way, I've kept Penhallow alive with the gorse candle. Every time I light it, I will remember all the good things. All the rose-tinted things.

My business Christmas cards are lined up here, a row of colourful pictures and sweet messages, handwritten in curling scripts. I run my thumb over the one from Diana, a sleek jade-green tree against a gold background. Understated and fuss free, just like her. It's signed from Diana, Sarah and Sarah's two kids, and my heart grows just reading the names aloud. They were childhood sweethearts and I never even knew. And once they reconnected, Diana took the leap and drove back down to Cornwall. She has tiny hearts on certain dates on her work calendar and I know what they mean. They are the days she's booked off to visit Sarah. And her dad. And her mum's grave.

I keep getting Gran's handkerchief out of my pocket as I cash up, rubbing my thumb over her embroidered initials. She would have loved this, the busy hive of customers, the autonomy of a business I built from nothing. She would love the life James and I are building too. How we are talking more. How we've mended that bridge over the chasm that divided us. How I can call us a family now and it feels like home.

Even though she's the piece that's missing, only living in my photo album. In my heart. I still miss her so much sometimes,

I can't breathe. Every corner of my life holds her tucked-away smile, her knowing eyes. There's a tether between me and her, a cord that binds us together. Sometimes, I'm sure I can smell her perfume when I enter a room, as if she has only just left it. Before, it would have floored me. Sent a hairline fracture through my heart. But now I drink it in, taking a moment to say hello to her before I carry on with my day.

A knock sounds at the door and I run over, twisting the lock open, and find James there, holding an overly large bunch of flowers. Lilies, Hallie's favourite.

'You've got... three minutes,' he says, consulting his watch with a grin.

I grin back, ushering him in, away from the frost-dusted pavement, the sharp chill of midwinter.

I reach up on tiptoes, rubbing my nose against his. 'You're freezing.'

'Warm me up?' he murmurs, brushing his lips over mine.

It sends tiny sparks dancing through my veins and I chuckle softly, lingering for another kiss. 'Just wait until I get you home later...'

He grins. 'Now you've only got *two* minutes, you flirt. Chop-chop.'

'I can be ready in two!' I say, dashing away from him, back to the till to finish cashing up. I straighten everything out before moving to the shadowed back to grab my coat. It still gives me a thrill, knowing this is all mine. And that James is with me, every step of the way as I grow.

'Did you get the card?'

I double back, picking up a pink envelope. Pink, with a card inside. We decided to celebrate every milestone. Every step in her journey. Tonight, we're going to Hallie and Kian's for a little Christmas party, to eat minced pies and drink mulled wine in their cosy lounge as the snow drifts slowly down outside. We'll hang a tiny red felt stocking on the tree just for her, for Kayleigh. And for the boy they lost last year.

It hasn't been easy, this past year, and we are hoping like hell that this one sticks. I can already picture her, a mouth all gummy and wide. She will be the most precious gift, Hallie and Kian's baby with her short black curls, her brown skin. Her eyes shaped like Hallie's, her mouth as generous and bubbling with chatter as Kian's. Hallie and I talk often about it. We meet up, walk along the riverbank at Richmond and it's like it was before.

We've found our way back to each other.

And one day, we will have our own baby, James and I. But until then, *he* is my family. Everything we are, we build together. And that backbone of us brings me so much courage. So much strength to keep trying. To keep talking it out, and fighting for us.

I hold on to a daydream. That one year, when the snow dusts the moors, when the long summer, and the nausea and the scans and hospital trips are behind us, we will take our own tiny human to Penhallow at Christmas. I will bundle them up, discard my phone on some side table and whisper to my gran at midnight, clutching her handkerchief in my fist. I will leave a slice of Christmas cake out for her, just the way she likes it with the thick marzipan and white icing.

I will whisper about all the ways she was right. And how grateful I am for her love, for that final time when her hand reached out to mine, when she kept reaching out, until I reached back. And I finally broke through to the other side. I am full of hope that my dream will come true. That one day, we will make more memories at Penhallow. That I will get to share with my child the story of the one Christmas that changed it all, like our own secret fairy tale.

I'm leaning into that hope.

Acknowledgements

You know how the saying goes: it takes a village. 'Thank you' will never seem all-encompassing enough, Maddalena Cavaciuti. You're the best agent I could ever hope for, regularly going into battle for me. Your enthusiasm is matchless. Thank you for loving this story so passionately. You made my dream come true!

To my editors, Mel Hayes and Ariana Sinclair, I don't know how I got so lucky to have such a dedicated, dream team. This story became a book under your expert guidance. Thank you for choosing it and fighting for it so passionately. Sorry (not sorry) it made you cry.

Huge thank yous go to the wider team at David Higham, particularly Margaux Vialleron, Emma Jamison, Sam Norman, Ilaria Albani, Alice Howes and Clare Israel. Thank you for fighting so hard for all my stories. The best team in the business.

Thank you to Allison Hunter for finding this book a home in the US, and to Natalie Edwards. You made what felt impossible, possible.

And to the teams at HQ and Avon, the copyeditors, the proofreaders, the cover designers, the marketing, sales, publicity and audio teams, particularly Becca Joyce, Lauren Gardiner,

Sarah Lundy, Stephanie Heathcote, Halema Begum, Angie Dobbs, Angela Thomson, Georgina Green, Sara Eusebi, Petra Moll, Rebecca Fortuin, Liz Hatherell and Eldes Tran. What a wonderful, passionate bunch you are, stretching across both sides of the Atlantic. Thank you for loving this book and sending it out into the wide world.

Thank you to my writing buddies, the people I have been on retreats with, shared my work with and who have been there at every step. The llamas, the snug girls, The MGical Misfits, the WWTS group, particularly Sarah Suk, Karina Evans, Susan Wallach, Kess Costales, Lorelei Savaryn, Marina Green, Jessica Rubinkowski, Cat Bakewell and Melissa Seymour. You're all awesome.

To Shea Ernshaw for celebrating every moment with me from my first full manuscript request. You have such a big heart. Rachel Griffin for offering advice, guidance and friendship from half a world away. I'm so glad we met in Ireland. Kate Rhodes for being a one-woman hype machine for a starry-eyed island writer! And Adrienne Young, I have learned so much from you. Thank you for WWTS, your advice and your friendship.

To Cyla Panin, I can't imagine writing a story now without you reading it, chapter by chapter. You've been the person I turn to and trust most for the past five years on this rollercoaster of a publishing journey. Here's to the next five years.

To Suzie Laud, the first person to read every chapter of that terrible first manuscript and then the very first to pre-order this book. I adore you. Helena Plowman, thank you for being excited for me at every step, and for learning all the publishing lingo. I would go on a thousand round-the-island walks with you.

Angie and Mark, where do I begin? This book would not be a book without you. You have held us up, supported us and fought alongside me at every step. You have never once wavered in your belief. Thank you for the many, many things you do for me, Joe and the girls. I love you so much. I didn't realise when I met Joe that I was also getting this big, wonderful family (and a café filled with cake!). And Mark, it's a deal, signed first edition of every book for unlimited childcare!

Thank you to Phil Greenlaw and Beth Dewer (or by the time this is published… Greenlaw!) for answering all my medical questions. And Beth, thank you for being one of the very first readers of this book. I am eternally glad he put a ring on it.

Thank you to all of my family for supporting me and for loving this book nerd. Nath, sorry there's no epic battle scenes in this one. I'll try harder next time. Audrey, I wish you could have read this. Gran was inspired by you. And to the wider Greenlaw and Creighton clan, thank you. I couldn't ask for a better team.

For my wildlings, Rosie and Izzy, you have the biggest hearts. I love you to the moon and back, and all the stars in between. Never stop being your fierce, feisty little selves.

Joe. There aren't words adequate enough to express what you mean to me. You are everything, the love of my life, my best friend. You are my person. You see all my worries, my sharp edges and still take my hand in yours. You are the best version of yourself every day, without even trying. My goon forever.

ONE PLACE. MANY STORIES

Bold, innovative and
empowering publishing.

FOLLOW US ON:

@HQStories